THE CHINA GAMBIT

JEFFREY JAMES HIGGINS

SEVERN RIVER PUBLISHING

Severn River Publishing
www.SevernRiverBooks.com

ISBN: 978-1-64875-705-1 (Paperback)

ALSO BY JEFFREY JAMES HIGGINS

The Nathan Burke Thrillers

The Havana Syndrome

The Khorasan Retribution

The China Gambit

The Uganda Protocol

To find out more, visit

severnriverbooks.com

For Cynthia, my wife and soulmate.

1

———

Imminent violence coiled Special Agent Nathan Burke's muscles and sharpened his mind—readying him to fight. He slipped his portable radio out from between the center console and the seat of the Ford Escape, a Bureau fleet car with 90,000 hard miles on it. He checked the volume knob for the third time to ensure he'd hear the call to action.

Beside him, Agent Osvaldo "Waldo" Falcón shifted behind the wheel as he checked football scores on his phone.

"Cowboys aren't gonna cover the spread, *amigo*," Waldo said.

"Get your head in this game," Nathan said.

Waldo was Nathan's new partner in FBI Group 346, where Nathan had transferred to investigate the Havana Syndrome. They parked on East 8th Avenue in Tampa's Ybor City District as groups of drunks wearing Halloween costumes roamed the streets. The din of music and merriment leaked out of the bars into the historic Cuban neighborhood.

Nathan watched the double-doored entrance to the Cubano Inn, where a Chinese covert operative known only as the Leopard holed up.

"What's taking these SWAT *mongas* so long?" Waldo asked.

"Waiting to confirm the Leopard's inside."

"But your snitch said he's there."

Nathan's stomach hardened. Having to sit on the sidelines and let the

FBI Tampa Field Office handle the arrest tweaked the control freak inside him, but that was protocol. Nathan and Waldo's group was based in DC, and this was Tampa's territory. The FBI Counterintelligence Division wanted a piece of this too, but a year ago, the Leopard had executed high-energy attacks against Nathan's girlfriend, FBI Supervisory Special Agent Meili Chan, and a dozen other Americans—and that gave his group partial jurisdiction.

His radio crackled. "All units, Charlie-Four, the manager confirms the occupant of room 321 went upstairs an hour ago."

"This is Charlie-One," the TFD's supervisor broadcast, "launch SWAT."

Nathan checked his phone. Nothing new from his source, Kei Choi, so he fired off a text.

Our boy still in his room?

I'm in LA. How I know? Kei responded.

Always helpful. At least Kei had discovered that the Leopard was active in the US again. The assassin was a lethal tool of China's Ministry of State Security, and he'd been a team leader during the Havana Syndrome attacks in previous years. Those attacks had paused after Nathan and Meili Chan exposed the Chinese government's complicity, so why was the Leopard back? It didn't matter. The Leopard had returned, giving Nathan his chance to catch a dangerous Chinese spy.

"Feels good to be back in Tampa," Waldo said.

"Lotta memories," Nathan said.

Both Nathan and Waldo had started as deputy sheriffs at the Hillsborough County Sheriff's Office before joining the FBI, so even though they'd worked there at different times, their pairing made sense. The trip down from DC was their first assignment together.

"Here they come," Waldo said.

The SWAT team's two unmarked vans rolled down the street. Nathan's pulse quickened as the vehicles stopped twenty feet from the hotel's entrance. The vans' doors flung open, and FBI agents wearing full battle rattle leaped onto the street. None spoke as they stacked up and pointed their weapons outward. Drunken revelers floated by, carrying plastic cups, laughing and drinking, and most didn't seem to notice the quiet professionals preparing for battle.

One of the TFD agents who'd been conducting pre-surveillance stubbed out a cigarette and led the tactical team into the hotel lobby. "Charlie-Four, entry team's inside. Heading up." He sounded excited, and he should. The TFD got to execute the best part of a case Nathan had labored on for two years, though his involvement had mostly been unofficial.

"We're as useless as bureaucrats in a crisis," Nathan said.

"We get to sweat him after they slap on the cuffs," Waldo said.

"If they catch him."

"You don't think he's in there, *Papi*?"

"Kei's intel is usually spot on, but it took too damn long for SWAT to arrive."

"They needed approvals and—"

"I never arrested anyone waiting for red ink to dry."

Waldo shrugged.

Nathan sighed. "Bad guys don't do paperwork. We need to be nimble and adapt. All I'm saying."

"I heard stories about you."

Nathan winced. Waldo knew about Eddie, Nathan's former partner. Waldo was only twenty-six and fresh out of the Academy, and it would take time for federal experience to jade him. Maneuvering around the law and FBI policy was like tiptoeing through a minefield, but Nathan couldn't show Waldo too much. Eddie's death had taught him that lesson.

"Drive around back," Nathan said.

"Huh?" Waldo looked at him.

"Twelve agents with body armor and carbines just marched through the lobby. If the Leopard's in there, he won't escape through the front."

"TFD's covered the perimeter," Waldo said. "It's their scene."

Was Waldo afraid or lazy? "If you want to sit here with your thumb up your ass, go ahead, but I'm heading around back." Nathan cracked open his door.

"Okay, okay. Don't get *loco*."

Waldo waited for a group of college kids to pass, then pulled out and turned down the next block. Signs trumpeting Gavin Harrison's presidential bid wallpapered a brick wall. His political ads covered the city like playbills on Broadway, which made sense, because he'd been Tampa's mayor for the past eight years before becoming the Democratic Party's official nominee.

"Charlie-Six, I've got eyes on 321," an agent transmitted. The TFD agents ran the surveillance on one channel, while SWAT used another. Coordinating both the surveillance and tactical entry would have caused too much traffic.

"Entry team's moving up the west staircase," someone responded. "Two mikes out."

Waldo squared the block and turned onto East 7th Street, where an agent wearing an FBI windbreaker climbed out of a car and stood on the corner. At the next intersection, another agent did the same. Both had their guns holstered. Waldo continued past.

"They're visible from the windows," Nathan said.

"They gave up the surprise when SWAT stormed the lobby."

"Standing in the open is a good way to get shot."

Thirty hotel rooms with ornate wrought-iron balconies overlooked the street. Most curtains were drawn, and lights glowed inside. On the bottom floor, sheer curtains covered the expansive windows in the dining room beside a fire door with a keypad lock. A food supply truck parked in the loading dock.

"Stop here," Nathan said.

Waldo pulled to the curb, and Nathan opened his door.

"Yo," Waldo said. "We're supposed to sit back and watch."

"I'm trying to be useful and fill holes."

Nathan stepped out and stood behind their car. He wore jeans, hiking boots, and a light bomber jacket to cover his Glock 23 handgun and extra magazines. The Leopard stayed in room 321, a south-facing unit. If their suspect looked out, he'd spot the agents wearing raid jackets. Nathan focused on the center rooms. It must be one of those. A few had lights on.

"At the door," Charlie-Six broadcast. "Ready to make entry."

The next thirty seconds would determine if they caught the man responsible for attacking American agents and diplomats with directed-energy weapons. Frustration bubbled up. This was his case, with personal stakes, and he should be kicking down the door, not relying on SWAT.

The food truck left the loading dock and edged past the perimeter agent, blocking the agent's view. Nathan's focus darted to the building in the agent's blind spot.

The truck continued down the street, giving the agent a clear view. Nathan scanned the windows. Nothing.

"Door breached," an agent reported in a breathless voice.

Movement caught Nathan's eye. A man raced out of the dock. Nathan sprinted toward him without thinking. The guy stopped in the middle of the street.

"What's up?" Waldo yelled.

Nathan ignored him and reached the man at the same time as the perimeter agent. Nathan didn't have a photo of the Leopard, only Kei's description, but the heavyset white guy wearing coveralls wasn't the muscular Asian operative they sought.

"My truck's gone," the man said.

Nathan chilled. His radio crackled. "Charlie-Six, all units. Negative package. Room's empty."

Nathan stared down the road. The truck was gone. *Shit.* Nathan turned and sprinted back to the car. He'd heard all he needed to know.

The Leopard had escaped.

Nathan's radio filled with TFD agents' frantic calls reporting negative sightings. Nathan raced toward Waldo and lifted his handheld radio, trying to break in to the chatter. Agents should shut up and only report emergency traffic. They didn't sound like they'd been cops before joining the Bureau, and if they had police experience, sitting behind a desk had made them rusty.

Waldo leaned out his window. *"Que pasa?"*

"The Leopard stole the food truck," Nathan yelled. He jumped into the passenger side and pointed east. "That way."

Waldo screeched away from the curb and roared down East 7th Street.

The agent interviewing the hotel employee in the loading dock raised his walkie-talkie to his mouth as they flew by him. "Charlie-Nine to all units. I've got a report of a delivery truck theft that occurred two minutes ago."

Nathan keyed his microphone. "Break, break, Whiskey 34-06, agents in pursuit. Wholesome Eats food truck last seen eastbound on East 7th Street. It's a white box truck with the company name and a loaf of bread drawing on the side."

Drunk young people in slutty Halloween costumes glared at them as they sped past.

"There," Waldo said.

Three blocks away, a white truck barreled around the corner and headed south.

"Whiskey 34-06," Nathan broadcast. "We may have the truck southbound on . . ." He read the approaching street sign and counted up ". . . North 19th Street. Notify Tampa Police."

"Copy 34-06," a TFD agent responded. "We're heading for you. Keep eyes on."

"Request an airship from TPD, and have them roll K-9," Waldo transmitted.

Nathan scanned the floorboard for a blue light, then leaned around the seat to check on the floor. If the loaner car had come equipped with emergency equipment, it was probably in the trunk. *Damn.* He should have prepared better, but being in a vehicle pursuit hadn't occurred to him when the TFD supervisory special agent had told him to stage nearby and wait for SWAT to capture the suspect. *Stupid, stupid, stupid.*

The truck blew through a red light and entered a busy intersection on Adamo Drive, with five lanes of east-west traffic racing past.

Waldo jumped on his brakes and the Bu-ride fishtailed to a stop as the intersection devolved into chaos. The truck careened through the intersection and vehicles skidded out of control with screaming brakes and blaring horns.

The food truck smashed into a Hyundai, spinning the tiny car in a circle. The truck plowed into three lanes of eastbound oncoming traffic. An armored car slammed on its brakes and slid sideways.

The truck swerved, narrowly missing it—but it turned too hard. It leaned over, and its passenger-side wheels came off the ground. The driver cut the wheel back, and the truck righted itself, but its shifting load kept it in motion and it canted in the opposite direction.

A minivan's tires smoked as it tried to stop. It collided with the food truck's tailgate. The truck toppled onto its side, and twisting metal screeched like a dying animal as the vehicle slid across the road. Its back doors snapped open and pallets of bread dumped onto the roadway.

Cars swerved and stopped in both directions. Smoke rose over the street. Plastic and metal debris littered the intersection.

"Caray!" Waldo said.

"Get over there, fast."

Waldo pulled into the intersection. Cars in the westbound lanes inched around the wreckage. Drivers gawked at the broken vehicles, and spinning tires drew their attention like magnets. Waldo swerved through the tangled mess of cars, drawing honks and anger. A woman in a minivan flipped them the bird.

The food truck lay on its passenger side, with the undercarriage facing them. Its wheels spun and oil and gas wet the street. No sign of the driver. He might be injured after the high-speed collision.

"Suspect's Signal-Four at Adamo and 19th," Waldo transmitted, using the code for a traffic accident. "Dispatch ambulance and fire."

Waldo drove around the armored car's bumper that had been ripped off in the collision and blocked eastbound traffic twenty feet from the over-turned truck.

Nathan cracked open his door and jumped out before the car stopped. He brushed back his bomber jacket and drew his .40 handgun. At a mini-mum, the driver was a car thief, but the timing wasn't coincidence, and he must be the Leopard. Waldo's door slammed behind him, but Nathan focused on the truck, scanning for movement. He aimed up at the driver's door as he approached. If the Leopard wanted to fight, he'd pop out there.

Whoosh. Flames flickered around the truck's cab and rippled across the gasoline coating the pavement.

Nathan jumped back. He jogged around the truck, giving it a wide berth. He rounded the cab as flames licked the chassis. The spider-webbed windshield lay on the street. The air reeked of diesel. Nathan edged around the engine, aiming at the driver's door.

Nathan squinted through the smoke rising off the engine. The cab was empty.

Nathan whirled around.

Across Adamo Drive, an Asian man sprinted down 19th Street under the elevated Selmon Expressway. He wore gray slacks with a black turtle-neck and carried a black knapsack. He must be the driver.

"Got a runner," Nathan yelled.

He dashed across the street and beneath the expressway. The hum of cars echoed under the bridge. His suspect continued down 19th Street, thirty yards ahead and pulling away.

They ran into an industrial district on the south side of the toll road. Nathan reached for his radio, but he'd left it on the car seat.

Damn.

Nathan wanted to check if Waldo followed, but he concentrated on the fleeing man and tried to keep pace. The Leopard was a block and a half ahead. He'd probably set the fire as a distraction. The guy was good.

Nathan dashed past a construction supply store. Pain radiated down his arm from his old bullet wound, making his fingers tingle. Swinging his arms exacerbated his symptoms, which had forced him to stop his daily jogs, and his poor fitness hurt him now. His breath came hard and his legs ached—his body had been dormant for too long.

Ahead, the spy broke right and dashed toward a fenced industrial property. Massive, circular storage containers rose into the sky, and exposed pipes connected them to a biodiesel facility. The property hummed with machinery, but looked unoccupied.

The operative bounded like a gazelle and landed halfway up the chain-link fence. He climbed with little visible effort and vaulted over the top. He hit the ground like a gymnast and raced toward an inner fence.

Nathan reached the property as the Leopard climbed a second fence and shrugged off his jacket. He spun it like a cape and flopped it onto the razor wire atop the fence. He hurdled it and dropped onto the grass. He smirked at Nathan, then turned and disappeared behind a cement structure.

Nathan peered through the fence links. The operative hadn't hesitated. Was he fleeing out of fear, or did he know where he was headed? Nothing about him had appeared out of control. The Leopard had an escape plan.

Sirens came from the north, either FBI or police. Probably both. What took them so long? Nathan touched his belt where his handheld should have been attached. His fault. He glanced back as Waldo lumbered down the street huffing and puffing, with no radio in his hand. If he hadn't called in their direction of travel, the cavalry wasn't coming.

Nathan scaled the fence, and it swayed beneath his weight. He fumbled over the top, and an exposed strand of wire ripped into his forearm. He landed on the ground with his shoulder on fire. He raced to the second fence, taking off his jacket as he neared.

He scrambled to the second fence and used his jacket to protect him from the razor wire as his suspect had done. He climbed down into the facility as Waldo reached the outer fence. Nathan pointed to the building where he'd last seen the Leopard, then he raced into the facility.

Nathan drew his Glock as he approached the cement structure. The man likely fled with his freedom on the line, but he could be lying in ambush. Shooting Nathan would help him escape, but it would also increase the stakes. What if the Leopard had diplomatic immunity? Nathan shook away the thought.

He slowed and edged around the building's corner, slicing the pie. Clusters of thick metal pipes connected the building to stacks paralleling the industrial storage tanks. The Leopard was nowhere to be seen.

Waldo struggled to climb the first fence, and his thirty extra pounds of weight didn't help. On the street behind him, an FBI car with a blue light on the hood screeched to a halt. They needed to set a perimeter, but Nathan had the best chance of catching their suspect.

Nathan pivoted and jogged parallel to the fuel tank. He aimed his Glock at the disappearing edge of the cylinder, but his attention flickered to the surrounding machinery. The man could pop up anywhere. He moved from cylinder to cylinder, raking his barrel in wider and wider circles. The operative could have fled in any direction, or even doubled back.

Nathan reached the property's edge. Beyond an empty grassy area, two docks poked into the black water of Tampa Bay.

Nathan looked back at the facility. Off to his left, another cluster of older fuel storage tanks provided more perfect cover. Nathan jogged to them and peeked into the blackness. No movement. The Leopard could be hiding, but a professional wouldn't do that. He'd put distance between him and his pursuers. Nathan stopped and listened. The din of traffic racing down the highway merged with droning machinery.

Footsteps pounded on the concrete. Nathan aimed toward the sound as Waldo came into view. Nathan depressed his barrel and waved. He scanned the area.

The operative had disappeared.

Waldo reached him and braced his hands on his knees. Sweat poured down his face. Nathan didn't feel much better, and his shoulder hurt so much, his teeth ached. The FBI needed to increase their fitness requirements. Agent candidates were put through a wringer at Quantico, but once they reached a field office, their physical fitness deteriorated. They needed regular training and standards, but the people in power who made those policies probably didn't want to be subjected to those tests either. It would never happen.

"Nothing?"

"He's in the wind," Nathan said. "Get on the phone and have them set a perimeter."

Waldo took out his cell and dialed. "*Qué carbón.* What you think he had in his knapsack?"

"A go-bag. He was ready to flee if he felt pressure, and he made the surveillance."

Waldo barked instructions into his phone, but a feeling of hopelessness passed through Nathan. He walked to the dock where the rusting wharfs jutted into the Ybor channel. The sound of an outboard motor buzzed in the distance.

"Get Harbor Patrol too," Nathan said. "Have them look for something small and concealable with one or two occupants moving away from the city."

"Roger," Waldo said. He transmitted their location and asked for a marine unit to respond.

Nathan looked back at the lights from heavy traffic transversing the Selmon Expressway. A hundred cars must pass by every few minutes.

He sighed. The Leopard was a trained special operations professional who'd used his cunning to slip past an FBI SWAT team. He'd fled to the warehouse district for a reason. Whether he had a car or boat waiting, he'd prepared for a rapid exfiltration.

The Leopard had escaped.

3

***

General Ming Zhao paced behind his desk inside the Guóăbú, the Chinese Ministry of State Security. His headquarters was located in the Haidian District near the Summer Palace in northwestern Beijing, and he stared out his window at the pea-green water of Kunming Lake that bordered the intelligence compound. He'd never seen a lake in the mountainous Shanxi Province, once the ancient city-state of Zhao that had been named after his powerful family. Water would always be an oddity to him. A dozen ships transversed the lake, likely either carrying tourists or doing the business of government. In the end, all business belonged to the government—as it should.

The Second Bureau's administrative offices were located inside the primary headquarters building, but much of the Bureau's work happened in buildings situated along the southern edge of the intelligence compound. The eleven primary intelligence bureaus within the ministry specialized in domestic, foreign, semi-independent islands, technology, local, counterintelligence, circulation, research, countersurveillance, science, or computers. Other subcomponents included foreign affairs, politics affairs, personnel, education, and other activities, but Zhao's Second Bureau was China's intelligence star.

And within the Bureau, Zhao's prized possession hummed with activity.

The gem of the operations bureau—the Division of Disintegration Warfare. China's future depended on it. So did Zhao's career.

And his life.

Someone knocked. He glared across his expansive office at the cedar door as annoyance stiffened his jaw. He'd asked not to be disturbed. He raked his fingers through his shining hair, combing it across his bald pate. A horseshoe of hair was not the image he wished to present. He sucked in his gut and tugged his belt over his potbelly, another unwelcome manifestation of age and too much time spent behind a desk.

"Come," he said in Putonghua, the standard Mandarin dialect used throughout China's government.

The door opened and Jìng Qí flowed into the room with the grace of a dancer. As usual, she'd pulled her black hair back into a bun that exposed her long neck. She wore a blouse and a tight skirt that reached her knees, but even conservative attire couldn't hide her spectacular form.

An image of her naked body writhing beneath him floated behind his eyes. A beauty like her would never look twice at a fifty-nine-year-old man with a bulging stomach, but Zhao possessed the greatest aphrodisiac of all —power. She pretended everything he said carried wisdom and every moment in sexual congress was bliss, but he knew she lied. It mattered not, if she kept her feelings to herself. The moment she showed disdain, or worse, sympathy, he'd have her drowned in the lake. His previous mistress had learned that lesson.

Jìng stopped at his desk. "General Sun is here to see you."

A frigid breeze blew away Zhao's carnal thoughts and replaced them with icy fear. Donghai Sun was a ranking member of the Politburo's Standing Committee, a nine-member decision-making body of the most powerful Politburo members. These men controlled the National Congress's Central Committee and embodied the Chinese Communist Party.

"Send him in immediately. Never keep him waiting."

"But you instructed me to hold your calls and—"

"Bring him."

Jìng nodded and hurried from the room. Zhao remained standing. He straightened his shoulders, then caught himself and scowled. Sun may be one of the nine most influential men in China, which made him among the most dangerous people in the world, but Zhao deserved to be on the Standing Committee more than he. Sun was smart, that much was certain, and devious too, but he didn't possess Zhao's cunning. Or his ruthlessness. Zhao would make his way into the inner circle, eventually.

He'd do anything to reach the summit.

General Sun breezed into the room like a man used to commanding every space he entered. He marched across the room and stood before the desk. It no longer felt like Zhao's office.

"Your strategy isn't working," Sun said without preamble. He'd stated it flatly, as if failure wouldn't destroy Zhao.

"It's a long-term strategy," Zhao said, "and we need time to reap the rewards of our labor."

"Perhaps, but using drugs to attack America was a disastrous tactic. The FBI dismantled the Phantoms of Khorasan, and they seized hundreds of millions of yuan worth of carfentanil. Worse, they linked the shipments to our homeland. The political fallout will damage us for years."

Zhao averted his eyes. "The Islamists create chaos. It is true they failed to achieve all their goals, but they damaged—"

"They brought Americans together for the first time in decades."

"That will not last. Losing the Phantoms, and especially the Slayer, set us back, but utilizing drugs as a weapon of war proved effective and our opioid attacks caused economic damage."

"Short-lived harm. Their economy has rebounded. In many ways, our attack strengthened their polity. It scarred over their open partisan wounds. That wasn't your intention of drug warfare, was it?"

"Increasing Americans' fentanyl usage has drained labor from their economy, committed law enforcement resources, and tarnished their perception of themselves. Addiction has spread misery across their land, created animosity with their police, and caused political rifts. I'll keep the drugs flowing, but we won't attempt similar terror attacks."

Sun eyed him with a face as hard as a quarry stone. The clock ticked in the corner. The moment elongated, as if Sun's will stretched the fabric of time.

"Their president threatens new tariffs, and if they do that, we lose our largest market. An economic war would devastate us."

Zhao had accomplished much by commanding the CCP's foreign intelligence apparatus, but Sun controlled the country, one step away from replacing Xi Jinping as the general secretary. Sun was ten years Zhao's junior, and yet he'd done all this. He could make one call and everything Zhao had earned would disappear like the mist over Lake Kunming. They both knew it, and their power differential dripped from every word spoken.

Zhao nodded and tried to moderate his tone. "I understand the danger of America severing ties, but that is why political tactics are crucial to disintegration warfare. Our next phase will give us the upper hand."

"You predicted victory from the Phantom's terrorism too. Why should I believe your political tactics won't backfire as well?"

"We will control the country from the top. We will pull the strings and turn the United States into our puppet."

Sun remained still as a terra-cotta soldier. "You risk much with this."

"We will succeed."

"You'd better."

4

Nathan reclined in his favorite leather chair beside Meili Chan in the tower office of his three-story condo built in a former church in Northeast Washington, DC. She stared out the turret's lofty windows at the Supreme Court and Capitol ten blocks to the east, and beyond them, the Washington Monument's bluestone glowed in spotlights. Meili had been staying at his condo more frequently, and she finally seemed comfortable.

He mentally scrolled through a list of things he needed to complete in his cases, as if a mystical checklist followed him wherever he went. His mind floated to the memory of the Chinese spy disappearing behind the building. His failures ran on a constant reel in his mind whenever his thoughts wandered.

"Still stewing over Tampa?" Meili asked, snapping him back to the moment.

"We had him in our grasp," Nathan said. "We should've done the op ourselves."

"Not in Tampa's backyard. It wasn't your call."

His stomach tightened. "Frigging goat rope."

"How'd he know SWAT was coming?"

"He's a covert operator, a black ops expert. He prepared contingencies."

"Not much of a getaway plan."

"Feels like improvisation," Nathan said. "He might have seen them outside, or he had electronic surveillance in place. Whatever happened, he received warning and acted decisively. He's bold . . . and now he's in the wind."

She flashed a sad smile. "You wear your heart on your sleeve."

"It matters. I took an oath to defend our country, and I take it seriously."

"You're a sheepdog, and I mean that in a good way. You protect the herd."

He nodded. "It's what I do."

Some people let their jobs define them, but the opposite was true for him. Protecting the weak expressed his core identity, and his job was an extension of that. But his failures lingered.

She sighed. "Your dedication impresses and infuriates me."

"Meaning?"

"When you catch the scent of a bad guy, that becomes your priority. Nothing else matters."

"It's important."

"You'll get him," Meili said. "You usually do."

Nathan snorted. "We'll see."

"Don't forget, I'm leaving for Taipei tomorrow afternoon."

The room darkened. "For how long this time?"

"Five days. I'm meeting with Taiwanese intelligence officers, and I'm hoping to debrief some of their sources."

Nathan sighed. "We haven't seen each other much lately."

"It's the job."

Meili was Nathan's supervisor, and she was also his girlfriend. At least, that's how he referred to her. A divorced man calling a grown woman his girlfriend felt childish, but "lover" sounded creepy and "significant other" or "partner" was sterile and lifeless.

"I have a girlfriend and simultaneously don't have a girlfriend—like I'm dating Schrödinger's cat."

"Funny. I know all the travel sucks, but I can't miss this opportunity to develop a high-ranking source."

Nathan raised an eyebrow. "Havana Syndrome?"

"The attacks have slowed, and Russia's more involved than China right now, but that's why I need to uncover the CCP's evolving strategy. They're targeting us in numerous ways, and I need sources on the inside to illuminate their plans."

"Isn't this under counterintelligence?"

"It's Havana adjacent." She smiled. "I'm picking up your bad habits."

"I prefer to think of them as *unconventional*. I prioritize mission over policy."

"That's why I'm going."

Nathan moved to the bar cart and refilled their wine. They clinked glasses. "This the same source you met before the Chinese targeted you?"

"I'm getting briefed on the Taiwanese investigation, and they're offering access to their people. And we don't know that the Chinese came after me. We picked up countersurveillance, but their intentions weren't clear."

"Clear enough for the FBI to pull you out of country."

"That was a precaution . . . and we may have overreacted."

"You know my thoughts on that—better safe than sorry. Now that I'm officially assigned to the group, how about I come with you?"

"You've got plenty going on hunting the Leopard, and what about Amelia?"

"The Leopard's probably back in Beijing by now, and Amelia can stay with Reagan."

"Dan will be there to cover me."

Nathan scrunched up his face as if he'd bitten into a lemon. "The same Dan who asked you out for a drink?"

"I told him I was seeing someone."

"You mean me."

"I'm trying not to advertise it. If the Bureau found out, they wouldn't let us work together."

"We barely see each other anyhow."

"I need to go. Taiwan's National Security Bureau and their national Police Agency both have information about Chinese disintegration warfare. You're getting surly. Why don't we—"

"Dad, you up there?" Amelia called from downstairs.

"Meili and I are having a drink."

"You, uh, is this a bad time?"

"C'mon up," Nathan said.

Amelia padded up the stairs in her socks. Her blonde hair poked up as she followed the curving stairwell, then her blue eyes peeked over the railing.

"Hey, kiddo," Meili said.

"Hey." Amelia's eyes narrowed. She'd seemed to tolerate Meili when she'd thought she was just a co-worker, but when Nathan and Meili had announced they were dating, Amelia's attitude had cooled. Amelia desperately wanted Nathan and Reagan to reunite, but that ship had sailed when Vince Cabrera married Reagan.

"What's up?" Nathan asked.

Amelia climbed the last few stairs and walked across the tiny office to him. She wore baggy jeans and a purple fleece with sleeves a little too short. She'd been growing fast, and he needed to milk the most out of her clothing. With Reagan's salary gone, his finances tightened. His expensive mortgage and condo fees hadn't changed, but he didn't want to leave their home after the divorce. They needed stability, and moving might be too much for Amelia. And for him.

"Why's Mom supporting this whack?"

"Who?" Nathan asked.

"The old guy running for president. He's having a Menty B."

She held her phone up so Nathan could see the ChatteringHen social media application, then she hit play. A video of a gorgeous woman, probably only twenty years old, sitting at a desk beside a monitor facing the camera.

"This is Ashley Morris, back for another cultural update. Today's frowny face goes to Presidential Candidate Gavin Harrison. He claims to be a Democrat, but he sounds like another warmonger threatening China and the world. And I'm like totally shook by what he's planning. Get this, he wants to shut down ChatteringHen. Guess this old, white male wants even more control."

Beside her, the monitor displayed a montage of unflattering photos of Harrison, from his eyes crossed, to mouth open, to him biting into a hot pretzel.

"He's leading in the polls," Ashley continued, "so if you're old enough to vote, you should write in your own name. Seriously, this guy's a clown. Super cringe. This is Ashley with your morning update."

"That's delulu," Amelia said.

"Delu-what?" Nathan asked.

Amelia rolled her eyes. "Totally cray. Ashley always comes with the wig snatch."

"What language are you speaking?" Nathan asked.

"Harrison's ancient."

"Your mom's a Democrat, and as an elector, it's her job to support the nominee."

"But he's gassing us. Even my teacher said something's wrong with him."

Nathan scowled. "Teachers shouldn't discuss politics with impressionable fourth graders."

"Remember," Meili said, "your teachers have opinions like everyone else, but their expertise in whichever subject they teach doesn't translate to economics or political philosophy."

"It's facts."

Meili didn't respond. Nathan and Meili had never defined the rules for her interactions with Amelia. She might want to guide the girl, but she probably worried about overstepping her bounds. Introducing his love interest to a child of divorce could be fraught with danger.

"There's more to politics than sound bites and bad pictures," Nathan said. "Who's this podcaster anyhow?"

"Da-ad, she not a podcaster. This is news."

"That was opinion."

"About the news." Amelia stared at him in earnest.

"Politics is complicated. If you're really interested, I'd be happy to discuss the issues with you, or better yet, since I'm not voting for him, why don't you ask your mom why she's supporting Gavin Harrison. Listen to both sides, think critically, and make your own decisions. Don't let any talking head sway you with illogical arguments. Use your ability to reason."

"What-evs." Amelia headed toward the stairs.

"Say goodnight to Meili."

Amelia stopped. "Why? Won't she still be here for breakfast?"

"Don't be rude," Nathan said.

"Goodnight, Meili."

Meili waved.

"Night, pumpkin," Nathan said, then when she'd disappeared into the stairwell, he turned to Meili. "Some of those pictures looked manipulated."

"You can't trust anything online, and AI can create video indistinguishable from reality."

"Deepfakes?"

"People are gullible, and deepfakes look real."

"That podcaster isn't the only talking head bad-mouthing Harrison," Nathan said. "And ChatteringHen is a pretty left-leaning platform. I wonder why they're going after the Democratic nominee?"

"He says silly things, which makes him an easy target. Everyone's hunting for clicks, and going viral generates money."

Nathan nodded and sipped his Bordeaux. "This is nice."

"Disinformation and propaganda?"

"Having you here."

She looked away.

He cleared his throat. "I think it's time"—his voice sounded tight—"for us to consider moving in—"

"Let's not ruin a good thing," she said.

Her words cut him, and he winced. "How would you living here *ruin* anything?"

"Getting serious too soon never ends well."

"It's been a year . . . sort of, I mean, we don't see each other much."

She took his hand. "Be patient."

Her cell vibrated. She glanced at the screen, then took the call.

"Uh-huh . . . uh-huh . . . What kind of negative reporting?" She sighed as she listened. "The source is ready to meet? Okay, I'll rearrange the trip."

Nathan raised his eyebrows.

"Submit the travel request," Meili said. She hung up.

"Something breaking?"

"My new Chinese source requested an urgent meeting."

"Who is it?"

"We haven't met her in person, but she goes by Xuannü. We think it's a code name based on Jiutian Xuannü, the goddess of war, sex, and longevity. We've tentatively identified her as Shen Wang, a high-ranking intelligence official. The agency has some reporting on her."

"Want me to debrief her with you?"

"Dan left for Taipei, so I could use you. Come with me to CIA in the morning. I want to know what we're walking into before we go."

"Where's the meet?"

"Macao."

5

Reagan Cabrera's mind reeled from the morning news. The presidential general election was only weeks away, and Arthur Ambrose, Gavin Harrison's vice presidential pick, had dropped out of the race. He claimed he'd done it for personal reasons, but his health seemed fine. As a Democratic Party elector, Reagan had the inside scoop on much of the political machinations behind the election, but she and everyone she knew had been blindsided by Ambrose's withdrawal.

What the hell had happened?

Reagan pressed the intercom outside Nathan's condo, a place she'd once called home.

"Morning, Reagan," Meili responded.

Reagan's chest tightened at the sound of another woman's voice. She looked up at the surveillance camera. "I'm here to collect Amelia. She ready?"

"Always late. Thanks for taking her while Nathan and I are TDY."

Always late. Meili's familiarity made Reagan's eye twitch. Who was Meili to pretend she knew Amelia? Meili may have been in the picture for more than a year, but she didn't know anything.

"I can wait down here."

"Nonsense. Come up."

The elevator door opened, and Reagan's stomach tightened as she rode it up. Dealing with her ex-husband brought a default level of tension, but having to make small talk with Nathan's lover wasn't an ideal way to start the morning—especially when she needed to focus on political ramifications.

The elevator opened and Meili stood there holding a steaming coffee. The aroma of French roast hung in the air.

"Coffee?" Meili asked.

"I need to get going. Nathan here?"

"Still in the shower."

A pang flashed through her chest. They stared awkwardly at each other. Reagan had no reason to be jealous. She'd left Nathan for another man, and Nathan had pined for her for ages before finally moving on, so how could this bother her? Besides, she and Vince were happily married, at least most of the time. But this peek into an intimate, domestic setting between Meili and Nathan prickled her skin, and this would be the new normal until Amelia was old enough to drive. Perhaps the stress of political upheaval made everything feel worse. Or maybe it was something else.

"I need to take Amelia to school and then do damage control."

Meili's eyes widened, seemingly happy at the change of subject. "I know. This is crazy. Has a VP ever dropped out this close to an election?"

"I don't think so."

"Did you have any warning it was coming?"

"No."

Was Meili sticking it to her by outing Reagan as a party outsider and making her admit she'd been no better informed than anyone? Reagan had been a delegate at the Democratic Convention, and then she'd been selected by the party as one of thirteen electors in Virginia. Her selection signaled the party valued her, probably because her past life as a State Department official had given her valuable experience and perspective. The party approved of her, and they'd already discussed her running for office during the next election cycle.

"What happens now?" Meili asked.

"Harrison will select someone else."

"Won't people vote again in another primary?"

Meili seemed generally curious, and she'd hit on the central issue. With the election so close, there'd be no time for voters to weigh in. "Harrison will choose a partner, and the party will anoint them."

"Won't that disenfranchise voters?"

That would be the Republicans' criticism, and they'd trumpet it to suppress Democratic voter turnout in the general election. Meili had said she was a Democrat, which was unusual for a federal agent, and her concern probably echoed what was on the minds of most voters.

The pipes squeaked upstairs as Nathan shut off the water. Reagan had heard that sound a thousand times, but now . . . it felt different.

"Harrison and Ambrose won the primary in a landslide," Reagan said, "which gives Harrison a mandate. We're a representative democracy, so people shouldn't be upset when he selects a new VP. Besides, people vote for the top of ticket, not the vice president."

"Who will he pick?"

Reagan shrugged. "That's the question of the day."

Harrison could select one of the other primary candidates, or he could pick someone out of left field. Selecting a VP was a mechanism for rewarding party loyalty, but it also helped sway specific voter groups and set up a career for a future presidential run. If Harrison was smart, he'd choose a popular politician from a swing state to lock up those electoral votes.

Amelia pounded down the stairs in her socks, carrying her backpack. Reagan's shoulders loosened, as the uncomfortable inquisition by Meili came to a close.

"Almost ready, Mom."

"You're late again."

"I know, I know."

"What did I tell you about respecting other people's time?"

"Sorry." Amelia slid on her shoes.

"Don't forget a jacket."

"I'm not a kid."

"If you weren't a kid, I wouldn't be waiting to drive you to school."

Reagan turned to Meili. "I hoped to say goodbye to Nathan."

"He should be out soon."

"I can't wait. How long will you be out of the country?"

Meili sipped her coffee. "At least five days. Depends on what happens."

"Anything you can talk about?"

Meili shook her head. "Sorry, but honestly, it sounds like you have the more interesting job this week."

Reagan's phone vibrated. A call from Liz Washington, the DNC Party's deputy leader in Virginia. "Gotta grab this."

"Sure."

Reagan stepped away and answered.

"Quick update," Liz said.

"This is nuts. When did—"

"It's a crisis, I know. I've got dozens of calls to make, but I wanted to let you know, Harrison is announcing his VP pick any minute."

"Do you know—"

"Darcy Lemon."

"Who the hell is Darcy Lemon?"

Meili looked up and raised her eyebrow. *Shit.* Reagan should have lowered her voice.

"She was the Director of the Office of Science and Technology under the last Democratic administration, before the last four years of Republican oppression. She toed the company line back then and kept a low profile."

"I assumed Harrison would pick a governor of a battleground state. How'd he select her?"

"He didn't. It came from the DNC. Ambrose's withdrawal took everyone by surprise. There are rumors about something in his past the vetting committee missed. The DNC didn't want another disaster, so they told Harrison who to pick."

"He push back?"

"What choice does he have? The election's in two weeks. If we lose this thing, we won't see a Democrat at the helm for another four years."

"And Darcy Lemon is a good choice?"

"She's a black woman, so she checks two intersectional boxes. Voters will have another chance to vote a woman into the presidency."

"I mean her positions. Where does she stand on the issues?"

"I told you everything I know about her. Gotta go."

"Thanks for the heads—" The call disconnected.

Reagan looked at Meili.

"Sorry to eavesdrop," Meili said, "but who's Darcy Lemon?"

"That's what all of America will be asking."

6

Nathan and Meili stood outside the main entrance to CIA headquarters in Langley, Virginia, and waited for their escort to lead them into the super-secret records archives. Meili wanted to read what the agency had on her new source before their face-to-face meeting in Hong Kong. No one had debriefed the woman in person before, making this their most dangerous contact. The chance of a double-cross loomed.

Nathan had perused the limited intelligence reports on the initial contacts with the source, safely locked away inside a top-secret vault in the FBI's Hoover Building. The new source, codenamed Xuannü, a woman believed to be Shen Wang, was a senior member of the CCP's Ministry of State Security. China's government had always been misogynistic, and despite women accounting for half the population, females only occupied eight percent of leadership positions. For Shen to have risen in China's intelligence service meant she was either incredibly good, or seriously connected. Why would she risk it all to pass information to the United States?

Unless she was a double agent.

"What's Xuannü's motivation?" Nathan asked.

"She claims she's fed up with Maoism. She caught a taste of how free enterprise could lift China out of poverty, even with intense regulation and corporatism, then she witnessed Hong Kong implode under the boot of communism. It doesn't take a genius to notice that centrally planned economies with few property or individual rights fail—no matter where they're tried."

Nathan nodded. That's how he'd feel in Shen's shoes, but he'd been raised in a Western democracy with Judeo-Christian values, a legacy of personal freedom, and a government restricted by a constitution. Shen lived under a communist regime that had been in power since 1949, and the government had propagandized her every day of her life and quelled public dissent and opposing voices. How did she develop the intellectual honesty to break free from group-think? Was something else behind her treason?

"Shen approached our Beijing office without enticement, correct?"

"She did a brush pass with the LEGAT as he exited a restaurant. He wasn't expecting it, but she bumped into him and dropped it in his pocket. Surprised the hell out of him, but he had the composure to get back to the office before he retrieved her message."

"The legal attaché has twenty-four hour counterintelligence surveillance," Nathan said. "That was a risky approach."

"She seems to know what she's doing."

"Why didn't she go to CIA?"

"Her note claimed she had information about Havana Syndrome. I assume she thought our LEGAT was the right contact at the US Embassy."

A steady stream of people entered the agency through the front door. They looked no different from people arriving at any other corporation. Even the business of national security became routine.

"Remind me how you identified her?"

"I sent a source to the restaurant where the brush pass occurred, and Shen Wang was on the reservation list at the same time the LEGAT dined there. That's a hell of a coincidence, and coupled with her level of access in the Second Bureau, makes it highly probable she's our source."

Nathan had read the reports, but it still didn't make sense. "She's a high-ranking intelligence official seeking to betray her country. Approaching the CIA would have made sense. She had to know the FBI would inform the ambassador and the CIA."

"Her note asked for a dead drop location, and in that next exchange, she claimed she had access to internal documents in the Ministry of State Security. She passed an internal memo, and we used it to narrow down people with access—which included Colonel Shen Wang."

"The CIA would never allow an in-person contact without verifying her identity."

"Neither would our counterintelligence folks, but they're not calling the shots and neither is the CIA."

"I'm surprised the agency didn't insist on taking control," Nathan said.

"They're involved, to say the least. Our people notified me because Xuannü claims she has Havana Syndrome intelligence. She demanded to speak to the FBI's Havana Syndrome group and asked for me by name."

A twenty-something preppy guy with wavy blond hair, tan suit, and a shimmering smile walked up to them. "Agents Chan and Burke, I'm Milo, your escort. Credentials please."

They handed him their credential cases and badges. He read each and matched their photos to their faces, something people rarely did after glancing at their gold badges.

"Please follow me."

Milo led them inside and through screening. Nathan's claustrophobia built with each layer of security they passed, from the checkpoints on the perimeter to the interior entry posts. The faces on the surrounding people were closed books.

Deep inside the building, on the floor they could only access with Milo as an escort, Nathan and Meili stopped outside the vault where digital files contained reports from human intelligence. CIA case officers ran agents all over the world—spies who provided information for various motivations ranging from money to revenge—and their debriefings were stored there.

These were the agency's most closely held secrets.

Light flickered behind the peephole, and Nathan glanced at the camera staring down at them from the corner. They held up their badges, and the door opened.

A young woman in a tan pantsuit smiled at them. "Welcome, I'm Tricia." She checked their identification again.

"Good day," Milo said to them. "They'll call me when you're finished." He headed back down the hallway.

"This way," Tricia said. She led them inside and stopped outside a classified documents handling area. They would not be allowed inside the inner sanctum. She opened the door and led them into a viewing room with two rows of desks, each with a computer terminal.

"Have a seat," she said. "The Librarian will bring the files you requested."

Nathan started. "The *Librarian's* meeting us?"

"She thought it best to handle this herself."

Meili slipped into a chair and Nathan sat beside her. Trisha left and shut the door with a double-click.

"She locked us in," Meili said.

"Security."

"This place stresses me out."

"It's important to see what they have on your source."

"That's why I'm here, but I don't have to like it."

Their terminals didn't look like commercial computers. They were black and irregularly shaped, connected to the desk with thick black wires. Whatever they viewed would be recorded somewhere. The CIA held many secrets, but the identities and debriefing reports of their human sources were the agency's crown jewels.

The CIA didn't like sharing source information, but Meili built a criminal case against Chinese actors behind Havana Syndrome after she and Nathan had exposed China's involvement in attacks on US soil. Assistant United States Attorney Robert Felix had submitted a Prudential request for any information the CIA had on Colonel Shen Wang or her chosen codename, which required CIA to provide any negative reporting on the source. Felix had filed similar requests with every federal agency. They didn't have enough evidence to prosecute yet, but uncovering negative reporting would be less damaging now than on the eve of trial.

The door opened, and a frail woman entered wearing a blouse buttoned high with an ivory brooch. She'd pulled her hair back in a tight bun and wore stylish glasses. Almost the stereotype of a librarian. In fact, that was what she was—the agency's custodian of all human source documents. Nothing was released without her approval, and her presence sent a signal that Meili's source had value to the agency. Or that's what they wanted the FBI to believe. Intelligence work involved layers of motivation and misdirection, and dealing with the agency was often like peeling an onion—it took time to get to the center, and the process often caused tears.

"I'm Lydia," she said. "We have reporting on your source."

"How bad is it?" Meili asked.

"That's for you to determine."

7

———

The Librarian stood before Nathan and Meili in the records viewing room in the bowels of the CIA. She was responsible for keeping the identities of the agency's spies secret, and if her face tightened anymore, her skull would rip through her skin. The law required federal agencies to provide any exculpatory or derogatory information they possessed about government witnesses, and both Prudential and Brady requests were formal mechanisms for intelligence sharing, but the Librarian didn't seem to approve.

The door opened, and Tricia entered carrying a CD. She used a key to unlock a hard drive, then inserted the CD into a slot and pressed a series of buttons.

"They're set on terminals four and five," Tricia said.

"May I see your credentials again please," Lydia asked.

Meili and Nathan complied. Checking and double-checking would normally annoy him, but protecting human source identities saved lives.

Lydia noted their names on a digital notebook. "Take as much time as you need, but no copying material, and I'll need to inspect your notes before you leave."

"Thanks," Meili said, then turned to Nathan. "Here we go."

She opened her terminal, and Nathan did too.

Four reports referenced Xuannü, proving the source had passed information directly to the CIA in the past. The first report was a summary of earlier information she'd sent, and the second was a debriefing of another agency source discussing Shen Wang, which they believed to be Xuannü's identity. The last two reports were copies of the recent notes Shen had passed to the LEGAT. The CIA didn't control Meili's source, but they'd either been given full access or obtained the information through alternative means.

Nathan opened the first two files, since he'd already read Shen's recent correspondence. Both Shen's intelligence exchange and the other source debriefing had been conducted in Beijing two months before Shen's first contact with the FBI.

Xuannü's first contact had been with a CIA case officer operating under Non-Official Cover. The NOC, Ellen Wassermann, worked the vice president of Longfellow Consulting, a private British company that handled legal issues with tariffs, Chinese quotas, and the legal labyrinth around importing and exporting goods from China to the European Union. She worked closely with the Chinese Ministry of Commerce to keep European companies in line with Chinese law. Wassermann reported shifts in the international market that affected the global economy, and her position allowed her to report both on what major industries planned to do and what people said behind closed doors. Her reporting would have been used to stay ahead of Chinese tariff and legal changes.

According to Wassermann's report, she'd exited her Beijing office and walked to her car in the company's private underground garage. She deactivated her alarm, unlocked her car, and climbed into the driver's seat when her nylons brushed against a sealed envelope leaning against her seat. She opened it and found a note from someone calling themselves Xuannü.

Nathan read the note, a four-page essay on how the CCP made a concerted effort to cast any criticism of China's market manipulation and tariffs as acts of racism. Xuannü claimed the Second Bureau had implemented a strategic plan to influence Americans by inflaming students' anger across universities and by coloring media coverage. They nudged journalists to ignore the economic pitfalls of government market manipulation, and they reframed criticism of Chinese policy as bigotry. Most damning, the report said US Representative Chelsea Winters had been bribed to further this narrative. The CIA had forwarded the bribery accusation to the FBI.

What was most surprising about Xuannü's note was not its contents but that she had known Wassermann was a NOC. The choice of Wassermann as recipient had sent a message that Xuannü was a member of Chinese intelligence, and let CIA know that Wassermann had been compromised. Had Xuannü intended that warning as a gift for taking her note seriously?

Nathan opened the second report, the in-person debriefing of another agency source in which their CI mentioned Shen Wang. CIA Case Officer Elliot Brown controlled an asset in Chinese State Security, an economic analyst named Yuanyun Guo. According to the report, Guo had limited access to higher-ranking officials, but in June, his boss had been in Shanghai for a family funeral, so Guo attended a weekly meeting of department heads. Guo had delivered the summary of his department's report on Taiwanese microchip prices.

Nathan scrolled to the next page, where Guo summarized what he had told the committee, but most sentences had been blacked out. He forwarded through pages of redactions before reaching Guo's summaries of what other department heads had reported. Just noting what each department decided was important to share gave deep insight into the priorities of various sections of Chinese intelligence. But those pages had been redacted too.

Nathan looked over at Meili. Her forehead wrinkled, and she scowled as she manipulated the document. She didn't seem happy the CIA had failed to share the report in its entirety. Context mattered, and this type of report would only contain peripheral details about Shen. Nathan continued through pages of unreadable text until he reached two uncensored paragraphs.

The source listened to Colonel Shen Wang, the deputy division chief of operations in the Ministry of State Security's Second Bureau. Source noted that while the Second Bureau handles foreign intelligence collection, Colonel Wang's responsibilities focus on foreign trade with a concentration on ocean shipping. Wang read an executive summary of the week's intelligence collection to the group noting a drop-off in Western shipping. She stated that two American, one Austrian, and one Spanish transshipment company had altered their shipping routes to avoid the

South China Sea. Her analysis suggested this could be due to fear of a blockade of Taiwan. She stated this fear may be caused by the Second Bureau's influence operations inside the United States. She recommended reducing the rhetoric about Taiwan until a military decision has been made.

The source noted that both Colonel Shen's intelligence and her analysis were incorrect. The exact motivation for the change in sea routes by the transnational companies could not be attributed to any single intelligence operation, and the actions of only four companies in a massive global industry do not reach the level of statistical significance. The source further stated that Colonel Wang's recommendation to reduce the level of propaganda disseminated inside the United States would have no discernible effect on the companies she noted or on the overall shipping business. The source believes Colonel Wang made an unsubstantiated and dangerous recommendation. The source further found her presentation troubling, and he would recommend to his boss that her report be ignored.

Nathan read it again, then waited for Meili to finish digesting the report. She looked at him.

"It's nothing," he said.

"He says she's unreliable."

"It's his opinion."

She sighed. "Still, an agency asset believes Shen provided bad information based on incomplete intelligence and incorrect analysis."

"Maybe he's right, and maybe not. He's a junior analyst in another division who doesn't know her, and he isn't privy to the totality of her intelligence collection that led to her conclusion."

"It doesn't matter. It's still negative reporting by a source about the validity of our source's information."

Why was she taking this seriously? "But it's not based on contradictory evidence or proof. It's a junior officer taking shots at a senior official. He might be trying to impress his case officer and puff up the importance of this meeting. And I wonder how much Shen being a woman had to do with his disregard for her information. If we saw the rest of his report, we could tell if he criticized the other division representatives."

"It doesn't matter," Meili said. "If we use her as a source and this case goes to trial, we'd be forced to turn over this unflattering appraisal to defense counsel."

"But it's not based on anything. There's nothing in this debriefing that shows Shen is unreliable or manufacturing evidence. He just doesn't *think* it's true."

"There's no exemption for bad opinions. The issue is we'd never be able to turn this report over to defense, because the agency's source is active. The CIA would never allow it, and they wouldn't be wrong."

"We still need to hear what she has to say."

"We'll debrief her, but we can never use her as a witness."

Nathan smiled. "Nobody said federal cases were easy."

8

Reagan shifted uncomfortably in her boardroom seat as Liz Washington chaired the Virginia Democratic Party briefing for electors. The presidential election loomed, and with an unpopular Republican president seeking a second term, Democrats had a viable shot at retaking the White House—especially with the charismatic Harrison ginning up support around the country. At least their chances had been good until the vice presidential nominee withdrew. The DNC had installed Darcy Lemon as Harrison's running mate, but nobody knew her, and her relative anonymity created hesitancy in the populace. At least that's what a recent poll had shown.

"The broad strategy," Liz said, "will be to focus on Harrison and—"

"Lemon can't hide until the election," Finn Morrow said. All eyes turned to him. Finn had been an elector for a decade, and before that, he'd been lieutenant governor. He wielded significant political power in Virginia.

"She's not hiding, Mr. Morrow," Liz said.

"She hasn't done a single interview since she became the nominee. It doesn't look right."

"Lemon has promised to do an in-depth, one-on-one interview before the election," Liz said. "She'll explain—"

"Not good enough," Finn said. "This election is razor thin, and were fighting for independent and undecided voters. This thing will come down to a few thousand votes in swing districts, and now, we're fielding an unknown. She needs to define herself, before the Republicans do it for her."

"Nobody cares about the bottom of the ticket," Liz said. "People vote for the president. Don't worry, Lemon's not a freak and she doesn't have any skeletons in her closet. The vetting committee made sure of that."

Reagan hadn't been outspoken in these meetings, and she needed to assert herself more, especially if she aspired to higher office, something the Virginia Democratic Party seemed inclined to support.

She inhaled a deep breath of courage. "Finn is right." Everyone looked at her, and Reagan's pulse thumped in her neck. "The unknown is scarier to voters than being drunk at a sorority party or flip-flopping on a position. Lemon needs to hit the campaign trail hard."

Liz scowled, making Reagan's chest flutter. Had she shot herself in the foot by challenging the committee head?

Fuck it. Reagan wanted to run for office, and that required daring. She had to speak her mind, otherwise, what was the point?

"Lemon should be giving multiple interviews every day," Finn said. "She needs to reassure voters she's not a whack job."

"Swapping the vice presidential candidate is unprecedented," Liz said. "She'll share her positions, but the focus must remain on Harrison."

"How about posting a similar platform to Harrison?" Reagan asked with more confidence. "Her job is to support Harrison's positions, so why not double down on them. It seems an easy enough lift to post a web page reaffirming her commitment to Harrison's political priorities."

"That's the VP's decision," Liz said.

"The DNC picked her," Finn said.

"Then it's national's decision," Liz said, "not ours."

The electors stilled around the table and flashed looks of concern. A few murmured quiet comments to each other. Clearly, no one was comfortable with this midstream change in horses.

Liz raised her hands to settle everyone. "Listen, everyone take a beat. I hear your concerns, and I'll forward them to national. These are unique times. Picking a former cabinet official was an unconventional move, but the beauty is, she doesn't have a controversial record we need to defend. As director of Science and Technology, Lemon basically executed the former administration's policy. She's a blank slate.

"That's what worries me," Finn said.

9

The call to prayer echoed out of speakers across downtown Hamtramck, making the city feel like a foreign country. Nathan paused on the sidewalk and scanned the densely populated urban area. Waldo stopped beside him, and they let a group of women wearing burkas pass. Across the street, men wore kaftan shirts and Sufi caps.

The City of Hamtramck lay on the outskirts of Detroit in Wayne County, Michigan. Five miles outside downtown Detroit, the city was an enclave for radical Muslims. The average income was under $15,000 and more than a third of the population lived in poverty. Most foreign-born residents came from the Middle East and Southern Asia, creating the United States' first Muslim majority city. Its poor population hadn't assimilated to American values, making it a feeding ground for radical clerics seeking to sow dissension and terror.

"Every woman I've seen is wearing a headscarf or a burka," Waldo said.

"That's why the sheikh based here. He has an ample supply of recruits and a sympathetic populace to provide cover."

"Think we'll get him?"

"I wouldn't have dropped everything to come if I didn't."

"I mean, is the intel good?"

The DEA Special Operations Division had received a tip from NSA indicating criminal activity had been intercepted on a telephone transmission, and while US law prohibited that information from being directly used by law enforcement, the intelligence community was allowed to pass the tip. DEA agents had independently developed probable cause and dropped a wire on the line. The subscriber turned out to be a drug trafficker, and one of his contacts was a weapons dealer who mentioned Sheikh Omar Yemeni on a call. DEA brought in the FBI's Detroit Field Office, and forty-eight hours later, they'd identified a potential location for the fugitive who'd helped orchestrate the worst terrorist attacks on American soil.

"HRT is staged and ready," Nathan said, referring to the FBI's Hostage Rescue Team, an elite unit used for high-risk operations, especially those targeting high-value terrorism targets.

"I can't believe he's still in the country after you rolled up the Phantoms."

"It's probably a sign he's planning something else."

Waldo scratched his head. "The Hamtramck Police didn't want a piece of this?"

"We just notified them. We couldn't risk word leaking out."

"They pissed?"

"I didn't make the call," Nathan said. "I doubt they want to be proactive, and I can't blame them, the way they've been targeted by politicians playing racial politics."

"Racial bias is a real thing in law enforcement."

"I know it happens," Nathan said, "but the narrative of cops disproportionately shooting black people is totally wrong. When you account for variables like group crime rates, the racial difference evaporates. In this climate, the data shows cops hesitate to shoot black suspects, like they do in simulated training scenarios. Who knows how many cops have been injured or killed because of that hesitation."

"Maybe . . ."

"Read the data. It's a provable thesis."

"You'd think these *pingas* would want a piece of a terrorist."

"There are plenty of good officers here, but the politicians have their boots on their necks. The guys from the precinct will back us up if we need them."

"They better."

"Targeting police criminally and civilly for doing their jobs will have lasting effects. The quality of recruits will decline. Cops will refuse to do anything proactive, and when they respond to calls, they'll do the minimum. Crime rates will soar, especially in minority areas where citizens need more police, not fewer."

Nathan and Waldo crossed the street and entered a hardware store. An FBI agent met them inside and led them upstairs to an apartment where the owner lived. Luckily, the shop owner was a cousin of a new agent in the Detroit office, so they'd been given covert access to the space to use as an observation post. Agents in plain clothes had moved equipment into the store through the loading dock using unmarked boxes, but despite the congested urban area, an influx of fit young people in proximity to their target would eventually set off alarm bells.

They needed to move fast.

A stocky woman in her mid-forties with olive skin crossed the room and extended her hand. "Melissa Pettorossi, SSA."

Nathan and Waldo introduced themselves and shook her hand. "Thanks for rallying your troops so fast," Nathan said.

"When DC calls with the location of a terrorism suspect, we don't screw around."

"Let's hope he's there."

She looked down in thought, then back at him. "How confident are you in the intel?"

"Why did everyone ask that?"

"It sounds credible, and surveillance caught three males entering the house, one of whom matches the description. It's possible."

Nathan knelt in front of a screen they'd hung to cover their movements inside the room. He stared at six monitors that showed various surveillance camera feeds focused on the target apartment, which was across the street and three doors down. They could have watched the feed from the FBI's tactical command vehicle, but that had parked half a mile away to avoid drawing attention.

An HRT operator monitored communications in the corner. He cocked his head as he listened to a transmission. "Red six copies. Stand by." He looked at Pettorossi. "Entry team's in place and ready."

Pettorossi turned to Nathan. "Green light?"

Nathan's stomach hardened like always before an operation. "Do it."

Pettorossi keyed her walkie-talkie. "All perimeter units, get ready. We're launching HRT." She gave the thumbs-up to the HRT operator.

He keyed his radio. "Red six to entry team."

He waited for a response, then transmitted, "Operational approval received. Execute, execute, execute."

Nathan looked at the monitors. Time suspended. The air stilled, like before a thunderstorm. He stared at the screen showing the front of the townhouse and didn't blink.

Two unmarked vans rolled up and the HRT entry team disembarked. Patrol cars and FBI sedans with flashing blue lights blocked the road in both directions. Muscular men loaded with heavy gear leapt from the vehicles like professional athletes and stacked up as they moved toward the location. An agent with a penetrator ram posted beside the door as the entry team covered the door and windows.

The breacher swung his ram and connected above the doorknob. Wood shattered and the locking mechanism popped into the air. The door swung inward, and the breacher stepped back.

The number-one man in the stack shouldered through the opening with his muzzle pointed forward. He broke left, the second man broke right, and the third pushed straight forward. The entire team shuffled forward and disappeared inside, leaving the perimeter operators to cover the street.

"Let's get down there," Nathan said.

"We can wait here," Pettorossi said.

Nathan ignored her and jogged downstairs. His badge hung on a chain around his neck, and he freed it from beneath his shirt. He dug out his crumpled raid jacket from his pocket and slipped it on. He crossed the street and waited outside with the perimeter units.

Five minutes seemed like an hour, then the call came over the radio.

"No joy," an HRT commander broadcast. "We detained three males, but our target is not here."

Nathan deflated.

They should have waited and continued surveillance on the apartment longer or tried to insert an undercover, or . . . Second-guessing was endless. And pointless. They'd only had a few sentences on a wire intercept and surveillance had been difficult, yet they'd seen a suspect matching the description. Going in had been a reasonable call, but it hadn't panned out. That happened.

At least the other Phantoms and the terror supporters who'd facilitated their attacks had been either killed or convicted. The sheikh was the last significant player on the loose.

Waldo kicked an empty Coke can across the street. "I'm getting tired of losing."

"You can't hit a home run without swinging."

"We better connect soon before something bad happens."

Nathan nodded. They'd keep trying, but one thing was for sure. Sheikh Omar Yemeni was in the wind.

10

General Zhao stared at the picture of the Central Committee hanging on the hallway wall outside his office. These men ran one of the world's most populated and powerful countries, and though the People's Republic of China's communist government was barely over one hundred years old, its real power came from the historical memory of their five-thousand-year-old empire. That culture had inculcated in the Chinese people the belief that they were the chosen people, and among them, Zhao had risen to a position to usher them to victory.

No, it was more than that.

Zhao's cunning had enabled him to devise a bold strategy to defeat the Americans, and he'd deftly executed the early phases, but his growing power came from somewhere deeper. Since his birth into the affluent Zhao family, he'd been groomed for leadership. They didn't name cities after weak bloodlines, and his ancestors had influenced everything in the Shanxi Province since the formation of the Zhao kingdom over two thousand years before. The power of his lineage preordained his rise to power.

Zhao was destined to lead, and the gods had chosen him to be their instrument—a weapon to return China to world dominance.

Zhao showed his identification to the guard in the secure elevator down the hall from his office. He entered the war room in a bunker located in the bowels of the Second Bureau, and six staff members leapt to their feet.

"Sit," he commanded with a wave of his hand.

The five men and one woman returned to their terminals. He pretended not to care about formalities, but their outward displays of respect would mold their perception of him over time, and their fear was necessary for him to wield unchallenged power within the Bureau. Besides, their subservience filled him with strength. Life was simply a power struggle, and those with authority won—and everyone else became slaves.

He sat at the head of the map table as Colonel Ying Luo approached carrying a thick folder. His eyes fell to her trim body. He'd selected her for his intelligence cell because of her beauty, as he had with every female officer in his inner sanctum. Perhaps he'd take her as a personal assistant when he grew tired of entertaining himself with Jíng Qí.

"General Zhao," she said.

"Report."

She stacked his daily briefing materials before him, then opened her folder and read from a printed page with colored tables and charts. She cleared her throat and straightened. "We have achieved a new high in fentanyl crossing the United States' southern border. As predicted, the American Border Patrol has been consumed with handling asylum requests, and the areas outside the checkpoints are essentially unguarded."

"How much was intercepted?"

She shuffled through her papers. "The Sinaloa Cartel reported a three percent loss last month."

"Acceptable," Zhao said.

He didn't show his pleasure, because he needed to keep his subordinates in a constant state of anxiety, but excitement vibrated inside him. His plan to undermine the integrity of the US border proceeded with the added benefits of undermining American culture and flooding their voting rolls with illegals. Americans' thirst for recreational drugs resulted in 100,000 overdoses every year and drained their economy. Surreptitious drug warfare worked, despite the relative failures of the Phantoms' overt terror attacks.

"As you directed, we've increased internal enforcement actions."

"Statistics?"

"Domestically, police have enforced the new analog laws twelve times, resulting in the seizure of a dozen laboratories."

"Anything significant?"

She scanned the report again. "All single-operator facilities. One of the arrestees had been identified by American drug enforcement. They issued a Red Notice."

"Excellent. Make sure we agree to every extradition request. Throwing them small fish will keep their DEA happy."

"Yes, General."

Previous to recent events, China had paid lip service to American concerns about opioid manufacture, but after the Phantoms' fiasco, they'd been forced to acquiesce to American demands for increased enforcement of illicit opioid manufacturing. The FBI had forced their hand by linking China to the terrorist attacks, even though China had denied knowing the Phantoms' intended use of the opioids.

It seemed incomprehensible that the Americans didn't understand China's lack of incentive to curb the flow of opioids. China made billions of dollars from the drug trade, and cracking down would damage their economy, but more importantly, forcing America to expend resources to combat the scourge of drugs was a drag on their capitalistic machine. Why would China stop when drug addiction hurt American morale, cost the United States a fortune, and ate away at their culture?

"Back to work."

He watched Colonel Luo return to her desk, then he opened his briefing materials. Disintegration warfare had succeeded beyond his wildest expectations, though the long-term effects wouldn't be realized for years.

That's why he risked his bold new strategy. The coming days would show whether he succeeded or not, and failure would mean more than a professional setback. He risked everything by upping the stakes. If he succeeded, he'd have his chance to advance, but if he failed, he'd be finished.

11

———————

Birds chirped in the backyard of Vince and Reagan's sleepy neighborhood in Falls Church, Virginia. Reagan sipped a French roast coffee, a habit she'd acquired during her years married to Nathan. The aroma brought back flashes of lazy Sunday mornings with Nathan and Amelia.

"The GOP is losing their minds," Reagan said. "Changing our VP candidate at the last minute threw a monkey wrench into their strategy."

"Can't say I blame them," Vince said. "You dumped an oil slick on the road fifty yards before the finish line."

"You'd think Republicans would be happy. Our entire strategy's in disarray. And we only changed the bottom of our ticket, but those nuts claim we're disenfranchising voters by adding an unelected candidate to the ballot."

"You know, they're technically right. Nobody voted for Lemon."

"It's brutal for us too. I mean, just getting paper ballots reprinted around the country is almost impossible, and voters have already submitted hundreds of thousands of mail-in ballots."

"What happens to them?"

"There's no way to identify them, return them, and get people to vote again. Even if we could, there isn't time. Our only choice is to count the votes as submitted."

Vince scratched his head. "Seems sketchy. State Department officials who voted absentee from overseas for Harrison and Ambrose will now have their votes cast for Harrison and Lemon?"

"The DNC didn't ask Ambrose to withdraw," she said. Why did Vince always seem to take the opposing side of arguments? Was it male characteristic to seek conflict? Nathan had done that too, always playing devil's advocate. It annoyed the hell out of her then as well.

"It's how the DNC responded that caused concern."

A dull pain throbbed in her temples. "Insinuating the Democratic Party is undermining democracy throws fuel on the fire. We're doing our best under difficult circumstances, and Republican accusations damage people's confidence in the system."

Vince cocked his head. "The DNC appointed a VP who didn't receive a single Democratic vote, but conservatives noting it's anti-democratic is the real threat to democracy?"

"Republicans would do the same thing."

"That doesn't make it more palatable. Besides, other than a few interviews from Republican pundits, most of the grumbling I've heard has come from people I know at the State Department, and they're Democrats."

Reagan cocked her head. "Now that you say that, I haven't seen much coverage either. I'm deep inside baseball and sitting in strategy meetings, so anything Republicans say hits my radar. Regardless, Republicans are complaining about media coverage too. What's new?"

Vince poured himself another cup of coffee. He stared into the dark liquid.

"What?"

"I'm a lifelong Democrat," Vince said, "and I'm uncomfortable defending Republicans— with whom I disagree on practically every issue, but ..."

"Spit it out." Her words came out more acidic than she'd planned, but she didn't need to fight at home too. Whatever happened to her safe space? Had she even had one? She shrugged away that thought. She had to deal with enough darkness for now.

"Replacing a VP candidate a couple of weeks before the election has only happened once in American history," Vince said. "This is a significant political moment, and Darcy Lemon has been in hiding since the DNC added her to the ticket. Republicans may be complaining, but they're right about their criticism of the media coverage."

"Meaning?"

"All the networks, including cable news, made Republican complaints the story, not what they're upset about. It's 'Republicans pounce' all over again."

"But their undermining the integrity of—"

"Republicans may be exaggerating the problem, but their arguments aren't reaching the American people."

She sneered. "That's a bad thing?"

"Normally, I prefer people didn't hear the crazy conspiracy theories those whack jobs circulate, but this is a historic moment and Lemon's hiding from public scrutiny. More troubling is when Republicans object, they're attacked as radicals . . . like what you're doing now."

"I didn't call anyone radical."

"You're blaming them for subverting the democratic process because they complained about the DNC doing that very thing. It's Orwellian."

"Mainstream media doesn't need to agree with them."

"Hell, I don't agree with them," Vince said, "but Republicans are being censored. If you can believe the data right-wing pundits share, their posts on social media have been throttled by almost every platform."

"Then we might have a chance in the election." She tired of the argument.

"At what cost? If we can't have a robust debate, how can we ever find truth?"

"Since when did you become a mouthpiece for the Republican Party?"

Vince shook his head. "I guess I'm pissed. Most of my friends are overseas, and they didn't vote for this woman, yet there she is on the ballot—"

"Not yet—"

"She will be, and that feels wrong. I don't know who the hell she is, and if I don't, neither does anyone else."

Reagan started to object, then stopped herself. *Shit.* He made a point she couldn't argue. God, it sucked when he was right.

12

The interior of the Diplomat Hotel in Macau oozed affluence. Big money. Nathan and Meili strolled through the opulent lobby, a towering room constructed from marble, steel, and glass. Black streaks in polished macassar ebony wood punctuated the stark contemporary design. He could never afford to stay at this near five-star hotel on his own, but they offered the government discount, which sent up a red flag. Had Macao dangled the affordable rate to lure foreign officials into its swanky accommodations?

They followed the porter, who wore a maroon uniform and a gold cap, as he pushed the luggage cart. Nathan always insisted on carrying his own bags overseas because intelligence services and criminals targeted foreigners, but the porter had insisted and making a scene would draw attention. But he kept his eyes on their belongings and held his briefcase tight against his body.

"It's gorgeous," Meili said.

"So much for staying under the radar," Nathan said.

"The Chinese knew we were coming when we applied for visas, and we need some level of diplomatic immunity."

"We're traveling on official passports," he said, "but only permanently assigned agents have diplomatic status."

"No kidding, but traveling here as on-duty FBI agents will prevent them from calling us spies and locking us up."

"In theory."

Macau was the world's most densely populated region, with over seven hundred thousand people living in the former Portuguese territory. The region covered approximately twelve square miles south of Hong Kong. The island retained a degree of autonomy as the Macau Special Administrative Region of the People's Republic of China. Macau had its own political and economic systems, but that was smoke and mirrors. The Chinese controlled it.

"The police confirm our meeting?" he asked.

"Lincoln texted that we're scheduled for the Macau Security Force tomorrow morning."

They'd asked Lincoln White, the FBI's LEGAT in Beijing, to set a meeting for them with the Public Security Forces of Macau. They'd claimed they wanted to discuss illicit narcotics shipments passing through the region, but that was a cover for them to secretly meet with Xuannü.

The porter waited near the elevators as they stood in line at reception. Nathan glanced around, then leaned close to Meili.

"Is Lincoln meeting us?"

"He wasn't happy with our plan," she whispered. "I think that's why he's sending Tony Wong instead of coming himself. Tony's supposed to pick us up and drive us over."

Lincoln had balked at doing anything that could upset his relationship with his Chinese counterparts, and Meili had needed to send the request to contact Xuannü through headquarters before Lincoln complied. Lincoln had passed the in-person debriefing request to Shen Wang through a dead drop, and she'd agreed to meet, but only outside of mainland China.

"Think Lincoln will cause trouble?" Nathan asked.

"He's already complaining to HQ, and he probably whined to the Ambo too."

As an FBI agent, Lincoln reported to the Bureau's hierarchy, but every agency stationed at the US Embassy served under the US ambassador, and Lincoln briefed him and the other agency heads during weekly country-team meetings. Classified operations were only shared with the ambassador or the deputy chief of mission, as needed.

"He better not fuck this up for us," Nathan said.

"He's been here for years and has a tight relationship with the Ambo."

"What about Tony Wong?"

"Never worked with him before. He's only been in country for a month."

They stepped up to the desk, and Meili checked them in. Nathan handed her his passport while she spoke to the receptionist. He was accustomed to taking the lead, but she was still his boss, and this was her show.

Nathan scanned the room, pretending to admire the design, but he memorized the faces of everyone in the lobby. A trained surveillance agent could radically alter his or her appearance with a simple wardrobe change, like adding a wig and switching jackets, so Nathan noted body types too.

Meili finished checking in, and Nathan paid for his room on his government-issued credit card, then they took the elevator to the twenty-third floor and stood outside their side-by-side rooms as the porter brought their luggage inside. They needed to keep their professional distance to create the illusion they weren't dating. Only asking for reimbursement for one room would draw questions from the FBI administrative section.

"I'm jumping in the shower," Meili said. "I'll meet you downstairs in thirty. Tony should be here soon."

"No rest for the weary. Want a quickie before we get started?"

Meili looked around. "If State Security discovers we're dating, they'll use it against us."

He sighed. She was right, but he didn't always think clearly when it came to sex. "Might be worth the risk."

"See you downstairs." She disappeared into her room.

Nathan tipped the porter and entered his room. The lights had activated automatically, and he stopped inside the threshold. The door to a black-and-white tiled bathroom stood open in the short hallway opposite a closet. Nathan listened to the quiet, taking in the space. The heater hummed across the room, violating the stillness of the empty room. He moved down the entryway into the ornately appointed bedroom. Maroon-and-gold decorative pillows covered the duvet opposite a delicate writing desk, and a love seat filled out the room.

Foreign intelligence monitored rooms rented to foreigners, which made audio surveillance almost certain, and cameras possible. Anything Nathan locked inside the room safe would be inspected the minute he exited the hotel, which was why he carried nothing sensitive on overseas trips. He'd leave a notebook and his watch in the safe so his watchers would have something to investigate, but anything of substance would stay with him. Always.

He freshened up in the bathroom, then slung his briefcase over his shoulder and headed downstairs. He rode the elevator alone. A bubble camera with a tinted cover had been affixed to the ceiling. Being under constant surveillance created a base level of tension that tightened his stomach.

Nathan removed his travel itinerary from his briefcase as he exited the elevator into the lobby. He pretended to read it while he scanned people sipping coffee, at reception, and most importantly, hanging near the entrance. A half dozen staff members milled around. The woman at the concierge desk met his eye, then quickly looked away.

Another elevator dinged behind him, and Meili exited.

"Tony texted. He's outside."

The concierge picked up the hotel phone as Nathan and Meili crossed the lobby. She didn't look at them again, but Nathan had seen enough. They exited the main doors into a light mist. On an island, the weather changed without warning.

A lanky Asian man leaned against a creme-colored vehicle outside the hotel's revolving door. He straightened when they saw him, revealing his height. Nathan was six foot even, and Tony had a couple of inches on him.

"Tony Wong," he said, extending his hand. "Welcome to Macau."

Meili and Nathan shook his hand.

"What time's our meeting?" Meili asked.

"I called MSF and postponed it to the morning."

Meili cocked her head. "Wait, what?"

"Xuannü contacted us last night. She's moved up the meeting."

"When?" Meili asked.

"Now."

"Why didn't you tell us?" Nathan asked.

"You were on the flight, but it doesn't matter. She left a draft email in the encrypted server we told her to use. Her schedule has changed, and she has a short window. She can only meet tonight."

"Where?"

"The Madeira Casino during their Halloween party."

Nathan looked at Meili. This was getting strange. "We don't have costumes."

"Got that handled," Tony said. "We better hurry. It's now or never." He unlocked a boxy vehicle that looked like the offspring of an SUV and a station wagon.

"What the hell is this?" Nathan asked.

"Toyota Sienta, a Japanese mini multipurpose vehicle. They sell 'em in Hong Kong."

"Bu-ride?" Nathan asked.

"Rental. It blends in, and I actually fit inside it."

"It looks like a toaster with wheels," Nathan said, climbing into the back seat.

Tony pulled away from the curb, facing the wrong way in the left lane, or at least it felt that way. In the former Portuguese colony, everyone drove on the left side.

Nathan shifted in his seat and pointed out the window at the hotel facade, as if commenting on it, but he shifted his eyes and glanced out the back window. A black Mazda with dark tinted windows pulled away from the curb and fell in behind them.

"I think we've got company," Nathan said.

Tony glanced in the rearview mirror. "They're always on me, but they're pretty obvious about it."

"They show you what they want you to see," Meili said. "Worry about the agents you don't see."

"I'll get separation before the meet," Tony said. He accelerated through traffic.

The game was on.

13

———

Reflected lights from hotels and businesses glowed in the Sienta's windows as Tony drove around a traffic circle in downtown Macau. His windshield wipers squeaked over the wet glass, and moonlight shimmered off Nam Van Lake. Tony navigated through a swarm of Corollas, Hondas, and Hyundais, which all appeared well-maintained, like the buildings and roadways. Macau swam in money, and it showed in Ferraris, Rolls-Royces, and Teslas that glided through traffic past glittering glass towers.

Nathan sat sideways in the seat and used his peripheral vision to monitor traffic behind them. Even in the dark interior, a surveillance agent would be able to see his head turn if he looked back. If the surveillance agents suspected they'd been compromised, they'd up their game and be harder to spot. Not revealing he'd seen his watchers gave him an advantage.

The car rocked as Tony maneuvered through cars and mopeds.

"You're new here, right?" Meili asked.

"Three weeks and two days. I transferred from LA Field Office. I've only been on the job a few years, so I couldn't believe they selected me."

"*Nǐ láizí zhōngguó?*" Meili asked.

"Naw, I grew up in Santa Monica, but my folks came from Zhongshan, not too far from here. They spoke Cantonese in the house, and they made me learn Mandarin too, which has helped me more than I knew when I was a kid. I minored in language at UCLA."

They weaved through thick traffic on a circle, then the road opened and Tony drove onto the San Van Bridge, a cable-stayed structure spanning the outer harbor that connected the Macau Peninsula to Taipa Island.

"Impressive," Nathan said.

"This is nothing," Tony said. "The HZMB is fifty-five kilometers long."

"HZ what?"

"The Hong Kong-Zhuhai-Macau Bridge. Three cable-suspended bridges and an underwater tunnel that link Macau and Hong Kong across Lanni Bay. It's a trip, man."

They rose up the roughly mile-and-a-half-long bridge, and at the midpoint, Nathan glanced back. The black Mazda stayed four cars behind. At least it looked like the same car. At night, and with so many similar vehicles, it was hard to be sure. The bridge lights illuminated silhouettes of two men.

"How much farther?" Meili asked.

"Five minutes. Taipa's small, but it has a few high-end casinos."

"Our watchers are still behind us," Nathan said.

"I scoped this out before I met you," Tony said. "I'll drive down the main strip, which has hotels and casinos on both sides, and I'll do a fake drop at the first one. They might bite. Then I'll let you out at the second. Hustle through it and exit out the back. There's a walkway that leads to the Madeira."

"How do we find her?" Meili asked.

"Her note said she'll wear a pink dress with a golden butterfly mask, and she'll be sitting in the garden in the center atrium. Use the phrase 'the lilies are wilted,' and she'll respond, 'but still beautiful.'"

"And our costumes?" Meili asked.

Tony reached into the glove compartment, removed two venetian half masks, and handed them to Meili and Nathan. Her gold mask sported black feathers, and Nathan's was silver with a pointed nose.

"Seriously?" Nathan asked.

"They'll give you some cover," Tony said, and they'll throw off facial recognition software. The costume party was a stroke of luck."

"As long as I don't die wearing this thing," Nathan said.

Tony drove along the multi-lane roadway beneath an elevated train that curled overhead like a hamster tunnel. He turned down Estrada do Istmo, where massive hotel-casinos lined the street. His eyes flickered to the rearview mirror, then he cut the wheel hard. Their tires screeched as he pulled under the overhang outside a hotel, drawing a glare from the valet.

"Duck down," Tony said.

He watched his mirrors, then accelerated away from the entrance as the Mazda pulled in. Nathan peeked over the seat as the passenger jumped out of the Mazda and hurried into the casino. The Mazda came after them.

"Get ready," Tony said.

Their tires screeched again as he pulled into the next hotel. The car jerked to a stop. Nathan grabbed the handle and flung open the door. Nathan raced through passengers disembarking from taxis and limousines with Meili on his heels. The front doors whooshed open, and they entered the casino lobby.

"Out the back," Meili said.

His heart thumped as he fast-walked through the thick crowd across the gaming floor. The jingle jangle of slot machines clamored around them. Nathan hurried past a group of businessmen to cover their egress and slipped behind a row of blackjack tables. He moved toward the exit sign.

Part of his excitement came from the fun and games of outsmarting an adversary, but screwing with a foreign intelligence service meant the stakes could be deadly, especially for a foreign national source who risked her life to reveal classified information. That responsibility rested heavily on him and sharpened his focus.

He reached the door and glanced back at the gaming tables. Two men in dark business suits entered the casino and scanned the crowd. Were they intelligence agents or businessmen searching for friends? Always assume the worst.

Nathan led Meili outside, and they climbed a ramp onto an elevated pedestrian walkway. Meili's shoes clicked on the hard surface as they hurried away from the casino. They crossed an undeveloped lot of grass and sand and moved onto the sidewalk circling the Madeira Casino and

Hotel. The main entrance faced the street, where other surveillance units could be searching for them, so he led Meili toward a side access point.

"Mask up," Nathan said, and they donned their masks. Nathan's smelled like an old cigar.

Glass doors opened automatically as they neared, and they entered a wide hallway with vaulted ceilings, crisp air-conditioning, and soft carpeting. Nathan led her past partygoers bedecked in elegant costumes and signs written in Mandarin and English advertising the masquerade party.

The drone of a mingling crowd grew louder as they approached the Grand Ballroom. Nathan paused at the open entrance doors. Inside, guests packed the space, and masked servers wearing tuxedos and black cocktail dresses roamed through the crowd carrying trays of hors d'oeuvres. Musicians with classical instruments played traditional Chinese music, and the Guangling Melody drifted through the ballroom.

Meili touched Nathan's elbow. "This way."

They moved down an expansive hallway with alabaster statues mounted on pedestals. Marble stairs led down to the atrium, a grotto filled with orchids and exotic plants around benches and iron café tables. Several people wandered around, many carrying twenties-style cocktail glasses filled with colored liquids.

"There," Meili said, "behind the plant." She nodded at a woman seated at a table beside a flowering hibiscus plant. The woman wore a formfitting lavender dress with dangling pipa sleeves and a golden mask shaped like a butterfly.

"Must be," Nathan said. "I'll approach."

"She looks younger than I expected."

"We don't have a picture."

"Be careful."

Nathan sauntered across the room and paused a few feet from the woman. "These lilies are wilted."

"But still beautiful." The correct phrase.

"Where do you—"

"Sit at that table behind the plant," she said without looking at him, "and don't acknowledge me." Her voice sounded tight.

Nathan made eye contact with Meili and nodded at the closest table. They sat, and an awkward silence weighed them down.

"We're here," he said, pretending to talk to Meili but loud enough for Xuannü to hear.

"Were you followed?"

"Of course. We don't have much time."

Chinese intelligence probably didn't expend many resources on two FBI agents supposedly meeting with Public Security Forces of Macau about narcotics trafficking, but then again, both Nathan and Meili had been instrumental in revealing China's role in the Havana Syndrome. The CCP would throw more bodies at the problem, and it would only be a matter of time before they spotted them.

"We have entered a dangerous time," she said. "My country plans aggression."

Nathan's chest constricted. "They've already done that. China supplied carfentanil to the Phantoms and facilitated the deaths of thousands of Americans."

"That part of their strategy has ended. They were displeased the Islamists' attacks didn't have the intended effect. In fact, just the opposite."

"The CCP is no longer using Islamists to export terror?"

"Perhaps that has finished. . . for now, but fentanyl is still an effective weapon of drug warfare."

"With increased manufacturing?" Meili asked.

"Deeper than that. We produce most of the world's opioids, and the Second Bureau works in concert with Mexican cartels to spread our fentanyl throughout your country. Our leaders understand how addiction reduces your productivity. It kills your citizens and costs billions of dollars in healthcare and law enforcement."

"DEA and the State Department addressed that at high-level meetings between Washington and Beijing," Meili said. "China promised changes in your laws and more enforcement to curb the flow—"

"It's all lies."

A couple walked by, and the man laughed too loudly, the way people did when alcohol poisoned their brains. Nathan scanned the room as he waited for them to pass.

"It's too dangerous meeting in person," Meili said. "Let's establish a unique electronic link for you to pass information to me."

"I have come here . . . I risk my life to express the urgency of what is happening."

"Do you have proof of Chinese government complicity?" Nathan asked.

"This is of no importance."

Anger flamed inside him. "No importance? We lost thousands of people—"

"Please . . . my government will continue flooding your country with poison, as long as your citizens demand it, but I must warn you about what is coming."

A chill tingled his spine. "Something worse than funding Islamic terrorism?"

"I asked you to meet because our unrestricted warfare has been a slow process, an eroding of your country's strength, but that is about to change. They are transitioning to phase two."

"Meaning what?" Meili asked.

"My government has been fighting you since long before I was born, but we are about to enter a new phase . . . of more overt warfare."

"Meaning what?" Meili asked.

"Disintegration warfare. The CCP already exerts influence on your politicians, and in your universities and media, but now, they seek outright control."

"How?" Nathan asked.

"They have contributed to the rise of collectivism in America since our Communist Party came to power, and now, they have reached a tipping point where they can overtly drag America into socialism."

"Our own politicians are doing that for them," Nathan said.

"They do it for us. You do not understand how far the communists' tentacles reach inside your political apparatus."

"You're saying our leftist politicians aren't just ideologues, but tools of the CCP?"

"Both things can be true."

"Ideas aren't illegal in America," Meili said. "If politicians push a socialist agenda and people vote for it, there's nothing we can do."

"It's not your people. The hand of China controls them like *pi-yung xi.*"

"Like what?" Nathan asked.

"Shadow puppets," Meili translated.

"They plan a bold strategy . . . to control you from the top, suspend your Constitution, turn your country into a dictatorship—like China . . . and controlled by China."

Was she serious? Her claims seemed outlandish. Could this be a disinformation ploy dreamed up by Chinese intelligence? To what end? Did they want the FBI to overstep its bounds and spread panic to discredit the Bureau?

"What you're saying seems too extreme to be credible," Nathan said.

"It will happen, whether you believe it or not. Disintegration warfare does not require your approval to succeed."

"Why didn't you take this to the CIA?" Meili asked.

"They cannot be trusted. Our infiltration of your intelligence services runs deep. We've emplaced moles everywhere, from your universities to the Capitol."

Deep lines creased Meili's face. "You have proof of this?"

"I printed internal emails. I will leave them under my chair. Read them and take heed."

Movement caught Nathan's eye, and he looked up as a bald man stumbled in from the opposite hallway. Sweat streaked down his face as he scanned the room. A second man wearing a suit came in and stood behind him.

"We've got company," Nathan said. "The watchers found us."

Xuannü stood.

"Wait," Meili said. "I need to give you contact instructions."

Xuannü hurried away without acknowledging her.

14

Reagan bubbled with anticipation. She'd attended several Democratic National Party Committee events and a few for the Virginia delegation—but this time was different. Their presidential nominee would have lunch with her and twelve other electors from Virginia. She could highlight things that would matter in the upcoming election. Until today, any suggestion she'd made inevitably became lost in the bureaucracy and probably never reached the candidate's desk, and if it did, someone else likely took credit. That didn't matter, because having better policy would be its own reward—but this was her chance to be heard.

She exited the Metro's Blue Line at the Roslyn station in Arlington. Presidential Candidate Gavin Harrison was coming to them to show their opinions mattered, whether that was true or not. The New Delhi Café served high-end, contemporary Indian cuisine, which everyone knew was the former mayor's favorite. He dined at the same spot in Roslyn at least five times over the past four years, raising suspicions that the food group running the restaurant had contributed to his campaign, but nothing came of the grumbling.

Traffic inched down the street, unusually gridlocked, even for the DC Metro area. The Secret Service had to be close. Personal protection had stepped up in recent years, and opposing party candidates rated similar levels of Secret Service protection to the sitting president. The political climate had heated for decades, and the last thing the country needed was another assassination attempt.

Would presidential races ever return to civility? Had politics ever been genteel or did nostalgia taint her view of the past? Candidates seemed less educated and more bombastic with each passing election cycle. At least Harrison appeared to break that mold. He'd been an effective mayor of Tampa by any objective metric, and his ability to govern separated him from the cult of personality that had dominated the presidency.

The founding fathers had envisioned a president as an administrator, not a king—George Washington had made that clear—but voters seemed more and more inclined to vote for charisma over substance, glitter over experience. The Republican president, Dean Hereford, was a classic example of that. He'd been married to a movie star and run a tech company before dipping his toe into politics. Unlike most Republican presidents, his contacts in Hollywood ran deep, and he'd used celebrities to woo the public. He'd won all the swing states, albeit in extremely close races, and he'd won the popular vote too, which was unheard of for a Republican.

Reagan rounded the corner onto Lee Street a block from where the Francis Scott Key Bridge spanned the Potomac and connected Virginia to Washington, DC. She walked faster as she neared the restaurant. Despite the shining sun, the New Delhi Café's lights glistened. The owner must have known Harrison stood a good chance of winning and wanted him as an ally—though Harrison's chances had dropped after his VP dropped out.

An Arlington Police Department patrol car activated his lights and turned sideways, blocking traffic at the corner. A siren yelped, and another cruiser blocked the street behind her.

Reagan's pulse accelerated. Whoever won the presidency would become the most powerful man on earth, wielding the most powerful military in history. She transformed into a schoolgirl meeting a pop star, silly for sure, but how many chances did the average person have to influence American politics? She'd worked in the State Department for years and had done little to change policy, other than submit reports that were summarily ignored. Like the way State had dismissed the Havana Syndrome as a psychogenic illness.

This was an opportunity to make a difference. To matter.

Liz Washington stood outside the café speaking with an older woman with thick brown hair with dyed blue streaks and a pinched face.

Reagan approached them. "Hey, Liz."

Liz looked at her and her features cooled. What was her problem? Did she not like Reagan, or did she fear Reagan's political ambitions? Reagan had been encouraged to run for State Senate, and when she'd floated the idea of seeking congressional office, many party officials had supported her. But not Liz.

"Let me introduce you," Liz said. "Reagan Cabrera, meet Gail Haverhill. Gail's our DNC National vice chair."

"Of course I know who you are," Reagan said, ignoring Liz and shaking Gail's hand. "I appreciate you coming for this."

"We organized it," Gail said with a chill to her tone.

Had Liz already poisoned Reagan's reputation?

Two black Suburbans with flashing red lights rolled off the bridge and edged around traffic. Reagan stopped and watched, tingling with excitement. The first vehicle stopped next to her, and the other parked behind it.

"What does the mayor think about Havana Syndrome?"

"Don't touch that subject," Liz said. "He's got bigger fish to fry. We all do."

A familiar frustration sizzled inside Reagan. "If he wins."

"He'll win," Gail said. "He must." Her eyes turned to burning embers in a face of stone.

"What's his position on China?" Reagan asked.

"That's not on the agenda either," Liz said.

"Tonight or ever?"

Four tough-looking men wearing suits and earpieces climbed out of the SUV and spread out on the sidewalk, their eyes roaming the street. Secret Service. Another agent exited the café and spoke into his sleeve.

"It's time," Liz said. "We should go inside."

Gail turned to Liz. "Give me a moment with Ms. Cabrera."

"I really think—"

"You go ahead," Gail said. "I'll join you in a moment."

Liz's body tightened, but she smiled, turned, and walked into the restaurant.

"She doesn't care for you," Gail said.

"I picked up on that."

"She's intimidated by you."

"Intimidated—"

"You just entered politics, and already, you've attracted attention. You have a shot at what she's always wanted."

"And that is?"

"Power."

A third Suburban stopped outside the café's front door, a few feet away. The security around the dignitary's visit drew the attention of thirty pedestrians. A Secret Service agent exited and opened the rear door.

Mayor Gavin Harrison stepped onto the sidewalk.

"That's our best shot at regaining power," Gail said. "Take it easy inside."

"I can't speak my mind?"

"Say whatever you want, but every word will be scrutinized, and your political future hangs in the balance."

"I know what I'm doing. Sort of."

Gail smiled, more genuine this time. "Trust your instincts, but don't forget to listen."

Harrison flashed a beaming smile—a lighthouse of charisma—and waved at the crowd.

A few people applauded. Someone booed. Then Harrison and his bodyguard disappeared inside.

"Ready for the show?" Gail asked.

"Can't wait." Nerves tickled Reagan's stomach.

Gail winked and headed for the door. Reagan followed. Would she impress Harrison? Would he win the election? Would this be the beginning of her political career?

Blinding light filled her eyes. Thunder plugged her ears. The air left her lungs. She flew backward through the air.

She lay on the sidewalk and waves of heat washed over her as her mind fought to understand. Her back throbbed. Her joints ached. The air stank of charcoal and chemicals. She coughed and spat out thick black mucus.

Everything had become fuzzy, confused. What happened?

She tried to sit up, and lightning flashed through her spine. She rolled onto her side. Gail lay next to her, unconscious.

Heat warmed Reagan's face. She raised her hand in defense and squinted. Flames gushed out of the shattered restaurant facade. Broken glass littered the sidewalk. Black smoke choked the air. The restaurant had been demolished. No one could have survived.

Harrison was dead.

15

Nathan cracked the Chevrolet's window and slapped his magnetic emergency light onto the roof as he muscled through brutal DC traffic. Waldo braced against the dashboard as Nathan jerked between lanes.

The capital had crawled to a stop since Gavin Harrison's assassination —or his presumed death since rescue personnel hadn't recovered or identified every charred body inside the New Delhi Café. The Secret Service blocked streets around the White House, and emergency vehicles raced around the city. The chaos allowed Nathan to use his emergency equipment in violation of FBI policy without much chance of getting caught. Not that he cared.

"Reagan said she was fine," Waldo said. "You can slow down."

Reagan had claimed she only had bruises and scratches, but the memory of her seizure on the floor of the US Embassy in Santo Domingo danced behind his eyes. His neighbor, Betty Cook, watched Amelia and their dog, Bruno, so at least they were safe. Nothing mattered more than his family.

"I won't relax until I see her."

Nathan nosed into oncoming traffic to pass a truck, then swerved back into their lane. Waldo stomped on the floor as if he had a passenger-side brake. Waldo glared, but Nathan ignored him and focused on the road.

"What did Meili say?" Waldo asked.

"She's still in China. After we met her CI, she went to Beijing to establish protocols with the LEGAT and handle any fallout from the debriefing. We gave Chinese intel the slip, so they knew we were up to something, but I don't think they caught the meet."

"Hotels have cameras."

"Everyone wore masks. The Halloween party thing seemed dramatic . . . amateurish, but it was brilliant. If our CI stayed covered during her approach and departure, they won't ID her."

"China monitors everything," Waldo said.

"They can't be sure what we were doing. We stayed at the party for an hour to throw them off the scent."

They entered Washington Circle, and the Chevrolet's tires screeched as Nathan hugged the inside lane. He lurched to a stop in front of the George Washington Emergency Hospital. He flipped his FBI placard onto the dashboard and bolted from the car.

Federal agents, police, and rescue personnel loitered on the sidewalk waiting for more victims of the blast, but from Reagan's description, nobody else would get out alive. The people inside the restaurant never had a chance.

"I'll wait out here and give you some privacy," Waldo said.

Nathan badged his way into the Emergency Department and identified himself to a nurse, who opened the doors to the patient care area. Nathan weaved past medical equipment and nurses and doctors tending patients. The ER didn't seem overly busy, but tension crackled through the hospital as everyone awaited victims. Burn victims would be taken to the Medstar Health burn unit in Georgetown, but most of the others would come there, the closest emergency room.

Nathan edged around a gurney opposite the nurse's station and yanked back the curtain to room 6. Reagan sat upright in bed with an IV in her arm talking to her husband, Vince, who slouched in a worn plastic chair.

Nathan's legs weakened with relief. "How you feeling?"

"Minor abrasions." She smiled, and the hint of their past love warmed him without the baggage of their destructive relationship. Had he grown?

"And a mild concussion," Vince said.

"They'll release me tonight," Reagan said.

Nathan moved beside her. "What can you tell me?"

A cloud darkened her face. "It was horrible. The worst thing I've ever seen."

"Dozens of people witnessed it," Vince said, "and someone caught the explosion on their phone."

"The news is running the footage on a loop," Nathan said. "They're calling it an assassination."

"That's premature," Vince said.

"We can't assume it was an accident," Nathan said. "And the timing is suspicious."

"The fire's out," Vince said, "but we won't know anything until forensics gets in there. Could've been a gas leak."

"All those people . . ." Reagan's voice sounded tiny, distant. "The waiters and cooks . . . Liz. It was . . ."

"What?" Vince asked. He sounded irritated.

"Unthinkable."

"How close were you?" Nathan asked.

She teared up. "I was right outside talking to Gail—"

"Gail?" Nathan asked.

"Haverhill. We were about to start lunch, but when Harrison went in, Gail asked to speak to me."

"She held you outside with her?"

"She expressed support for my political career."

"What career?" Vince asked.

She glared at him. "My political ambitions."

"How long before—"

"Like thirty seconds," Reagan said. "Then we turned to go inside and . . . it happened."

Thirty seconds. A chance conversation. That's all that had saved Reagan from the abyss. Life could disappear in a fleeting moment. In a breath.

"I'm . . ." His voice felt shaky. He'd been in hand-to-hand combat with terrorists, fought for his life, been shot—but his loved ones in danger was a different level. "You survived, and that's what matters."

"So many victims," Reagan said. A tear streamed down her cheek.

"I'm more worried about how this will affect the election," Vince said.

Reagan shot daggers at him. "This isn't the time—"

"We're ten days away from a presidential election, and not only did we swap VPs, but now the presidential candidate is dead."

"We'll deal with the political fallout," Reagan said, "but people lost loved ones."

"This could ignite a civil war," Vince said. "People are shocked . . . and pissed."

Nathan looked from Vince to Reagan. He'd been so consumed with worry about her that he'd compartmentalized the politics—but this was a historic event. The Democrats had a vacancy at the top of their ticket, and the vice presidential candidate was an unknown.

"I'm glad you survived," Nathan said. "I'm sorry you lost people—"

"Every Virginia elector," she said. "Except me."

"Now's not the time to worry about that," Nathan said. "FaceTime Amelia. She won't relax until she sees you with her own eyes."

Reagan smiled. "Like her father."

Vince pulled out his vibrating phone. "Trouble."

"What?" Nathan asked.

"The president activated the National Guard."

16

The Second Bureau's underground war room hummed with activity as a dozen officers monitored classified communications networks while Zhao and his top advisors conferred around the map table. Zhao had implemented a critical operation in his strategy, and the air tingled with electricity. His plan rode on this bold move—a daring strike at their enemy.

Any moment now, they'd know if the operation had succeeded. Either Zhao would triumph or he'd have made a mistake with catastrophic consequences for the motherland. And for him.

This moment had been fated. Zhao didn't follow the Taoism of his ancestors, because the Communist Party was his god, but the opposing forces of Yin and Yang were real, and the American belief in democracy and individual rights stood in opposition to China's ascendancy. Ideology was the enemy, and Zhao was the hammer that would crush them.

Zhao's heart pounded inside his chest, so loud everyone must hear it. He leaned back and watched Colonel Luo monitor her computer. A bead of perspiration wet his brow. He ground his teeth to keep his worry off his face. If he couldn't maintain a flaccid exterior, he'd project a hard one.

She looked up with wide eyes. She stood and approached him.

"Well?" he asked, his voice sounding frailer than he liked.

"It's done."

Zhao couldn't keep the smile off his face. He liked to hide his emotions, remain a mystery to his subordinates, but this was momentous. This act would change history. He had changed history. The Central Committee watched Zhao's every move with suspicion and worry, and a failure at this stage would have derailed his accelerated strategy—but his assassination of the American presidential candidate had succeeded.

"Thank you, Colonel."

"May I . . ."

"Speak."

"How will they respond?"

He eyed her. His immediate staff in the Second Bureau's inner sanctum had knowledge that no one else in Chinese intelligence or anywhere in the government knew, except the Central Committee, and even their knowledge was limited to the broad strategy.

"They will reel from the attack. They will blame each other. They will lose trust in the system."

"A brilliant operation. Congratulations, General."

He nodded, and she returned to her workstation. Even the sight of her young body couldn't surpass his jubilation, and he had not mentioned the most important outcome.

But she did not need to know everything.

Anyone privy to the details of Zhao's disintegration warfare plan posed a potential threat—a double-edged sword he could not avoid. Training, supply, logistics, coordination, and communications added a long tail to their operations. His black ops teams required five times as many people to support their work behind the scenes. These people around him must be involved, but they only needed enough information to do their specific jobs.

The most brilliant part of his plan remained secret.

17

Nathan stood with Waldo in the shadow of the J. Edgar Hoover Building and watched a mob of protesters march down Pennsylvania Avenue. Did *mob* describe them? They expressed anger over Harrison's assassination, but they weren't violent—at least not yet. Who could blame them? The United States had endured assassinations of candidates and presidents before, but this had come in the wake of the VP's surprise resignation—the reason for which remained a mystery—and the country reeled from the violent deaths of Harrison and the Virginia contingent.

And the election was only nine days away.

Waldo stared at his phone. "Shit."

"What?"

"Last-minute field goal. Now I need Detroit to win."

"How can you gamble when DC's about to riot?" Nathan asked.

"This one is a lock. One big score, and I'm back even."

A car alarm wailed down the street. The mob grew more aggressive.

"The country's on tenterhooks," Nathan said. "The administration needs to release information about the assassination to ease the tension."

"Our people are on it, and so is the Secret Service and half of federal law enforcement."

"Conspiracy theories are everywhere. The White House should counter misinformation with facts."

"It's too early to know anything."

Nathan shook his head. "Then they should say that. Their silence feels like a cover-up."

A bottle smashed nearby. Across the street at the Department of Justice, a uniformed security guard walked toward a group of angry young people on the sidewalk. The situation heated, and the threat of violence crackled through the crowd. It would erupt eventually, and if not at this protest, then somewhere else. And soon.

"You hear what they found, *Papi*?" Waldo asked.

"It's not for public consumption," Nathan said. "They're still analyzing data . . . Hell, they're still identifying bodies, but someone packed a massive amount of explosives inside an interior wall of the restaurant."

"What kind?"

"C-4. The owner remodeled after a plumbing problem two years ago. Whoever did this planned ahead."

"Two years . . ." Waldo scratched his head. "How would they know a presidential candidate who liked that cuisine would be running?"

"It seems like a leap, but the evidence points to the explosives being pre-staged during the construction. That means either they booby-trapped a lot of restaurants, or—"

"Those *pingas* knew Harrison would run years before he announced."

"And that would make it an inside job. Someone knew the DNC would support Harrison's nomination, which brings up other questions."

"Like?"

"Who could be certain that not only would he run, but he'd win, and the big question—why would someone want to kill him?"

Waldo rubbed his neck. "If I wanted to off him, I'd have whacked him in Tampa before he won . . . when he had less protection."

"So many questions."

Nathan's phone vibrated, and he answered.

"I'm watching the protest on TV," Amelia said. "They're marching right past your building. Why don't the police stop them?"

"It's their constitutional right."

"I'm worried about you."

Amelia hadn't slept well since Harrison's assassination. Political upheaval stressed everyone, but children needed safety and stability. The constant replay of the assassination footage and protests on the news didn't help. Media thrived on violence.

"I'm fine, sweetheart."

"I don't want anything to happen to you."

Amelia had always been concerned with his carrying a gun for a living, a fact he hadn't fully realized until he'd been shot, but Reagan's brush with death had surfaced Amelia's anxiety. Families of cops and agents paid a deep price—invisible casualties.

"Stop obsessing," he said. "Turn off the TV and read something fun. Distract yourself from politics."

"You taught me not to ignore problems."

Smart kid. She had him there. "You're not old enough to vote, so don't fret about things you can't change."

"I never would have voted for that clown."

"Don't talk like that. Harrison gave his life for the country."

"Not for me. He hated women."

"That's absurd. Why would you say that?"

"I saw it on ChatteringHen."

"You should turn that crap off too."

A fistfight broke out in the crowd, and three DC Metro officers pushed through the throng to break it up.

"Everyone says we're better off without him," Amelia said.

"That's a horrible thing to say, and no one believes—"

"And now we can vote for a woman."

"Gender means nothing when picking a leader, and you're too young to vote."

"I'll be allowed to vote in a few years."

That jolted him. Amelia was smart, but like her friends, she ingested news from ChatteringHen where content creators didn't know more than their audience. They preached simplistic ideas through an addictive app, and most of their information was wrong.

"ChatteringHen spews nonsense."

"It's better than TV."

She might be right, but could Amelia and her friends discern right from wrong? Her teachers should teach them to spot logical fallacies, but instead of training kids *how* to think, they told them *what* to think.

"Shut off your phone and go read a book."

"C'mon dad."

Another bottle shattered on the street. A woman screamed. The situation deteriorated.

"Gotta go, honey."

"Bye, Dad."

He hung up and scanned the crowd. People shouted, but kept themselves in check, but that could change in a second. The threat of violence hung over the crowd like a cloud.

"She okay?" Waldo asked.

Nathan turned to him. "This administration needs to get in front of this before the country spins out of control. Where are the DOJ press briefings they hold when they're targeting political opponents?"

"Main Justice ain't saying shit."

"We need to look at that more closely."

"We do?"

"If not *us*, then who?"

"I don't like that look in your eyes."

"People need answers, and I don't think we've seen the worst of this."

Nathan's phone buzzed again with an incoming email. He opened an email from CorrLinks, a notice from the Federal Bureau of Prisons. The message requested approval to accept communication from an inmate housed at the United States Penitentiary Florence ADMAX—a maximum-security prison in Colorado that held the most dangerous criminals in America.

Only one of Nathan's arrestees was housed in Florence—the former CIA officer who'd unknowingly colluded with China to carry out Havana Syndrome attacks.

Trent Hamilton.

18

———

The autumn sun cast shadows on the US Capitol's alabaster granite steps as Reagan headed toward Gail Haverhill. Eight days from the presidential election, the Democratic Party had devolved into chaos. The media played a bystander's cellphone video of the explosion on an infinite loop. Assassinations had violence and drama—everything the media craved—and they spread fear. Television news used the footage to lure eyeballs to their broadcasts.

Reagan waved and climbed the steps to Gail. A bandage covered Gail's forehead where a shard of glass had lacerated her and required a dozen stitches to close.

"She chose Senator James," Gail said without preamble.

"I just heard that on NPR," Reagan said.

"Archie's well liked, and he's respected on both sides of the aisle."

"At least people have heard of him."

Gail frowned. "You don't sound pleased."

"Don't forget our Virginia state motto," Reagan said, "*Sic Semper Tyrannis* . . . Thus always to tyrants."

"What's your point?" Gail asked.

"Two weeks before the election, we appointed Darcy Lemon as VP, a relative unknown, and after the assassination, she takes the reins and selects her own VP."

"Everyone likes Archie," Gail said. "He's been a senator for decades, and he's moderate, which will appeal to independent voters. He can reach across the aisle."

"I agree he's a good pick, but nobody voted for him either. We have a presidential ticket that didn't receive a single primary vote."

"They have overwhelming party support."

"That's the problem. People perceive party elites anointing a government."

"By *people*, you mean you?"

Reagan maintained eye contact. "It troubles me. Changing the ticket without voter input puts people on edge—and they're not wrong. We're asking them to vote for candidates who didn't go through the primary process."

Gail scowled. "Thanks for the civics lesson, but we didn't expect our candidate to turn into a burnt marshmallow."

Reagan jolted. The vivid image of Harrison's body being retrieved from the wreckage of the restaurant flashed in her mind, and Gail's callous comment raised the tiny hairs on her body. How could Gail speak that way about the popular mayor they'd championed?

"Harrison had a family . . . a three-year-old son."

Gail snorted and looked at the sky. She cracked her jaw, then leveled her gaze on Reagan. "Are you on our team or not?"

Her flat tone sent a chill through Reagan. Politics was a bloodsport, and those that entered it were either rabid narcissists or they sought power . . . or both. She needed to tread lightly around Gail. Without Gail's blessing and DNC's support, Reagan could never run for national office. At least not as a Democrat.

"I'm amplifying a concern I've heard, and not only from Republicans and Independents, but from our people—the voters we need to win."

"Nobody anticipated losing our entire ticket weeks before an election. We didn't have time to organize a second primary. What would you have had us do?"

"We could have selected the highest vote-getters from our primary to show we respected people's input."

"Senator Jones came in second, but he's a crank. The votes he received were a symbolic protest against DNC positions. Nobody wanted a fringe character to represent our party, and there's no way we'd approve him. We brought in professionals who could right our sinking ship."

The senator from Oklahoma, a Republican firebrand, stalked up the steps near them with his entourage in tow.

"Okay, okay," Reagan said, lowering her voice. "But let's acknowledge voters' concerns. We installed a new ticket after a shocking and horrific event, and I think they'll understand if we explain it to them and—"

"We've had talking heads on every news show."

"But Darcy Lemon still hasn't given an interview. She should answer questions and let voters get comfortable with her. They need time to accept her."

Gail scowled. "It's only been a couple of days. You're asking for a miracle."

"Nobody likes change, and this has been abrupt. Let's help voters embrace our new team. Many Americans don't want four more years of Republican governance. Let's do a better job of introducing our candidates. Archie James can help do that. People trust him."

Gail cocked her head, appraising Reagan. "Now you're making sense. I want to see more of that."

"More what?"

"Being a team player. You have a bright future, and there's a world in front of you, ready for the taking."

"I don't want power," Reagan said. "I want change."

Gail's eyes narrowed. "Then get on board. You can only affect change if we win."

19

The flabby corrections officer's keys jingled as Nathan and Waldo trudged behind him down an unending sterile hallway inside the USP Florence ADMAX, an administrative security penitentiary in Florence, Colorado. Either the fluorescent lights had too much wattage or the glossy linoleum magnified the light. The glare and odor of industrial cleaning solvents stabbed Nathan's brain like needles.

Trent Hamilton, the former CIA manager Nathan had convicted of being an agent of a foreign government had sent Nathan an email via TRULINK, a monitored system inmates used to correspond with the outside world. His message had been cryptic.

I need to speak with you urgently. I know what China's doing.

Through a series of TRULINK messages, Hamilton claimed he possessed intelligence about a nefarious Chinese plot and time was running out. Was the infamous federal inmate trying to trap Nathan into admitting he'd coerced Hamilton's confession to seek a retrial, or could he actually help? He might want to cooperate to reduce his sentence.

The flight to Denver had taken four hours, and by the time they'd rented a car and driven another two hours to the maximum-security facility in Florence, visiting hours had almost ended. The trip was a grind and a serious time suck based on scant information, but Hamilton had insisted they meet without his lawyer and the AUSA. He'd promised it had nothing to do with his incarceration, which was doubtful, because inmates met with agents for one reason—to get out of jail—but they'd know what he wanted soon enough.

The lure of information had been too much to resist.

"You got here late," Officer Dorf said over his shoulder. "Shoulda come sooner."

"Last-minute trip," Nathan said.

Dorf turned, showing them his seventies-porn-style mustache. "And we're supposed to have approval forty-eight hours in advance."

"We didn't know we were coming," Nathan said.

Nathan suppressed the anger bubbling inside him, something he'd been trying to control. Who knew the pressure Dorf was under, or the health problems and horrors he'd experienced? Everyone faced hidden battles, which often exhibited as bursts of rage, like a demon lurking in the shadows.

Or Dorf could be an asshole.

"*Oye*, does Isabella got a man?" Waldo asked.

"Who?" Dorf asked.

"Officer Ramirez. She checked us in."

"Dunno."

They passed through a series of doors, stopping and staring at cameras as they waited for them to be remotely unlocked. The deeper they descended into the prison's bowels, the more Nathan's chest constricted. He wasn't claustrophobic, but being locked inside a facility, with no way out, restrained his soul the way free men never experienced. Could he ever survive prison?

"This is it," Dorf said. "You only got fifteen minutes."

Dorf opened the door to an interview room and escorted them inside a ten-by-ten room with sterile, white walls, a stainless-steel desk, and metal chairs bolted to the floor. They sat and waited.

"Hamilton's been locked up for two years," Waldo said. "What possible information could he have about China?"

"He did their bidding for years," Nathan said. "He used high-energy weapons to kill Americans who opposed China. He's likely the highest-placed Chinese spy ever arrested."

"But they manipulated him with a false-flag operation."

"Either way, he ran technical operations for the agency, and he has decades of institutional knowledge."

"But why talk now? Didn't he have a chance to cooperate before?"

"No way the US attorney would've recommended a lighter sentence," Nathan said, "and no judge would have approved a lenient plea deal. The corruption ran too deep. A national security advisor worked for the Chinese and used the CIA as a weapon against Americans. Politically, Hamilton couldn't have avoided a life sentence."

Waldo smirked. "I thought the justice system operated outside politics."

"Yeah, right."

"He could be hoping for commutation or a new trial. He's got appeals going, right?"

"His attorneys appealed using every conceivable theory. None gained traction. If he wants to get out—"

A key jingled in the lock, then the heavy door swung open and two officers led Hamilton inside. He looked older, worn out, like a Dickens apparition of his former self. He'd lost thirty pounds, his hair had gone gray, and his skin had a yellow pallor. Prison had not been kind to him. Hamilton glared at Nathan as the guard sat him down and handcuffed him to the metal loop affixed to the table. This maximum-security prison held the worst and most dangerous federal inmates in the country, and procedures were put in place for a reason.

The guards left and Nathan and Waldo waited for Hamilton to speak. Hate radiated from his eyes, and Nathan shifted in his seat. The trip had been a mistake. Hamilton wanted to overturn his conviction, and he'd known the promise of inside information on China would be too much for Nathan to ignore.

"You asked for me," Nathan said, breaking the silence, "and we're here. What's on your mind?"

"China killed Gavin Harrison."

The statement hung in the air, too absurd to believe and too outrageous to ignore.

"I'll bite," Waldo said. "How do you know this? You've been locked up in a hole with only your attorneys visiting. I know, 'cause we checked the logs. You got ESP?"

"Mock all you want," Hamilton said. "China's responsible for that bombing—"

"We haven't confirmed what happened," Nathan said. "Forensics is still evaluating evidence."

Hamilton stared at the ceiling, exasperated. "Of course it's a fucking bomb. You think a plate of chicken tikka exploded?"

"Gas leaks happen," Nathan said, even though he didn't believe it.

"We don't have time to dick around," Hamilton said.

"Seems to me," Waldo said, "you got all the time in the world."

Hamilton looked at him for the first time. "China forced the vice president off the ticket and replaced him with Lemon, then they killed Harrison."

"I hear *ifs* and supposition," Nathan said. "Unsubstantiated theories that you're not in a position to prove. You're probably the least likely person on earth to gather evidence on China. What's your proof?"

"I gamed similar scenarios at the agency. The national security advisor and I had a similar plan for another country."

"Which country?" Waldo asked.

Another glance at Waldo. "Israel. We had a hypothetical plot to force regime change and install our own prime minister."

"Israel's an ally," Nathan said.

"Don't be naïve."

"Screwing with foreign governments ain't new," Waldo said. "We've done it all over Latin America."

"The events leading to Darcy Lemon and Archie James on the Democratic ticket follow the exact sequence we plotted with our Israel plan. The timing is more than coincidental. This is how China operates. They've been scheming and seeking this for decades."

"But you worked for them," Waldo said.

Hamilton's face reddened, and he looked at Nathan. "They used me. You know that. For two years, I've been trying to figure out how they did it and how deep their penetration went."

"Humor me," Nathan said. "What'd you discover?"

"They're into everything. They're manipulating our universities, media, and government. They dictate curriculum in classrooms and brainwash our children. The infiltration is so deep and pervasive that politicians openly accept money from them and defend China without worrying about political backlash or legal consequences."

"Not to beat a dead horse," Nathan said, "but you don't have evidence, right?"

Hamilton clenched his fists. "That's not how intelligence works. I banked a lifetime of analyzing our adversaries, and I've been on the inside of a Chinese false-flag operation."

"You've had a change of heart?" Nathan asked. "Now you want to defend our country."

"I thought I was doing that all along. They duped me."

"You don't defend the country by subverting the Constitution with extralegal executions of American citizens with whom you disagree."

Hamilton stared at his hands. "I'm being punished for my crimes. China has been my obsession since you sent me here, and I know more about what they're doing than anyone."

"From researching on Google?" Waldo said with a smirk.

"Last year's terror attacks weren't a figment of my imagination," Hamilton said. "Fueling the opioid epidemic is only a tiny piece of their unrestricted warfare."

Unrestricted warfare. There was that term again. "How do opioid attacks relate to influencing candidate choice?"

"Those terrorist attacks were only the beginning. When you linked China to them, you deterred that type of overt action, but you may have triggered unintended outcomes."

"Meaning?" Nathan asked.

"Best guess, they'll double down on covert warfare and to undermine our institutions."

"*Guess* is the right word," Waldo said. "You don't have evidence. You dragged us to Colorado to hear jailhouse theories."

Hamilton's face hardened. "I'm here forever. I know that. I'm not delusional enough to think I'll ever get out from behind these walls, but China needs to be stopped."

"That's rich," Waldo said, "coming from the man who acted as their puppet for years."

"I won't deny it," Hamilton said. "They used me. They stole my life, and I can't go back in time and fix it. But I want those assholes. I must expose what they're doing."

"How do you plan on doing that?" Nathan asked.

"I can't," Hamilton said. "I need you to do it for me."

20

Nathan parked outside a tiny ranch-style house in North Potomac, Maryland, and turned off the ignition. He looked at Amelia in the passenger seat. "You sure you're fine with this?" He held his breath waiting for her answer because he had no other options.

"Why can't Betty watch me?" Amelia asked.

"Because she has doctors' appointments, and I'll be out of town, and your mom and Vince are gone too."

"I never met Meili's mom."

"It's only one night. Your mom will pick you up tomorrow, then I'll be back the following day."

Amelia narrowed her eyes. "I'll probably need a psychiatrist when I get older."

"Excuse me? Where did you hear that?"

"On ChatteringHen. I'm a latchkey kid, right?"

"You have more people who love you and want to take care of you than anyone I know."

Amelia looked down.

What he'd said was true, but guilt sickened him. Every time he shuffled Amelia from house to house, it brought back self-doubt about his divorce.

Had he been so unbearable he'd driven Reagan away, or had she been selfish? Sometimes shit happened, and no one was to blame.

"I'm sorry about this scheduling snafu," he said, "but it doesn't happen much. Be a trooper and roll with it, okay?"

The front door opened and Meili waved from the stoop.

"Let's go," Nathan said.

"Whatevs."

He grabbed her backpack, locked the car, and led her up the sidewalk. The grass had browned and weeds poked out from between the slabs of concrete. Meili's mother, Yimo, had lived alone for twenty years, since her husband's death.

"Welcome," Meili said.

Nathan pulled Meili into an embrace and kissed her on the mouth.

"Come on, Dad," Amelia said. "Not in public."

"You'll understand one day."

"Ew, gross."

Meili broke their embrace and held the door open for them.

Amelia peered inside. "Did you grow up here?"

"My parents moved here when they immigrated from China. I was born in this house, and I didn't leave until college."

"Yet your mother doesn't speak English?" Nathan asked.

"Her friends are Chinese and it's an insular community. Montgomery County has the largest Chinese population in the DC Metro area. She doesn't need English."

They went inside and Meili introduced Nathan and Amelia to Yimo. The woman stood less than five feet tall, and she'd retained a lean body, which was a good sign for Meili, since children often turned into their parents. Despite being in her mid-sixties, Yimo showed no sign of cognitive degeneration, and intelligence radiated behind her eyes. She eyed Nathan like a falcon tracking a mouse.

"Welcome, Amelia," Yimo said with a heavy accent.

"You'll be able to communicate?" Nathan asked her.

Yimo nodded.

"She understands more than she lets on," Meili said. "They'll be fine."

"You good?" Nathan asked Amelia.

She nodded and put on a brave smile, but she didn't appear comfortable.

"Call me anytime."

"I'm chill," Amelia said with too much bravado.

"I better get going," Nathan said. He turned to Meili. "See you in a couple days?"

"As soon as I'm home."

"*Zhège nánrén shénme shíhòu qǔ nǐ,*" Yimo said.

"*Wǒmen hái méi tánlùnguò tā,*" Meili said.

"*Nǐ niánjì dàle, wǒ xiǎng yào sūnzǐ.*"

Meili waved her hand dismissively. "*Zhīhòu.*"

Yimo rattled off a string of Mandarin. Not understanding language drove Nathan crazy, but Mandarin was complicated to read, write, and speak. He'd picked up some Arabic and Pashto, at least enough to follow terrorist interrogations, but Chinese dialects remained a mystery.

"What did she say?" Nathan asked.

"Nothing," Meili said.

"Sounded like something."

"Later."

She'd tell him if he wanted, but from the expression on Yimo's face, she hadn't been impressed with him—yet another obstacle to deepening his relationship with Meili.

"Gotta run," Nathan said.

"I'll walk you out," Meili said.

Nathan kissed Amelia on the head, then followed Meili outside.

"You're sure this will work?" he asked.

"Mom loves kids, despite her rough exterior. I wouldn't have agreed if I didn't think it would go well. I want Amelia to trust me." She rubbed her temples.

"Jet-lagged?" Nathan asked.

"It's been a constant state. I love travel, but it's getting old."

"We could transfer to a small office and work bank robberies and white-collar fraud," he said.

"We'd go nuts."

Nathan looked around, confirming they were alone. "I saw your report from the embassy. You weren't able to set another meet with Xuannü?"

"Lincoln begrudgingly contacted her. He's afraid of making waves over there."

"What did she say?"

"She didn't seem comfortable communicating via encrypted messages, so I suggested email drafts from a new account, and she agreed."

"Old-school," Nathan said.

"She said China's entering a new phase of disintegration warfare, but she didn't tell me much, which makes me suspect she's testing us. She didn't trust CIA, and now she's cagey with us."

"A double agent?"

"Wouldn't surprise me," Meili said. "She claims the Second Bureau will continue drug warfare, which is weird, because DEA announced new analog laws in China."

"The CCP floods American streets with opioids," Nathan said. "Stopping one analog forces new drugs to market. It's obvious they haven't taken any serious enforcement action."

"Not to the State Department," Meili said.

"State diplomats view everything through the lens of optimism, as if they believe China wants to help. Or they know it's bullshit and they're propping up the Chinese propaganda for other reasons."

"Always the conspiracy theorist."

"Occupational hazard," he said, "and my paranoia has proved accurate in the past."

Meili yawned and ran her fingers through her hair. "If my source isn't lying, how do we counter drug warfare?"

"It must be a political response. We're a free society. If we want to stop Chinese opioids, the CCP needs to help."

"How do we make that happen?"

Nathan shrugged. "What else did she say?"

"She said our communications are compromised. She said we're deeply infiltrated. Most troubling, she suggested China's unrestricted warfare will become more overt."

"Meaning?"

"She said China's manipulating our elections."

The hair rose on Nathan's neck. "That's what Hamilton said."

Meili cocked her head. "Trent Hamilton?"

"Long story. He contacted me while you were traveling, and Waldo and I flew out to see him. He claimed China assassinated Harrison."

"I'll need to see your report. I'm shocked the ASAC approved the interview. That case is a political red ball."

Nathan smirked.

"You're shitting me," Meili said. "Tell me you received approval for the trip."

"I was the acting supervisor while you are gone, and I ran the travel request through the acting ASAC while the ASAC was in a White House briefing."

Meili closed her eyes and rubbed her neck. "That will cause serious problems with—"

"Hamilton said it was urgent, and I didn't have time to jump through administrative hoops. Hamilton told me about his assassination planning at CIA, and frankly, he didn't want anyone to know we talked."

"His defense counsel?"

"He insisted we speak alone. I had him sign a waiver."

"The AUSA's going to lose his mind when he hears about this."

"Hamilton claims China assassinated Harrison, and now you've got a high-ranking source saying they're manipulating the election."

"A source who could be a double agent," she said, "and manipulation doesn't mean blowing up a restaurant."

"Anything new on that investigation? I've asked around, but everyone involved is closed-mouthed. They don't want anything leaking."

"I'll probably get a full briefing, after I share our source's allegations. The explosion's related to our case."

Nathan checked his watch. "I've got to run." He kissed her and took a step toward his car before stopping and turning back to her.

"Your mom doesn't care for me?"

"Why do you say that?"

"The way she looked at me. Her tone. Want to tell me what your mother said? Second thoughts about babysitting?"

"It's not about you . . . not directly. She's looking forward to having company. My mother's traditional. She didn't like it when I put my career before family. It's an ongoing battle."

"She must be proud of you. You're running a group, and you received a commendation from the attorney general."

Meili's eyes clouded, and her mind seemed to go somewhere else. "She wants me to marry, have a family."

Nathan's heart raced. "Is that so bad?"

"It's . . ."

"What?"

"She demands grandchildren now."

"In a way, you have a child—Amelia."

"I love Amelia. She's a great kid, and you've done an amazing job with her, but Mom wants her own biological grandkids."

"Do you want kids?" They'd never really discussed it, because every time Nathan pushed for more commitment, she'd resisted. He had tread easy.

"The timing's bad."

"It's always inconvenient."

"What would having children do to my career?"

"It's about choices . . . priorities."

"Taking maternity leave would kill my cases, and possibly my career, and when it was time to return, would I want to leave my baby?"

"Children change what's important. It isn't a bad thing."

"My culture and genetics drive me to procreate, but how would I afford childcare?"

"We could do it together." His nerves tingled.

She chewed on her lip. "That would mean moving into your place with the memories of your ex. And I don't know if I even want to do the *mom* thing."

"Living together is an interesting idea."

Meili grinned. "She asked when you planned to propose."

Nathan couldn't breathe. "I didn't know you were waiting for that."

"I'm not," she said a little too forcefully.

Nathan's mood darkened, and he looked away.

"Let's talk about this later," she said.

"Your mother brought it up."

"She cares about me."

"I care about you too."

She took his hand and kissed him, more passionately this time. He headed for his car with a full heart.

21

California offered perfect weather, a spectacular coast, and the glamour of Hollywood—a state that dangled aspirations, hope, and magic—and it lived in her dreams. But downtown Los Angeles evoked none of that enchantment.

Reagan stood outside the three-story office building where Democratic Party officials congregated for an emergency meeting to salvage an election strategy. Reagan breathed in the fresh air, then coughed. She'd come outside to escape the recycled air, but the light breeze tasted polluted. How did people live in LA? Other than cultural outposts like the Arts District, Chinatown, and Little Tokyo, the city was bleak—simmering concrete, soulless office buildings, and deserted streets—where impossible wealth and shattered lives existed side by side in a creative wasteland.

A handful of politicos smoked cigarettes away from the entrance, in compliance with California law. Reagan had never taken up the habit, which now seemed like a political liability. How much political maneuvering and cementing of alliances happened in those informal smokers' gatherings between meetings?

Reagan scanned the street for a coffee shop. Graffiti covered the walls of a store with haphazardly stacked merchandise in its window, as if a child had graduated from a lemonade stand to run the business. Even Malibu

Beach houses that sold for millions of dollars looked unkept. Everything around LA felt unpolished, except the bodies sculpted by plastic surgeons.

But Reagan had come because this Democratic machine meeting was an opportunity. Politics lured her with its promise of fame and power, but it also offered the ability to make the world a better place. Running for office appealed to her for both personal gain and altruism. She wanted it. Bad. And winning the party's support was the key to success.

"Reagan Cabrera?" a woman said behind her.

Reagan snapped out of her fog of ambition and turned to the stunning Asian woman smiling at her. She wore a leather-and-denim skirt and powder-blue, embroidered boots with distressed fabric. Adorable.

"Have we met? I'm sorry, I don't—"

"No, no, I haven't had the pleasure," she said, extending her hand. "Ruoxi Ko with The Modern Democrat."

Reagan shook her hand. "The Modern . . . ?"

"Democrat. We're an online editorial magazine dealing with our changing political environment."

"I see . . . and how do you know me?"

"It's my job to understand who's who. We air a companion podcast that features movers and shakers in the Democratic Party"—she cocked her head—"including up-and-comers, like you."

Did Ruoxi flatter everyone in LA's superficial culture, or was she sincere and wanted to use her influence to vault Reagan into the limelight?

"I love your shoes," Reagan said. "Are those Ferragamos?"

"Christian Louboutin. I spotted them in a window and had to own them."

The group of smokers headed toward them, including Gail Haverhill. That signaled the end of the break. Reagan stepped away from the door to allow the group to pass.

Gail reached out and grasped Reagan's hand as she passed. "Don't be late."

"Right behind you."

Ruoxi held the door for the group, then fell in beside Reagan as they entered. "We'd like you to write an op-ed piece for us and appear on the show."

Reagan slowed. "An editorial about what?"

"Whatever you'd like. Issues you find important."

Reagan could talk about the Havana Syndrome and foreign operations on American soil, or . . . so many things needed fixing, and the Democratic Party had skewed hard left, sometimes making things worse instead of better. A respected platform could amplify her voice and spur change, not to mention increase her credibility in political circles.

"Why me?"

"You're a new face in the party, and since the accident, you're the only legacy delegate in Virginia."

"You mean the assassination."

Ruoxi smiled, but not with her eyes. "The tragic incident in Rosslyn, whatever the cause."

"What's the format?"

"Long-form, at least forty-five minutes. The time allows people to move beyond sound bites and dive deeper into issues."

Reagan inflated. "Could be a good opportunity."

"We don't ask just anybody. We've aired many of our most illustrious voices."

Reagan nodded. She'd never heard of the show, but why insult the woman? She could listen to their archives to get a feel for their style.

"Let's set a date for you to record in our LA studio."

"LA?"

"If travel's a problem, we can do it remotely. We also pay a stipend."

"You'd pay for an interview? Is that allowed?"

"Not for the interview, but to reimburse your expenses and lost income. It's ethical."

Reagan bit her lip. What expenses would a video interview require? They entered the central ballroom as senior delegates and party officials returned to their seats.

Gail stood behind the podium and tapped on the microphone. "Welcome back from break. This morning, you heard an overview of our election strategy and the talking points we want you to parrot. Now, we'll break into regional working groups, so you'll have a playbook to take back to your states."

"What are our chances of winning this thing?" a man shouted from a table close to the podium.

"It's close, by all polling data," Gail said. "But we can't expect the electorate to vote for our ticket if our party apparatus is still divided. We need to coalesce around our new candidates and speak with a unified voice."

"Good luck with that," the man said. A few people laughed.

Gail leaned her elbows on the podium. "Listen, we're all enthusiastic, and we have fractious elements, but need to come together. Diversity is good, but not diversity of thought, and not a week out from a general election."

The crowd murmured.

Diversity of thought was a *bad* thing? Cognitive dissonance tightened Reagan's neck and shoulders. She needed to speak up. She stood.

Gail's eyes darted to her. "Yes, Ms. Cabrera?" Her tone could have frozen the microphone.

"I'm a team player, and I agree we need to overcome our differences to achieve our common goals, but shouldn't we discuss what those goals are?"

Gail shook her head. "We had an entire convention to discuss our platform. Now's the time to figure out how to win."

"But we have new candidates. Does Darcy Lemon embrace the platform? What are her priorities?"

"Of course she supports our platform. That's why we installed . . . er, that's why we nominated her."

"Voters should hear that from her," Reagan said. "Are Lemon and James planning more public appearances?"

"They have a joint interview scheduled on network television."

"The public wants to ask questions. How about a series of press conferences and town hall meetings?"

"That's not our strategy," Gail said.

People's eyes bored into Reagan, and her face heated under their scrutiny. Did they agree with her objection to the "hide Darcy Lemon in the basement" strategy?

Gail snatched the microphone from the stand and came around the podium. She scanned the crowd. "I hear all your concerns."

Reagan sat down. Had speaking up been a mistake? In politics, the success of tactics often remained hidden until the outcome became known.

"We brought you here to take our strategy back to your states and unify this party," Gail said. "I understand your unease, but the time for doubt is over. We have 4,600 Democratic delegates, and we need all of them to commit to the Lemon-James ticket."

Gail locked Reagan in her stare. "If we want Darcy Lemon to be our next president, we need to do whatever is necessary to win."

22

Nathan and Waldo sat across from Trent Hamilton in Florence ADMAX penitentiary again. Hamilton looked more frail and gray than before, if that was even possible, but he'd requested the meeting.

"You sick?" Nathan asked.

"Sleep's hard to come by with inmates yelling and the night terrors."

What could Nathan say to that? "You have something urgent?"

Hamilton sighed. "You're interested in China's use of Islamists to spread drugs in the West, right?"

Nathan tensed. "The Phantoms killed thousands."

"Radical Islamists are a convenient tool for any ideology seeking martyrs. Did you know before World War I, Kaiser Wilhelm radicalized Muslims to use against Germany's enemies, and in World War II, Hitler used the Grand Imam? Islam and Nazism share much in common."

"We flew out here in the middle of our investigation, with the election looming. Can you get to the point?"

"You need to give China a reason to stop opioid production."

"It's a major industry, and China controls tens of billions of dollars of the global market. Curtailing production would damage their economy, and they won't do that to help us. The US is China's primary economic rival, and whatever hurts us, helps them. It's a zero-sum game."

"I'm speaking of illicit trafficking. They turn a blind eye to illegal labs, drug diversion from legitimate manufacturers, pill mills, fraudulent doctors and pharmacists, and criminal organizations."

"We've exerted political pressure and trade incentives, but nothing has worked. They pay us lip service about clamping down on illegal operations and new analog laws, but nothing changes. It's all smoke and mirrors."

"Then try something else."

"What would make China . . ." Nathan trailed off as the coal of an idea flared in his mind.

"China's unrestricted warfare utilizes numerous simultaneous tactics to undermine us, and you need to counter all of them, from election interference to spreading addiction."

"We're trying to—"

"I'm giving you a source."

Waldo's head jerked up. "Who you got?"

"I called him Emerald. He's a principal in a transnational criminal organization that smuggles everything from antiquities to precious stones to drugs."

"What can he do for us?" Waldo asked, suddenly interested.

"Emerald deals with corrupt officials across China. We used him to collect information but also to plant seeds. He affected Chinese strategy without officials recognizing the hand that manipulated him."

Excitement bubbled inside Nathan. "How highly placed were those officials?"

"The highest. Emerald influenced Provincial police chiefs, mayors, and central government officials. Information placed in the right ear can travel all the way to the top. Whether the Central Committee acts on it is another question."

"The CIA must have changed his contact procedures after you, uh, left."

"I ran him off the books. He dealt with businessmen, criminals, and governments across the Golden Triangle, and he proved useful for black ops."

"You mean your directed-energy attacks," Waldo said.

Nathan flinched. Waldo had a point, but antagonism wouldn't help. He waited for Hamilton to respond.

Hamilton leaned back in his chair and rolled his tongue inside his mouth. "I won't discuss anything about my case. I'll never win an appeal, but I must maintain hope."

"Yet you're introducing us to your source?" Nathan asked.

"He won't incriminate himself, or me. But he can help you uncover the symbiotic relationship between drug traffickers, Islamists, and the CCP."

"How do we reach him?" Nathan asked.

"Put an ad in the *Shanghai Daily* newspaper's classified section. It's an English publication."

"What should it say?"

"Give me a pen and paper."

Nathan glanced at Waldo. The penitentiary's rules explicitly prohibited them from giving anything to an inmate.

"You need to word this properly."

Nathan opened his notebook to a blank page and pushed it across the desk with a pen. Hamilton scribbled furiously, then handed the notebook back.

"The pen?" Nathan asked.

Hamilton smiled and handed it to him. "Use that exact verbiage, then three days after your ad appears, meet him in Bangkok at the Sheraton Grand Sukhumvit. He'll be at the bar in the furthest seat away from the door. He'll pass you specific meeting instructions."

"We'll see," Nathan said. "We need to vet him and—"

Hamilton's face clouded, as if a storm had blown into the room. "You don't have time. We're at war, and if China isn't stopped, we're finished."

23

Bangkok's humidity opened Nathan's pores and dampened his clothes as if he'd entered a sauna fully dressed. Even in late October, the ninety-degree temperature clung to the earth. The sun hung low, casting shadows over buildings and tinging the smog-filled air a fiery red. Waldo walked beside him, and despite being raised in Tampa, sweat poured down his face.

Nathan stopped outside the Sheraton Grand Sukhumvit. Two-story palm trees lined its white-brick exterior and towering glass windows.

"Wait here," Nathan said, "and I'll see if Emerald is inside."

"And if he doesn't show?"

"That'll mean Hamilton was screwing with us, and we wasted five grand in taxpayer money and two days of work. If you spot countersurveillance, come inside and order a water, and I'll meet you back at our hotel."

Waldo gave a thumbs-up and pulled out his phone, no doubt to check football scores.

Nathan crossed the brick driveway under a black canopy, and the doorman opened the door. Nathan entered a spacious lobby of shiny marble, neon lights, and sparkling gold. He crossed a lounge and stepped up into the elevated area where café tables circled the bar. Three couples chatted at tables, and a single man in his fifties hunched over a drink at the bar. He met Nathan's eyes and didn't look away.

Nathan sat one seat away from the man and the bartender appeared before him.

"Drink, sir?"

"Do you know how to make an Emerald?" Nathan asked, using his source's code name.

The man smiled beside him. He'd received the message.

"No, sir, I don't," the bartender said.

"I'll take a Singha," Nathan said.

Emerald stood and set a pile of Thai baht on the bar. As he left, he slipped a napkin onto the bar beside Nathan. Nathan palmed it and held it in his lap to read it.

The Forest Club, Soi 23

Nathan wadded up the note and stuck it in his pocket as Emerald walked through the lobby toward the exit. Nathan left five dollars in baht and followed him out.

Nathan caught Waldo's eye and jerked his head toward Emerald. Their new source wore a gray summer suit and brown shoes—formal, but not ostentatious enough to draw attention.

Emerald headed down the sidewalk against heavy westbound traffic on Sukhumvit Road. A median separated the six lanes of traffic and the elevated train ran above, making following him by car difficult. In intelligence work, the little nuances made the difference between life and death.

Nathan alternated his attention between pedestrians and oncoming cars. None paid attention to Emerald. Nathan stayed fifteen yards back, close enough not to lose him, yet far enough to disassociate from Emerald. He glanced back over his shoulder. A handful of people trod the sidewalk outside the hotel, but no one watched him, and none looked the part, not that a professional would stand out. Waldo followed at a distance, moving casually.

They continued for a few blocks, and then Emerald crossed the pedestrian bridge to the other side of Sukhumvit and arrived at Soi 23—the beginning of one of Bangkok's red-light districts. They entered Soi Cowboy, a hub of go-go bars where strippers and prostitutes plied their trade. The district covered the area of four hundred yards long, and it glittered like the Vegas Strip. Bars lined the street, and gorgeous young women wearing skirts, short-shorts, or bikinis lured passersby into bars. Neon signs illuminated the mostly male throng. The air sizzled with booze, desire, and sex.

Emerald passed a food cart that offered fried bugs, and ignored two girls who tried to corral him into a bar. He pushed through the crowd and entered the Forest Club.

Nathan waited outside for Waldo to catch up. Petite women from across Thailand danced on poles in clubs like this, and most would go home with customers if men paid a service fee to the establishment and then compensated the women separately.

Waldo stopped beside him. "Seriously?"

"He wants to meet here."

"Too *pública*," Waldo said.

"It's all foreigners."

"Chinese are foreigners."

"Let's hope they don't frequent this place. Trust Emerald. He ran black ops with Hamilton for years."

"Go-go bars are crazy."

Nathan raised an eyebrow. "You've been before?"

"Business." Waldo grinned.

The high-pitched, tonal sounds of Thai hookers hawking their bodies punctuated the din. A woman wearing a short skirt and bikini top hooked his arm. She probably thought he was another creep ogling Thai women for sex. She squealed with fake elation as he slipped into the bar.

His eyes slowly adjusted to the dark, but the sleazy feeling lingered. Pretty women in various stages of undress danced on three stages as a heavy, rhythmic beat thumped through the room.

"Hello, handsome," a petite Thai woman said. She wore a silver micro bikini.

"Looking for a friend," he mumbled as he pushed past her.

Emerald sat in a booth in back. Nathan edged through the club with Waldo shadowing a few yards behind. Half the booths were occupied by middle-aged white guys. They fixated on the dancers like lions stalking elk —only their prey could be caught with a handful of twenties.

Nathan weaved his way to the back. Emerald didn't take his eyes off him, but his face remained unreadable. His eyes were emotionless black orbs. Nathan slid into the booth.

"You're not who I expected," Emerald said.

"Our mutual friend in Washington sent me."

Emerald eyed him suspiciously. "I heard he went away."

"I put him there."

Emerald's body tensed. He leaned back and assessed Nathan. "You CIA?"

"FBI. Special Agent Nathan Burke."

Emerald nodded with recognition. "Yes, of course. You caused our friend troubles. You ended a lucrative relationship for me."

"He said you can help me."

Emerald sneered. "Why would I do that?"

"Money. I can request a massive reward for you."

"Or perhaps you wish to send our friend a roommate."

"I'm not here to arrest you. I need your help."

Emerald clicked his tongue. "Then why is your associate hiding?" Emerald nodded at Waldo, who stood several tables away pretending not to watch.

So much for Waldo's surveillance technique. "He's making sure we weren't followed."

Emerald narrowed his eyes.

Time for honesty . . . or the perception of it. "And he's making sure you don't try to hurt me. We don't know each other. I'm here because of Hamilton, and he's not my biggest fan."

Emerald nodded, almost imperceptibly. "Why would he send you? I'd want you dead."

"He believes in my mission."

"Which is?"

"To deter China from flooding the United States with opioids."

Emerald smirked. "You think I can do that? China earns billions, and your citizens want their drugs. Americans' desire to get high creates the demand."

Nathan waved Waldo over. Waldo's shoulders sagged as he walked to the table.

"Emerald, this is my partner, Waldo."

Emerald appraised him, and Waldo nodded.

"You know the Chinese government's role in exporting opioids?" Nathan asked.

"They use many channels to distribute," Emerald said.

"Fentanyl?"

"Everything. They've built relationships with Mexican cartels and European traffickers . . . Anyone willing to flood America with toxins. And they're developing them as an underground army—criminals and terrorists dependent on China to fund them."

"For what purpose?"

"To destroy America."

Nathan looked at Waldo. This was bad, and they had to do something. "Who else is China using?"

"Everyone knows the connection to Islamic terror groups, but China also works with state actors like Iran. Anywhere they perceive a vacuum of power, they fill it. When the US withdraws or withholds aid, China sees an opportunity for influence. They're everywhere—Africa, Middle East, Asia —any region where they can influence governments, mine resources, or establish military bases. And they use immigration warfare to populate areas with Chinese immigrants to affect local politics and make countries friendlier to China."

"Specifically, who's transporting their drugs?"

"Trafficking groups across Southeast Asia, Europe, the Caribbean. Chinese intelligence —"

"I need China's policymakers to divest from drugs, and our friend tells me you have contacts inside the Second Bureau."

Emerald's eyes darted around the room, then settled back on Nathan. "If that were true, how would it help you?"

"I want the CCP to think the opioid epidemic will hurt them too."

Emerald shook his head. "They don't care about addiction. They throw users in prison."

"China doesn't want tariffs, economic sanctions, or foreign indictments."

"That doesn't scare them. Americans need cheap Chinese products. The demand for opioids is high, and hospitals need fentanyl."

"China supports the illicit industry," Nathan said, "and worse than that, they used opioids as a weapon against us."

"And nothing happened to them. Their strategy worked."

"It tarnished the CCP's reputation and made diplomacy difficult."

"But they damaged America's economy and terrified its citizens. That benefited China. They are your adversary."

Nathan sighed. Emerald was right. The US had used radical Islamists too, as a tool to bloody the Russians in Afghanistan. That strategy had not ended well. Especially on 9/11.

Nathan's mind lightened as an idea rushed into him.

"*Que pasa?*" Waldo asked.

"What if . . ." The idea congealed in Nathan's mind ". . . the Chinese government considered radical Islam a threat?"

Emerald smiled. "They support Islamists across the globe, but none have the power to threaten China. They don't have the technology."

"But they have opioids," Nathan said. "The fentanyl and carfentanil China sells them."

Emerald frowned. "They need China as a supplier."

"Islamists want a caliphate more than money. It's their endgame. What would China do if Islamists turn China's opioids into weapons?"

"That hasn't happened," Emerald said.

"But if it did, China might reassess their policy."

Emerald's eyes narrowed.

A waitress wearing a bikini that barely covered her stopped at the table. "You want drink—"

"Go away," Emerald said.

"You need buy two drink—"

Emerald's eyes flared. "Get away, woman."

"Bring us three whiskeys," Nathan said. He dropped one hundred baht onto her tray. She nodded and walked away.

"Let's not make a scene," Nathan said.

"You're planning a terrorist act inside China?"

"Plan is the word. I don't want to start a war with China. But if they believe Islamists are using drugs to support the Uyghurs and execute attacks across China, they may rethink their position on opioids . . . or at least restrict sales to legal trade."

"A sneaky plan."

"Would it work?"

"Perhaps, if . . ."

"*If* what?" Nathan asked.

"If you had the right contact on the inside, someone to sell your story."

"And you're that person?"

Emerald smiled. "For the right price."

24

Reagan sighed in front of her home computer as the weight of the assassination and party pressure depleted her energy. If her leadership demanded she support the Lemon-James ticket, what choice did she have? Democratic Party infighting would result in another four years of Republican governance.

"What should I do?"

She'd been talking to herself a lot recently. Vince remained in Santo Domingo on business, and Amelia frequently stayed with Nathan. She drummed her fingers on the desk while her desktop booted up. The screen came to life, and she opened her bookmark for her bank.

"Who the hell is Darcy Lemon?" she said.

Archibald James, Lemon's selection for vice president, was a long-term senator and a respected career politician with a reputation as a moderate. He'd developed strong relationships across the aisle, and he'd even voted against a few Democratic spending bills.

"Archie's okay," she said. "But Lemon's an unknown."

Her login box appeared, and a pop-up window appeared for her saved password service. "Amelia at twenty-eighteen," she mumbled as she typed. Password services scared her, because if anyone hacked that account, they'd have access to everything, but she couldn't remember dozens of unique passwords that she was forced to change every few months. Who could remember them all without writing them down? Encrypted online password managers were lifesavers.

Her home screen appeared, and she opened her bank account. Things had been tight.

"Twelve thousand in checking . . . sixty-two hundred in savings . . . shit."

She didn't have much cash, and Vince maintained his own separate checking and savings accounts, something she insisted on after divorcing Nathan. Keeping her own money and their finances separate gave her a sense of independence, though she wrote Vince a check every month for her half of their expenses. He'd been put off by her request at first, and it probably still bothered him, but this was the new Reagan, and she wanted to keep the money she earned, no matter how scant that was since she left State.

Her net worth had dropped every month since losing her fat government check. Being a delegate paid nothing, and she could legally raise little in contributions. She'd planned to run for the Virginia State Senate or House, but with her increased visibility and responsibility after Harrison's assassination, the promise of a federal office seemed reachable. Unlikely, but possible, and hope gave her reason to wake up each morning. As a junior congressperson, she'd make $174,000, a number that would solve her financial worries.

She stared at her accounts. She carried eight grand in credit card debt, a stupid waste of money. She should pay that off, but it would wipe out her assets.

"I need another consulting gig . . . fast."

Reagan checked her email and opened another message from Gail asking her to commit her vote to Darcy Lemon and Archie James.

"I know . . . I know."

If Reagan didn't get on board soon, she'd hurt her career. Politics was a fickle business, where perception meant everything. If she didn't act like a team player, she'd never receive the endorsement of Gail and other heavy hitters.

But her questions around Lemon remained.

She saved Gail's email as unread. She'd think about it and respond later.

The ramifications of her decision were too significant to make without serious contemplation. She needed coffee.

She maximized her bank website window to log out. Experts said you should do that because leaving them open made them more vulnerable to hackers, though her bank would log her out automatically after five minutes of inactivity.

She rolled her cursor over the logout button and stopped. The summary of her account balances on the home screen drew her eye.

Her checking account balance didn't make sense. She blinked and looked again.

The account now held over forty thousand dollars.

She clicked on it and examined the transaction log. Someone had deposited thirty grand into her account. Reagan opened the transaction details and read the name of the sender.

The Modern Democrat.

25

Nathan and Waldo walked down Sunthonkosa Road toward the Chao Phraya River in Bangkok. The organic odor of fetid water replaced the stench of carbon monoxide pouring out of motorcycles, tuk-tuks, and other vehicles.

"You trust this guy?" Waldo asked.

"Kei? Yeah, as much as it's possible to trust any snitch. He's a career criminal, but I have confidence in his intelligence. He risked his life infiltrating the Triads and ISIS, and if it wasn't for him, that passenger airliner would have exploded over the Washington National. Even though he did it to work off gun charges, he came through for us."

"Is it smart to introduce him to Emerald? What can he do?"

"Kei has contacts in Chinese intelligence and police agencies. He's operated in that gray area between organized crime and espionage for years. He knows the right people, and more importantly, he knows how the Chinese government thinks."

"Seems *peligroso* to expose sources to each other."

"They both have skin in the game, and their lives depend on keeping their relationship with us a secret."

"Why isn't Kei hiding after his last case?"

"He avoided exposure because the AUSA agreed to build the case without his testimony. It made things harder, but we got our convictions, and lots of pleas."

They passed between buildings and arrived at the Wat Khlong Toei Nok Pier, where the Chao Phraya's green water moved lazily past, as if the heat slowed it down too. Two long-tailed craft docked against the pier with their propellers dangling in the air. Beside them, a dilapidated houseboat bobbed in a slip. The aft door on the houseboat opened, and a man stepped onto the stern.

Kei Choi.

"Welcome to Bangkok, boss" Kei said.

Nathan grinned. Kei had risked his life to infiltrate the radical Islamists, and together, they'd saved hundreds of lives. Kei's inside information had also exposed China's involvement in the Havana Syndrome attacks.

Kei climbed down a short gangplank and met them on the pier. Nathan embraced him. "This is my new partner, Special Agent Osvaldo Falcón. Waldo, meet Kei."

"Hope you do better than Nate's other partners."

Kei kidded, but an image of Eddie's body flashed in Nathan's mind. A lead weight settled in his stomach, dampening his mood. He gazed at the water while Waldo and Kei shook hands.

"How'd you find a houseboat in Thailand?" Nathan asked.

"I know people, man."

"But I set this meet two days ago, and you don't live here."

"Bangkok's playground for Triads, traffickers, and spies. I do many business here."

Nathan swatted Waldo's arm. "See, that's what I'm talking about. Kei makes things happen."

"We should get moving," Waldo said. "The meet's coming up."

Nathan looked at Kei. "Emerald will introduce you to our target."

"Who is this man?" Kei asked.

"An opioid trafficker based in Shanghai."

"I buy the drugs from him?"

"You got it."

"If I didn't know you, I think you feed me to the sharks to make money."

"Kei, Kei, Kei. Now why would I do that?"

"Wealth, power, the usual reasons."

"He's not a normal human," Waldo said.

"We're not here to make money," Nathan said.

"Then why I buy drugs?"

"I'll tell you when you need to know," Nathan said. "Emerald brought the drug dealer to Bangkok. Guy's name is Quon Li. He wants to meet at the Wat Pho temple."

Kei cocked his head. "You tell me, never let bad guy set the place. You say that many time."

"In this case, it doesn't matter, and if you push back, he'd get suspicious."

"Why he in Thailand?" Kei asked.

"Quon Li runs a trafficking group in Shanghai that produces opioids for export. He brings his crew here for business and pleasure. He jumped on a plane the moment Emerald called."

Kei narrowed his eyes. "Why he come himself? He does not know me."

"Emerald has clout. He's a middleman between the CCP and these groups. He puts people together . . . same as you."

"Emerald worry me too."

"We need him," Nathan said. "I sent the prearranged signal for him to bring Quon to the Wat Pho Temple."

"What signal?" Kei asked.

"I can't tell you."

"He confirm?" Kei asked.

Nathan grimaced. "He doesn't respond. He shows up."

"We hope," Waldo said.

"Over here," Nathan said. He led Kei into the umbra of a building. "You know the drill."

Kei lifted his hands, and Nathan patted him down, searching his pockets for contraband, weapons, or anything a defense attorney could later claim Kei had brought to the meeting. Kei had nothing, except a billfold stuffed with Thai baht.

"You're an international drug transporter," Nathan said. "Meet Quon and negotiate for a large shipment of carfentanil—"

"That shit's so lethal, even China blacklisted it."

"Smoke and mirrors," Nathan said. "The illicit market is flourishing."

"I don't wanna touch that shit."

"Don't be a pussy. Tell him you want a kilo sample as a test, and if the quality's acceptable, you'll order ten times that every week."

"Where do I say I'm delivering it?"

"You don't."

"But—"

"We need him to supply the drugs. We'll handle the rest."

"You arrest him for dealing?" Kei asked.

"It's a buy-walk operation. Get the drugs."

"Too easy. Then what?"

"Emerald will introduce you to the Muslim Brotherhood."

Kei shifted his weight on his feet. "What you up to, cowboy?"

"Meet Quon and make a deal. He has product to sell, and you have buyers. Take it one step at a time."

"Through a field of mines."

Nathan led them back to Sunthonkosa Road where the two-stroke engine of a tuk-tuk puttered past. Nathan hailed a taxi and told him to drive to the Grand Place in southwestern Bangkok. They crowded in and stayed silent as the car weaved through raucous traffic and glittering lights. The sweet odor of carbon monoxide tingled his nose.

Ten minutes later, Nathan told the driver to stop a few blocks from the palace. They exited onto Sanam Chai Road, and Nathan slipped into a narrow side street between commercial buildings. The Chao Phraya River slunk past a block to the south, and to their north lay Wat Phra Chetuphon Wimon Mangkhalaram Rajwaramahawihan, a sixteenth-century temple complex commonly known as Wat Pho.

"Emerald will be here any minute," Nathan said, "then he'll walk you into the temple."

"Do the Thai police watch us?" Kei asked.

"No."

"Do they know?"

"No."

Kei nodded. "I make deal for a kilo of carfentanil in a country that executes drug dealers, and you do not share your plan with the police?"

"You're just talking."

Kei smiled, without warmth. "You arrested Golden Dragons for that."

"You're on the right side of this."

"So you say, boss man." He looked around. "Who will protect me?"

"You're looking at your cover team. Waldo and I will be close. If anything happens, we'll swoop in and extract you. But nothing will go wrong. Emerald has clout, and he's vouched for you."

"You carry a gun?"

"I need you to relax," Nathan said. "This guy's a trafficker, not a killer. He—"

"His drugs kill hundreds of thousands," Waldo said.

Nathan scowled at him, then refocused on Kei. "Take this phone and keep it in your front pocket. I'll dial in right before you meet him and listen to everything."

"But I'm Chinese, Emerald is Chinese, and Quon Li is Chinese. Won't we speak Mandarin?"

"If you're in trouble, say—"

"I know—egg roll."

Nathan smiled. They'd worked together for years and had locked up significant numbers of bad guys. Kei triggered feelings of gratitude in him, despite the axiom not to trust CIs. Nathan wanted to protect him, because if anything happened to Kei because Nathan had sent him into a bad situation, the resulting guilt would cripple him. Nathan hardened, a defense mechanism everyone in law enforcement developed—at least those that lasted.

He handed Kei the device, then plugged in headphones to his own phone and brought up the number in his contacts. One touch, and he'd listen in to everything Kei said.

Nathan's phone rang, and displayed Meili's number. He answered.

"Waldo withdrew five grand in operational funds," Meili said.

Nathan glanced at Kei, then held a finger up to Waldo and moved away from them to speak in private.

"That's a fine way to say hello," Nathan said.

"What's going on?"

"I authorized it as the acting group supervisor when you were out."

"For a source meeting?"

His stomach tightened. He should clue her in, but the more she knew, the greater liability she'd assume.

"Nathan?"

"A thousand is for CI information and services, and the rest is for a buy-walk."

"Drugs?"

"It's in the op plan."

"Which you approved?"

"Yep."

She sighed into the phone. "What are you doing?"

"Emerald is bringing someone we're interested in, and our guy is collecting evidence to prove his involvement. I shouldn't say more over the phone."

"I thought this was a meet." Her voice took a sharp edge.

"It's our best chance to corroborate Emerald's info, get inroads into the guys involved with our case, and get a charge on our target. A kilo is more than enough to hit the threshold for a minimum mandatory."

"The ASAC approved it?"

"Yeah, well, I briefed it with a couple of other cases. He was in a rush."

"I'm tempted to shut this down."

"We're meeting the CI now. It's about to happen."

"Don't screw it up. We'll talk about this when you get back."

He hung up and walked back to Kei and Waldo.

"All good?" Waldo asked.

"Let's make this happen. We won't get a second chance."

Nathan's phone vibrated, and he checked it. A text from an anonymous number. He opened it.

Ready.

26

Nathan led Waldo and Kei past rows of commercial buildings into The Siphon Alley. He texted the library name and address to Emerald, then moved inside a chedi, a pagoda-like gatehouse with a pitched roof that led into the property. The walls shielded them from view from the street. The Wat Pho temple lay a hundred yards away, which meant Emerald was close.

"Why is Emerald doing this?" Waldo asked.

"He had a long relationship with our friend in Florence. He's committed."

"And Quon Li will play ball?"

"The introduction is everything. Emerald vouched for Kei, so he owns whatever happens next."

"What'll happen to him when we make arrests?"

"You mean *if* we make arrests," Nathan said. "Our goal is to send a message to the CCP. I don't care about arresting another trafficker."

A minute later, Emerald stepped through the chedi and stared at them.

"Emerald, meet Kim," Nathan said, referring to Kei's alias.

Emerald narrowed his eyes and said something to Kei in Mandarin.

"English, please," Nathan said.

"I asked who he was," Emerald said.

"He's a drug trafficker looking to acquire a new supplier," Nathan said.

"That's all Quon needs to know, and that's all the information you need. When you meet Quon, keep the entire conversation in English. Tell him Kei's Indonesian and doesn't speak Mandarin."

Emerald looked at Kei. "You look familiar."

Kei shifted. "I do not know you."

Emerald clucked his tongue. "Did you work for the Golden Dragons?"

"No," Kei lied. He showed no outward reaction.

Emerald looked skeptical. "I will introduce you and assure him you will not steal his product, then I'll step away. The rest is up to you."

Kei nodded.

"Quon is waiting," Emerald said.

Nathan pressed send and confirmed his phone connected with Kei's fake cell. "We're set. After the meeting, Emerald will stay with Quon, and Kei will return here. If anyone follows you, I'll call and reroute you."

"Okay, boss," Kei said.

Emerald led Kei toward the temple along a curb painted red and white. Nathan stayed thirty yards behind, and Waldo paralleled them on the opposite sidewalk. Kei looked comfortable, like he did this every day. He'd always been a smooth talker, and his skills had improved under Nathan's tutelage.

They paused at the entrance to Wat Pho, paid a fee, and disappeared inside. Nathan increased his pace and reached the gate thirty seconds later. He paid two hundred baht and slipped inside. The temple's buildings stretched for fifty yards around a courtyard with prang tower spires pointing toward the clouds. Tourists wearing tee shirts and shorts removed their shoes as they entered the buildings. A smaller number of Thai visitors may have come to worship.

Emerald and Kei met a wiry, middle-aged Asian man with thick deep lines in his face. Did his gaunt appearance come from the stress of running a criminal organization or from a drug problem?

Nathan stopped at a garden twenty yards away and pretended to read a tourist sign. His earpiece crackled.

"Quon, this is Kim," Emerald said.

"*Hĕn gāox'ng jiàn dào nĭ,*" Quon greeted him.

"*Nín hăo,*" Kei said.

"Kim is Indonesian with imperfect Mandarin," Emerald said. "He prefers English."

"You live in Thailand?" Quon asked.

"New York City."

Nathan cringed. Kei's response would raise Quon's suspicion. Criminals knew the United States had long-arm statutes to charge traffickers around the world.

Emerald scrutinized the tourists around them, then gestured to the main building. "Let's speak in there." They walked past ornate statues to the entrance. They removed their shoes and placed them in green bags, then disappeared inside.

Nathan closed the distance and peeked inside. The golden feet of an enormous 150-foot-long Buddha statue glimmered inside. The ruffling of Kei's phone in Nathan's pocket came across the connection, so he didn't need to follow them inside. Listening to their conversation would be enough to corroborate Kei's testimony if the case ever went to court.

But it wouldn't.

Nathan drifted away from the entrance so they wouldn't see him when they exited. Waldo stayed close and pretended not to know him.

"This is the largest reclining Buddha in the world," Emerald said.

"Is there a lot of competition?" Kei asked.

Nathan shook his head. Kei couldn't control his sarcasm, and his sting operation depended on the success of this meeting. Without a drug purchase, nothing else would happen.

"I do not meet customers myself," Quon said, "but my friend requested I come."

"You won't be sorry," Emerald said. "Kim moves white powder for the Muslim Brotherhood."

"Who?" Quon asked.

"They coordinate Islamist organizations around the world and focus them on their common goal."

"And what is that?"

"Fealty to Allah."

"How do I fit into that?" Quon asked.

"We have drug suppliers," Kei said, "but I need something stronger."

"What do you want?" Quon asked.

Quon was biting. Nathan breathed faster.

"Carfentanil," Kei said.

Silence came over the line.

"Dammit," Nathan muttered. He should have followed them inside so he could read Quon's body language—but not burning the surveillance trumped all. He stayed put.

"Pills?" Quon asked.

"Powder. We will press them at their final destination . . . if that's what my customer wants."

"Where is this going?"

"None of your business."

Nathan held his breath. Kei pushed back, which could sour the deal, but he played it like a trafficker. The supplier didn't need to know where the drugs were headed, and most traffickers wouldn't tell him. Quon could have asked to test Kei, or he could be feeling him out.

"It is my business if you get caught," Quon said.

He had a point. If Kei's drugs were destined for New York, Quon would open himself up to foreign prosecution.

"My customers live in twenty countries."

"Carfentanil is potent. What do they intend to do with it?"

Smart guy. Cagey. He'd been through this before, and after last year's terror attacks, he was being careful. Selling drugs created liability, but being part of a terrorist attack brought attention. Of course, that hadn't stopped him from supplying the Phantoms.

"They will dilute it and distribute the product to gangs to sell to addicts."

The murmur of other people came through Nathan's speaker, creating static. It sounded like they were moving. Did Quon smell a trap?

"How much you want?" Quon asked.

Nathan breathed a sigh of relief.

"We start with one kilo," Kei said, "and if the quality is good, we order regular."

"How regular?"

"Ten kilo every week, or more if things go good."

"That's a lot of powder," Quon said. "Is your customer established?"

"Also not your business."

A gong echoed across the temple and vibrated Nathan's eardrums. A young girl stood beside the instrument holding a mallet. She smiled and gave a peace sign as her friend snapped a picture with her phone.

"That's 36,000 yuan for one kilo."

"In US dollar," Kei said.

"$5,000."

"Too much," Kei said.

"That includes delivery to Thailand. You want ten kilos next time, the price is $4,000 each."

"How much to send to Chiang Mai?"

"$3,000. Where do you want it?"

"I will accept the first sample kilo in Pattaya City. I pay $5,000, then $2,900 each for ten kilos delivered next week."

"Uh, okay, yes. When?"

"Tomorrow."

"I can deliver in two days."

"Take my number," Kei said. "Text me when it is in Pattaya, and I'll send you my location."

"I need the money first," Quon said.

Kei's pockets ruffled. "Here is $5,000. You can count it."

"No need. I will send the product, but after this first deal, you won't see me again. I will introduce my associate, and you can tell him when you want more."

"Very good," Kei said.

Outside, Nathan relaxed as he moved closer to Waldo. "Deal's done. Money delivered."

"He fronted the cash?" Waldo asked.

"No other way."

"How many rules are we breaking?"

Nathan smiled. "Enough to accomplish the mission."

27

Victoria Harbor darkened from teal to gunmetal gray as the sun disappeared beneath the horizon and the water reflected Hong Kong's glass-and-steel structures. Glimmering lights made the city look like a floating casino. Nathan and Meili had roamed the streets for an hour cleaning themselves of surveillance before they entered the night market on Temple Street for their clandestine meeting with Xuannü. They strolled past fabric vendor stalls glowing with lights as a mass of shoppers flowed around them like a school of fish.

"She better show," Nathan said. "I need to meet my source in Thailand tomorrow."

"I can't shake the feeling you're taking advantage of our relationship," Meili said. "I wouldn't have approved that op, and you know it."

Nathan's chest tightened. "I'd never use our intimacy to manipulate you."

"I can't allow my personal attachment to affect my group. You used your position as acting to approve an operation the ASAC never would have green-lighted if he'd been in the building."

"I've pushed the envelope with every boss I've had, if that makes you feel better."

"It doesn't."

"You know this is important. I saw the opportunity to engage the drug trafficker who supplied the Phantoms with the poison that killed thousands of Americans."

"Or so Trent Hamilton says," Meili said. "We don't know that's true."

"We've corroborated Emerald has the contacts, and Quon agreed to the sale."

The clamor of customers and vendors rose around them as the scrum of humanity congealed into a squirming organism. Spotting a tail would be tough, but they'd started their route pretending to be tourists, then slipped out the back of a grocery store before continuing. Tony had flown in to cover them and he'd provided countersurveillance at their last waypoint and texted that they were clear. That was all they could do.

"Did you notify the Royal Thai Police about your buy-walk?"

"I informed my contact in Naresuan 261."

"Telling their Special Operations Unit's terrorism team isn't the protocol for a counterdrug operation."

"But I—"

"And we don't front money for drugs."

He sighed. "It's the way the traffickers work when they don't know you. Kei asked Quon to follow FBI protocol, but he balked."

"That's not funny."

"It's a little funny."

She smiled. Sort of. "How did your other bosses handle you?"

"They didn't, which is why you have me."

"Lucky me."

Meili nodded at a tiny restaurant and they slipped inside. The dark interior only held six tables. A waitress peeked around a curtain from the kitchen with an expression devoid of emotion. Nathan's eyes adjusted to the dark, and the silhouette of a customer came into focus.

Xuannü.

Nathan and Meili moved to the back and sat at her table. She looked younger closer up, but a scarf and tinted glasses covered most of her face.

"Were you followed?" she asked.

"Hope not."

She narrowed her eyes. "You make me uncomfortable."

"We can all end up in prison," he said. "You picked the place."

She looked at Meili. "What do you want to know?"

Meili leaned close. "For starters, how about evidence the CCP planned some of the Havana Syndrome attacks?"

"I care nothing of Havana Syndrome. It is a Cold War weapon."

A chill flittered through Nathan. "That's why you asked to meet."

"I mentioned Havana Syndrome to meet criminal investigators, not intelligence officers."

"You don't trust the CIA?"

"The CIA and FBI are deeply infiltrated. I only trust agents who hunt criminals. Your street agents are honorable, but your leadership is filled with corrupt politicians who the Communist Party manipulates like puppets."

Nathan tried to digest that. "You're accusing CIA and FBI leadership of treason. Where's your proof?"

"The evidence is right in front of you. China bribes your politicians in plain sight, and you don't seem to care. We invest billions in your universities, Hollywood, sporting teams, media organizations, and other American institutions."

A fifty-something man with a large potbelly came into the restaurant and glanced in their direction. Nathan turned his head to avoid staring, but kept the guy in his peripheral vision. The old waitress pushed through the curtain and led Potbelly to a table near the door.

"Is he a problem?" Nathan asked.

Xuannü stared at the man. "If he is intelligence, it's already too late. We don't have long."

"What's the point of China's bribery and influence?" Meili asked. "Do they seek a trade advantage, or do they want to limit American influence in the Pacific Rim?"

Xuannü's eyes narrowed like a snake's. "To destroy you."

Was she telling the truth, or did she inflate the threat to elicit a specific reaction? What was her endgame?

"For many years," Meili said, "American experts have said China wants to be left alone."

"We own many of them," Xuannü said, "and the rest are simpletons. Useful idiots."

Meili rolled her eyes. "Convincing politicians and academics that China's wary of the West doesn't sound like a plan to destroy the United States."

"Disintegration warfare is a broad strategy that seeks to neuter your country by undermining its institutions from within and crippling your power so you can be destroyed."

Meili's face had tightened. "The disintegration warfare theory has been floated for decades, but I don't see proof it's been implemented."

"The proof is everywhere," Xuannü said. "When sports leagues ban criticism of China, that is our influence. When American companies use Chinese slave labor to make products, but your Congress and the media ignore it, that is because we control them."

"What's the CCP targeting now?" Nathan asked.

"Everything," Xuannü said. "China has purchased large swaths of your country, and we use it to gather intelligence and launch covert operations."

"Which operations—"

"Intelligence gathering, corporate espionage, technology theft, psychological operations—"

"PSYOPs?" Nathan asked.

"China engages social media platforms to sow dissension among your minority groups. They poison the minds of your youth against your country. A divided America is a weak adversary."

"ChatteringHen?" Nathan asked.

"Another Chinese intelligence operation. It's designed to lower the IQ of your children by shortening their attention spans, normalizing childish behavior and psychological disorders, praising victimhood, and making them hate your country."

An image of Amelia flashed in Nathan's mind. "Your intelligence is behind it?"

"It goes much farther. They influence the US Congress to increase your national debt. You now spend more on debt service than defense, and China holds that debt. They use tariffs to limit your production and then subsidize Chinese industry to force you out of markets."

Cognitive dissonance ate away at Nathan. "But tariffs are bad for everyone—"

"This is not about free markets. China expends national treasure to dominate markets. Once they control specific industrial sectors, especially those related to national security, they can embargo the US."

"We could rebuild manufacturing," Meili said.

"Not overnight, and this warfare extends beyond your borders. China bought mineral rights in Africa. They threaten Taiwan, and if China ever dominates the semiconductor industry and microprocessor production, America will be unable to build new technology."

"These are long-term plans, and geopolitics changes all the time," Nathan said. "Whenever China gets an advantage, we can respond."

"That's your American thinking. Always in a rush. The party follows a thousand-year strategy to seek hegemony while your politicians work on two or four-year schedules. The party rules forever."

"Nothing is forever."

She nodded. "We can only hope."

That jolted him. It was the first time she'd directly criticized her political apparatus. His stomach hollowed. "Assuming all that is true, China is still a poor country. Sure, they have a billion people—"

"One point four billion," Xuannü said.

"More than us," Nathan continued, "but they are technologically far behind the West."

"Not for long," Xuannü said. "The CCP uses proxies to acquire financial interest in tech companies around the world, even in Silicon Valley. They appropriate research and—"

"You mean *steal* it," Nathan said.

"They make huge advances in technology through industrial espionage. The game changer will be when they solve the quantum computing problem first. If they—"

"All this conspiracy talk is fantastical," Meili said.

Xuannü stared at her before speaking. "We simply expanded on the KGB playbook."

"And you have proof?" Nathan asked.

"Of course, but Agent Burke has seen our influence firsthand." She looked at him. "You ferreted out one of our deepest moles when you killed your national security advisor."

One of? "I didn't kill him. A Bengal tiger did the work for me."

She smiled. "That one set us back more than you can know, and the party won't let it go."

He stilled. "It's been almost two years."

"They want payback."

"Meaning?"

"They plan to kill you."

28

Zhao and his commanders reviewed a formation of his officers who marched in the courtyard outside the Second Bureau. His heavy coat protected him from the frigid early morning air, but the dampness burned his ears below his cap. The frozen ground muted the thumping boots, but the sound of so many officers in step projected strength and inspired him.

One third of his staff was overseas doing the hard work of foreign intelligence, so those that remained in his headquarters were command and support staff—officers who led the machine and kept it running—but not warriors at the tip of the spear who executed the Bureau's plans. *His* plans.

The troops moved in uniform step, a result of regular training—time poorly spent in his estimation—but even with daily practice, they still didn't match the precision of the military units he'd previously commanded. Officers in intelligence thought differently, more freely. They acted outside expectations and learned to move upstream against the flow while staying in the shadows. That mindset inserted itself in their muscle movements, unlike other units that reacted without internal scrutiny and perspective. In a perverse way, his people had been trained to question everything, and that made them insider threats, whether they knew it or not.

A lieutenant exited the building and marched toward Zhao. The man was one of the few officers remaining in the Bureau to monitor communications during the weekly exercise. If World War III broke out, Zhao needed to know immediately. The man carried an envelope sealed with classified tape.

The formation moved at a right angle, then settled into one long formation, many rows deep. He would have stopped this weekly charade, but he kept it going not because it bred discipline but because his officers hated it so much. Forcing them to march in the cold reminded them he was in charge. It solidified their position in his organization and added an element of physical discomfort that reminded them he could inflict pain. And he could do it whenever he chose.

The lieutenant stopped beside Colonel Ying Luo. She stayed at attention as she listened to him, then she stepped out of formation. She held out her hand, and the lieutenant handed her an envelope. She ripped it open with a practiced motion and read its contents.

The formation halted and stood at attention. Hundreds of eyes stared straight ahead. It was time to review the troops, but Zhao wouldn't move until he knew what news the runner had brought. His officers could stand in the cold all day if that was his desire.

Luo looked up and met his eyes. She took a half step back, spun on her toe and headed for him. She marched with stiff movements, obviously aware that everyone watched her. She executed a right turn and faced him. "General, we received a message I think you should hear."

Zhao stared at her, letting uncertainty seep into her decision to break formation. He nodded. "Follow me."

Zhao stepped away and led her out of earshot. "What has happened?"

"A communique from Quon Li."

"Who?"

"The trafficker we used to support drug warfare operations in America."

Zhao glanced around ensuring no one could hear. Mentioning that operation outside the secure facility was forbidden, because the United States possessed advance technology for audio surveillance. But he had asked the question.

"What is the problem?"

"Quon Li's Shanghai Group has been approached by the Muslim Brotherhood."

"The Brotherhood?"

"Command and control for every Islamic terror group."

"Yes, I know." Annoyance seeped into his tone. "Why do you bother me with this?"

"They want to purchase large quantities of opioids from Li."

"Quon Li has sold fentanyl for years," Zhao said. "It's why we chose him. The man is a useful tool."

"The Brotherhood wants carfentanil."

Zhao frowned. That could mean many things. He had introduced the tactic of using carfentanil as a weapon of mass destruction against the United States, and he'd employed the Phantoms to do it. That Afghan group had no affiliation with the Muslim Brotherhood, as far as he knew, but perhaps the Phantoms fell under the Brotherhood's direction. Or perhaps he had inadvertently given the Brotherhood the idea for a new terrorist tactic.

"How will the Brotherhood employ it?"

"They told Li they will sell it to customers to fund operations. He assumed they meant jihad."

"Where?"

"They didn't say, but they asked for delivery in Thailand. The Brotherhood's representative insinuated they'd send it somewhere in the West."

"Who is that man?"

"Unknown."

"Identify him."

"Yes, General. If the drugs are going to America, it will advance our drug warfare."

"Unless they plan to use it for an attack."

"That would still fall within our broader disintegration warfare. It's what we did."

She was correct, of course, but he didn't need her to state the obvious. She'd become too willing to share her unsolicited opinions.

"I don't need you to recite my own plan to me."

"Yes, General."

More attacks would hurt the West. Unfortunately, the FBI had unofficially linked the Phantom's attack to China, and coming a short time after exposing China's culpability in Havana Syndrome, it had caused a diplomatic kerfuffle, from which the fallout hadn't been fully realized. Another carfentanil attack would be blamed on China. But if the Brotherhood distributed the dangerous drugs to American users, it would cause death and economic destruction with only their own impotence to blame.

"Should I give approval for the sale?" Luo asked.

Zhao had gone all in with his accelerated strategy. Hesitation now would only limit his success ... or failure.

He set his jaw. "Do it."

The Fine Print

29

___

Reagan parked a few blocks from the Capitol and headed for the National Democratic Club. She dug out a business card from her purse and dialed the number Ruoxi Ko had given her in LA. The Modern Democrat, Ruoxi's podcast, had deposited thirty thousand dollars into Reagan's checking account with no explanation. Reagan had called five times and left three messages, but so far, no response.

"Modern Democrat," Ruoxi answered.

"Uh, hi," Reagan stammered. She hadn't expected Ruoxi to pick up. "This is Reagan Cabrera from—"

"Good to hear from you. Did you get the money?"

"That's why I'm calling."

"Oh, yay," Ruoxi said. "I'm so glad you received it."

"I didn't . . . what's that for?"

"The interview we discussed."

Reagan opened her mouth, speechless.

"We're excited to feature you. With everything that's happening, voters crave hearing from a young, fresh voice in the party."

Young? "I, uh, thanks. I appreciate the opportunity, and the money . . . I mean, wow, but I don't understand . . ."

"What can I clarify?"

"I know your podcast is long-form, but I didn't expect payment—"

"It's to reimburse your time and expenses."

How much did Ruoxi think it would cost to fly to LA for the day? "I'm not sure when I can break free to come out there."

"Then we'll do it remotely. We prefer to record in person, but we can use a DC studio, or worst case, link to your computer."

Reagan glanced around, making sure no one heard her. She wasn't doing anything wrong, but something made her want to keep this secret. She turned her back to the townhouse beside the club and lowered her voice. "I won't have thirty grand in expenses . . . not even close."

Ruoxi giggled. "The rest is for your time and effort."

"But it's only a podcast, uh, I don't mean to belittle it, but I've never heard of making that kind of money for an interview."

"Happens all the time, especially in politics. Don't undervalue yourself. You have an important message, and we're here to help you get it out."

Her chest swelled. She did have vital information and the Democratic Party needed her vision. Her ideas would help America.

"I don't know . . ." She and Vince could use an influx of cash . . . or at least she could. Vince seemed to be solvent, but while keeping their finances separate had been important for her independence, it had stranded her on an economic island as she struggled to earn income and reimagine her life after the State Department.

"Listen," Ruoxi's tone cooled. "I know this is new to you, but you're a rising star, and we want to elevate your status in the party and amplify your message."

"How do you even know my positions?"

"We're plugged in. You're pushing the party to move in new directions, and we think the establishment needs fresh ideas. We believe you're the candidate to back, but if you're uncomfortable with that, we have a list of other officials who'd love the chance to accelerate their careers."

"No . . . I'll do it."

"That's what I hoped you'd say. I'll email you the details."

Reagan thanked her and hung up. Thirty thousand dollars for her to share her ideas with a wider audience. She would have done it for free.

Hell, she'd have paid for the opportunity. Reagan smiled. This could be the moment her political career took off.

She approached the club building where a handful of people sipped coffees at outdoor tables, but instead of going inside, she continued past it and climbed the brick steps to the Erickson Townhouse, a two-story building used by the Democratic Party for events.

Why had Gail wanted to meet there instead of inside the National Democratic Party's dining room? The club offered excellent food, and the one time Reagan had dined there, she'd felt like an insider. Had Gail chosen the townhouse because Reagan remained on the outside of political power.

That might be about to change.

Reagan knocked, and a young woman opened the door as she balanced a stack of papers and squeezed a cellphone between her ear and shoulder. "Hold on," she said into the phone, then to Reagan, "May I help you?"

"Reagan Burke for Gail Haverhill."

"In the living room," the woman said and looked in that direction.

Reagan entered, and her feelings of self-importance from the call vanished. She remained a Virginia delegate, and she'd need to work hard and use her acumen to politic if she ever wanted to rise onto the national scene.

She entered a room that had been decorated like a Virginia mansion, replete with velvet curtains, crystal glassware, and paintings of stallions on the walls. Gail sat at the table wearing a creme-colored scoop-neck shirt under a blue blazer with a Democratic National Committee donkey pin on her lapel. She waved her over.

Reagan nestled into the seat beside her. The cherry table glistened with polish. Reagan set her purse on the floor and leaned it against her chair leg, self-conscious about resting it on a chair.

"We're in crisis mode," Gail said. "I need you working around the clock from now until the election."

"What can I do?"

"Virginia is more purple than ever. It hasn't been a swing state in years, but your governor and legislature are turning red."

"Doesn't feel that way," Reagan said.

"That's because you live in Northern Virginia. We have an overwhelming blue majority from Loudon County to Alexandria and in every major city, but we could lose the state. If Virginia votes Republican, we're finished."

"I'll do whatever I can to—"

"Mobilize the machine. The party's apparatus is in full swing, but as the only surviving delegate from the assassination, I need you out in front to be the face of the delegation. That means media and public appearances at school boards, candidate events, anywhere we can reach voters."

Reagan nodded. "I won't flip independents or undecideds by attending Democratic events."

"You're not getting it. We need to get the vote out. Our party's in disarray. I need you generating enthusiasm among our voters, people we already have, and make sure they vote. I'm worried all the upheaval and chaos will keep people at home."

"You want me to assure them we have things under control—"

"Exactly. I'll send you a list of interviews on local and national television, and Tanya, the woman who let you in, will handle scheduling. She'll send you our event schedule for Virginia. Attend every one and advocate for our team."

"I accepted a podcast interview request from The Modern Democrat."

Gail nodded as if she already knew, but how would she? Had they asked her for approval before floating the offer? The DNC must influence who they let speak for the party.

"Virginia wants to vote democratic, but they're scared of the unknown. They spent a year getting comfortable with Harrison and Ambrose, and now, we have new names on the ballot. Convince people it's safe to vote for a Lemon-James ticket."

Reagan beamed. "I'll do it."

30

Pattaya Beach bordered the Gulf of Thailand, ninety miles south of Bangkok, and the city had become a destination for parasailing, bar hopping, and prostitutes. Nathan and Waldo strolled down Walking Street past go-go bars and seedy hotels—an eastern capital of debauchery. They passed under an arch onto Beach Road, where beyond the white sand, sun glistened off blue water, creating a million points of light. Natural beauty merged with the seedy underbelly of human desire, as beggary and desperation collided with affluence and carnality. Pattaya was Malibu Beach with a red-light district.

Twenty yards ahead, Kei and Emerald crossed the street and settled at an outdoor table at a go-go bar. It was only noon, yet thumping music resonated from inside. Nathan had searched them before they left to meet Quon and receive a kilogram of carfentanil. They'd already delivered the money, so the risk to his sources was low, and it was a buy-walk, so the Royal Thai Police wouldn't make an arrest. The fact that the police didn't know about the deal made things easier.

Nathan and Waldo joined Major Paitoon Shinawatra on the patio of the Sunset Bar, thirty yards from Kei and Emerald. Paitoon led a five-man tactical team in Thailand's Special Operations Unit Naresuan 261, and he'd assisted Nathan with several counterterrorism cases when Nathan had been assigned to the FBI's Afghanistan-Pakistan group.

"Thanks for coming, Pai," Nathan said. "This is my partner, Waldo."

"My sympathies," Pai said.

Waldo snickered.

Nathan pulled out a plastic chair and its legs scraped against the concrete. He kept an eye on Kei and Emerald—no contact yet. Nathan scanned the restaurant. An old man stood behind a counter inside, and a petite waitress wearing shorts approached their table. Her pointed ears imbued her with an elfin quality.

"*Khun tongkan aa-han rue beer mai?*" she asked.

"Two coffees," Nathan said and raised two fingers.

She smiled and walked into the back. Nathan adjusted his earpiece and confirmed his phone remained connected to Kei's rat phone.

Pai shook his head. "You're always making trouble. The Narcotics Suppression Bureau should be here."

"I'm covered as long as I have host country law enforcement present."

"That won't help me if they find out. Do you ever follow the rules?"

"Only when they advance the mission," Nathan said.

"An American cowboy."

"No joke," Waldo said.

"Tell me again how this is related to terrorism?" Pai asked.

"The Chinese national who's selling opioids to our source is the trafficker who supplied the Phantoms."

"And why don't you want to arrest this man?"

"It's . . ." Nathan hesitated. How much should he confide in him? "We'll nab him, eventually."

"Why not arrest him with the drugs?"

"We're, uh, sending a message. I'm recording the conversations, and you'll keep the evidence for a future prosecution, but right now, this is more of an intelligence mission."

"That is your role now?" Pai asked.

"No, it isn't," Waldo said.

"Not exactly," Nathan said, "but we're trying to force a reaction."

Pai sighed. "Okay, cowboy. I'll be your pawn ... again."

"I appreciate—"

"Target's here," Waldo said.

Quon and an Asian male walked down the sidewalk. The other man's shoulders bulged under his shirt and his biceps stretched his sleeves. Quon trusted Emerald, which was why he delivered the drugs himself, but he wasn't taking chances moving through Pattaya alone carrying thousands of dollars of drugs. He rolled a small suitcase behind him. Was the kilo inside?

Nathan turned his head and listened. He'd record the undercover conversation through the device in his pocket. Normally, he'd have put a high-quality digital recorder on Kei, but having the buy-walk go off without a hitch and letting Kei maintain his cover took precedence. The rat phone that transmitted from Kei's pocket would have to be enough.

"Which one is your target?" Pai asked.

"The older guy," Nathan said. His earpiece crackled. "Hold on."

Quon and his goon joined Emerald and Kei. Quon scrutinized the street, not trying to hide his suspicion.

Nathan watched with his eyes hidden behind his tinted glasses. He increased his phone's volume.

"Is everything good?" Quon asked.

"Of course," Emerald responded. "This is the beginning of a strong partnership. I came today to show my faith in both of you, but I will not be involved with further dealing."

"Nor will I," Quon said. "This is Somsak, my man in Bangkok. You will call him with your orders, and he will deliver anywhere in Thailand."

"And if I need delivery elsewhere?" Kei asked.

"Where?"

"Central America, perhaps."

"Tell Somsak and we will arrange it. Somsak acts on my authority."

"You have the package?" Kei asked.

Quon rolled the suitcase in front of Kei.

"May I," Kei asked. He pulled the suitcase onto his lap and opened it. He jerked his head up. "It's empty."

Nathan's heart jolted. He surveyed the street. No sign of trouble.

"It's not in the suitcase," Quon said. "It's *inside* the suitcase."

"I don't understand what—"

"The powder is concealed in the handle and frame. It's packed tight, so it will appear to be solid plastic in the X-ray machine, in case you plan to fly it out. It's packaged for transportation . . . as you requested."

"How do I know it's, er, the correct amount?" Kei asked. "How can I check its quality?"

Good man. Kei couldn't care less if the carfentanil was the proper quality or weight, but a real trafficker would, and he had to act the part. The plan depended on it.

"You have my personal guarantee," Quon said.

"But—"

"I have worked with Quon for many years," Emerald said. "As distance tests a horse's strength, time reveals a person's character."

Quon nodded. "A promise is worth a thousand gold pieces."

"Very well," Kei said.

Quon handed something to Kei. "This is Somsak's number. Once you verify the quality of my product, call him with your order. Refer to the product as flour and multiply each amount by ten over the phone. Then meet him twenty-four hours later at the place where you first met me and give him the money. Your product will be delivered two days later."

Kei extended his hand, and Quon shook it. Quon turned and departed left, with Somsak hurrying to catch up.

"I have done what was requested," Emerald said to Kei. "Tell our mutual friend I will expect payment." Emerald stepped off the porch and disappeared down a connecting street.

"Deal's done," Nathan said. "The product's in the suitcase. We'll follow Kei to the drop-off and—"

Nathan's phone rang, and he took the call. "Good job."

"Hey, boss, we got trouble."

"What's wrong?"

"The police," Kei said.

Nathan's eyes darted to the street where a motorcycle cop had stopped along the sidewalk and climbed off his bike.

"Move to our debriefing location."

Kei rolled his suitcase off the patio and headed down the first side street.

"The cop is headed your way," Nathan said, "but you're out of his view."

"What should I do?"

"Run."

31

———

The American presidential candidate was dead. Zhao smiled as he exited his black sedan and walked toward the Imperial Ancestral Temple outside the Palace Museum in downtown Beijing. The American Democratic Party had selected a new candidate in authoritarian fashion that would have made Mao proud, but that caused conspiracy theories to fly across the internet, and the United States teetered on the brink of a constitutional crisis. Chinese involvement hadn't been discovered and Americans pointed fingers at each other, throwing fire on the political turmoil.

Everything went according to plan.

Zhao's driver remained in his car, and in a trail vehicle, his assistant, Jíng Qí, waited with Colonel Luo, who carried communications equipment in case of emergency. Zhao had forgone his security detail. These trips caused logistical problems, but he needed time away. Zhao wore a padded green overcoat to cover his uniform as he often did when he paced the *Taimiao* temple grounds, because the gold stars on his shoulder boards would draw unwanted attention from tourists—and he came there to be alone. He needed to think. Mist hung in the early morning air and chilled his bones. Harvest time seemed colder each year.

He paused at the temple's stone steps. Many more tourists visited the enormous palace complex behind it, but the temples clustered around the courtyards connected him to the past in a way that the royal palace did not. The temple was located on the outskirts of what had been the Forbidden City, and during the Ming and Qing Dynasties, it had honored China's ancestral legacy. It still did.

The sloped Xiēshān resting hill roofs and the building's symmetrical design were economical and aesthetically pleasing—physical examples of living with purpose. They comforted him. The site contained spirit tablets and royal records, documenting China's imperial legacy. Once, ritualistic sacrifices had been used to honor the past, and that lesson meant everything. The lingering memory of death tainted the air—an invisible force that reached out from history and raised the hairs on his arms.

He paced the courtyard, a form of walking meditation that centered his thoughts. China continued to prevail over the centuries because its leaders did what was necessary to survive. Victory went to the bold leaders who had risked everything to make China the world's hegemonic power.

As Zhao did now.

He reached into his jacket's inner pocket and withdrew a sealed envelope with *Juémí* markings indicating top-secret contents. He shouldn't have classified documents outside his secure facility, but he was the boss. Sure, he reported to the Politburo's Standing Committee, but they weren't present. Power had its advantages.

Zhao ripped open the message from the Sky Fox, one of the Second Bureau's most valuable assets and a key to Zhao's plan succeeding. His spy had embedded inside the US government and had spent years rising through the ranks to a position that afforded access to America's most sensitive information. Zhao's moles had infiltrated the US Department of Defense, every branch of the military, and even the Pentagon, but the Sky Fox observed the inner workings of federal judicial cases, and that revealed more opportunities for political influence than even Zhao had imagined. His mole had proven to be the intelligence gem of the Second Bureau.

The Sky Fox had infiltrated the highest levels of the US Department of Justice.

Zhao read the message, which had been automatically decrypted by China's most powerful algorithm on their most guarded computer in the most secure intelligence building. He finished reading and stared at it without breathing. His heart thumped in his chest until he could hear it pounding in his head. He inhaled and blew out a long stream of vapor into the icy morning air.

The reverberations from the assassination threatened to destabilize America, and politicians wrestled for control as the political ground swayed beneath them. Everything followed his plan, but the outcome was far from given. Rogue elements within the DNC pushed back against party leadership. Zhao hadn't anticipated that. Americans were undisciplined, but this level of resistance against their superiors seemed irrational. How could they defy party orders when they fought the Republicans? With people threatening riots and the country teetering on civil war, who would weaken their party apparatus by ignoring directives?

Americans really were cowboys.

Zhao needed to push harder to achieve the desired outcomes of his radical strategy. Failure would not end well for him. He must activate every resource and utilize every weapon. Fear and hesitation were the traits of losers, and Zhao was a warrior destined to lead China to victory.

Zhao turned on his heel like a soldier on the parade ground and took out his encrypted cellphone. He dialed as he walked. The line rang twice and connected. It clicked as the communication traveled through encrypted gateways. It beeped, and the sound changed.

"Colonel Luo."

"Meet me in the courtyard."

He hung up. He didn't need to say his name—not that he'd use anything other than his codename over a wireless phone, encryption or not —but she knew his voice, and even if she wasn't sure, she'd come running. He'd cultivated an institutional culture of fear to breed blind obedience.

Boots thumped on the stone, and he turned as Colonel Luo raced across the bricks. She carried a thick messenger bag that contained a radio that allowed communications with every office from the Central Committee to the Tactical Operations Center. She came to attention and saluted. Her breath created puffs of vapor.

"Do not salute here," he said.

She flinched at the reprimand. "Yes, General."

"And keep your voice down."

"Yes, General."

"Send the Leopard a message."

"But he has been compromised—"

"I know that, you dumb egg. Your job is to listen and report, not question."

"Forgive my disrespect. I am ashamed."

He stared hard at her. "It is time to apply pressure to American electors inside the Democratic Party."

"Yes, General."

Her voice had carried the timber of fear. He glared at her, and her eyes widened. Fear.

Excellent.

"There can be no room for error. We need maximum pressure. Send the Leopard the codeword to execute operation *Hundun*."

"Go on Operation *Hundun*. Yes, General."

He'd named the operation after the faceless mythological creature that represented chaos in the universe before the creation of man. The perfect entity to sow confusion in America. He turned back to her.

"Do it now."

"Yes, right way, General."

She nodded, almost a bow, and hurried back to the vehicle. He'd struck fear into her, but her eyes had betrayed her doubt about his plan.

He snorted. He didn't need the approval of a colonel. Who was she to judge the strategies of their ancestors? And if she failed to execute his orders, there were plenty of cells available in the prison beneath the courtyard.

32

Nathan draped his arm over Meili as they sat on his couch. Amelia had gone to bed, leaving them alone for their first date in a week—but Meili seemed preoccupied.

"Want to tell me what's bothering you?" he asked.

"You wouldn't understand," Meili said.

"Try me."

She sighed and her shoulders slumped. Whatever psychological conflict she experienced had worn her down.

"I can help," he said.

"I'm Chinese."

"Oh my God. You're right."

She pursed her lips. "See, this is why I don't come to you with touchy-feely stuff."

A pang of guilt stabbed his chest. "Sorry, humor's my default reaction."

"No kidding. I kinda noticed that."

"I can't support you if I don't understand what's wrong."

She sighed again. "I'm first generation. My mother barely speaks English, and she raised me in a neighborhood populated with Chinese, eating ethnic food, and hearing Mandarin everywhere, including at home. I'm American, culturally and ideologically, but I'm also Chinese."

"Everyone's influenced by their family's culture."

"It's intrinsic to who I am. But beyond the comfort food and rich tradition, some aspects of Chinese society infiltrate me. People in China think differently, and I've inherited some of that. It could be genetic or a sociological influence, but it's part of me."

Nathan nodded. "That's a good thing. My great-grandparents immigrated from Ireland, and when I visit the country, I feel a kinship to the place . . . and to the people."

"We're not at war with Ireland." Her voice had an edge to it. She looked away. Whatever this was, she really struggled with it.

He put his hand on her leg, tentative, as if she might explode. "I get it. You feel disloyal, like you're targeting your own people."

Her eyes watered, and she bit her lip.

"Chinese culture made you who you are, and your ancestors called China home. Now, you're targeting the Chinese government and people who look like you."

She nodded. "I know it doesn't make sense. The Chinese Communist Party is evil. They oppress their people and enslave Uyghurs. They force abortions and stifle political dissent. They oppose everything I believe."

"But they rule a country where your ancestors lived for thousands of years."

"I'm not tribalistic. Or racist. My connection is to the culture, which is distinct from the dystopian political nightmare China's population endures."

Nathan mulled that over. He had to tread lightly. "The FBI's a sprawling organization. If this is causing you too much turmoil, you could transfer and investigate something else."

"When I joined the Havana Syndrome investigation, I honestly thought it was a psychogenic illness, or government employees fraudulently claiming disability. When we learned more, I assumed Russia was behind it—"

"They're responsible for much of it."

"True, but then we exposed China's involvement, and the Phantoms' opioid attacks used drugs manufactured in China, and—"

"Their involvement is deeper than that."

"That's my point," she said. "Now, all I'm doing is targeting China."

"You need a change?"

Meili picked lint off her skirt. "They're trying to damage the United States—my country. I swore an oath to protect us from enemies, foreign and domestic. It's my job."

"We have no shortage of enemies. You can protect us in other ways, fight different dragons."

She looked down. "I can't shirk my responsibility. Not now. I want to target China, because I don't want the communists torturing my people with their regressive ideology. I'm driven to help the Chinese people, both here and in the homeland."

"You're a sheepdog too."

"I know the culture, and I'm fluent in Mandarin. That makes me a powerful weapon."

"It also makes you a target. Do you think your ethnicity contributed to China's decision to target you with a high-energy weapon?"

She scrunched her face. "It's possible, but we'll never know the answer. My ego wants me to believe they attacked me because we came close to the truth."

Tension built inside him. "How can I help?"

"You already did."

He raised an eyebrow. "How?"

"By listening."

The Municipality of Shanghai sat on China's eastern coast, where the Yangtze and Huangpu rivers emptied into the Yellow Sea. Towering buildings rose above the Fengxian District and looked out over Hangzhou Bay. Shanghai's twenty-five million inhabitants made it the third most populated city in the world, yet the streets and sidewalks sparkled. Where were the homeless? Where was the litter, the detritus of millions of people?

People stared as Nathan and Waldo followed Tony through the Changning District's congested streets. Foreigners lived in Shanghai, but Caucasians in Western clothing still stood out, and curiosity filled people's eyes. No, it was more than inquisitiveness. Citizens looked at them with suspicion. Were they concerned about American spies, or their own government seeing them in proximity to Americans. Did neighbors inform on each other out of fear of staying silent? Populations living under the boot of totalitarianism became insular and distrustful—anything to avoid a knock on the door from the state security.

Nathan's phone vibrated, and he answered.

"The stone is cut," Emerald said.

"He's coming?" Nathan asked.

"Any minute."

"And you made the other call?"

"Yes," Emerald said. "They know it's happening."

"Who was that?" Waldo asked.

"Emerald."

"We good?"

Nathan nodded. "Just making sure we're not alone."

"They bite?"

"We'll find out."

Kei had safely slipped away after he received the kilo of carfentanil in Pattaya. The motorcycle cop who'd arrived during the deal had been a patrol officer stopping for lunch. Luckily, Kei hadn't panicked—another reason Nathan had assigned his most reliable CI. Kei was cagey with a track record of success, but more importantly, he'd shown loyalty to Nathan—a requirement for an operation that wasn't as it appeared.

Now, they had to keep Kei alive.

Tony stopped opposite the café where they'd set the meeting. "That's it."

"Kei and Emerald are inside," Nathan said.

"They should meet somewhere more private," Tony said.

"Kei's posing as a trafficker," Nathan said, "and Emerald is introducing him to a customer. We'll debrief Kei somewhere else."

"You said *we* were meeting a source," Tony said. "You didn't tell me this was a meeting between a CI and a suspect."

"Not a suspect," Nathan said. "Not really."

"Running an undercover operation without an op plan or higher approval is a problem, especially without host nation involvement."

"The fewer people who know about this, the better," Nathan said.

"Who's the customer?"

"Hasan Yakuf, a member of the Turkistan Islamic Party."

"Are you shitting me?" Tony asked. "Your source is meeting with a TIP terrorist, and you didn't think I needed to know that."

"They're only talking."

Tony grimaced. "I'm calling the LEGAT. He should know what we're doing."

"If he gets squeamish, he may shut us down," Nathan said, "and this is too important."

Nathan's and Waldo's visas permitted liaison with the FBI's country office to conduct business, and they'd openly discussed a fact-finding mission to Shanghai—a city with transnational criminals, from drug transporters to human traffickers. Chinese intelligence was always listening.

At least Nathan hoped they were.

"Don't think of it as an operation," Nathan said. "Our CI is meeting with a local on his own time, and we're debriefing him after. Your boss knows we're meeting a source, and what the source does before that is his own business."

Tony grimaced. "That's not how it works."

"We're not covering the meeting . . . not really."

"We're here."

"We're nearby . . . in case there's a problem."

"If this blows up, I'll get kicked out of the country, and I just got here."

Nathan rested his hand on Tony's shoulder. "Listen, this is critical. The trafficker Kei met in Thailand was responsible for the drugs that killed thousands of people, and this guy's a terrorist who might want to do the same thing. We can't let that happen."

"But he—"

"Our CI's only having a discussion. If anything happens, it's on him . . . and me. Help us stop more attacks."

Tony stared at the tops of his shoes, and a flicker of guilt passed through Nathan for lying to him. But this could prevent more attacks.

Tony met his eyes. "Okay, but I didn't know anything about the CI meet. I came to assist with the debriefing."

"That's what we're doing," Nathan said.

Meeting bad guys in foreign countries was fraught with danger, and Shanghai was as dangerous as anywhere. And they operated without the knowledge and consent of the CCP. They sat on a bench two doors down from the café where Emerald and Kei waited to meet a ranking member of the Turkistan Islamic Party, a radical Islamist group run by the Uyghur minority. The group sought to create an Islamic State inside China and across Central Asia.

Emerald's and Kei's voices came through Nathan's earpiece.

"Here he comes," Emerald said.

Nathan's eyes darted to the entrance of the café as an Asian man at least six feet tall pushed through the door. He wore dark cotton pants and a plain shirt—the uniform of the communist proletariat. The sound of Kei's phone shifting in his pocket rustled in Nathan's ear.

"Yakuf, this is Kim," Emerald said. "He can supply product."

Trent Hamilton had given Nathan the spark of his idea for this operation, and his CI made it possible. Emerald knew everyone. Relying on one source was risky, and Emerald's connection to Hamilton amplified the stakes.

"You look Chinese," Yakuf said.

"And you look like a giant," Kei said. Kei's humor would get them killed one day.

"You are from here?" Yakuf asked.

"Where I'm from doesn't matter," Kei said. "You want powder, I can deliver."

"You worked with him?" Yakuf asked.

"He is trustworthy," Emerald said. "You want a product for a good price, and he has this. I make an introduction, and then you are on your own."

No one spoke, and only the sounds of clinking plates and Kei's breathing came through the rat phone.

"How much carfentanil can you deliver?" Yakuf asked.

"How much do you need?" Kei asked.

"A few kilograms, then more later."

"I can do."

"How much?"

"Twenty-two thousand yuan per kilogram," Kei said. "Highest quality."

"Too much."

"Then go somewhere else."

"Eighteen thousand," Yakuf said.

"Why you need carfentanil?" Kei asked. "You want make your camels sleep?"

"Why do you think?"

"I don't care. My only interest is making money. It will cost you twenty-two thousand per kilo, delivered here. Take it or leave it."

"You can deliver ten kilograms of powder next week?"

"Give me a few days to prepare, then I can deliver that every week."

"Deal."

Yakuf exited the café, followed by Kei and Emerald. Yakuf looked around, then hurried up the street. His head bobbed above everyone else until he turned the corner and disappeared into the urban maze.

Across the street, a young kid on a motorcycle snapped pictures of Emerald and Kei.

The bait was set. Now, Nathan had to wait.

Nathan gazed out his home office windows at the Capitol's dome, and beyond it, the Washington Monument. Spotlights illuminated the structures that represented why Nathan risked his life. Not the buildings, but the government. No, that wasn't correct either. The government had become almost as statist as any European country, but he'd die to protect the original ideals on which the government had been created—individualism, property rights, limited government, and freedom. No country in the history of mankind had ever been founded on the idea that citizens should control the government. Limited government. Free people.

Fucking brilliant.

His eyes dropped to his laptop screen and the encrypted tunnel through which he had accessed his email. A dozen email subject lines advertised bureaucratic deadlines and reporting requirements. Nothing interesting.

He opened a browser and logged into the commercial email account he'd set up with Meili and given to Xuannü to communicate directly with them. The end-to-end commercial encryption was more than enough for what they sought to do, especially since they communicated through the draft folder without launching emails over the internet. This communication was a violation of FBI policy, since they used a commercial email account instead of an official FBI server, but the rules didn't account for modern technology. Until recently, US embassies had used teletypes, for crying out loud.

Bypassing the Beijing office minimized the chance of Chinese interception, but it also avoided interference from the LEGAT. Lincoln White was not on board with their operation, and his concern over his fiefdom being invaded by two agents from DC had been almost palpable. Agent Tony Wong seemed to understand, but he didn't want to start off his new assignment on the wrong foot. Risking Tony's career would be unfair—but the stakes were higher than professional advancement. The United States was under attack and American lives at risk. People depended on the FBI to defend the homeland.

He opened the draft folder. A new email caught his eye. The subject line was a single word: *Interesting?*

An email from Xuannü.

His pulse quickened. The paperclip icon indicated attachments, so Nathan opened his malware and virus software—supercharged protection the FBI had given him. The scan showed all clear, but China intelligence had serious spyware. Recruiting informants inside the Chinese government brought risks. At least his standalone laptop contained no personal information and wasn't connected to his home router.

The email contained a cryptic note: *"Does this look suspicious to you?"*

Nathan opened the attachment, and a video played showing a beautiful woman smiling at the camera and complaining.

"Life in America is unfair," she said. "Inequity is everywhere, and the system must be torn down to fix it. Women can't succeed in this misogynistic and patriarchal society. You have no chance of advancement if you have girl parts."

As she spoke, cartoon emojis popped onto the screen and stars flashed to punctuate each point. "Women make like eighty-four cents on the dollar. Does that sound fair?"

Nathan's jaw stiffened. Her argument had the tinge of truth, but her conclusions were wrong. American women had been historically oppressed, but now they did far better than men. More women graduated from college, and they had higher starting salaries in the major cities. The salary disparity disappeared when variables like job types and experience were factored into the equation.

"You'll never earn enough to buy a home," she said, "because the system has already given the wealth to rich, white men."

Nathan ground his teeth. Every element of her message was flawed starting with the Marxist idea that wealth was handed out instead of being created through innovation and hard work. And the fixed-pie, zero-sum theory that one person's gain meant another's loss was complete nonsense.

"If you aren't achieving your dreams, it's not your fault. Failure is unavoidable in an inequitable society that keeps you down." She spoke directly to her audience, which probably targeted women from preteen to young adult.

"And girls of color have no chance at all. It's like a total waste of time to even try in a systemically racist society."

Her message was simple—and wrong. Racism existed but not like in the past. Black people in America did better economically than anywhere on earth, and decades of affirmative action provided entry and advancement beyond what merit indicated.

Nathan leaned back. Logical fallacies and inaccurate facts permeated her argument, but she delivered it with glitz and polish. She played on ego. If viewers didn't achieve everything they dreamed, blame someone else. That made failure easier to accept. This sexy young woman affirmed what people wanted desperately to believe. They didn't need to work harder or smarter, because their failure was the system's fault. Without agency, people lacked motivation. Why work if failure was a forgone conclusion?

The messaging was pure evil.

The woman finished her rant, then stared deeply into the camera with her beautiful brown eyes.

"So what can you do?" She paused for effect. "Don't be part of the system. It's time for revolution. Capitalism is dead, and democratic socialism is the answer. Vote, vote, vote. Speak out in school, become an activist, and bring down the white man's capitalistic system."

Nathan snorted. That was their answer to everything from climate change to racial inequity. Tear down the system.

Nathan clicked on another link and started an interview with a man in a tweed coat and a bad haircut speaking on stage at a think tank event. The chyron listed him as Dr. William Sanford, an evolutionary biologist and social psychologist.

"All behavior is vulnerable to influence," Sanford said. "Decades of research in social psychology explains how people learn, what draws their attention, and what makes them take action. Couple that with behavioral economics, and consumers can be manipulated. Corporations utilize this from slogans to pitches to affect consumer decisions."

The interviewer raised a finger. "You're talking about marketing techniques correlating to sales, but your latest book, *Control the Masses*, focuses on political influence."

Sanford smiled. "There's no difference." He stayed quiet, waiting for the interviewer to ask the inevitable question.

"No difference between politics and selling a widget?"

"None whatsoever. Both employ behavioral economics to direct individuals to take specific actions. The tactics and techniques for each desired outcome differ, but the strategies are similar. Both businesses and government agencies develop brands to draw interest. They frame problems to make them resonate, then they offer a solution. They create subconscious pathways that encourage people to do their bidding, and whether it's buying expensive sneakers or voting for a candidate, the science is the same."

The interview clip ended where Xuannü had clipped it.

Nathan clicked the next attachment and played a clip from a Sunday news show where the anchor interviewed DNC Vice Chair Gail Haverhill.

"I'm glad you asked that," Gail said. "Darcy Lemon represents the change we need to bring equity and fairness into a corrupt system."

That clip ended and another from a popular network comedy that Amelia watched started.

"I can't buy a new cell without money," one teenage girl said to another, "and I can't find a job."

"Nobody can," the other girl said. "Somebody's got to make a change."

"No kidding. There's no equity in hiring. It's so unfair."

The clip ended, and Nathan stared at a dozen more email attachments. He scrolled through them, listening for a few seconds, then moving to the next. They all used the same language—equity, fairness, inclusion, and change—as if one person wrote commercials, television, movies, podcasts, and political talking points.

He opened the last link, a compilation of anchors from local news stations across the country. They all reacted with the exact same language to incidents. The stories changed, but the responses did not. Dozens of ostensibly independent news outlets read the same copy, using the same buzzwords, and all with the same meaning—America was bad.

Nathan stared at the screen. "Holy shit."

Birds took flight inside Reagan's stomach as she waited to speak at a Democratic Get-Out-The-Vote event in Arlington. Public speaking had terrified her, since seventh grade when she'd rooted to her chair when it was her time to deliver a presentation on the pilgrims.

She had always been eloquent and persuasive addressing small groups —her high IQ helped—but now, hundreds of potential voters waited for her. At least they were Democratic voters, a friendly crowd who'd taken time out of their schedules to attend a campaign event. That meant more this close to the election, because they'd been inundated with political commercials and donation pleas for months.

I can do this.

"And now, speaking for the Virginia delegation, please give a warm welcome to Reagan Cabrera."

Her intestines gurgled.

She climbed the aluminum steps onto the prefab stage, and her footsteps clanged on the metal as the tepid applause wound down. These people didn't know her, and hers was one of many speeches they'd endure this afternoon.

She stepped to the podium and looked over people filling the elementary school parking lot. Her throat tightened.

"Thank you, Tom," she said. A pang of fear sliced her chest. Had she remembered the event organizer's name correctly?

She looked out over the silent crowd. Everyone stared at her. Her fingers tingled, and she resisted the urge to flee. "Thank you for the opportunity to speak."

A few people turned their ears to her. Her voice had been too low. She cleared her throat and pulled the microphone down. She leaned forward and spoke directly into it.

"I, uh, I'm here to tell you our party is unified. We lost most of our Virginia delegation during the assassination, and as the last original delegate, I want to assure you our new slate of appointed delegates have your best interests at heart. Rule 13J of the Delegate Selection Rules reads, 'Delegates elected to the national convention pledged to a presidential candidate shall in all good conscience reflect the sentiments of those who elected them.' I'm here to promise that we will represent you."

Everyone watched in silence. She'd expected applause when she'd practiced her speech at home.

"The haters won't stop us," she said. "Darcy Lemon and Archie James have taken the reins, and in them, we have two capable leaders. We can retake the White House, but we need your support to do it."

Did she believe her own words? Doubt lingered.

These voters didn't know Darcy Lemon, because she hid from public scrutiny and had only relented to a few interviews, all über-friendly outlets who fawned over her. She hadn't answered a single adversarial question. Would people vote for an unknown, no matter how much they hated the Republicans? Would switching candidates midstream make Democrats stay home on election day? Early ballot numbers showed low voter turnout. Reagan needed to assuage fears, but she harbored the same concerns. How could she urge them to be comfortable with a candidate that she herself didn't know?

"Now is the time to set aside our internecine disputes and come together as a party . . ." She continued her speech, her confidence matching her passion for saving the country. An image of her speech outline floated behind her eyes, and she hit each point, being careful to enunciate. Her presentation meant as much as her content, which was unfortunate, but that was reality.

". . . and in conclusion, let me reassure you that we are back on track and ready to bring about a bright future for America. Send in your ballot today, and help us retake our country!"

People clapped but with little enthusiasm. Her speech had contained more platitudes than information, but how could she defend a candidate she barely knew? She'd referred to James's record as much as possible without highlighting her lack of information about Lemon. The applause died down.

"Thank you all for coming. I hope—"

"What about social media?" a heavyset man in the front row called out.

Did the organizers want her to take questions? They'd asked her to speak for five minutes about the qualifications and integrity of the Democrat candidates, and she'd done that, but if they wanted her to alleviate concerns, shouldn't she respond?

Reagan glanced at the moderator who'd introduced her. He smiled, giving no direction whatsoever—but everyone had heard the question.

"We encourage you to speak out on social media," Reagan said. "Use your platforms to spread the word."

The man stood, and his face puckered. "That's not my question. I want to know why social media silences users who criticize Lemon."

"That's not happening," she said. "I've read critical pieces."

"They're suspending people who question the way the DNC installed Lemon without a vote."

Her speech wasn't processing as planned. "Sir, I'm not aware of any censorship—"

"You gotta be shitting me. Republicans have complained about being silenced for years, and now they're doing it to us."

"If that's true—"

"You bet your ass it's true. I can't post my opinion about my own party without getting suspended."

The event organizer mounted the stairs and headed for her. Thank God. Reagan didn't need to handle the heckler alone. Did this count as heckling? If the man told the truth, he had a right to be angry.

The organizer reached the podium and stood beside her, ready to step in, but Reagan couldn't look weak. If she couldn't handle constituent complaints, how could she hope to win a bigger election?

"Sir, I'm outraged about censorship in any form, whether it's done by the government or private companies that control the digital town square. Private corporations have the legal right to curate content, but silencing political speech is unethical."

"Yeah, so what will you do about it?"

The organizer leaned in, trying to edge Reagan away from the microphone, but he wasn't building a political career. This was her future at stake. She needed to learn to handle dissension and do it with a smile on her face.

She inhaled a deep breath, then pointed at the man. "I promise to investigate your claims and present your accusation of censorship to the DNC."

A smattering of applause gave her courage. People agreed with her. She looked out across the crowd. "And I'll make a promise to everyone. If any government agency pressures private companies to censor users, that's a first amendment violation, and I'll make sure we stop it. This country was founded on free speech, and we won't allow the suppression of citizens' voices. Not here. Not in my America."

The crowd applauded and flooded her with endorphins.

The organizer applauded too, then he gently nudged her away from the podium and leaned into the microphone. "Let's hear it for Reagan Cabrera."

More applause. It filled her. Their feedback affirmed her belief in herself. That was what had drawn her into politics. She'd used her moral compass and reason to determine the best path forward and articulated it in a way that resonated with voters. Maybe she could do this.

She waved to the crowd and climbed down the stairs. People around her applauded and grinned as she passed. They approved of what she'd said. They approved of her.

She might have a future in politics.

Nathan walked through the passenger terminal in Shanghai Pudong International Airport as he and Waldo waited for their China Eastern flight to Hong Kong and connecting flight to DC. Nathan scanned the crowd, but nobody paid attention to him. Video surveillance also covered every inch of the terminal—except the restrooms.

Nathan eased past a throng of teenagers and entered the men's room. The Italian design features sparkled, having been cleaned spotless. He moved to the last stall and slipped inside, as planned.

Footsteps echoed across the tile, then Emerald entered his stall and shut the door. He moved away from the opening where his feet wouldn't be visible.

"We only have a moment," Emerald whispered.

"I need you to push the Second Bureau."

"I have no authority there."

"Your people do. Use your contacts to nudge them to act."

"You make that sound simple."

"Make a decision-maker believe illicit opioid trafficking will fund the Uyghur insurgency and a wider Islamic revolt. Drug profits will be used against them across China and their interests abroad."

"They know drugs fund terrorism."

"But opioids haven't been used as weapons inside China. The marriage of TIP terrorists and traffickers will cause significant problems for the CCP."

"Yes," Emerald said, "but will they believe it?"

"Their drugs are real, and so is the Islamists' money."

"Will you let Yakuf strike inside China?"

"You mean using the opioids we're selling him?"

"Of course."

"We can't allow that," Nathan said. "I can't support a terrorist act on Chinese soil."

"It's the push the Chinese government requires to take action."

"I won't be responsible for the deaths of innocent people."

"You will be thousands of miles away with no risk of jail."

Nathan moderated his voice. "If our role is uncovered, we'd start World War III."

"Then your efforts may not achieve your desired results."

"That depends on your intelligence sources," Nathan said.

Emerald nodded and exited the stall. Nathan waited for him to leave, and his mood worsened. He couldn't let Brotherhood operatives execute an attack or even receive the full order of drugs. His plan spiraled out of control, and his chance of success dwindled.

Would their massive risk be for nothing?

37

Reagan shifted in a stiff wooden chair in the DNC's Erickson Townhouse as she waited for Gail to explain why she'd been summoned, but from Gail's pinched expression, she wasn't happy. Reagan had participated in seven public appearances over the past twenty-four hours, and she'd energized every crowd. Or at least not offended them. Gail certainly couldn't be angry about her effort.

"The polls have us down one percent nationally," Gail said.

Reagan had seen the most recent data too. "That's within the margin of error."

"Swing states decide elections, and Democrats dominate behemoths like California and New York, so if we're close in national polling, then we're behind in places with even voter distribution."

That made sense, but what did Gail expect her to do about it? Reagan hadn't forced the vice president to drop off the ticket. She hadn't assassinated Harrison and eighteen other people. She'd stepped up during the crisis and at great personal expense. She hadn't seen Amelia in four days, forcing Nathan to drop Amelia at his girlfriend's mother's house. What kind of parent had Reagan turned into? And what would happen if she ran for higher office? Could she handle grueling hours on the campaign trail or governing and still be a good mother and wife?

"I'm doing everything I can to help us in Virginia," Reagan said.

Gail stared daggers at her. She rolled her tongue in her mouth and tapped her fingers on the table, then stared at the ceiling, as if needing a moment to control herself. Finally, she lowered her gaze to Reagan. "Does your vision of helping us include telling voters that the government censors their speech?"

Ah, that was it, a nothing burger that she could easily explain. Tension melted out of Reagan's shoulders. "I didn't say that. A voter claimed he'd been suspended from social media for questioning the Democratic Party's decision to install a new ticket."

"That's bullshit."

Gail's tone startled her. She'd never sworn in front of her, not even after the bomb exploded a few yards from them.

"I didn't acknowledge his claim of censorship was true. I acknowledged his concern that if social media censored people critical of the Democratic Party, it would be a problem for—"

"You said, and I'm loosely quoting here, that you would ask for an investigation to determine if the government pressured social media to silence people."

"He made that allegation in front of hundreds of people. I couldn't ignore it."

"What you said was worse than ignoring it."

"Worse?"

"More damaging," Gail said. "You gave his allegations credibility by suggesting an official investigation."

"Republicans have complained about this for years," Reagan said. Anger crackled in her chest like a spark engulfing kindling. "One of our voters accused social media of silencing him for criticizing us, and if that's true, his rights were violated to protect our party. It's a valid complaint, by the way."

"That's what this is about, isn't it? You're still upset by the way we appointed candidates after the assassination. Are you unhappy with the delegates we selected in Virginia as well?"

"I haven't hidden my concerns about the way the DNC handled that,"

Reagan said, "but I've also kept my criticisms private. I haven't spoken out publicly about what I thought should have happened."

"And what is that?" Each of Gail's words had been sharpened on a stone.

"We should have had some kind of vote—"

"There wasn't time."

"Not a normal election, but what about online polling, internal polling, or even another mini-convention where delegates voted?"

"Two weeks from an election?"

"I didn't say it would be easy," Reagan said, "but at least we would've made an effort to enforce the will of the people instead of decreeing who their candidates would be without input."

Gail's nails clicked against the tabletop, like a trigger being pulled over and over. "You entertained this man's dissatisfaction in public to let him voice your views, because you're too afraid to do so yourself in public."

Her vision reddened. "I'm not afraid. I've held my tongue because I'm a team player, but this man made a serious accusation, and if I ignored it, it would look like we're covering up our party machinations. I had to address it, and frankly, the party should get in front of this. And remember, we're not the administration. If the government applied pressure, then the Republican administration's guilty of censorship, not us."

"And if it's true?" Gail asked. "If social media companies chose to throttle certain voices or suspend people based on content that was bad for us, who will the public blame then?"

"Social media companies are private, which will give them a legitimate argument about curating content, but that's for courts to decide, not us, and certainly not for CEOs to determine which ideas are suitable for public discourse."

"But the criticisms were of *our* party. Those CEOs did it for us. Voters aren't stupid, not completely, and they'll figure it out. If we open an investigation days before the election, voters will focus on our censorship."

The way Gail said it sounded like she knew it happened.

"That won't be good for us," Reagan said, "but it'll be worse if we try to cover it up. If social media companies ran interference for us, they are guilty, not us, unless . . ."

"*Unless* what?" Icicles hung from Gail's words.

"If we asked them to do it or pressured them to tip the scale, we deserve whatever comes next."

"There's no evidence," Gail said, "and we're trying to win an election."

"I want to win as much as you, maybe more, but some things are more important than winning elections."

Gail shook her head as if she spoke to a child. "Oh, and what is that, my dear?"

"Free speech. The US Constitution. The rule of law. The belief that our system isn't manipulated by a small group of elites. If we lose trust, our democracy is finished."

38

Nathan leaned against a cubicle inside the Hoover Building and sipped a strong black coffee while he waited for FBI Special Agent Randall Blanc to hang up the phone. The plastic-coated paper cup burned, but he didn't set it down. Caffeine addiction created daily rituals, and he needed three cups of coffee to function. He should quit and reset his tolerance. He should do a lot of things, but life demanded his attention.

Randal hung up. "Gotta make this quick, and it's sensitive, so keep a close hold."

"I appreciate the brief."

"Harrison was assassinated, and we suspect the plumbers that fixed a leak in the café's wall two years ago. Forensics confirmed the C-4 exploded near a small access trap."

"Could someone have slipped the C-4 through the trap?"

"Unlikely. The assassin configured the explosives against the far side and directed the blast outward. Forensics determined that from the burned timbers and melted plastic. The plumbers concealed the explosives in a frame, so only the Y-connection and shutoff valve was visible."

"How much C-4?"

"They estimate fifty pounds of C-4 could have fit between the studs."

Nathan rubbed his neck. "How did the plumbers get access to the restaurant? What's the connection?"

"The Felix-Nelson Corporation acquired the Capitol First Plumbing Company two years ago."

"Who are they?"

"An LLC out of Delaware, registered by an attorney, Aaron Wink," Randall said. "They outbid the restaurant's regular plumber for the restoration two years before the assassination."

"They planned this after the Republicans took office. How could they know Mayor Harrison would run? It's unusual for a mayor to be a serious presidential candidate. How certain are we the plumbing company was behind the assassination?"

"Nothing's proven," Randal said, "but it's suspicious as hell. When the restaurant's pipe burst and leaked through the wall, Capitol First Plumbing called and offered to do the work for much less. It's like they were waiting for the call."

"Or they caused the leak."

Randall widened his eyes. "Huh. Hadn't thought of that."

"If they did it, this was planned years ago. It feels unlikely. Too many variables would have to come together."

"There's no other way someone could have planted those explosives, unless they cut open the wall last week and concealed it before Secret Service's site visit. Most of the employees perished in the blast, and two who were there the previous night didn't notice anything unusual."

"Did you bring Aaron Wink in for questioning?"

"He'd dead."

Nathan cooled. "Accident?"

"Hit-and-run outside his home a month ago."

"The timing seems coincidental."

"We've asked the State Police to reopen their investigation. They'd assumed it was a drunk driver, but Wink lived on a suburban street with low traffic volume. A vehicle struck him when he went to his mailbox. Paint chips are consistent with a Chevrolet Suburban."

"Who else was involved in the Felix-Nelson Corporation?"

"Wink registered it as a single-member LLC."

"Business records?"

"We have his tax returns and state filings, but they don't show much. We're trying to track down physical records, but his apartment and office were cleaned out. It looks like a shell corporation."

"Someone cleaned it up. He wasn't alone. What about contract employees? Who were the plumbers who showed up to do the work?"

"Still running that down, but we're hitting dead ends."

"That alone tells us something."

Randall raised an eyebrow.

"This assassination wasn't some crazy lone wolf. This thing was well executed and planned."

"Why would people conspire to eliminate Mayor Harrison? Why was he a threat?"

Cognitive dissonance tingled Nathan's brain. "I've no idea."

"To stop him from enacting a certain policy? Maybe a special interest group or—"

The idea hit Nathan like a thunderbolt. "What if he wasn't the only target?"

"Eighteen victims died and another six are seriously—"

"I mean this thing was planned years ago, when the killers could only guess he'd be the nominee, but what if they didn't want to kill Harrison specifically?"

"You mean they targeted someone else in the restaurant?"

"What if they planned to kill whoever the nominee was?"

"But they planted the explosive years ago?"

"Then we need to look at the other front runners in the primary and see if any of them were targeted."

"How do we—"

"They ambushed Harrison with explosives in a restaurant he frequented. Let's check the favorite haunts of the other primary leaders."

"That could be hundreds of restaurants and other venues."

"You can do most of it over the phone. See when candidates gathered support, then call the places they frequented."

"And ask what?"

"Whether they had any plumbing work done."

39

———————

Reagan opened her front door and cinched her housecoat around her neck as Nathan pulled into her driveway. Amelia jumped out of his car and waved, filling Reagan's heart. She hadn't seen her daughter in days. Amelia raced up the walkway with that half-scurry, half-prancing run she had whenever her happiness bubbled over. Reagan embraced her and lifted her off the ground like a mama bear.

"I missed you," Reagan said. She set her down.

Amelia looked up at her. "Mom?"

"What is it, baby?"

"Is your internet fixed?"

"We're done with our reunion?"

"I need to do schoolwork."

"Sure you do. Go ahead—"

Amelia ran into the house. Reagan looked at Nathan and rolled her eyes. He laughed and joined her on the stoop.

"Sorry I couldn't watch her this week," Reagan said.

"Election has you busy?"

"It did?"

"Did?"

"I've decided not to stump for Darcy Lemon anymore."

Nathan canted his head. "You're coming over to the dark side?"

"Nothing like that. I can't get behind a candidate who refuses to do interviews and hides her positions. Even when she answers softball questions, she issues empty platitudes."

"Are there any other kind?"

"I know politicians have done that, but hiding from scrutiny seems like a trend. We've hit rock bottom with our candidates, but I'm an insider and I don't know her positions."

"As a small-L libertarian, I don't like either party," Nathan said. "They both offer expansive government, central planning, and regulation. Neither party represents individualism or the Founders' vision for our country."

"What's worse," Reagan said, "is my party rules with less and less voter input."

"Backroom dealing has always been part of politics."

"At least it had the patina of democracy. Now, elites dictate policy from on high."

"Both parties may be guilty of that."

"I can't vote for someone who may hold ideas antithetical to my values, to what made this American experiment work, but this is a deeper failure. People vote based on their general impressions of a candidate. He's tall, she's pretty, they seem like a leader. But all of that is crap. What they do once they take power is what matters. I need to understand a candidate's ideology, epistemology, and core values. Those elements that will bring a country to greatness—or destroy it."

"You've thought about the ramifications?" Nathan asked.

Reagan sighed. "My plan after I left State was to become a delegate, then seek tougher office."

"Still thinking about the House?"

"I am, and that's why I pulled my public support from Lemon."

"Won't you run afoul of the DNC?"

Her stomach tightened. "That's why I'm struggling with this. I can't in good conscience endorse a candidate I know nothing about, but I also can't alienate the party machine, because I need them to support my future candidacy."

"Do you even want to run as a candidate for a party that's behaving that way?"

She peered at the sky. "The party has moved far left in recent years, but I consider myself a blue-dog Democrat. I believe in a safety net and compassionate governance, but the entire system feels more autocratic, more distanced from the people than ever before."

"You've bailed on your speaking engagements?"

"I withdrew my public endorsements. I'm happy to support the Democrats, but I agree with voters who feel disenfranchised, and I'm suspicious of the party's efforts to conceal Lemon's intentions. Why isn't the media complaining?"

"They're complicit. Mainstream media are activists, not reporters. I'm shocked when they do actual investigative journalism or criticize a Democrat. They treat Republicans and Democrats differently, and they manipulate interviews to propagate narratives and make their chosen candidates look better."

"It's chilling," she said. "When our constituents complain about being silenced, I know we're in trouble. Where can voters find the truth?"

"It's a bipartisan problem," Nathan said.

"What's the answer?"

"We need to teach children to use logic and reason and interrogate narratives. But education has been corrupted too. Teachers train their students to be change agents instead of teaching them to think critically."

"At least we got Amelia into private school."

"It's better, but not perfect," Nathan said. "They're still inculcating the students in whatever social justice initiatives they support. It's up to us to teach Amelia how to separate fact from fiction."

"She's too young to understand the issues."

"But she's old enough to learn to distrust people who argue without facts. I've got faith in her."

"What about me?" Reagan said.

"You?"

"Am I making the right decision?"

"I don't have enough information to advise you, but I know one thing—

if you want to change things, follow your conscience and do what you believe is right."

Reagan nodded. "Then I'm in for a fight."

40

———

Waldo sat across the interrogation table from Hamilton and seemed chipper after flirting with Isabella again. At least that was better than gambling. Nathan paced behind him, unable to sit. The combination of the early morning flight and long drive stiffened his muscles, and he stayed in motion to burn off his frustration. Not knowing what was happening made him antsy.

"We identified a Chinese black ops asset," Nathan said. "He slipped away from us in Tampa."

"How did you locate him?"

"Through investigation."

"How, specifically?"

"That's law enforcement sensitive."

"I had the highest security clearance in the country."

"That was before I arrested you for treason. You don't need to know our means and methods."

"Then why tell me?"

"The operator was part of China's Havana Syndrome attacks—the clandestine team you supported."

"Not intentionally."

"Let's not re-litigate your case. He was doing something in Tampa, then someone assassinated Harrison."

"You think that operative was involved?"

"Harrison was the mayor of Tampa, and a Chinese assassin was down there before someone murdered him. The coincidence is hard to ignore."

"Why would the Chinese assassinate an American presidential candidate?"

Nathan shrugged. "Dozens of reasons. We're an impediment to China's global hegemony."

"Harrison's death has thrown our country into political chaos."

"Chaos might be their goal—"

"If the Chinese are behind it," Hamilton interrupted.

"—but if the Chinese wanted a candidate who was friendlier to the CCP," Nathan asked, "why kill Harrison so close to the election and decrease their candidate's chance of winning?"

"Maybe they wanted the Democrats to lose," Waldo said. "Republicans should be suspects."

"You have it backwards," Hamilton said. "The timing proves the Chinese government was behind this."

What did he mean? "I don't understand."

"Look at the timeline," Hamilton said. "If the CCP eliminated Harrison during the primaries, his chief rival would have won."

"Then why didn't the CCP back him?"

"He's a nut. Everyone knows it. They needed a candidate they controlled."

"Darcy Lemon?"

"If they killed Harrison after the primary, but far enough from the general election, the DNC would have time to debate his replacement and possibly even hold a special election. If the CCP did this, they needed to install their VP candidate and force the party to make the switch because they had no other option."

"You're saying China forced the first VP out of the race?"

"Obviously."

"How?"

Hamilton shrugged.

"We need to talk to Arthur Ambrose," Nathan said.

Hamilton smirked. "He won't talk to you. Why would he? If China influenced him, he has nothing to gain and everything to lose if he informs the FBI."

"Unless we can free him from whatever pressure they're exerting," Nathan said.

"Not gonna happen," Hamilton said.

They sat in silence. Waldo shifted on his chair. Hamilton looked bored.

Nathan sighed. "It's worth a shot. All he can do is decline the interview."

Hamilton smirked.

"What?" Nathan asked.

"You have no idea how deep China's roots have burrowed into the United States."

"Then we'll yank them out."

"You may be surprised at what you find."

41

Reagan glanced at her cellphone on her nightstand as it played "One Sweet Day" by Mariah Carey and Boys II Men, a tune that transported her back to childhood. She sat in bed with her laptop on her thighs, a habit Vince hated, because he claimed bringing the outside world into the bedroom through the internet disrupted his sleep. For a tough FBI supervisory special agent, he could be a delicate flower. Everyone used the internet in bed. How else could she keep up with her email? But Vince had traveled to the Dominican Republic for work, leaving her alone, so she'd do what she pleased.

She burrowed under the covers to ward off the chill and reread her email to Gail for a third time. In it, Reagan claimed she'd come down with a bug and couldn't attend her scheduled appearances. Normally, calling in sick wouldn't be a big deal, but bailing during crunch time could hurt their chances of winning. She wasn't really sick, just fed up with endorsing an unknown candidate and supporting a party that acted in an undemocratic fashion.

"No choice," she said.

She clicked send, and the email whooshed across the ether. Done. A flicker of fear passed through her and she fidgeted, second-guessing her action. At least she made a decision. Her nerves settled, and she breathed easier. She glanced at the clock. Almost midnight. Now, she could get a good night's sleep, and tomorrow—

Her phone rang.

Who'd call so late? She knew but hoped she was wrong. She leaned over and checked her phone. Gail Haverhill.

Shit.

She could ignore it, but she'd just sent the email, so Gail knew she was awake. Not answering would make their inevitable conversation more uncomfortable. Her stomach cramped. She sighed and picked up.

"Hi, Gail," she said, moderating her tone to sound sick. "You saw my email?"

"You need to speak at that event in the morning."

"I'm ill. I think it's the flu."

Making excuses made her feel dishonest, but she wasn't really lying about being sick, since the party leadership's behavior made her want to stay in bed and hide under the covers. She was fed up with politicians and their power plays. Did the average voter feel the same?

"That's convenient timing after our last discussion," Gail said. "If I came down too hard on you about the heckler, I apologize, but you needed to understand the ramifications of your public declarations."

"He wasn't a heckler."

The line went quiet. Had she pushed back too hard? If her plan was to pretend she was sick, falling back into the censorship argument wasn't smart.

"You're not happy about how we've handled this crisis."

"No."

"Is this your way of acting out?"

Acting out? Was she a teenager? "I don't feel well. I've been pushing hard, and I need time to recover."

"We all need a break, honey, but the election is next week."

"I'm sorry . . . I don't think I can make it." She should admit that she couldn't support a candidate who avoided questions, nor could she sanction the party's authoritarianism and tacit approval of censorship. But that would ruin her political aspirations.

"This is it. Win or lose. We need all hands on deck."

"I'll take something and reassess in a couple of days."

More silence.

"Are you still on our team?" Gail asked.

That was the question, wasn't it? She'd been a lifelong Democrat, but the party had moved far left, and in many ways it no longer represented her values. Free speech had historically been a liberal hallmark, but they'd become the party of censorship. The movement felt icky.

"I'm on board, but I'm not comfortable with Lemon ducking the press or how we installed her without a vote. And if accusations of censorship are true, it makes everything we're doing seem dictatorial."

There, she'd said it. Being honest felt right, whatever the ramifications.

"You've made that clear. If you abandon us now because of this . . ."

Her implied threat hung in the air. If Reagan didn't stump for Lemon, she'd be finished. Perhaps she could navigate a middle road.

"I feel strongly about everything I said, but I'm really sick." In a sense. "I'll take a bunch of meds tonight and reassess tomorrow."

"You'll go to the event?"

More fluttering in her stomach. "There's no way I can commit based on my condition, but I'll let you know when I can come off the bench."

"I'll wait for your call."

"Okay."

"And Reagan?"

"Yeah?"

"Don't make the wrong decision."

42

Nathan reclined in the passenger seat of Waldo's Bu-ride outside Arthur Ambrose's private residence in northwest DC. The colonial house was palatial—a contradiction of style and size—but its boxy shapes hinted at the structure's many additions. Since the former vice presidential candidate had withdrawn from the race, he'd remained out of the public eye, hiding in seclusion.

"This is another bad idea, *Papi*," Waldo said.

"No choice."

"He rejected our interview request."

"He didn't reject it," Nathan said. "He ignored it, and he doesn't want to force us to get a grand jury subpoena."

"We can't drag him into a grand jury. He hasn't done anything wrong."

"Not that we can prove, and he doesn't know that."

The wrought-iron gate surrounding the Ambrose estate opened, and a black Lincoln Town Car exited onto Arizona Avenue and headed north.

"Follow him," Nathan said.

Waldo started his car, and they trailed Ambrose's vehicle. Waldo drove in silence, and didn't look at Nathan.

"The ASAC ordered us not to interview him," Waldo said.

"That's because Ambrose's people must have called HQ. If he had nothing to hide, why would he pull political strings to prevent us from talking to him?"

"Nobody wants FBI questions. If he calls HQ, *estamos jodidos*."

"*Jodidos?*"

"We're screwed."

"Maybe."

"That's all you got to say? I'm working on a career here."

Heat rose in Nathan's neck. "And I'm trying to protect our country."

"That's bullshit. Ignoring the boss's orders will get us suspended."

"I took his comment as more of a suggestion."

"He told us to call off the interview."

"And we did. This will be a friendly conversation—"

The Lincoln slowed in front of a granite sign that announced The Rockwell School. Ambrose's car turned onto school property and followed the circular drive around to the private elementary school. It stopped outside a building that resembled an English manor. Politics came with perks, but how did elected officials amass so much money?

"How do we know he's in the car?" Waldo asked. "He picks up his daughter himself?"

"Parent-teacher conference day."

Waldo sighed. "This keeps getting worse." He parked behind the vehicle.

The driver's door opened, and a man with a weightlifter's physique exited. He wore a gray suit and dark sunglasses, and a weapon bulged inside his suit jacket.

"Told you he'd have people for this."

"Wait for it."

The driver walked around and opened the rear passenger door. A man stepped onto the sidewalk.

Arthur Ambrose.

"C'mon," Nathan said. "Let's stop him before he reaches the school."

Nathan jumped out and jogged up the sidewalk. Waldo followed. Nathan pulled out his credential case as he closed on the former VP candidate.

"Mr. Ambrose?" Nathan asked.

Ambrose stopped and turned. His driver stepped between them with hands at waist level, ready to engage.

"Easy, tiger," Nathan said. He showed his FBI credentials, letting the cloth flap fall and reveal his badge. The gold badge allowed him to get close. "FBI Special Agents Burke and Falcón."

The gorilla's eyes flickered to the badge, then he appraised Nathan and Waldo. He watched their hands, which revealed police or military training.

"What's this about?" Ambrose asked, peeking around his hulking bodyguard.

"We have a few questions," Nathan said.

"Is this in reference to the interview request I received yesterday?"

"Affirmative," Nathan said, using his most official voice.

"It was my understanding that this interview had been canceled," Ambrose said.

"And why would you say that?" Nathan asked.

Ambrose frowned. "You're welcome to schedule an appointment at my office. I keep a suite downtown where we—"

"This will only take a minute of your time."

"As I said—"

"We want to know why you resigned," Nathan said.

"I issued a complete public statement," Ambrose said. "I withdrew to spend more time with my family."

"Nobody quits this close to an election. You hamstrung your ticket, and it looks like sabotage."

The muscles in Ambrose's jaw bulged. "When did political decisions become illegal?"

"It was more like political suicide . . . a murder suicide."

"I disagree, but it's still not illegal."

"There's been interference by foreign powers."

"Are you accusing me of something?"

Nathan needed to be careful. He had no evidence of wrongdoing—only a gut feeling. Meili had wanted to come, but Nathan had convinced her to avoid the potentially career-ending encounter. Good thing she'd listened to him.

"I'm trying to understand what happened. Did anyone influence you?"

"I have no obligation to answer that," Ambrose said, but he made no move to leave.

"Then why are you talking to me?"

"I've always supported the FBI."

"Not if you don't answer our questions."

Harrison scowled. "I responded."

"Yet you've said nothing."

"I can't tell you things I don't know."

"You can start by explaining the real reason why you dropped out in the bottom of the ninth inning."

"I told you. Personal reasons."

"Bullshit. That means nothing. Who pressured you to quit?"

Waldo cleared his throat, clearly uncomfortable.

"No one."

"I'm trying to figure out what scared you," Nathan said.

"I'm not afraid of anything. I just want to be left alone to take care of my family."

"Did anyone threaten you?"

Ambrose's eyes glistened. Had Nathan hit on the truth?

"Nobody threatened me."

Nathan studied him, like reading a poker player at the table. Reading body language was not an exact science, because people reacted differently, and one emotion could appear to be another—like fear and anger. Ambrose exhibited numerous tells that indicated nervousness, but they could be caused by many things. But he seemed afraid, and that's what Nathan bet on.

"Is your family in danger?"

"Leave it alone."

It. Nathan was on target.

"We can protect you and your family."

"Nobody is in jeopardy. You're sailing into dangerous waters that you know nothing about."

"Then help us understand what—"

"Enough."

"Is it blackmail?"

Ambrose froze, then shook it off. "I'm done talking."

"But—"

"Any further communication can go through my attorney."

"Don't fight this alone."

"And don't think I won't call your director." Ambrose stormed away with his bodyguard at his side.

"Fuck," Waldo said. "That got us nowhere."

"Are you kidding?" Nathan asked.

"He denied everything."

"He said 'leave *it* alone,' and he practically crumbled when I mentioned blackmail. Someone pressured him to drop out of the race."

"For what purpose?"

"That's the question."

Waldo cleared his throat. "We better figure it out before we're both standing in line at the unemployment office."

43

———

Nathan pressed his cellphone against his ear, and the line crackled from the overseas connection. Across from him, Waldo spoke on his desk phone and shuffled papers.

"You hear me, boss?" Kei said.

Nathan covered the microphone and looked at Waldo. "It's Kei."

Waldo raised his finger as he scribbled notes. He thanked whoever he was talking to and hung up, then came around the desk.

"I got you," Nathan told Kei. "What's happening?"

"I hear from the guy," Kei said.

"We good?"

"He is waiting for the thing."

Nathan sighed. Conversations with sources were always like this, word salads with vague phrases and no specifics. More information transferred through what was not said. He'd read hundreds of wiretap transcripts, and bad guys talked like this too. He should have been a doctor.

"Does he have everything?" Nathan asked. Yakuf wanted the carfentanil sample.

"He has money, and he's ready for the stuff."

"The sample?"

"Yes."

Waldo raised an eyebrow, and Nathan flashed him a thumbs-up.

"Okay, set it up as we planned. We'll fly over to cover it."

"Uh, okay," Kei said, doubt clouding his voice.

"Problem?" Nathan asked.

"I, uh, this one is strange," Kei said. "I mean, we never give stuff away before."

"We're charging them."

"I mean, these are bad people and they will keep the stuff."

Nathan's chest tightened. He'd done buy-walks of drugs and weapons before where he'd bought product and arrested his suspects much later—but this was different. He was selling Quon's drugs to a Chinese rebel. Would Yakuf distribute it and use the proceeds to finance terrorism?

"It'll be fine," Nathan said.

"You won't arrest him?"

"No."

"And I will not be in trouble for this?"

"You're acting at my direction," Nathan said. "And the local guys will be there." Did Kei understand he meant Thai cops?

"Okay, boss. I'll set it up."

Nathan hung up and turned to Waldo. "Yakuf's ready. Kei will give him the time and place."

"This could cause *un gran problema*," Waldo said.

"We're highlighting the terrorist threat from opioids."

"After the Phantoms, everyone knows that."

"The Chinese need to think they're targets too."

"We gonna support a Uyghur attack?"

"Of course not. But for this ruse to look dangerous, Yakuf needs to order a huge load of carfentanil, which means we need to show we have quality product and can deliver. Letting him walk will prove we're not cops."

"We ain't in policy, and we might be breaking the law."

"Technically, it's a Thai law enforcement operation and we're just observing. As long as they're running things, we don't even need an op plan."

"Does Pai know he's in charge?"

"It's a gray area."

Waldo smirked. "I get it, but we're taking a big chance here."

"The stakes are too high not to make this work."

"Why not come clean with Meili and make this official?"

"HQ would never approve it."

"You're gonna get us shitcanned."

"I'll take the heat."

Waldo sighed. "I know you mean that, but if this goes sideways, we're both gonna get burned down. *Comemierda*."

"What's that?"

"We're gonna eat shit."

Waldo was right to be afraid, but one hundred thousand Americans died every year from overdoses, and the Chinese did little to stop the flow of opioids. China made tens of billions of dollars from opioids, and drugs hurt the US, so why would they stop?

Nathan needed to do something.

"Why are you going through other case files?" Nathan asked.

"They're all related to China. I'm looking for similarities. This can't be the first time they've interfered. There's gotta be something in there we're missing."

"Find anything?"

"*Nada*."

"Who'd you have on the phone?" Nathan asked.

"Randall Blanc," Waldo said. "He located a barbershop in Bethesda where Governor Samson meets constituents when he's running."

Excitement grew inside Nathan. Randall had followed through with Nathan's request.

"Why did you ask about the governor?" Waldo asked. "He won't run again for three years."

"He came in second in the primary. I asked Randall to check regular haunts for the other primary candidates. He find anything at the barbershop?"

"They had a leak in their bathroom and had a major plumbing repair two years ago."

"And?"

"The plumbing company was owned by the Felix-Nelson Corporation, Aaron Wink's company behind the Harrison assassination."

"You mean—?"

"They found sixty pounds of C-4 in the barbershop's restroom, enough to incinerate everyone inside."

"I knew it." Nathan pumped his fist in the air. His hunch had been right.

"If they wanted to assassinate the governor, why didn't they do it?" Waldo asked.

"He didn't campaign at the shop in the early days, and he was never in contention. The assassins waited for a primary winner. If Samson had won, he'd be dead now."

"Samson and Harrison had different policies," Waldo said. "That should help us nail down what the killers wanted."

"I don't think that's it at all. The assassins went to great lengths to prepare. They didn't care about policy, they just wanted to eliminate the nominee."

"Because they were both Democrats?"

"Let's find them and ask them ourselves."

44

Reagan slouched at her kitchen table nursing a coffee and feeling hungover, despite foregoing alcohol since the assassination. She'd simply been too busy with daily public appearances, and as much as she'd wanted to crack a bottle of wine, she needed to stay sharp.

She sipped her coffee and scrolled through her phone. No call from Vince in Santo Domingo—which disappointed her—but also no calls from Gail, and that was a welcome relief. She'd emailed Gail earlier with a single line. *Still sick*, then she'd blown off the DNC's get-out-the-vote event at a car dealership in Arlington. Gail wouldn't be pleased, and she hadn't believed Reagan's excuse. But making moral choices was hard. The most important decisions always were difficult. Taking a stand made her feel better, despite the consequences.

Someone rang the bell.

Reagan jolted and spilled coffee on her lap. Luckily, she hadn't bothered to dress yet. She dabbed a napkin on her sweatpants, wrapped a housecoat around her, and went to the door. She peeked through the peephole and gasped.

Ruoxi stood on her stoop.

What the hell was she doing there? And how did she know where Reagan lived? A tingle of fear tickled her stomach.

Reagan opened the door.

"Good morning," Ruoxi said. "Bad time?"

"I'm, uh, under the weather."

Ruoxi looked her up and down. "You don't look bad, just underdressed."

"I overdid it the past few days."

"We have you booked on the podcast tomorrow morning."

Reagan's chest tightened. "I know . . . I'm sorry, I don't think I can do it."

"We leased time at a production studio on K Street, so you don't need to fly to LA."

"I appreciate it, but it's not possible."

Ruoxi's eyes narrowed, and the angles on her face seemed to sharpen. "May I come in?"

"Uh, well . . ." Reagan glanced down the hallway, searching for an escape. She returned her attention to Ruoxi. "I'm not feeling well, and I don't want to get you sick."

"Nonsense," Ruoxi said. "I have an iron constitution." She bladed her body and slipped past Reagan into the entryway.

Reagan stood in the doorway and watched her with a feeling of help-lessness. Entering Reagan's house uninvited was a violation, an invasion of her personal space, but Reagan had burned enough bridges for one day. How should she handle this woman?

Reagan shut the door and faced Ruoxi. "Really, I hate to cancel. I was looking forward to the opportunity." *Was* became the operative word, since being the face of the Virginia delegation and championing Darcy Lemon no longer felt palatable. Or ethical.

"Is there anything else I should know about?"

"I don't know what you mean."

"We selected you as an up-and-comer out of numerous delegates and political hopefuls."

"I appreciate it, really—"

"People who are hungry to succeed. People who want to make it. Were we wrong to think you deserve a place in the national spotlight?"

She spoke as if she pulled the levers of power, picking winners and losers. And who was the *we* to whom she kept referring? The political podcast wasn't part of the DNC. Was she puffing to give her company added credibility, or was she collaborating with the DNC?

"I take my responsibility as a delegate seriously, and more so now that I'm the only remaining Virginia member who voters actually chose."

"I'm not talking about being a delegate."

"I plan to run for higher office," Reagan said.

"You can't run in a vacuum," Ruoxi said. "You'll need donations to fund your campaign, political endorsements, guidance, and above all, publicity. We're offering you that."

Conflict raged inside Reagan. She wanted this so badly. Since Havana Syndrome had struck her down, she'd been lost, and her foray into politics had given her hope . . . but could she play for a team she distrusted?

"I'm deeply appreciative, but I'm really ill."

"You need to play hurt and show up even when you're not one hundred percent."

"I can't continue . . . not now."

"This is politics," Ruoxi said. "You must make compromises to succeed."

"I can't."

Ruoxi glared at her.

"I don't know what else to say," Reagan said.

"You're disappointing a lot of people, benefactors who believed in you."

"It's not my intention to disappoint—"

"And worse, this will be an incredibly close election, and without the support of delegates, the Republicans will win."

"I don't want that but—"

"You're letting down the party and your constituents . . . and others."

"I can't do it. Not now. Can we reschedule?"

Ruoxi's eyes turned to ice. "You don't understand the consequences of your actions. This isn't a game." She turned and raged out of the house, slamming the door behind her.

Reagan stared at the closed door, and dread built inside her. Had she made the wrong decision and damaged her career, or did the fear seeping into her bowels come from something else?

45

———

Nathan knocked on Meili's condo door and waited for her to open it. She obviously didn't feel his level of anticipation after being apart for days. Or was he reading too much into it? Their crazy schedules had forced the separation, and despite all they'd been through together, their romantic relationship was too new to endure long absences.

The door swung open and Meili smiled at him, evaporating his worry. She wore black leggings and a white sweater beneath a fur coat. Something stirred inside him. She attracted him with more than physical beauty and intelligence. At her core, she radiated decency, honesty, and virtue. She had a righteous soul.

"Long time, stranger," she said.

He steeled himself. "Don't get mad, but I emailed you another travel request. Waldo and I need to leave soon."

Meili frowned. "You're returning to Thailand?"

"The cops are covering a meeting between our narco trafficker and a terror suspect."

"Come inside."

She let him in and led him into her living room. The lights of Clarendon glowed through the floor-to-ceiling windows.

"Are Islamists preparing for an attack?"

"That's what we're monitoring." He hated lying to her.

"Who's running the surveillance?"

"Major Paitoon Shinawatra."

She nodded. "I'm swamped anyhow, so it's not like we'd be hanging out. Want a drink?"

"Got scotch?"

"I bought it for you. Your favorite." She moved to a bar cart against the far wall and poured herself a glass of white wine. "We had a Chinese national walk into the division and claim he has information about Havana Syndrome and Chinese interference in the election."

Something about that didn't sit right. "How would a source have access to two radically different Chinese operations?"

"He claims he's a defector from China's Intelligence Bureau of the Joint Staff Department."

"Running HUMINT?"

"SIGINT," she said, "but he handled communications from their moles here."

"Credible?"

"Maybe."

She poured him three fingers of Macallan.

"Isn't our Counterintelligence Division all over this?"

"Yeah, the China branch claimed jurisdiction, but the guy came in leading with Havana Syndrome, which makes him ours. It'll be a turf battle, but we won't get completely shut out. Best guess, we debrief him together and each unit runs a different aspect of the investigation."

"That'll make for tense cases . . . unless it all turns out to be bullshit."

She handed him a thick tumbler of brown liquid. He wanted ice, but he needed to know about this new source.

"Cheers," he said. They clinked glasses, and he sipped. He swished the scotch in his mouth and the oaky aroma filled his sinuses. It burned going down, then warmed him inside.

"I met the CI this morning," she said. "He claimed he saw communications between the Second Bureau and one of their top black operators codenamed the Leopard."

"If he's telling the truth, that's our guy."

"It's a big *if*, but he knew information about the high-energy attack against me, which we never released. That indicates inside knowledge."

"What inside—"

"He claimed the Leopard pulled the trigger from a mobile unit in a van. The description matched a vehicle the team spotted on surveillance footage but never located."

"Who's your source?"

"Kaiyan Wang. He works as an adjunct professor for Jefferson College in the District."

"A NOC?"

"Apparently. CIA didn't have any information on him. He took a big chance revealing himself to us."

"Unless he's a double agent."

Meili bit her lip and drank.

"Does he know where the Leopard is now?" Nathan asked.

"He thinks he's still in the country."

An icy chill tickled Nathan's spine. "For what purpose?"

"Wang didn't know, so I tasked him to find out."

"Then you're keeping him in place?"

"We need him to develop actionable intel, but he wants to defect. He plans to steal whatever he can and bring it to us, then he wants protection."

"Could be a scam . . . or a plant."

"We're still evaluating his credibility." She slipped onto the sofa. "I've had enough work talk today."

"Hazards of working together." He sat beside Meili and put his hand on her leg. Being close to her calmed and energized him at the same time, and being alone in her condo felt intimate on a different level. She never invited anyone from work into her inner sanctum, and after they'd slept together, he'd soaked in everything in her bedroom from family pictures to a jewelry box she'd had since childhood. Amelia meant everything to him, but his relationship with Meili enriched his life in other ways.

"We haven't had much alone time," Nathan said.

"We're talking now."

"I mean intimate contact."

"You keep jetting back and forth to Thailand."

"You've been traveling too. I get we're busy, but we need to make time for each other. It's . . ."

"What?"

He sighed. "Long separations are tough on a new relationship." God, he sounded like a teenage girl.

"This is intimate."

"We could head into the bedroom."

She smirked. "So that's what you mean by intimacy? I should have known."

"It couldn't hurt."

"When you come back, I want you to take me on a real date first."

"I'll take what I can get."

She swatted him on the arm. "We knew this would be complicated. It's difficult for agents to date, and your working for me complicates things. It's hard to see each other when we're investigating serious cases."

He nodded. "There's a way we could have both."

She stiffened. "I'm not ready for anything serious."

"I'm not talking about marriage. I haven't been divorced that long, and I need to consider Amelia."

She exhaled. "Good. Let's not rush—"

"What if we moved in together?"

"I have a drawer at your place."

"We're not teenagers," he said. "I know how I feel about you, and stealing moments once a week isn't cutting it for me."

"Things'll slow down."

He snorted. "No they won't. I told Reagan the same lie year after year while I missed birthdays, anniversaries, and every other significant moment. You know it won't get better."

Meili stared at the floor.

"What's going on?" he asked.

She shifted in her seat.

"Tell me," he said. "We need to be honest with each other. Do you feel differently about me?" He held his breath.

"That's not it," she said. "I care about it you . . . but I'm conflicted."

He quelled his discomfort and forced himself to stay quiet. She didn't express herself as openly as he did, and he wanted to understand the conflict raging inside her.

"I've always focused on my career," she said. "My parents beat the need to make a living into me all the time, and I internalized that work ethic, but when I entered law enforcement, they discouraged it. They wanted me to do something more womanly, whatever the hell that meant, and they share the Chinese community's cultural distrust of law enforcement. Their resistance motivated me to succeed at being an agent even more."

"Youthful rebellion?"

"A little of that, at least at first. Then the chauvinism inside the Bureau drove me harder. I've been doing this for a while, so I guess it's become part of my personality."

"I get it," Nathan said. "Believe me, I do. I love what I do, and it's more of a calling than a job, but my prioritizing my career killed my marriage."

"What you're saying makes sense," she said, "and I'm not getting any younger. I feel the biological urge to settle down and start a family, but moving in together and going public with our relationship will impact my career. They'll transfer one of us to another group . . . or another division."

Cold seeped into his gut. He didn't want that. He couldn't pull Amelia out of school and relocate to another state, not that Reagan would allow it. What if they transferred him to some white-collar group?

"We need to keep our relationship in the shadows?" he asked.

"Can you live with that?"

He sighed. "I guess we don't have a choice . . . for now."

46

Nathan's phone interrupted a disturbing dream in which some kind of horrible threat bore down on him. The details dissipated as he clawed for the cell on his nightstand.

"Did you see this fucking shit?" Meili asked.

"Morning, sweetie," he said.

"Someone accused my new source of rape."

Nathan sat up straight in bed. Rape accusations had a way of doing that. "Who are you talking about?"

"The defector I told you about last night at my place. Some woman accused him of rape, and the DC Police questioned him. They leaked it to the press."

"What are you saying? They arrested him?"

"Worse. They questioned him without an attorney, and his accuser went public. She must've called every media outlet inside the Beltway. Her story is plastered all over the internet."

"Is she identified?"

"Not in the online stories or in the papers, but I have her name from the police report."

A pounding headache started in his temples. Not the ideal way to wake up. "Is the allegation believable, I mean, do you think there's anything to it?"

"You're not understanding," she said with an edge.

"I'm still in bed."

"Sorry," she softened. "The woman went public, which means the Bureau will never let me use my source in court . . . not with that kind of baggage."

"I've put witnesses on the stand who've committed murder. Your AUSA needs to buttress their credibility when he discloses their past criminal behavior to the jury."

Her voice tightened. "I've been on the job as long as you, and I know how it works, but flipping a member of a criminal organization and having them testify against their co-conspirators is different from having them impeached for unrelated behavior. Sexual allegations carry more weight than ever. Especially rape."

He nodded. Her analysis made sense. FBI upper management wouldn't want the Bureau to have anything to do with a CI accused of a violent sex crime.

"He could be a CCP plant anyhow," Nathan said.

"Maybe."

"But you don't believe that."

She expelled a long breath. "He seems credible, and he's inside Chinese black ops in the US. He could be the source we need to start bringing charges, or at least use to disrupt Chinese disintegration."

"But not if he's a pariah."

"Exactly."

Nathan sighed. "Give me the accuser's name."

47

Zhao leaned his elbows on stacks of folders and papers that littered his desk. The sun had set long ago, without him noticing. The moving parts of his strategy required his complete attention, because while he delegated individual tasks, only he saw the big picture. Even those familiar with the broad strategy, like General Sun, didn't possess the foresight or imagination to understand Zhao's genius. And he hadn't shared everything with the Politburo's Standing Committee. Zhao had learned long ago that information equaled power. General Sun and the committee members also didn't have the courage to act without fear. Only Zhao had been gifted that mandate by the unstoppable advance of destiny.

Zhao rubbed his eyes, and they creaked in their sockets. The strain of his bold strategy wore him down, while oddly energizing him with each success. But every minor victory came with more opportunities for crushing failure.

A knock on the door drew his attention.

"Come."

Jíng Qí opened it with two officers standing at attention behind her. Zhao knew them, but their names floated away, refusing to land. He should stop working for the night. Perhaps it was time for a glass of baijiu. He could let the white liquor transport him.

"Major Wang has arrived with a fresh group of eight prisoners," Jíng said. "He requests permission to process them."

"The intake form," Zhao said, sticking out his hand.

Jíng strode across the office and handed him the paper. Zhao scanned the names. Something as simple as admitting new political prisoners into the prison beneath his compound shouldn't require his signature, but he insisted. Incarcerating the wrong person or failing to extract that critical knowledge from someone in his grasp would be fatal errors. Some tasks could not be outsourced when fighting in a political arena.

His life depended on success.

Zhao scanned the names and recognized the nephew of the Qinghai Province's governor. The young man had dabbled in the sex trade, and while Zhao might have forgiven that indiscretion, he needed the governor to fight the Uyghur insurgency, and holding his nephew was leverage.

Zhao grinned.

He read the charges against the others, then handed the form back to Jíng. "Have them interred, but keep number four isolated. I don't want him harmed. At least not yet.

"And the others?"

"The usual." Zhao's psychiatrist interrogators used advanced methods that yielded fast results. They broke men in record time—the ultimate expression of his power.

Jíng turned on her heel and gave his orders to the officers. The men saluted and disappeared down the hallway. Jíng reached for the handle.

"Come here," Zhao said.

She returned and her eyes fell to the reports covering his desk. "Yes, General?"

"Phase one and two are complete," Zhao said. "We eliminated a dangerous adversary and emplaced our agent. Now, we must prepare the battlefield to give her a chance to win."

"How do we provide this advantage?" Jíng asked.

"It is time to consolidate support within the party and then influence their general election. My plan requires victory."

"What are your orders?"

"Have Psychological Operations enhance their social media influence—"

"Yes, General."

"—and remove the hacker team's restrictions. I want full penetration of media, academia, and anyone with political influence."

"I will see it done."

He nodded. "We cannot leave the expression of Americans' will to chance. We must tell them how to act."

48

Reagan stretched outside her house wearing black tights and a pink running jacket as the mid-morning sun glowed in the distance. She unlocked her phone and tapped the fitness application, which would record the time, distance, and pace of her run. It didn't open. Weird. She tapped it again, and the data displayed on the screen. She pressed start and broke into a slow jog.

Her sneakers clopped on the pavement as she glided through her neighborhood, a deathly quiet, tree-lined sanctuary during the day when everyone was at work—like she should be. She'd canceled every speaking engagement as she struggled with her ethical dilemma. She'd made her choice, and she'd need to deal with the consequences.

She slowed at an intersection and shielded her eyes from the sun before continuing through. She veered around a dark-blue Nissan parked at the curb. As she passed, a man in the driver's seat looked at her. Why hadn't he parked in a driveway like everyone else?

Reagan shook off her irritation. She wasn't mad at some stranger. Her situation put her on edge. She replayed her conversation with Ruoxi in her head. Something about that woman scared her. Would The Modern Democrat reschedule the interview after the election? Things could change, and

Darcy Lemon could reveal more about herself, or she'd lose and her mysterious positions wouldn't matter.

God, she hadn't exercised in ages, and her muscles warmed beneath her tights. Movement cleared her head, and might help her find a path forward. Or not. At least the physical exertion vented the frustration building inside her.

What if she'd screwed up, and the podcast shunned her? Gail hadn't contacted her again either, and without the DNC's support, Reagan's career would be over.

The money. *Shit.*

If she didn't give the podcast interview, would The Modern Democrat make her return the $30,000? She'd never asked for the money, and how they'd obtained her bank account number remained a mystery, but they'd paid for an on-air interview. She'd be morally and legally obligated to give it back.

She hadn't spent that money, per se, but cash was fungible, and her account balance decreased every day. Though she hadn't planned on the windfall, she'd relaxed once she'd received it. Thirty grand gave her breathing room, and if she returned it, she'd have practically nothing left.

Reagan opened her bank app, entered her password and checked her bank balances. The money was still there. She relaxed. Of course it was, because only she had access, but she'd need to deal with it. And soon. She'd agree to an interview, but how would she respond to questions about Lemon? They wanted her to vouch for the candidates, and in return, they'd give Reagan visibility and much-needed publicity she'd require to run for the House. That was the unspoken deal. The Modern Democrat would anoint her as a legitimate political prospect—a rookie with superstar potential.

She wanted it.

A film of sweat coated her body, and her breath came harder. Her fitness had really declined in the weeks she hadn't run. Jogging hurt, but in a good way. She swiped to switch back to her running app, but the phone had turned off.

"What the hell?"

Her phone was relatively new. She'd spent so much time in bed recovering that she allowed herself the extravagance of buying a new one with a big screen to make surfing the internet easier, and it had worked perfectly until now. Now, she couldn't afford a new one. She should have paid for the insurance.

She slowed at the next intersection and powered on her phone.

Reagan wanted to become the fresh face of the party. She certainly had different ideas, and the party needed to change. Her experience of the past weeks had shown her that. In some grotesque way, Harrison's brutal murder had created the environment for radical change.

But change wasn't always good.

What if the party used the assassination to consolidate power and become more dictatorial? The idea chilled her.

Her breath came hard and lungs burned as her muscles called for more oxygen. She slowed. She checked her phone. It had turned off again.

"Dammit."

If she had to shell out for an older model, she'd be pissed. She rebooted it and it flicked to life. Her app showed the first mile had taken ten minutes. Short and slow, but her quads and calves ached like she'd run ten. She needed to return to daily exercise, but no sense in overdoing it. She'd improve through incremental growth, one day at a time.

"Take it slow," she said.

Talking to herself had become a habit. Spending time alone while Vince traveled made her crave companionship. She'd traveled too when she was married to Nathan, so she couldn't complain. That was how she'd met Vince.

The thought jolted her.

Would Vince meet someone else during his extended work trips to the Caribbean? No, that was silly. He'd never cheat. But he'd slept with her when she'd been married. True she and Nathan had been separated, but not officially, and though she'd wanted out of the marriage, Nathan had been in the dark. She wasn't proud of her affair—but life happened.

Would Vince think the same way?

Time to head home. She'd take it easy on her way back. She glanced over her shoulder to make a U-turn. The Nissan she'd run past earlier rolled slowly down the street. She watched it pass her. Sweat rolled down her forehead.

The Nissan stopped at the next intersection, then turned right without signaling. She glanced after it. The car turned at the stop sign and disappeared. Strange. If he was headed to work, why was he trolling through a residential neighborhood?

Silly to feel vulnerable in a safe residential neighborhood with practically no crime, but criminals targeted women and her senses had been on alert since Vince left. She picked up her pace.

Reagan cleared her mind and focused on her form. Efficient strides cost less energy and produced more speed. Her pulse thumped harder, perspiration dripped down her face, and her muscles fatigued as she closed on her house. She sprinted the last twenty yards, then held up her phone to check her time.

The screen blinked and went black.

"Shit."

That wasn't a good sign. Not good at all.

49

Gina Harris had accused Meili's defector of rape. The twenty-two-year-old bombshell had starred in dozens of ChatteringHen viral videos and had over 200,000 fans. She was gorgeous, charismatic—and from what Nathan could determine—a congenital liar. Nathan followed her car into the parking lot of a gym in Bethesda.

Gina's videos brimmed with disinformation that characterized the United States as an immoral, imperial power. Her glitzy videos contained nuggets of truth, but she twisted and exaggerated facts to reach unjustifiable conclusions. She played all the hits from patriarchy to racism. Podcasting wasn't cheap, so how had she grown a massive audience around that content?

Gina drove past the front of the gym and moved slowly up a row looking for a parking space. Dozens of empty spots ringed the lot's outer edges, but she looked for something closer. Why did people planning to work out avoid walking?

Gina's rape accusation wasn't supported with any corroborating evidence, so the police couldn't charge Meili's source—but the taint from rape allegations would stick to him, and even without a conviction, public perception could damage his reputation. She'd rendered him unusable in court.

Gina found a spot and parked. Nathan stopped in the row behind her and watched her through his rearview mirror as she fiddled with her makeup. Who wore makeup to the gym?

Public perception wasn't the worst part. Both the DOJ and FBI leadership were populated with political climbers who'd never approve of using an accused rapist as the centerpiece of a case. Even if the Bureau signed off and an AUSA agreed to go forward, they'd get pushback from the DOJ's Criminal Division.

Gina's door opened. She stepped out and slung a gym bag over her shoulder. Nathan jumped out and approached her.

Meili was right to worry. The allegations would sink her source before the case even started. She'd only conducted an initial debriefing and hadn't officially signed him, but she wouldn't get ASAC approval to use him. Few supervisors wanted an accused rapist working for them. Even if the crime didn't happen, it didn't look good.

Gina moved with purpose and she'd almost reached the gym before he caught her.

"Gina Harris?" he asked.

She flinched and faced him, looking askance. "Yes?"

He flashed his badge. "Nathan Burke, FBI."

Her eyes widened, and she deflated. She glanced around as if she expected the Hostage Rescue Team to rappel out of helicopters.

"What . . . was I speeding?"

She was dumber than he'd anticipated.

"I'm a federal agent, not a traffic cop. I wanted to speak to you about the allegations you made against Professor Wang."

"You can ask my attorney. He'll answer any questions—"

"You're not a suspect, and you're not under investigation. At least not yet."

She leaned away, wanting to disengage. "How'd you find me?"

"I'm a federal investigator."

"Is this . . . are you . . . did I do something wrong?" Fear of authority figures often made people mentally stumble.

He studied her, letting the silence grow heavy. "You know you did."

She inhaled sharply. "I reported what he did to me after class. He—"

"Enough," Nathan said. "I read the reports, and your accusation doesn't match the facts."

"But I—"

"Professor Wang wasn't in town the day you claim he assaulted you."

Fear flickered across her face. "He attacked me. He—"

"He interviewed a historian in Baltimore half an hour before the alleged rape. His E-ZPass tolls and cellphone tower connections corroborate that, and the subject matter expert confirmed his presence. I only spent two hours fact-checking, and I can prove your accusation is bullshit."

Wang had already been suspended by Jefferson College. A system that demonized the accused before they'd had the opportunity to defend themselves was unfair and un-American, but it had become common practice in academia.

"I got the time wrong," she said. "He raped me." Her tone lacked conviction. She sounded like a child lying about eating the last cookie.

"I read your witness statement. Lying to police on an official report is a crime."

"I didn't lie—"

"And beyond potential criminal charges, Wang could sue you for everything you own."

She flinched. The corners of her mouth dropped. Everyone feared losing something, and wealth was her vulnerability.

"Am I in trouble?"

"You could go to jail."

"I didn't—"

"Save it. Your story falls apart on first glance. It's obvious you lied, but the question is why."

"My lawyer—"

"It took me an hour to find your connections to China. You became famous on ChatteringHen, and that's a Chinese intelligence operation. It's not your only connection. Your advertisers use Chinese financing, which comes from the CCP."

"But I—"

"I uncovered this in one afternoon. Can you imagine what I'll find if I really investigate you?"

"I didn't mean to hurt anyone."

Her lower lip quivered, and a wave of empathy washed over him. She was a twenty-two-year-old woman with no real-world experience. But she'd falsely accused an innocent man of rape and had done so at the behest of a foreign adversary. His empathy vanished, replaced by anger.

"Who told you to do this?"

"I can't . . . please."

"Tell me who ordered you to accuse Wang, or I'll make sure you spend the next five years in jail."

"They paid me thirty thousand dollars."

"The Chinese?"

She nodded and tears streamed down her face.

"Who are they?"

"I don't know their names, and I can't reach them."

She'd undermined their source, but her admission should allow Meili to sign him. "Help me find the men who paid you."

"They'll kill me."

50

———

Reagan's cellphone alarm pierced the silence, and she shrugged off her covers and reached for it, her mind clinging to a world of nightmares. She fumbled for the phone, knocking it off its holder. She hit the snooze button and lay back in bed.

Another shitty night of sleep.

She yawned and checked the phone. At least it powered off by itself. She scrolled through her email, looking for emergencies. Nothing from Vince, and nothing from Gail. She relaxed and started to close the app when an email jumped out at her.

The subject line read, *Open Me Now.* The message came from someone called YourPoliticalFuture@yahoo.com. A paperclip icon indicated an attachment. Was it spam? Opening attachments from people she didn't recognize wasn't smart, but she could read the message.

She clicked on it.

Dear Reagan,

You have reneged on your election promise and betrayed both your party and your constituents. You pledged to support the Democratic Party when you ran to become a delegate, and people voted for you expecting you to fulfill that oath.

You need to properly discharge the duties of your office and unequivocally support the candidacy of Darcy Lemon and Archibald James. If you do not comply, I'll send the attached pictures to everyone on your address list. You must act today.

Reagan's blood ran cold.

Her stomach hardened into cement as she hovered her finger over the attachment. Could the message be a scam to lure her to open a document and download a virus? That's how malware entered systems, but this wasn't a form letter sent to thousands of potential victims. The sender had addressed her by name and knew she was a delegate who had withdrawn her support of the presidential ticket.

She tapped it and downloaded a set of JPG photos. She gasped.

In the first photo, a younger version of herself stood naked on a beach. A section of South Beach on Martha's Vineyard. A nude beach.

She flipped her phone across the room, as if it had bitten her. It clattered across the wooden floor.

She trembled with fear and eyed the phone as if watching a poisonous snake. How had the sender found those photos buried in her old computer's hard drive? She'd never transferred them to her new devices or shared them with anyone. Had they automatically uploaded to her cloud storage during a backup? And how had someone accessed them?

Reagan needed to see the photos.

She climbed out of bed and crossed the room on shaky legs. She picked up her phone, and her hands shook as she scrolled to the next photo that showed her skipping toward the water away from the camera.

She knew what was coming.

Reagan had dated a guy after college, and after drinking too much, he'd snapped a few nude photos of her. Even in her intoxicated state, she'd had enough common sense to make him use her phone. He never possessed the photos.

She flipped to the next photo. It showed her naked, on her hands and knees. A weight compressed her chest, and she couldn't breathe. She advanced through the series of her posing on the hard-packed sand wearing only a silly grin. She'd laughed about it then. The next one showed her on her back.

It was her. Clear as day. What had she been thinking?

She gawked at the last photo, which showed everything. Why hadn't she deleted the pictures from her archive? Too late now.

"No, no, no."

Could she explain away the photos as a youthful indiscretion? What had made her do it? Her body numbed.

Whoever sent the pictures made their demands clear—but she wouldn't endorse Lemon. She'd already refused and endangered her budding political career, so why would anyone think blackmail would work?

But if she didn't comply . . .

What would happen if they emailed these to her family, friends, and colleagues? What would people think about her? She could never show her face in public again. Her political career would be over before it really started, and—

Amelia.

Her daughter would see these. Would the images change how Amelia felt about her? How she thought about sex? She'd be scarred for life.

Would these monsters follow through with their threat? She lightened. They wanted to scare her enough to change her position, and maybe they wouldn't send the pictures to anyone.

She frowned. Her tormentors had gone to great lengths to acquire compromising photographs. Nothing indicated an idle threat. They'd destroy her if she didn't do as they asked.

How many others had they blackmailed?

A text dinged on her phone. Now wasn't a good time to chat with anyone, but Vince's overseas travel and her constant worry about Amelia necessitated her checking. She opened the message.

Tick tock.

Below the words was a picture of her, naked from the waist up in her bathroom. The camera angle came from the countertop where she'd set her phone while getting dressed. The photo was recent. They'd hacked the camera on her phone.

She covered the lens and powered off her phone. They'd been watching her. What else had they seen?

Bile rose in her throat. She turned her head and vomited.

Zhao tried to ignore the thumping headache behind his eyes as Jíng filed intelligence reports in his office safe. He hadn't been sleeping well, and lack of rest caused more physical ailments than when he was younger. He refocused on his morning intelligence briefing. He read the summary and straightened.

He held up the report for Jíng to see. "What is this?"

Jíng shut the safe and moved to the other side of his desk. "We intercepted a communication from an unknown drug trafficker in New York to a CAIR representative—"

"The Muslim Brotherhood?"

"One of their front groups. In the email, the drug dealer specifically mentioned opioid revenues would be funneled to a Uyghur independence group."

Zhao scowled. "We're supplying opioids to Brotherhood operatives, and you're telling me we're funding our own insurgency?"

"There's no way to know where the Brotherhood's drugs originated, or where the money was diverted from the supply chain."

"But it's possible."

"Probable," she said. "We're trying to identify the trafficker and ascertain the details of the transaction. Our people in New York are on it."

Zhao nodded. Every action he took to undermine the United States caused ripples and unexpected outcomes. Financing of radical Islamists to target the West had created chaos, but if they funneled money back to Islamists in China, he'd subsidize domestic dissension and terror.

"Should I instruct Quon to suspend deliveries to Brotherhood affiliates?"

Zhao rubbed his chin. Taking action unleashed a cascade of reactions and further actions, and changing course could exacerbate things. He needed to fully understand the scope of the problem before ordering interventions. He'd learned that lesson the hard way.

"Stay the course . . . for now."

52

The Toyota HiAce van reeked of curry, garlic, and stale tobacco, and the pungent odor filled Nathan's sinuses. Waldo sat beside him in back of the parked van, both concealed by a sheet hanging behind the driver's seat. Nathan peered through the heavily tinted rear window at the Night Market in downtown Chiang Mai. The northwest Thai city lay only a few hundred miles from the Myanmar border. The Doi Suthep mountain, the highest peak in Thailand, rose above the lush jungles of Doi Suthep-Pui National Park.

Captain Paitoon Shinawatra sat in the row behind them, representing Special Operations Unit Naresuan 261. Pai gave them legal cover for the drug deal, though he stretched his authority. He'd taken possession of the kilos of opioids Quon had provided Kei, and then returned them for this controlled delivery to Yakuf. Pai had skimmed over the details of the plan with his higher authority, portraying it as an intelligence collection operation. He took a risk, because selling illicit opioids could bring the death penalty.

The tonal sounds of spoken Thai resonated above the din of traffic. Thousands of people strolled down the street, browsing vendor carts brimming with clothing, crafts, and jewelry. The majority were Thai as the number of tourists dissipated farther from the sea.

"All set, boss," Kei's voice squawked out of the receiver beside Nathan.

Nathan had checked out tech gear, because the delivery of Quon's opioids to Yakuf held significant evidentiary value, and FBI management expected documentation. Nathan complied, though the case would never reach court.

"Public spot for a drug deal," Waldo said.

"Chiang Mai is perfect for this," Nathan said.

He'd chosen Thailand because Naresuan 261 could facilitate his operations, but also because of Chiang Mai's proximity to western China. Drug traffickers spider-webbed routes across the Golden Triangle connecting China, Myanmar, Laos, and Thailand. It's why Yakuf had agreed to receive the contraband there.

"We can't let the bigger shipment slip through our fingers," Nathan said.

"Then why risk it?" Waldo asked. "And why buy the dope from Quon?"

"Kei needs to deliver the drugs to Yakuf or both he and Emerald lose credibility. If we snatch him with the sample, they'll know Emerald set them up."

"Then let's lock up Quon too."

"Not until the CCP realizes the danger in Islamists acquiring opioids."

"But Quon's dope killed thousands of Americans."

"He'll have his day. These kilos will make Yakuf comfortable, then Kei can set up a larger deal. We'll prosecute Quon later, hopefully without needing Kei."

Waldo rested his hands on his hips. "Why risk delivering it to Yakuf? He could use the carfentanil to kill a lot of people."

"He won't use a sample as a weapon, and we need to win his trust or the Chinese won't buy our ruse. The best way to corroborate the CCP's fear is by showing TIP terrorist's want carfentanil."

Outside, A uniformed Royal Thai Police officer parked his Honda motorcycle and set the kickstand. He climbed off and adjusted his gun belt as he scanned the street. Pai provided the legal cover for the operation, sort of, but he hadn't informed the local police, because the risk of compromise was too high.

And what they were doing wasn't strictly legal.

Waldo nodded. "What will the Chinese do to Yakuf when they catch him?"

The air stilled. The CCP was ruthless to anyone who threatened it. "They might jail him for life."

"They'll whack him," Waldo said.

"Yeah, probably."

Nathan glanced back. The motorcycle cop was gone. Nathan leaned around the seat. The officer walked toward them—thirty yards away. Was he ticketing vehicles? The FBI's Bangkok office had rented the van for their surveillance, so it had legal plates, but what if the cop spotted them inside? A confrontation would burn their surveillance.

And that would ruin everything.

"We're setting up Yakuf," Waldo said.

"He's a terrorist."

"How do we know that?"

"Emerald."

"Selling him carfentanil is entrapment."

"He wanted drugs, which is why Emerald brought him. His prior behavior invalidates an entrapment defense."

"But we're feeding him to those *cabrónes*."

"He's a radical Islamic terrorist who needs to be removed from the board. Even if he escapes, our goal is to convince the CCP that opioid sales can backlash."

Waldo nodded. "Still—"

"A man is watching me," Kei's disembodied voice came out of the speaker.

Nathan lifted a digital camera and pressed the telephoto lens against the glass.

A thick man with a hard face stood beside a stack of bejeweled purses and stared at Kei. The guy didn't attempt to hide his interest in Kei, which probably made him Yakuf's soldier. Or a crook eyeing Kei's bag. Or worse. Yakuf could have double-crossed them and had sent an operative to rob Kei —or kill him.

The man strode toward Kei.

If things went to shit, Pai would have to intervene. Nathan brought a collapsable baton, but it would be useless against armed terrorists. The operation would have been safer with the FBI's Bangkok office on board, but informing the LEGAT they planned to walk two kilos of carfentanil would have been a career-ender.

The man stopped in front of Kei. "You here to meet someone?"

"I am Kim."

"Yakuf send me." He pointed at Kei's knapsack. "That is for me?"

"Where is Yakuf?"

"He told me to take from Kim."

"Where is the money?"

The man reached into his jacket.

Nathan tensed. Would he withdraw money or a gun? Having the money and drugs together wasn't safe, but an illegal operation required compromises.

The man handed a thick envelope to Kei. Kei turned his back to the crowd and stepped into the space between stalls. He dug inside the envelope.

"It's all here," Kei said.

"The product," the man said.

Kei shrugged off his knapsack and set it in the dirt.

The man looked around, then snatched up the bag. He unzipped it and peeked inside. "You better not fuck us."

"It's strong," Kei said.

Nathan glanced back at the motorcycle cop. The officer inspected a car two spots away. Nathan returned his attention to the trafficker. The man slung the knapsack over his shoulder, looked Kei up and down, then turned and stomped away.

"It is done," Kei whispered.

The man weaved through the crowd but maintained a casual pace. He kept his cool—a professional.

"The perp took it," Waldo said. "We could grab him."

"We're not doing that."

"That dope will go into users' arms."

"They may want to test that it's potent enough to use as a weapon, like the Phantoms."

"Any blood they spill is on us, *amigo*."

Nathan's chest tightened. He'd never done anything like this. "If our ruse works, the endgame justifies the risk."

"But—"

"It's done," Nathan said. "You should have objected sooner."

The guy carrying the knapsack stopped beside a food cart. He spoke to someone. Who was he—

Yakuf stepped out of the shadows. He looked in Kei's direction, then surveyed the street. His eyes landed on Nathan's van and lingered there.

Nathan didn't breathe.

Yakuf's attention moved to the vehicles behind their van. He froze when he spotted the motorcycle cop ticketing a moped. Yakuf scrutinized the surrounding crowd. He seemed satisfied and said something to the man with the drugs. They walked around a stall and darted down a side street.

Nathan exhaled. "Whew."

"I almost shit myself," Waldo said.

"Why do I take chances for you?" Pai asked.

"You'll be a hero when you arrest him with a huge shipment."

"What now?" Waldo asked.

"We have Quon deliver a hundred kilos of carfentanil, then we persuade Yakuf to pick them up in the Kingdom of Thailand."

53

Nathan leaned back in his business-class seat on their return flight from Bangkok. They'd had a short layover in Munich where they'd switched to the Boeing 777 for the final leg back to Dulles International. Eighteen hours in the air. The back-and-forth travel across time zones took a toll. DOI policy required government employees to purchase coach seats, but he'd used his frequent flyer miles to upgrade. Climbing the waitlist and finally getting bumped up had felt like winning the lottery. The difference between eighteen hours in coach versus business was night and day. Poor Waldo was stuck in the back.

He stretched and yawned.

A female flight attendant wearing a fitted uniform eased down the aisle, the sound of her movement covered by the drone of the engines. She inspected each row and smiled at him as she passed. He returned it, and she continued on. Was selective memory misleading him or were the flight attendants in business and first class in better shape than those in coach?

He reclined his seat and glanced around the cabin at the other passengers who either dozed or zoned out watching on-demand movies. The Polaris flatbed seat could lie flat, but he never slept on planes. He cherished uninterrupted time alone with his thoughts. Having a smartphone with access to the world's knowledge gave people abilities that would have been considered magic a hundred years before, but being electronically tethered to a device prevented deep thought. Being cut off from the constant influx of information, communication, and distractions created a respite for his mind. He always thought better in the air, either from the isolation or the pressurized cabin screwed with his head. Whatever it was, he needed time to distill what had happened.

They'd brokered a deal for narcotics in a buy in a quasi-approved operation. It had been a desperate attempt to demonstrate the danger of opioid trafficking to the Chinese. The operation's chance of success wasn't as high as the probability he'd land in hot water for bending the rules, but the situation required risk.

The political turmoil at home triggered more stress. While he focused on a foreign adversary, the United States struggled with a constitutional crisis, and the level of Chinese penetration into American institutions would make a conspiracy theorist blush.

A shadow enveloped him, and he looked up.

"*Qué pasa, amigo?*" Waldo said. "You awake?"

"You're not supposed to be up here."

"Couldn't sleep."

"Explain that to the attendant when she throws you out."

"This shit is twisted. What are we doing?" Waldo leaned close and lowered his voice. "We let two kilos walk."

"Technically, Naresuan 261 did that."

Waldo's eyes narrowed and the corners of his mouth dropped. "Not how the front office gonna see it."

"You know the stakes."

The aircraft hummed around them. A flight attendant in the galley peeked around the curtain and noticed Waldo. She frowned.

"I get we want the Chinese to worry the poison they're spreading around the world will hurt them, but if Yakuf gets away, he could murder people—and we'd be responsible."

The flight attendant scowled at Waldo as she marched down their aisle.

"Then we better not let that happen," Nathan said, "or we could start World War III."

54

Nathan passed through US Customs at Dulles and headed out into the main terminal with Waldo somewhere behind him in the queue. Nathan's roller bag tugged at his shoulder like a box of rocks. Air travel back and forth to Thailand had done a number on his old injury and on his internal clock. He craved sleep. He rounded a chute that funneled past friends and family waiting behind barriers.

Meili waved to him from across the terminal. His heart warmed, and he quickened his pace. As he approached, Meili's face tightened. Something was wrong. Nathan's elation evaporated. He reached her with dread coiled in his stomach like a rattlesnake.

"Is Amelia okay?"

"She's great, and welcome back."

"What's happened?"

"Can't a woman meet the man she's dating at the airport without something being wrong?"

He cocked his head and wrinkled his nose.

Meili sighed. "I came because I miss you, but I also stumbled on something strange."

The snake tensed inside him, ready to strike.

"I had coffee with Reagan when you were gone, and we—"

"You hung out with my ex-wife?"

"Don't get mad. She asked me to meet her."

He grimaced. "Why—"

"It wasn't about you."

His eyes widened. "Amelia—"

"I told you she's fine. Calm down, and I'll explain."

Waldo dropped his bag beside them. *"Hola, jefa. Qué pasa?"*

"Welcome back, Osvaldo. Let's find a place to talk."

Waldo glanced sheepishly at Nathan the way Bruno did when Nathan returned home to find a mess on the floor.

They followed Meili through the terminal to an empty corner. She perched on a metal bench with the grace of a ballerina and crossed her legs in a way a man could never do. Waldo flopped down beside her, and his shoulders sagged.

Nathan remained standing. "Meili has news."

"I met Reagan while you were—"

"Your ex?" Waldo grinned. He seemed relieved Meili wasn't there to reprimand them.

Nathan ignored him. "What did she want? It's been a long flight."

Meili scowled. "She called right after you left—"

"You should have told me."

"It had nothing to do with you. The DNC asked Reagan to help register a large group of new residents arriving in Virginia."

"Illegals?"

"No, at least not technically. Some had asylum status and others had been paroled under the CHNV program, but some already had green cards."

"How many people we talking about?"

"She was supposed to register 2,852 individuals seeking Virginia residency."

The number hit him like a hammer. "Mostly new arrivals?"

"That's what's so strange. Half of them had already established residency in other states."

"So why move?" Waldo asked.

"I had the same question, so I dug into it."

"And what you discovered made you drive all the way out to Dulles?" Nathan said.

"I had our analyst research new resident data in all fifty states. Virginia isn't the only state with a spike in both new residents and voter registration."

"The DNC is trying to flip red states?" Nathan asked.

"They're sending more immigrants to Democratic states than those with Republican majorities."

"What's the point?" Waldo asked.

"More residents in blue states gives Democrats extra congressional seats and electoral votes," Meili said.

"That accusation isn't new," Nathan said.

"This looks more sinister."

The snake in Nathan's belly moved. "I see where this is going, but I hope I'm wrong."

"Six states saw disproportionate swings in new residents this election cycle, including Arizona, Michigan, Nevada, North Carolina, Pennsylvania, Virginia, and—"

"Wisconsin," Nathan said.

She nodded. "You get it."

"Swing states?" Waldo asked.

"Yes, but the relocation is targeted specifically at purple counties within purple states."

The snake struck. "That's brilliant . . . and dark."

"A party may be millions of votes behind in the popular vote, but tens of thousands of voters in swing states can capture all their electoral votes. Some of those purple counties can be won with a few hundred votes. It doesn't take much to tip the scales."

"They're moving people from other states into counties that can turn states blue."

"They're fighting to win," Waldo said, "but it ain't illegal."

"It might be election interference if they're using federal funds," Meili said, "but it's illegal if they're encouraging illegals to vote."

"But this is a Republican administration," Nathan said.

"The moves are sponsored by NGOs," Meili said. "The money trail is complicated. Bureaucrats in the various agencies could be working against the administration's interests."

"Is the DNC paying these immigrants to vote a certain way?" Nathan asked.

"Unknown, but that's not all of it."

Nathan hung his head. "You're not the best welcome committee. What's your other great news?"

"Half the new residents Reagan was asked to register in Virginia . . . they're Chinese."

55

Reagan shifted on a wrought-iron chair in a noisy coffeehouse that kept the temperature too cold. Could they make it any more unpleasant to sit and drink a coffee? The shop was cute, the furniture trendy, and the coffee was usually good, though overpriced. She sipped her eight-dollar latte, which they'd over-brewed and burned the beans. She set it down and caught a glimpse of her reflection in the window. Her face had pinched tight with the pursed lips of a bitter old woman.

What the hell was wrong with her?

She should be grateful to have the resources to drive a $30,000 car to a café and drink a warm beverage on a chilly and windy day—but her bad mood came from being blackmailed—and she needed to tell someone about it.

The bell jingled above the front door and Nathan entered. He waved, and as he beelined for her, fear and shame battled to control her. Should she tell him? She couldn't share the sordid details with anyone else.

"I don't have much time," he said, "but from the look on your face, it's serious."

She slid a black coffee across the table, a gift for his time. He slipped into the seat and took it, never taking his eyes off her.

She stared back, unable to speak.

"Is this about Amelia?" His body tensed while he waited for her answer.

"No, well, it'll affect her, but this is about me."

"Are you sick?"

She smirked. "Just with myself."

He waited.

She gazed out the window at people hurrying down the sidewalk, most bundled in warm clothes. Winter was coming. Around them, customers munched on baked goods and drank expensive coffees, as if nothing was wrong, as if her entire life wasn't about to implode.

Reagan sighed. "I'm being blackmailed."

His eyes widened. "When did this happen?"

"This morning. They emailed me."

"Who's they?"

"I don't know."

"What are they threatening?"

She'd dreaded this moment since receiving the photos. Telling Nathan would make it real. But he was the only one. When Havana Syndrome had incapacitated her, he'd been the only one who believed her. Then he'd found the people responsible and made them stop. He'd saved Amelia from terrorists too. He protected them.

"They have pictures of me."

Nathan grimaced. "Compromising photos?"

She nodded.

"From where?"

She averted her eyes, unable to meet his stare. Was he judging her already? Her chest tightened and her throat closed.

Don't cry.

"Reagan?"

She fixated on the table. "Someone sent me revealing pictures of me. They're intimate."

"Intimate?"

"Explicit."

Nathan set his coffee cup down. "Who took them?"

"An old boyfriend, from college. We were drinking on the beach, a lifetime ago."

"How did the blackmailer get them?"

"They hacked my phone or my computer and accessed my cloud storage. I'm not sure how the photos got onto my cloud. I had them on my old phone, so they must have uploaded years ago."

"Could your old boyfriend have posted them?"

"He'd never do that, and he used my phone to take them."

"He could have emailed himself a copy or—"

"This happened years ago. If he stole them, they'd have surfaced long before this. We didn't date for long, and I'm trying to figure out how the blackmailer knew about him. And they hacked my new phone's camera—"

"What?"

"They controlled my phone's camera and snapped a photo of me getting dressed in my bathroom."

Nathan glanced at the table. "Where's your phone?

"It's off and stuffed in a shoebox in my closet."

"What about your computer?"

She jolted. She hadn't thought of that. Had they hacked all her devices? "My laptop's on my nightstand."

"Assume it's compromised. They could access your camera even when it's off."

"Shit." She needed new devices, but would they hack them too?

"What did Vince say?"

Her gut tensed. "I haven't told him."

Nathan nodded. "You're worried how he'll react?"

"No . . . yes, I don't know. It's not the kind of thing I want to discuss with my husband."

"Everyone has a past."

"Yeah, but everyone doesn't have their worst decisions recorded for posterity."

A young couple walked behind Nathan and set their coffee cups on the table beside them. Their chair legs scraped on the floor as they sat down.

"How bad is it?" Nathan asked in a lower voice.

"As bad as you're imagining."

Nathan cracked his neck. "Okay, how much money do they want?"

"They don't want money."

He arched an eyebrow. "What then?"

"They want me to publicly endorse the Lemon-James ticket. That's their ask."

"This is bad."

Her insides twisted, and her heart raced. How was this real? She'd wanted to make the country a better place, and now, they jeopardized her reputation, her career—her everything.

"Agreeing to pose for those photos was stupid. What was I thinking?"

"You weren't thinking. You were a kid full of hormones and booze. It happens, but you shouldn't suffer for it."

"What do I do?"

"I take it you decided not to support Darcy Lemon?"

"I can't. She's a mystery, but beyond that, I don't approve of my party's actions. The way they anointed her was wrong, and now they're . . ."

"What?"

Should she tell him about the censorship? Gail had all but admitted complicity, but that was internal party business, and Nathan wasn't a political ally. "The party machinations aren't transparent, and they're doing things I consider wrong."

Nathan nodded, but didn't push her.

"I don't know what to do."

He locked eyes with her. "You can't comply."

"They'll ruin me. How will Amelia react? Kids will tease her in school. Oh, God, all the parents will see me."

"It doesn't matter."

"I'm an elected delegate, and I've been in the news. If this thing blows up into a scandal—"

"They're asking you to betray your oath. You made a reasoned decision to withdraw support, and voters expect you to vote your conscience."

"My loyalty is to Amelia."

Nathan kept his voice even. "If you give in to them now, they'll own you forever. Who knows what they'll demand next? That can lead to treason."

"Treason?"

"We don't know what they'll want. Once they own you, you're at their mercy."

"But—"

"If you change your position, they can hold your corruption against you. That's worse than a few indecent photos."

Tears filled her eyes. "They show . . . everything."

He leaned forward and took her hand. "I understand this is hard. Your choices are difficult, but there's only one path forward."

"You mean . . ."

"Rip off the bandage. Call their bluff now, before things worsen."

"They'll distribute the pictures."

"Maybe, maybe not."

She gazed out the window. "This is a disaster."

"You could get in front of it, issue a public statement and come clean. You're a victim. You didn't do anything a million other young people haven't done. Voters will appreciate your honesty. They'll trust you."

"They'd crucify me. How could I show my face in public? Can you imagine the opposition's ads if I run for the House?" She buried her face in her hands. "These pictures will finish my career."

"Then I'll float another idea."

A glimmer of hope bubbled inside her. "Anything will be better."

"Agree to their demands, but insist on getting the photos back. Tell them you need assurances they'll destroy the copies."

"But you said I shouldn't—"

"You won't actually capitulate. We'll start a criminal case and catch these bastards. You're an elected official, so the FBI has jurisdiction. This is an attempt to manipulate the election. It's blackmail, but it's also election fraud."

"For the Democrats' candidate," she said. "Do you think the party is involved?"

"It could be special interests, insiders. Who knows?"

"If I report this, FBI agents will see my photos. Your colleagues."

"If we don't report it, everyone will see them. Submitting to blackmail isn't an option."

A tear trickled down her cheek. He'd said *we*. He stood by her side. And he was right, as usual.

"Take some time and think—"

"I don't need any more time," she said. "Let's catch these assholes."

56

Nathan and Meili dug through the case files in the Moser safes in a cubicle behind their group's bullpen. They leafed through old investigations searching for suspects that matched Gina Harris's description of the men who'd paid her to accuse Meili's defector, Kaiyan Wang. Their electronic database searches hadn't born fruit. Nathan's surprise interrogation outside the gym had shocked Harris into confessing she'd made up the rape allegation, and her admission had helped Meili sign Wang as a source.

Meili and Nathan had different skill sets, but they worked well together. This relationship had a solid foundation, except he was fresh off a divorce. And he needed to be careful with his daughter. And they worked together, and worse, she supervised him. Not to mention her reticence at getting more serious, which bordered on commitment phobia. Come to think of it, they weren't doing that well.

"Shit," he said.

"What is it?" she asked.

"Uh, nothing. Just frustrated."

"I'm not seeing anything in here either," she said. "Her descriptions don't match anyone on our radar."

Agents Jimmy West and Tom McAvoy chatted as they entered the bullpen on the other side of the cubicle wall.

"Nationals looked good this year," Tom said, "but they need pitching."

"You say that every year."

"It's always true," Tom said.

Nathan dug through another file and flipped to the indexing section. No matches to Wang's description.

"You free to interview a new snitch with me?" Jimmy asked.

"I got a couple of hours before I gotta meet the AUSA," Tom said. "Who is it?"

"Another Chinaman," Jimmy said. "Chinese commies have infested DC."

Meili jerked her head up and stared at the cubicle wall.

"Let's go now," Tom said, "so I can get back in time."

"Let me grab my notes."

Their footsteps receded.

Meili frowned, appearing more hurt than angry, and it broke his heart.

"He's an asshole," Nathan said, his anger surfacing. "I'll say something—"

"Let it go."

"But you can't allow your people to talk like that."

"I notice the way Jimmy looks at Asians," Meili said. "If agents investigate criminals of any ethnicity long enough, they form opinions."

"It's racism."

"I wonder what they think about me?"

"Your ethnicity has nothing to do with what we're fighting."

"I can't ignore it. My ancestors came from China. I was born there, and it's part of my identity."

"Your family has history there, and the culture influenced you, but that's different from the evil communist-totalitarian ideology that's trying to conquer the world. Most of your family's history in China predates the government we're investigating."

"People look at me and see the enemy."

"That's not true."

"Listen to them," she said. "The more China's imperialism and strategy become public, the more people will distrust Chinese. Look what happened to Japanese Americans in World War II."

"There'll always be racists who see race and ethnicity instead of individuals, but we can't internalize their hatred."

"Easy for you to say."

She was right. He could intellectualize arguments against bigotry, but he'd never been targeted by vitriol and tribalism. He understood the concepts, but he'd never suffered the deep emotional cuts of someone attacked for their genetics—immutable characteristics they couldn't change.

"I know it's tough to listen to assholes like Jimmy, but he's the exception. Everyone *sees* race and ethnicity, because cultures differ, but most people don't prejudge. They don't look at you and see a Maoist terrorist."

"I wish that was true."

"Who's more vilified in today's climate than racists? Racism will always exist. People are tribalistic and form group associations based on the tiniest commonalities, from which baseball team they support to physical characteristics, but the era of blatant racism is gone for the vast majority of Americans."

Meili's mouth tightened, and she stared at the file cabinet. Nathan's heart ached. Why were people so careless with their words? Rage erupted inside him—a familiar cocktail of chemicals and testosterone that clenched his fists. He wheeled and headed for the bullpen.

"Where are you going?" she asked.

"To tell Jimmy to shut the fuck up."

"No, don't. Nathan, wait—"

He blew through the group like a storm. Tom stood outside a cubicle laughing at something Jimmy had said. Jimmy sat in his chair grinning as he removed his notebook from a drawer. Nathan's chest tightened in anticipation of confrontation, but righteous fury propelled him forward.

"I heard what you said, you prick."

Jimmy flinched. He looked up and cocked his head, clearly not understanding what Nathan was talking about. Tom stepped back.

"What—"

"That crack about Chinese people."

Tommy's eyes lit with recognition. "Hey, I didn't mean—"

"That's some racist shit, and if I hear it again, we're gonna have a big fucking problem."

Tommy's face hardened. "Whatever, man. I wasn't even talking to you."

"One more time, and we'll settle this down in the garage."

Jimmy glared, but stayed silent.

Nathan spun around and headed for Meili's office. She stood outside her door. She must have heard. He searched her face for a reaction as he approached.

She waved him into her office.

Nathan blew out a stream of air, venting adrenaline and tension. He had enough enemies without fighting agents in his group, but some things required action. The occasional act of social terrorism kept assholes in check.

He entered her office and shut the door behind him. "I think he got the message."

"Let's not discuss this again. I won't say anything to him, and when you go back out there, act like it didn't happen. Let's put this behind us. I don't need dissension in the group."

"Got it."

"Oh, and Nathan?"

"Yeah?"

"Thank you." She beamed, and warmth filled him.

"I won't let anyone hurt you. If—"

His phone buzzed with an email notification. He read the message.

"It's Hamilton. He's got something urgent to tell me."

57

Reagan wanted to be anywhere else except staring across the conference table at Agent Rick Davis inside the Department of Justice's Criminal Division's Public Integrity Section. Beside him sat AUSA Samuel White, who Nathan had insisted be involved, and six DOJ attorneys and FBI special agents from the Election Crimes Branch—the unit that handled election fraud.

Vince stirred in the chair beside her, looking uncomfortable. He'd returned from Santo Domingo when she'd informed him about the blackmail, and now he sat in a room full of men discussing his wife's pornographic photographs.

"The plan is for you to encourage communication from the blackmailers," Sam said, "and give our agents time to track them down and identify them. We need to develop evidence to bolster a criminal prosecution . . ."

Reagan nodded. She tried to listen, but his words sounded muted, as if he spoke underwater. Every man in the room had seen her naked. She'd turned over the emails and text message, and who knew how many agents had viewed the photos of her? Those pictures were awful, but they'd been taken long ago and she'd detached from that person—but the shot of her naked in her bathroom had been recent.

That one bothered her the most.

"…and that's why the method of collection is vital," Sam continued.

Wait, what had he said? She refocused. This was important. Her future balanced on the outcome of this case.

"I've written the response email for you," Agent Davis said.

He slid her new laptop across the table. Reagan had purchased it herself, at their request because they wanted her to use her credit card in case her purchases were monitored. The FBI tech guys had loaded it with anti-malware and virus protection. The software wouldn't prevent a hacker from controlling her computer, but it would track him and send the data to the FBI forensic team.

She read the email response.

I'll do it. I'll support Lemon, but I need assurance the pictures will be returned to me. I won't do this unless I know it ends here.

Simple and to the point. Would it enrage her blackmailers? Would they refuse? Would they release a single picture to pressure her? Had this been the right decision? Questions swirled in her mind, and the ground moved beneath her.

She sighed. Too late now. She'd reported it, and the FBI wouldn't walk away, even if she begged them. She'd committed to an investigation. This would have to work, or her career and reputation would shatter.

"What if they geo-locate her and see she's at Main Justice?" Vince asked.

"We spoofed her GPS to show she's at home," Davis said, with a hint of pride in his voice. Clever boys wanted credit.

"What reaction do we intend to elicit?" Vince asked. He sounded annoyed.

"The more they talk, the more data we acquire," Davis said, "and the better the chance they slip up."

"From a prosecutor's perspective," Sam said, "We want as much incriminating evidence as possible. We want them to state their motive and acknowledge they're engaging in illegal behavior. These conversations will drive them to plea out later."

Did any of that make sense? Agents and prosecutors lived in the criminal world, but the legalities eluded her. Was their plan clever or foolhardy?

She didn't know any of them, but Nathan had vouched for Sam, who'd prosecuted his most important cases. Nathan had wanted to attend the meeting, but Vince hadn't been comfortable with that. Nathan would do anything to protect her, he'd proven that before, but she didn't want him to see the photographs. For some reason, she still craved his respect.

"What are the charges?" Reagan asked.

"All federal, obviously," Sam said. "Bribery, corruption, and a host of crimes involving campaign finance, voter fraud, and civil rights violations, but I'll make charging decisions after the facts are in evidence."

"We have evidence of attempted bribery now," Davis said. "Ideally, we arrange for a meeting where the photographs are exchanged."

"They're digital pictures," Reagan said.

"Then we manufacture a reason for a meeting."

Even if they caught the criminals and seized the photos, the case becoming public was a forgone conclusion. Any prosecution for election interference involving the blackmail of a delegate would make national headlines, especially when the salacious photographs dropped. The photos may be disseminated, but the details would come out in criminal complaints, and her career would be over. Hopefully, she could protect Amelia from seeing the photos.

Vince leaned forward. "If you screw around with these guys, they'll release the pictures and ruin us."

Sam and Davis exchanged looks.

"To be frank, they may do that either way," Sam said. "I know that's not what you want to hear. Our mission is to identify the suspects, develop a prosecutable case, then arrest and convict them. If we don't acquire more evidence, none of that will happen."

"You mean, I'll endure all this embarrassment and stress, and they may still send the pictures to tabloids."

"They'd post them online," Davis said, drawing a stern look from Sam.

"It's possible," Sam said, "but you had no choice. I knew that the minute Agent Burke explained the circumstances to me. If you'd done anything but officially report this, you'd open yourself up to charges."

Vince snorted. "What charges do you—"

"Someone's extorting Mrs. Cabrera to change her vote," Sam said. "That behavior undermines the integrity of the presidential election. She needs to cooperate completely. Full transparency."

"I reported it," she said.

Sam nodded. "And that's why you're a witness and not a defendant."

58

———————

Nathan watched Waldo and other agents and analysts typing away at their computers. The FBI employed 38,000 people, of which close to 13,000 were gun-toting special agents, yet the bureaucracy tied everyone to their desks. If made king for a day, he'd force every agent onto the streets. It wouldn't matter if they met sources, interviewed witnesses, or followed perps. Anything would be better than filing red tape and filling safes with reports nobody would read.

Only results mattered.

The endgame with Yakuf approached, and they'd know soon if their ruse would work. He picked up the single-use cell he'd purchased for Kei and dialed.

"What's up, boss man?" Kei said.

"Any word from our guy?"

"He wants delivery."

"Is he impatient?"

"He suspicious if we wait too long."

Nathan's stomach tightened. "We need to stall. Tell them there's a short delay."

"He will not be happy. It may kill the deal."

"I need more time."

"But he expects—"

"Keep him dangling on the line," Nathan said.

"Dangling?"

"Keep him talking. Let me know when he reaches out."

Nathan hung up and called Emerald on a number they'd promised to only use for emergencies.

"*Gěi wǒ yī diǎn shí jiān*," Emerald answered.

"It's me."

"A moment."

Rustling came across the line, then the sound of traffic. "It is dangerous to speak."

"What's happening inside the Second Bureau," Nathan asked.

"They observed the meeting."

"What are they planning?"

"They ordered surveillance on Yakuf but—"

"No names," Nathan said.

"—but they're having difficulties."

"What kind?"

"He's back in Xinjiang, where the Bureau's reach is poor."

"What will they do?" Nathan asked.

"The meeting with the trafficker worried them. They are gathering intelligence and deciding how to react. At least that's what I believe. My little mice don't see everything."

"It's taking too long," Nathan said.

"I don't control the Second Bureau."

"Send a message the second you hear anything."

Nathan disconnected. They'd executed the plan as designed, but the CCP hadn't reacted as they'd hoped. Didn't Chinese Intelligence recognize the peril of the Turkistan Islamic Party negotiating with traffickers for carfentanil, especially after the attacks in the United States?

"What's up?" Waldo asked.

"No response. If the Second Bureau doesn't sound the alarm, our little unauthorized op will fail."

"We risked our careers for nothing?"

"And Yakuf expects carfentanil. Failing to deliver puts our CIs at risk."

"Why isn't the CCP all over him?" Waldo asked.

"TIP threatens them, but mostly in the Xinjiang region."

"Western China, right?"

"Yeah, but the insurgency has national implications. The central government wants to squash them, or at least contain them to prevent the rebellion from spreading."

"What happened to the commies' zero tolerance for dissent?" Waldo asked.

"Xinjiang is semi-autonomous and . . ." A flicker of excitement tickled the base of his skull.

"And what?"

"You gave me an idea."

"Uh-oh."

"Dissension is contagious," Nathan said.

"Meaning?"

"Quelling an Islamic revolt seeking a caliphate is tough enough for the CCP, but what if that rebellion transformed into a broader anti-party movement?"

"*No es posible,*" Waldo said. "Chinese reformers aren't radical Islamists."

"They share a desire for self-determination."

"The party worries about Islamic terrorism, but they've contained it."

Nathan nodded. The amorphous clouds of ideas merged, and a plan appeared. He smiled.

"What?" Waldo asked.

"They need a push," Nathan said.

"You've got that look again, *hermano*."

"What look?"

"The one that says I'm about to risk my career again."

"Mission first."

Waldo sighed. "This ain't gonna end well."

59

Political tension electrified the country, including the City of Alexandria, five miles south of the White House. Reagan stood outside City Hall at lunchtime and watched groups of opposing protesters scream at each other. Alexandria's Registrar Office was across the street, and though early voting had begun, few people entered the building. Twenty Republican activists protesting a lack of election integrity stood in the historic plaza carrying signs that predicted a stolen election. Thirty feet away, Democrat counter-protesters screamed at them for suppressing the vote.

The air crackled with potential violence, and onlookers gawked at the spectacle from the perimeter. Why were people drawn to conflict? Didn't they sense the danger?

"Communists are stealing the election," a man shouted. He held a *Stop the Steal* sign.

"Racist," a woman screamed back.

Reagan's stomach knotted. She'd come to meet her blackmailers. The FBI still hadn't identified them, but after an exchange of terse emails, she'd finally convinced whoever had stolen her photos to provide them to her on a disk. The meeting was absurd theater, because digital photos could be copied, but she'd drawn a line in the sand and refused to comply unless they turned them over and assured her that when she supported Lemon, they'd stop. They must think she was naïve for making the request, or they suspected a trap.

A team of FBI agents had deployed to the area hours before, but none of them stood out. She was an hour early, which had seemed like a good idea when her handlers suggested it, but with the crowd's rage growing and her stress rising, it no longer felt smart.

She took out her phone and called Nathan.

"You okay?" he asked.

"I'm having second thoughts about this operation. I didn't anticipate a riot in Old Town."

"Looks peaceful so far."

Reagan scanned the area. Other than activists and a tiny group of spectators, a few people loitered around the plaza. A young couple ate ice cream, a homeless man slept on a bench, a man walking his dog—

Wait.

She studied the homeless man again. He lounged on a park bench wearing a ratty overcoat, a brimmed hat, and jeans. She'd skimmed right over him, the way people did with the homeless. Engaging with someone suffering from mental illness or drug addiction could invite harm, which was why she avoided people on the street. Nathan probably counted on that.

But she'd recognize Nathan anywhere, and that was him.

"Why are you here?" she asked.

"I want to make sure you're okay."

"They sent a team of agents—" She glanced around and lowered her voice. "It's not your job to protect me."

"You're not just my ex, you're my daughter's mother. I won't let anything happen to you . . . if I can help it."

The way he qualified that statement with an *if* chilled her. "Agent Davis will blow a gasket if he catches you here."

"It's a public place."

"That won't help."

"Davis wasn't married to you. I have a vested interest in your safety, and to be honest, this bribery thing pissed me off."

Ah, that was it.

"Does the possibility of compromising pictures of me going public bother you, or does a man threatening me make you feel impotent?"

He laughed. "Little of both, and let's avoid the word *impotent*."

"Fair enough." She smirked. He could be a Neanderthal, but his presence calmed her.

"How do you know your blackmailer is a man?"

That stopped her. She'd assumed it. Men committed most crimes, but what if—

A woman screamed.

The protesters closed within feet of each other, and two men scuffled. An Alexandria police officer—a petite female who probably weighed one hundred pounds—shouted at them with a command voice of a Marine drill sergeant. The men backed away, hurling insults.

The plaza became a tinderbox.

Could some protesters be FBI agents? The Bureau had infiltrated mobs before and later they'd obfuscated their role to Congress and the press. Collecting intelligence justified undercover work, but encouraging citizens to violate the law crossed a line. The depths of their involvement may never see the light of day. Rule of law was oxygen for democracy, and police enforced it, but the unchecked power of federal law enforcement loomed like a hostile army massed at the border. The threat of tyranny always existed. Safety for security, that was the trade-off, but too much and freedom disappeared. Governments loathed relinquishing power.

Reagan touched her clothing over where Agent Davis had adhered a concealed microphone to her chest with surgical tape.

When Reagan had been with the State Department, her colleagues had looked down on federal agents and considered hairy-armed, gun-toting colleagues a necessary evil.

Now, she depended on them to protect her life.

A presence weighed on her, and hair rose on her neck. She turned. A lanky white guy with a goatee and wispy mustache stood behind her. He wore jeans, a plaid wool shirt, and a knit beanie, like a grunge hipster from the nineties. She met his eyes.

He didn't move. "I'm here."

"You brought the disk?" Her voice sounded tiny and scared like a little girl's. Had he noticed?

He slipped a compact disc out of his back pocket and showed it to her. "Your glamour shots are all here." His eyes roamed over her body.

Yuk. She reached for it and he snatched it back. "They want you to confirm your public endorsement. You need to do it today."

They? "I agreed to do it. You're blackmailing me, so I don't have a choice, but this stops here. I won't be your slave." She'd said *blackmailing* like Davis had instructed her. Her heart pounded as she waited for an answer.

He leaned close. "You don't call the shots."

She looked over his shoulder. Were the agents watching? Was the FBI close?

"What are you looking for? You weren't stupid enough to call the police, were you?"

"I, uh, no. Why are you doing this?" That last line slipped out. Her emotions bubbled to the surface. Who were these monsters, and why had they targeted her? She'd never hurt anyone.

He scanned the crowd. "You know what'll happen if you rat on us. Did you tell anyone?"

Reagan froze. This meeting had been easier when she'd mentally rehearsed it, not that she'd thought they'd show. Why risk being arrested? For this crook to let her see his face, he must be a moron . . . or feel untouchable.

"Why won't you leave me alone?" Tension filled her. She wasn't a cop. Why had the FBI asked her to meet a criminal who'd seen her at her most vulnerable? She looked around again, desperately wanting help.

He noticed, and a trace of fear flashed behind his eyes. "If you—"

"Give me the disk," she said. Her fear masqueraded as courage.

"Shit. I told them . . ." He shifted his feet.

"I'll do what you asked, but you must destroy the photos."

"You bitch."

"What do you—"

He turned and zipped across the plaza, moving with jerky, spastic strides. He pushed through protesters and bystanders, drawing angry looks.

She turned in a complete circle, scanning the plaza. Why wasn't the surveillance team following him? She examined the rooftops, then the street. The agents were invisible. Ghosts.

Would they lose him? At least the meeting she'd dreaded had ended. The blackmailer bolted down the steps at the far end of the plaza and disappeared behind City Hall. He'd alluded to his co-conspirators. Would the agents identify them too? How deep did the tentacles of corruption reach inside the Democratic and Republican Parties? Was their leadership compromised?

She peered back at the bench hoping Nathan could help. He was gone.

60

Nathan strode down North Royal Street between the registrar's office and City Hall. He'd lost sight of the suspect, but if he'd sprinted across the plaza, he'd have flagged himself to even the most incompetent countersurveillance agent. He shuffled his legs but kept his upper body still to lessen his appearance of speed—an old surveillance trick.

The FBI's Special Surveillance Group had been in place before Reagan had agreed to the meeting. The blackmailers had tried to move the meeting to a remote venue, but Reagan had refused, saying she'd only meet in a public place.

Nathan reached the end of City Hall and rounded the corner onto Cameron Street. Four blocks away, the Potomac shimmered in the crisp air. At the other end of the building, the man who'd been arguing with Reagan crossed the street.

The blackmailer.

A man sat in a car parked at the intersection. The suspect glanced at him and then headed north and out of sight. The blackmailer must have flagged the car as surveillance. He'd be wary, especially after fleeing with the disk. If Nathan followed behind him, he'd get burned too.

Nathan jogged across the street and paralleled the suspect, one block to the west. His fingers tingled with fear. He increased his pace to reach the next intersection first, because if the suspect backtracked, broke into a run, or entered a building, Nathan would lose him.

Historic townhouses lined the street. Nathan reached Queen Street and peeked around the robin's-egg clapboard of a three-story residence. The sidewalk was vacant. He scanned the street.

Nothing.

Had he made a mistake? Had the suspect changed direction? Nathan's breath came faster. Panic fluttered in his chest.

The suspect popped into view.

Nathan breathed again.

The man turned onto Queen Street and hustled toward the water. No FBI watchers were visible, which either meant they executed a perfect surveillance or a terrible one.

Nathan crossed Queen and followed from the other side. Worried suspects checked their six, so Nathan stayed half a block behind.

"Where are you guys?" Nathan muttered.

The crook passed brick houses with the tatters of Halloween decorations clinging to stoops and windows until Queen Street dead-ended at Founders Park. Nathan allowed him to pull farther ahead, then he kept pace.

The man paused at North Union Street and looked behind him. Nathan resisted the urge to stop or hide as the man's eyes took in the street. Walking down the street wasn't unusual, unless Nathan exhibited strange behavior. But being a single man on the street would make the blackmailer consider him.

The blackmailer barreled across into Founders Park where a cool wind blew off the icy water, a harbinger of the coming winter. He followed the curving walkway, then turned at the marina and headed south along the water.

Nathan fast-walked across the Union and dove into the park after him. The man wouldn't see him run, but if others watched, they'd mark him. A flock of black-and-white geese floated on the river and honked as Nathan passed them. He turned at the boathouse where a handful of motorboats and sailboats bobbed at the pier.

No sign of the blackmailer.

The sidewalk forked with one path cutting beside a parking garage between two restaurants. Could he have parked there, or had he followed the other path along the water? The garage made sense, and Nathan needed to see the license plate. Nathan jogged to the structure and peered inside the small parking area.

The man was gone.

"Shit."

Nathan continued to Old Town's harbor, where sightseeing boats were lashed to the dock. Tourists huddled around the visitor information booth and rested on benches beside docked pleasure craft. Global warming hadn't hurt that industry. Nathan hesitated at the dock. If the blackmailer had followed the water, he'd be coming out—

The man came into view.

Nathan held his breath as the man traipsed past, his feet thumping on the wooden slats. He'd seen Nathan once, so he couldn't spot him again. Nathan needed to change his appearance. He shrugged off the tattered overcoat and took off his floppy felt hat. He scrunched them together and folded them into a tight bundle, then dropped them beside the restaurant's stairs. Someone might steal them, but that wasn't his concern. He had to keep eyes on his suspect.

Where the hell were the SSG?

The man crossed the dock to the Torpedo Factory Art Center, an old repurposed munitions plant. He paused at the entrance and glanced around. Nathan leaned behind two heavyset tourists carrying shopping bags. Nathan waited a beat, then stepped around the people as his suspect swung open the building's door and disappeared inside.

Nathan headed for the Torpedo Factory, but not directly for the entrance, because the sun reflected off the door's windowpanes and hid the interior from view. If the man had stopped and looked out, he'd see Nathan pursuing him.

Nathan reached the building and followed the wall to the entrance. It had been thirty seconds since the suspect had entered. He'd be nervous, struggling with his fight-or-flight response and wondering if he'd been followed. Half a minute would feel like an eternity.

Nathan opened the door and stepped inside. His eyes adjusted to the darkness as the man turned into the main hallway that ran the length of the building. He must've paused at the door to watch, but not long enough. The criminal conspiracy had displayed levels of technical sophistication, but this guy's countersurveillance technique seemed amateurish.

Nathan glanced out the door's windows. Nobody followed. The SSG was nowhere to be seen.

Dozens of artists' studios occupied the Torpedo Factory's two floors, offering the blackmailer hundreds of places to hide, or he could escape through exits on either side of the block-long building. Nathan needed to close the gap, so he picked up his pace as he entered the atrium.

The suspect navigated through twenty people who browsed art. Nathan started down the hallway, then stopped.

The suspect headed toward an exit door.

Nathan backtracked into the atrium as the man pushed through a heavy door onto North Union Street. Nathan raced to the main exit and climbed downstairs to the sidewalk. If his target headed toward him, Nathan would slip back into the building. He glanced down the sidewalk.

The man headed away from him, toward Founders Park.

A heavyset couple waddled past pushing a baby carriage. Nathan walked behind them, using their beef for cover.

The suspect entered Founders Park again. His behavior appeared to be a heat run where suspects move in circles to ferret out tails. Would this guy make another pass around the docks then double back?

Nathan's instinct said no. Meeting Reagan had been a massive mistake and not something a professional would risk. That, coupled with his crappy countersurveillance skills, exposed him as an amateur. But that didn't jibe with the expertise required to hack a delegate's devices. The conspiracy had to go deeper, but Nathan could resolve that contradiction later.

Instead of following the same path, the man headed north along the river. A smattering of people strolled through the park. A man played fetch with his shepherd. A woman stared vacantly at the water. He trudged past sharp rocks, waterlogged timber, and flotsam. Nathan crossed the grass and paralleled him from the street. He stayed fifty yards behind, pushing the boundary between going unnoticed and losing him, but unless the man had a boat waiting, he'd need to return to the street.

A memory flooded back to him of the water under the Woodrow Wilson Bridge and the sputtering of a motorboat disappearing into the distance as the Islamic assassin who'd murdered his CI escaped. He scanned the coast, but no boats moored in the river.

The man continued north among industrial buildings to Orinoco Bay Park. Nathan hung back because they were the only two people on the street. The suspect disappeared into the next park, and Nathan jogged after him.

Where was he headed? Rivergate City Park lay north of Oronoco, one of many public parks along the Potomac. Daingerfield Island came after that, and the blackmailer could easily disappear into its wooded wilderness. Beyond it lay another marina, then Washington Reagan National Airport.

The suspect glanced over his shoulder but didn't check Nathan's side of the street. Nathan's confidence soared, but how long could he continue a one-man surveillance?

No sign of the SSG, and no vehicles trolling the streets. That team was good, but not this good.

Nathan dialed Waldo.

Waldo answered. "Hey, partner—"

"I'm following the blackmailer who met Reagan."

"You're what?"

"Something happened," Nathan said. "The surveillance team let him walk."

"You're not authorized to be there."

"Good thing I was."

"If you burn this surveillance for them—"

"I came to protect Reagan, and because I didn't trust the team's competence."

"Because you're a control freak."

"I was right to worry," Nathan said. "We're headed through Oronoco Bay Park. He's executed a couple of heat runs, but I don't think he spotted me."

"This isn't your case. You'll be in serious trouble if—"

"I don't give a shit. Get on the horn with Davis and vector the surveillance team to me."

The suspect veered off the path to the Dee Campbell Rowing Center. He stopped and scanned the park. Nathan stayed on the road and paused behind a parked car.

Nathan waited for a beat, then peeked around the rear window.

The man was gone. Had he entered Rivergate City Park?

Nathan jogged down the street and entered the park. He slowed and surveyed the area from the shore to the parking lot. A few people wandered around chatting, but the suspect wasn't among them.

Uh-oh.

Nathan looked back toward Oronoco Park. The blackmailer wasn't there either.

The suspect couldn't vanish. Where—

His eyes landed on the boathouse. "Not again."

Nathan broke into a run.

61

———

Nathan raced toward the rowing center with self-doubt and aggression battling for control. The building sat on a tiny piece of land that jetted into Oronoco Bay. The blue A-frame structure housed rowing sculls and other boating equipment and provided a club for spectators to watch events. Where else could the blackmailer have gone?

Nathan's phone vibrated in his pocket, and he answered.

"Davis isn't answering," Waldo said.

"I lost the eye. I'm trying to reacquire him."

"I can't reach anyone on scene. Want me to call Reagan?"

"She won't know what they're doing. She's their protectee, not part of the surveillance."

"They'll debrief her after the meeting."

"She'll be taking a prearranged route they're covering to make sure she wasn't followed. I'm sure they haven't scooped her up."

"I could call—"

"This guy will be in the wind if I don't find him," Nathan said. "Why'd they let him walk?"

"They must've had a reason, *hermano*. I'd break off before you burn their case."

"I'm not letting him go."

Nathan hung up. He couldn't lose another suspect, not after the last one escaped, and certainly not an asshole who endangered his family. Well, his ex-family. How could he have let an amateur slip away? What was he doing there? Waldo was right, this wasn't his fight. Not officially.

But the blackmailer violated the integrity of the election and threatened Reagan. Taxpayers expected the FBI to catch crooks. Nathan stepped onto the rowing center's property.

Nathan visually examined the building. Empty boat trailers had been left beside the driveway, and towering shrubs lined the opposite side. Closed wooden doors protected the cargo hold where the boats were stored. A staircase rose to the second-floor entrance to a main room with windows overlooking the Potomac. Rowers would use three ramps to launch their sculls.

Nathan approached the building, and flashes of water peeked through the shrubs. The center appeared closed. Did people row in November?

He stopped and listened. Lapping waves rhythmically tickled the shore. Geese honked overhead on their way south. Why would the blackmailer flee there, and if the building was closed, where had he gone?

Doubt seeped into Nathan's bones. If he lost the guy, he'd hate himself, but if he burned the surveillance, he'd be screwed.

He grasped the wooden door's handle and tugged. Locked. The second-floor door appeared secure too, and the lights were off inside. Nathan scanned the park. No sign of his suspect. He sighed. Had the guy doubled back? Nathan edged around the building to view the park to the south.

The blackmailer stood five feet away.

Nathan jolted, unable to contain his surprise. The crook pressed against the wall and gawked at Nathan. The ruse was over. He knew Nathan had followed him.

Nathan brushed back his jacket and drew his Glock. "Thought I lost you."

The man's eyes widened. "I didn't do anything."

Every perp said that when Nathan had worked the streets. Nathan eyed his empty hands, then scanned his clothing. No bulges indicating a concealed weapon.

"Nathan Burke, FBI."

The man's eyes darted to the park behind Nathan. He contemplated running.

Nathan aimed at his chest. "Get on the ground. Do it now."

Nathan's heart raced. Was he doing the right thing? This wasn't his case, and he had no right to be involved—except his duty to his ex-wife and the morality he held above the law.

The blackmailer's eyes flickered from the park to Nathan's gun. Wheels turned in his head. He wore the conflict like a mask. This was the moment he'd either flee, fight, or submit. Nathan's muscles tingled with anticipation. If he went for the Glock, Nathan would shoot him.

What the hell am I doing?

Nathan took an athletic stance and aimed his barrel at the man's face. "I said, get down, asshole." Nathan deepened his tone to let the perp know he meant business.

The man's shoulders sagged as his body deflated. He raised his hands. Nathan kept his gun trained on him and stayed ready. The perp's body language projected surrender, but skilled fighters knew how to deceive. Feinting one move and then attacking with another could be the difference between life and death.

"Down."

"Okay, okay." The man knelt on one knee and then the other.

"On your stomach."

He complied.

"Extend your arms, palms up. Spread your legs."

The guy did as ordered.

"Turn your head and look away from me."

The man stared at the building's siding. "I didn't do anything."

"Don't move, or I'll shoot you."

Nathan stood near his head and pointed the Glock at him. With his other hand he dialed 911.

"Alexandria Police, what's your emergency?"

"Nathan Burke, FBI. I have a suspect at gunpoint at the Dee Campbell Rowing Center. I need a unit to assist. And call the FBI and have Agent Davis respond."

Nathan answered her follow-up questions, then hung up. He split his attention between the man and his surrounding area. If the guy had come to the boathouse to meet someone, Nathan didn't want to be surprised. The shrubs hid them from view, so no civilians noticed. That would change when backup arrived.

"What's your name?"

"Andre."

"Andre what?"

"I just talked to her."

"I asked for your name."

"Anderson."

"You have the right to remain silent. Anything you say can and will be used against you. You have the right . . ." Nathan recited the Miranda card from memory. "Are you willing to answer questions without an attorney present?"

"What's happening?"

"I can't explain unless you consent to talk to me."

"Fine."

Good enough. The guy probably wouldn't reveal much anyhow, but Nathan wouldn't have another chance to interrogate him. Davis would be pissed, especially if Anderson lawyered up.

"Who do you work for?"

"I was talking to the woman about the protest."

"I didn't mention any woman."

"I don't know anything."

"What were you doing at City Hall?"

The guy's agreeing to meet made little sense. He'd already shown Reagan the pictures, so she knew they had them, and they'd done it anonymously, so why risk the face-to-face? Sam thought they were desperate for Reagan to switch her vote, and Davis thought his ruse was brilliant. Neither theory made sense.

"I told them it was a mistake to come."

Nathan perked up. The guy didn't sound like a hardened criminal, and his defenses seemed penetrable. He might give up something of value—if Nathan handled him properly.

"You told who?"

He didn't respond.

"Who are you working for?"

"The ground's cold. Can I sit up?"

"Soon."

"It hurts."

"The people who sent you knew you'd get caught." Nathan floated an interrogator's trick, a foray by fire to see what would shake loose.

"It's not illegal to talk to someone."

"I know what you did, so let's cut the shit. Why would you agree to meet her after all your effort to conceal your digital trail?"

"I couldn't say no."

"To who?"

"I have to do whatever they ask."

"You mean—"

"They've got shit on me too."

That would be a potential defense at trial. If he'd been coerced, it could reduce his culpability, depending on the facts. An uncomfortable feeling spread through Nathan as his excitement diffused into shades of gray.

"Unless you want to take the fall for everything, you better tell me who's pulling your strings."

"The enterprise runs everything."

"Who are they?"

"The Deep State . . . oligarchs, the cabal of people in control. I don't know."

That probably wasn't entirely true, but if Anderson didn't know his conspirators, he'd go to prison alone.

Sirens wailed to the west. The police would arrive soon. So would Davis, and when that happened, Nathan would be on the outside of the investigation again. If he wanted information, he had to get it now.

"What do they want?"

"Come on, man. They want Lemon elected. Isn't that obvious?"

"Meeting Reagan risked their operation. Why send you? Was coercing her vote that important?"

He snorted. "The opposite."

"What's the—"

"They're blackmailing so many people, they don't care if they lose one . . . or if I get arrested. They're pressuring everyone. They're into everything. They're everywhere."

"They're not here. You are. They left you holding the bag."

Anderson didn't speak.

"If they swing the election to Lemon, what about the legal repercussions later when this comes out?"

"They're not worried about that, man. They don't care."

The sirens grew louder and a police car raced down the street.

Did the blackmailers have political or legal cover? Were they affiliated with the current Republican administration?

"Why Lemon?"

"I don't know anything about that, man. They paid me to do a job."

Nathan glowered at the back of Anderson's head. He seemed so glib about his role in undermining democracy. "If you don't cut a deal, you're looking at twenty years in a federal penitentiary."

"I didn't kill anyone."

"You broke a dozen federal laws and interfered with an election. They'll bury you in prison if you don't cooperate and help us catch them."

"They'll kill me."

"We'll protect you."

"I . . . I don't know what to do."

An Alexandria police car rumbled over the sidewalk toward them.

"We don't have much time. Once they know you were arrested, you won't be of much use to us. Tell me who paid you."

"Fuck. An old guy," Anderson mumbled.

"Who?"

"Never knew his name. He paid me twenty grand to hack Cabrera's computer and phone."

"Why?"

"You know, to look for stuff . . . private stuff."

"For what purpose?"

"To make them do things. Give me information or whatever else the old guy wanted."

Them. Nathan chilled. "How many times have you done this?"

Anderson's body tightened into a vise.

"Tell me," Nathan said.

"I don't know . . . twenty."

Nathan flinched. "You've blackmailed twenty people?"

"At least."

"And what did you force them to do?"

"All kinds of things, but lately, it's all about the election."

62

An autumn wind blew hard out of the northeast and lifted tiny waves on the normally placid surface of Kunming Lake in Beijing. Zhao hunkered inside the cabin of a thirty-foot junk sealed off by soundproof windows. He'd had the sea craft reproduced from an illustration of a two-thousand-year-old Han Dynasty boat that had captivated him as a child. When he'd risen to power, he used his substantial black budget to finance the project and have it docked behind the Second Bureau. The vessel required twenty-four-hour security and demanded maintenance, but Zhao justified the expense by entertaining government dignitaries on it. He'd named the ship *Tianma* after the mythological steed that flew through the heavens—another connection to China's past glory.

Colonel Luo briefed him as she balanced an electronic pad on her lap that contained her notes. Jíng Qí waited in the stern, watching for Zhao to wave her inside. If the cold breeze bothered her thin body, she gave no indication.

"The FBI has been far too aggressive," Zhao said. "Our moles did not predict the FBI would uncover our bribery scheme or our involvement in the assassination."

"Our analysts based their analysis on the FBI's previous reactions."

"Do not make excuses for them. They were wrong." Irritation made him uncomfortable in his own skin.

"I reread the latest intelligence reports," she said, then stayed silent.

"You may speak. Give me your assessment."

"Our sources' predictions and estimates were unanimously wrong."

"That doesn't help me."

"They failed to anticipate a stronger reaction, because they did not incorporate the mindset of the individual agents involved."

"That is a methodological error . . . and one they should have accounted for."

"True, but the agent who interfered with our plot to discredit our defector in Washington was not assigned to the case. He acted on his own. He's the same man who arrested one of our blackmailers and had clandestine meetings with a traitor."

"Who is this man causing us such problems?"

"Agent Nathan Burke."

Zhao stood. Fury swirled inside him. "The special agent who connected us to the Havana Syndrome?"

"The same."

"How did he find this turncoat?"

"Unknown, but according to our mole in FBI Headquarters, this traitor told Agent Burke about our plans to affect the election and summarized our disintegration warfare strategy for him."

"Who is that treasonous serpent?"

"Unknown, but they met in Macao at least once."

The news of yet another apostate to the realm twisted his stomach. How could his people betray all under heaven? He would identify the shrew that had burrowed into his house and eradicate it.

"We must seal the leak and stop this subversive snake from talking to this Agent Burke," he said.

"How?"

"Contact the Leopard."

"He is in hiding."

"Use our special intermediary."

"What are your orders?"

"Tell him to send the traitor into the void. It's time for the Leopard to eat."

63

Darkness fell over the Huangpu District in downtown Shanghai, casting shadows like a protective veil, but the watchful eyes of the CCP's security service were everywhere. Nathan and Waldo strolled through the People's Park across from the Shanghai People's Government building in People's Square. The naming committee had hit the communist theme on the nose. Cultural and government buildings dotted the neighborhood, and to the east, skyscrapers with neon lights lined the Bund along the banks of the Huangpu River.

The weather hovered in the fifties, which justified more clothing to conceal them. Nathan and Waldo wore local attire they'd purchased with cash from a bazaar. They'd carried the apparel in Waldo's knapsack, then changed under an overpass and donned N-95 respiratory masks and caps to conceal their faces. By tomorrow, Chinese security would analyze video from every security camera in the city.

That happened after a bombing.

They exited the park and rounded the government center. The building's massive structure looked like a gladiator helmet made of stone, and its brutalist architecture screamed dictatorship—the kind of place Darth Vader would call home.

"*Este tarado*," Waldo said.

"What does—"

"Crazy."

"We need to send a message," Nathan said.

"And die in a ChiCom labor camp?"

"It's your optimistic outlook that makes me happy we're partners."

"Fucking *loco*."

They circled the perimeter of the bureaucratic fortress that contained the governmental nerve center for Shanghai. The Administrative Agency was housed there, a political body with twenty-seven departments covering everything from Ethnic Affairs to the Public Security Bureau—the city's despotic brain.

The scar tissue in Nathan's shoulder burned, and he adjusted the straps on his backpack. The nylon dug into his skin as the pack's heavy contents bounced with each stride. The improvised explosive device inside weighed twenty-two pounds.

"This is two blocks from where we met Yakuf," Waldo said.

"I know."

Waldo's face brightened. "Ah, *comprendo*. You want to connect it to Yakuf."

"Yep."

Waldo's brow furrowed. "But the cops didn't know he came here."

"The Second Bureau observed his meet with Kei. They'll wonder what they discussed, then they'll connect it to the bombing."

"But how does intelligence know about the meeting?"

"I told them."

"How—"

"Emerald."

Nathan stopped on the south side of the building and looked over Waldo's shoulder. Two guards wearing green uniforms with red epaulets and braided dress caps stood at attention on pedestals beside the entrance.

"Not here," Nathan said.

"How about not anywhere?"

"We'll emplace it on the east side."

"What's in that thing?" Waldo asked.

"I packed the pipe with match heads and—"

"You built it?"

"China offers cheap labor, but the government frowns on foreigners detonating bombs here. It's a DIY project."

"But match heads?"

"Yeah, well, I don't have TNT or C-4," Nathan said. "I had to improvise. I could have used ammonium nitrate and fuel oil, but acquiring those here would have set off alarm bells, and I didn't want to use Emerald. The less he knows, the better."

Waldo stared at the device. "Who taught you how to do this?"

"You'd be surprised what's online, but I studied IEDs in the AF-Pak group. Terrorists don't need firearms to kill people."

"You brought that in your luggage?"

"I bought matches at the bazaar and packed them inside the PVC with marbles. I needed to include projectiles, or they'd figure out it wasn't serious."

"*Mucho* dangerous, *hermano*."

"Black ops are risky."

"How do you initiate the explosion?"

"A small PVC pipe contains the battery, and two wires run into the pipe containing the match heads. I spliced the wire and attached it to the timer's clock hands. When the hands meet at 12:00, they complete the circuit and the battery ignites the matches."

"Enough to make an explosion?"

"The end caps seal the PVC pipe, so the combustion has nowhere to vent. It'll make a big bang. I added a bladder of gasoline to amplify it and create a fireball."

Waldo shook his head. "If anybody gets killed . . ."

"We won't hurt anyone. We'll detonate it when the area's clear. C'mon, let's make this quick."

Waldo grumbled something as they headed around the corner. Vehicles motored down the thoroughfare behind them, and a smattering of people mingled around an exhibition hall to the east, but their target was unoccupied after business hours.

Surveillance cameras mounted on the third story focused on a side entrance. Nathan stayed out of its view, then surveyed the street.

All clear.

He lowered his head to hide his face from the camera and strode off the sidewalk toward the building. He knelt in the umbra of a towering hedge and shrugged off his backpack.

"This is a bad fucking idea," Waldo said.

"Everything rides on this," Nathan said. He unzipped his pack and used the backs of his hands to push the nylon fabric away from the device.

"We're breaking about a hundred laws."

"We've got to force the Chinese to stop producing opioids."

"*We* don't."

"Someone does."

"The Chinese will hang us as spies," Waldo said.

"They won't do that."

"Really?"

"They'll use a firing squad," Nathan said.

"Not funny, *Papi*."

"Keep a lookout."

Nathan lifted out the PVC pipes, then removed the gasoline bladder and set them on the ground beside the shrub. He placed the device on the bladder and aimed it at the wall. He leaned a saline bag against the device.

"What's that for?" Waldo asked.

"To direct the blast into the stone. I don't want it spraying the street."

"Won't that look sketchy?"

"They'll assume we're incompetent or we rushed the emplacement."

Nathan balanced the timer on top. He depressed the plunger and the metal minute hand started moving. They had two minutes.

"Time to go," Nathan said.

Waldo turned on a dime and headed for the street. Nathan followed, moving with purpose but not fast enough to draw attention. He caught Waldo, and they headed east.

They reached an exhibition center and blended into the crowd, but they didn't slow. The IED would shatter the evening calm in a minute, and once that happened, the police would lock down the city.

Foreigners on the street would be prime suspects.

Nathan stopped at the corner and stepped onto the street. He raised his hand, and a taxi with an illuminated sign pulled to the curb. The frequency of available cabs was another reason Nathan had picked a downtown target. If he had—

Boom.

The pipe bomb exploded and the gasoline bladder sent a fireball high into the sky. The sound echoed off buildings. People screamed. Nathan slipped into the taxi behind Waldo and gave the driver a hotel name across town. It wasn't theirs, but it was close enough.

A police siren wailed in the distance as their taxi turned onto a side street and headed away from the mayhem.

64

Reagan leaned against Vince on their couch and finished her third glass of wine. He'd barely spoken to her since she'd told him about the blackmail plot. The photos had upset him, which was why she hadn't wanted to show him, but he'd insisted, and now he pouted like a teenager.

The photos.

She unlocked her new smartphone and her fingers brushed the black tape that covered the camera. She'd replaced all her devices, opened new accounts, and changed every password, but her stomach still flipped whenever she opened her email. She'd been on tenterhooks since the blackmail. She scanned her messages, and nothing nefarious jumped out. She sighed and relaxed.

The photos of her hadn't been released.

Vince glowered at her, or did she misread his mood? Maybe if he talked more, she wouldn't need to guess. Why did men hold their feelings inside?

"What are you thinking?" she asked.

"You know what's bothering me."

"I can't change the past."

"I'm surprised they haven't posted your photos."

That question plagued her too. The FBI had arrested the hacker, thanks to Nathan, so whoever had sent him to dig up dirt on her must know she'd double-crossed them, so why hadn't they followed through on their threat? The guillotine hung over her neck, and the terror of waiting for it to drop might be worse than the act itself.

"At least we know why they agreed to meet me. They used a minion to insulate themselves in case it was a trap."

"But that doesn't explain why they haven't punished you for notifying the feds."

She upended her glass and let the last bit of cabernet drip into her mouth. "Nathan thinks they haven't released the photos because public attention would draw a bigger police response. I proved I wouldn't be coerced, so they'd only shine light on their broader campaign to—"

"I'm sick of hearing Nathan's opinion."

"If he hadn't been there, the hacker would have escaped."

"And if you hadn't posed nude, you wouldn't have been blackmailed."

Now, it was her turn to glare. She'd made a mistake. A drunken, youthful indiscretion, that she couldn't undo. She'd be upset too if the roles were reversed, but how long would he torture her?

"I screwed up, and I'm sorry to put you through this, but I'm the victim here. You can't keep beating me up about it."

He snorted. "I'm not thrilled my colleagues saw my wife doing porn."

That verbal arrow plunged into her chest. She'd hurt him, and understandably so. "Sorry this is uncomfortable for you."

"Give me time to wrap my head around it, and let's stop talking about it."

Another male tactic, but if he wanted to brood in silence, she'd let him.

They sat quietly, both immersed in their own thoughts, then Vince got up and went into the kitchen. Even before the incident, her hectic schedule as a delegate had made things tense between them, and so had Vince's lengthy travel. Their honeymoon period had ended, and they needed to adapt to marital life with two demanding careers—assuming her political aspirations survived the blackmail attempt and her resistance to the DNC.

Vince sauntered back into the living room with the bottle of wine and refilled her glass. He smiled at her, and she warmed. Did she seek his approval or a reprieve from her guilt for putting him through this ordeal?

The incident kept returning to her thoughts, like waves pounding the shore. If Nathan was right, and the blackmailers hadn't released the pictures because they wanted to stay under the radar, that meant they were doing other things. Bad things.

"Not to bring this up again," Reagan said, "but I was targeted to change my vote. The guy Nathan caught claimed he'd hacked dozens of computers, so there's a coordinated attempt to alter the election."

Vince sighed. "The FBI's running down the information he provided. If other delegates were compromised, they'll uncover it, and if any of them succumbed to the blackmail, we're in for a political scandal like this country hasn't seen before."

"I'm confident they'll identify whoever that sleazeball targeted, but not who employed him. How big is this election interference operation?"

"Republicans are complaining over social media about lack of voter ID, out-of-date voter rolls, and illegals voting."

"Nothing new there," Reagan said.

"I'm old enough to remember Democrats crying about foreign interference and a stolen election. Challenging election results has become an American pastime, but honestly, we've seen a dramatic shift in election rules. Whatever happened to voting on election day? Now, we have months of voting in some states and in others, anyone can vote absentee."

"It's about accessibility and avoiding voter suppression. There's no evidence of widespread fraud."

"More people vote in every election, which doesn't indicate voter suppression, and it's almost impossible to prove ballots are fraudulent when they're dropped into unattended ballot boxes. When security measures are removed, we can assume fraud happens."

"But not enough to swing an election," Reagan said. "The conservative in you is coming out."

"The amount of fraud may not be enormous, but it only takes a few thousand votes to turn an election."

"We have over three hundred million people, and half of them must vote."

"The math changes with the electoral college. Most states are red or blue, and the losing voters don't matter, because the popular vote is meaningless—"

"I wouldn't say that. It shows a president has a mandate."

"But only the swing states matter in a general election," he said, "and their cities are blue and rural areas red. Swing states can flip based on a handful of purple counties. Ten thousand votes can push a state into the other column and win an election."

Reagan took another sip. "I've been focused on my personal situation and worried about influence on other delegates, but now I'm wondering how widespread this election fraud goes . . . and who's behind it."

65

Zhao roared into the Tactical Operations Center in the basement of the Second Bureau, and Colonel Luo snapped to attention. She'd sounded nervous when she'd called him into their secure information facility to view a top-secret message they'd decoded.

"Report."

"General, we've received intelligence traffic from the Sky Fox."

"Give it," Zhao said, extending his palm.

She handed him a sealed envelope containing the message, and he glared at her. His temper had been growing like a beast inside him. The failures of his operation had fed the monsters, and he marshaled his willpower to maintain control. He ripped open the envelope and dropped his eyes to the report.

The Sky Fox had access to the most sensitive intelligence inside the US Department of Justice, but this most recent report detailed an internal poll from the Democratic National Committee. He skimmed the data. Despite what the DNC said publicly, they couldn't predict a win, because their poll showed the race too close to call. Their latest numbers had the Republican candidate up half a percentage point, well inside the margin of error.

The Democratic electors hadn't fallen into place as expected. They supported the appointed nominees, but not unanimously, and not without dissent, which had started behind closed doors, then moved into the public arena. That rebellion would never be tolerated in China, and if the Democratic National Committee wasn't willing to snap their people into line, then Zhao would need to intervene and do it for them. He couldn't rely on them to act with the severity necessary to achieve the desired results.

Everything rode on the upcoming election.

Jíng Qí entered the room, spotted him and hurried over.

"General, Donghai Sun has arrived."

Zhao's eyes flashed to the door. "Where?"

"He passed through security, and I directed him to the conference room to have tea while he waits."

Zhao's chest tightened. "He has no patience for waiting."

"I told him you were called to handle an urgent matter," Jíng said.

Good girl. "Well done, little flower."

Zhao handed the file folder to Luo and raced out with Jíng on his heels. She'd been with him longer than the rest, and though he'd begun to tire of her, she'd proved her usefulness once again. Perhaps he'd keep this one a little longer.

They took the elevator up to the floor below his office, and he rushed down the hall to the conference room where General Sun waited at the head of the table flanked by his latest aide, a major whose name eluded Zhao. He silently chastised himself. Remembering names and understanding the interpersonal dynamics of those within the circles of power were essential tactics to upward advancement. His understanding of his adversaries and alleged allies was critical to his survival. Yet the shifting parts of his strategy had taken too much of his time and attention.

Zhao forced a confident expression and tried to appear relaxed.

"You had an emergency?" Sun asked.

"In the Operations Center," Zhao said. "It's nothing that can't be handled. My apologies for not greeting you in person."

"I am less concerned about protocol than your plan backfiring and dragging us into direct conflict with the United States. It is too soon for that phase to occur."

"We are on track."

"Not from what I hear. You have a habit of wishing for profit but causing loss. Perhaps your ambition has outgrown your ability."

The room cooled.

"A few minor tactical setbacks," Zhao said, "but our strategy is sound, and we are on pace to achieve our goals—an outcome that will far exceed our expectations."

Sun's eyes narrowed. "Your chosen candidate will win the election?"

A direct question and one Zhao had to be careful answering. Making a black-and-white prediction could leave a deep and lasting wound if he proved wrong.

"Winning is a strong possibility, but either way, her influence will sway the party for years."

"If she loses, how will she exert political power?"

"No one will blame her. The unique circumstances of an assassination weeks before the election were unprecedented. She'll be lauded for stepping up to fight . . . even if she's not victorious."

"Your scheme to blackmail electors has faltered too," Sun said in a level tone scarier than a shriek.

Zhao had to tread cautiously. He shouldn't contradict him, because the blackmail strategy had brought unwanted attention. Damn the FBI again.

Zhao cleared his throat. "American law enforcement acted faster than our moles inside their organizations predicted." Had Sun noticed Zhao shifted blame onto his sources?

"They arrested your people."

"A minor setback. The contractor they apprehended had no direct link to us."

"The details are irrelevant," Sun said. "Focus on a single leaf and you miss the mountain. You utilized blackmail to solidify political support, and instead, your tactic brought scrutiny."

Zhao nodded. "It was not ideal, but the nomination proceeded."

"You are happy with the outcome?"

"I won't be satisfied until China reigns as the world's hegemonic power. That is what I bleed to achieve."

A glint flashed in Sun's eyes, and a wave of queasiness passed through Zhao.

"You understand the stakes?" Sun asked.

"More than anyone."

Why didn't they leave him alone to execute his strategy? Didn't they comprehend his plan and understand the need to strike now? Didn't they feel the hand of destiny?

Sun stood. "Then I will take my leave. I trust you will inform me of any news?"

"Of course." Zhao saluted.

Sun returned his salute and marched out with his aide in pursuit.

Zhao stared at Sun's empty chair. The Americans hadn't reacted as anticipated, and worse than outspoken resistance from electors, politicians, and pundits was the FBI's aggressive intervention.

Exasperation and fear blew through him like a storm across the South China Sea. They merged, cramping his stomach and sending pangs through his chest.

He rubbed his temples. Focus. Logic and strategy won wars, not emotions.

He reviewed scenarios in his mind, the players transforming into black-and-white stones on a Go board. He'd make his moles pay for that incompetence, but later, after he'd won. He needed to take pieces off the board. Seconds ticked away, and tactical variations grew in concentric circles with multiplying decision trees. Whoever could see farther in advance and predicted behavior better would emerge victorious.

"Do you have an order?" Jíng asked.

He hadn't known she'd followed him into the room. She'd witnessed him deep in thought, but did she recognize the window into his vulnerability? His cheeks reddened. He stared straight ahead.

"Send a message," he said.

"Yes, General. What are your instructions?"

"Tell Colonel Luo to execute Operation Rang." He smiled at the allusion to Yu Rang, the legendary assassin. "Tell her to punish those who stand in our way."

66

Nathan paced in Meili's office, too apoplectic to sit, and Reagan perched on the chair beside him looking uncomfortable. Meili watched him across her desk, sipping a green tea, appearing calm, but she leaned forward with drawn eyebrows, betraying her concern about the FBI operational failure.

"Reagan could have been killed," Nathan said. "Where the hell was the cover team?"

"They were called off."

"What?"

"A snafu. They claimed it was a miscommunication. An ASAC from HQ ordered them to maintain her security but not follow the suspect. He warned them not to burn it."

Nathan's face reddened. "The entire purpose of the meeting was to identify the suspect. Davis briefed the team and told them to follow the suspect away and have an Alexandria patrol car make a traffic stop to identify him."

"That's what Davis told me," Reagan said.

"Who was the ASAC who made the call to stand down?" Nathan asked.

"William Kremelberg, from public integrity."

"Why was he involved?" Nathan said.

"He's been in HQ for a decade, and he oversees corruption cases."

"You mean he covers for them."

"It was a bureaucratic fuckup," Meili said.

"I've assumed incompetence over conspiracy as my default position, but after the infiltration and subterfuge I've seen recently, I don't know . . ."

"You think someone at your headquarters undermined the surveillance?" Reagan asked.

A thought tingled the back of his head as it often did when pieces came together. "An ASAC intervened with tactical direction that contravened the point of the operation. It's a stretch to think it wasn't intentional."

Reagan's face slackened, and she blinked rapidly as the implications washed over her.

Meili leaned back. "You're alleging serious corruption. You think the blackmailers paid off Kremelberg to change the order?"

"It may be worse than that."

She sighed. "Explain."

"This might not be regular crime-related corruption where unethical agents seek monetary gain. Kremelberg may be part of an effort to undermine the election."

"You mean—"

"That ASAC could be a Chinese mole."

Reagan gasped.

Meili shrugged. "You're over your skis."

"Am I? We've heard directly from Chinese sources that their disintegration strategy involves infiltrating our institutions."

Meili glanced at Reagan. "I know we're all friends here, but Reagan isn't cleared for that intelligence."

"I've been targeted by them," Reagan said. "We're on the same side."

Meili smiled. "I know, but we need to safeguard our HUMINT. We can discuss this without revealing sources or specific intelligence."

"How would they even influence an election?" Reagan asked. "If the Chinese have compromised FBI Headquarters, where else are they?"

A twinge of pain flashed through Nathan's jaw. He'd been clenching his teeth again. He opened his mouth, and his joint cracked. "If they undermine the FBI, they'll destroy our ability to ferret out their infiltration. Kill the sheriff and outlaws run wild."

"You can't make accusations like that without proof," Meili said.

"Kremelberg's actions are documented," Nathan said. "Now we need to figure out what motivated him."

67

Reagan opened her front door for Nathan, and just seeing him made her feel safer. Being alone in the house while Vince traveled again took a psychological toll, and the support of a brave and moral special agent lightened her burden. She led him into her living room.

"Any news on your case?" Nathan asked.

"Every time I open a browser, I expect to see naked pictures of me, but nothing so far."

He flashed a sly grin. "That doesn't sound all bad."

She chuckled. Laughing at the situation helped, but if the lewd photographs dropped, her career would end. "Are you on the hot seat for nabbing the hacker?"

"Shockingly, no. Kremelberg was out of line shutting down the surveillance, so I saved the Bureau from a huge mistake."

"Do you think he worked with my blackmailer?"

"It's not a crazy assumption. He wasn't involved with your case, and he interjected himself at the last minute."

"Is he in trouble?"

"He claimed it was a misunderstanding, and he only wanted them to avoid getting burned, but the SSG team leader talked to me privately and said Kremelberg told them to stand down and not intervene."

"What will happen to him?"

"Nothing."

"But that's not fair—"

"He's a bad actor. I think he's either being manipulated, or he's a mole and a true believer."

"In what?"

"Money, or he's anti-American. Speaking out against the West is popular. Half of Congress hates American exceptionalism."

An uncomfortable fog of cognitive dissonance muddled her thinking, and she shifted in her seat. "Election interference is serious. How can the FBI allow him to keep his job? He almost let a blackmailer escape. If you hadn't been there . . ."

"No evidence. We can't prove the team leader didn't misunderstand the order. The conversation happened over the phone, and nobody else heard it. Even if the team leader had a recording, the ASAC could claim he made a mistake. The government rarely punishes employees for incompetence."

"Can't you expose him?"

"The team leader won't confront an ASAC directly. He knows nothing will happen, and then he'd have a powerful bureaucrat out to get him for—"

"Then there won't be any repercussions?"

Nathan grimaced. "I'm working on it."

Reagan got up and paced across the living room. "This whole thing . . ."

"How are you holding up?"

"Not great. I've had my privacy invaded in the most intimate way. DNC leadership is pissed at me, and my own party is headed off the rails. That, coupled with the assassination . . . I mean, this has been a crazy couple weeks."

"Politics is a shitty business," Nathan said. "It attracts narcissists and sociopaths."

"Someone accused me of taking a bribe. The Public Integrity Section's investigators checked my bank records and questioned the $30,000 payment from The Modern Democrat."

"It's a ridiculously high payment for a media appearance," Nathan said.

"Publishers and Hollywood pay politicians all the time. They give massive advances on books, and nobody blinks an eye, but suddenly, my payment is considered a bribe?"

"DOJ should take the allegation seriously," Nathan said. "It's normal for them to investigate big payments to elected officials. Anything over ten grand needs to be reported. It's clear to me that they targeted you for influence."

"You're assuming The Modern Democrat is involved in election tampering. They're a major player."

"Institutions have been corrupted," Nathan said.

"It doesn't make sense. It's not like I took a payment to change my vote. Both Gail and Ruoxi pressured me to support Lemon, and I refused. If Ruoxi paid me to get a political result, it didn't work."

"You'll be cleared, unless . . ."

Her belly cooled. "What?"

"The level of infiltration terrifies me. If they can turn an ASAC like Kremelberg, who knows how deep their infiltration goes?"

"You think I'm being targeted by someone inside DOJ as some kind of lawfare?"

"It's happened before."

Reagan scowled. "This keeps getting worse. I didn't even ask for the money. It appeared in my account. How did they even get my bank login information?"

"The tech guys checked your computer, right?"

"They checked all my devices . . . my printer, keyboards, everything. They didn't find malware, spyware, or viruses."

"Will you show me where you use it?"

That struck her as funny. "You saw me on my computer a million times when we were married. I'm not doing anything strange."

"Humor me."

"Not until you tell me what you hope to find—"

"My years in law enforcement taught me there's no substitute for walking the scene of a crime."

"But what are you looking for?"

"I won't know it until I find it."

She led him into the bedroom where she did most of her work. Having him in her private space felt intimate and familiar. They'd shared a bedroom for a lifetime.

"You don't work in an office?"

"I have a desktop in the spare room, but I spend ninety-nine percent of my time on the laptop in bed or at the kitchen table."

"Let's look at the kitchen next."

She rolled her eyes. "Whatever you say, Sherlock."

She sat on the comforter and rested against the backboard. "I'm not getting under the covers."

"Log into your bank account for me."

She opened her laptop and typed her password.

"Do you use a password aggregator?" he asked.

"Don't trust them."

"You've never given your password to anyone?"

"No."

"Never had someone from the bank call and ask for your password?"

"I'd never give that information over the phone."

"Did you write your password down anywhere? They could have broken in and found it."

Her eyebrows knitted together. "I don't write them down. It's a serious security violation at our embassies."

"Show me."

She opened her browser. "Account 364821—"

"You're saying your account number aloud."

She looked at him. "What?"

"You're mumbling, but you're saying the number as you type."

Her cheeks warmed. "I didn't realize. I've been alone a lot recently since Vince has been traveling, and I've gotten into the habit of talking to myself."

"Huh." He rubbed his chin.

"What?"

"Did the FBI search for bugs in your house?"

What was he suggesting? "They checked for signs that a hacker had gained control of my computer or accessed the camera on my phone."

"We know Anderson hacked you. He admitted it, but that doesn't mean they couldn't have been listening through your computer or even broke in here and planted a listening device."

She glanced around her bedroom. "You mean . . ."

"They could have been listening or watching."

Her skin crawled, and she hugged herself. "Could they have been watching me?"

"You need to have the tech guys sweep again. Crooks could have turned it off when the FBI swept your place."

"But either way . . ."

"You told them your passcode."

Her shoulders slumped, and the room darkened. She'd given them the passcode, because she talked to herself like a lunatic. Worse, her privacy had been invaded in a horrible way. Listening to her when she thought she was alone . . . Technology had eliminated her safe spaces. She hugged herself tighter.

"Why target me?"

"You're not just a delegate. This is a purple state, and it could become a swing state again, at least in this election."

"And I'm speaking out against the DNC."

"Exactly."

"If they're willing to target me for my minuscule influence, who else would they target? And how far would they go?"

"They're all in," Nathan said. "No one is safe."

68

Nathan sat on the metal floor of a Bell UH-1D helicopter with his legs dangling into the abyss. Waldo, Pai, and Naresuan 261's command staff surrounded him. The metal beast sliced through thick air, a few feet above the jungle canopy in northern Thailand. The seats had been removed to facilitate rapid disembarking, and the engine vibrated through the floor and into his teeth. The rotors thumped in his ears, and Nathan swallowed hard to clear them and restore equilibrium. This was Nathan's twentieth trip to Thailand, but the first time he'd flown in one of their helicopters.

Darkness shrouded hundreds of miles of wild jungle below as the flight of three helicopters headed for the border. Chiang Mai's urban congestion had thinned to a smattering of tiny cement homes with corrugated tin roofs, and then the countryside reverted to uninhabited jungle. The 140-million-year-old rainforest threatened to reclaim its reign over earth.

Waldo turned to him and said something, but the howling wind carried away his words. Nathan tapped the boom microphone in his helmet.

Waldo keyed his mic. "I said, we better not let this shit slip away. We lose one hundred kilos and we'll be more toasted than a Cubano."

"These guys are pros. The dope won't get away, but Yakuf's people might resist."

"Why fight?"

"Thailand will execute them for trafficking that quantity of opioids."

Somewhere on the road below, an undercover counterterrorism officer drove a load of carfentanil toward the borders with Laos and Myanmar. Kei had received the drugs from Quon, under the discreet surveillance of Naresuan 261, and now Kei would deliver the poison to Yakuf's TIP terrorists. Or at least that's what Yakuf anticipated.

Nathan would never let that happen.

The helicopter followed the Kok River, and in the distance, the muddy waters of the Mekong River serpentined through jungle and flowed through the boundary where Laos, Myanmar, and Thailand converged—an area known as the Golden Triangle. The Laotian city of Tonpheung lay across from Thailand's Chiang Saen City, and to the northwest, Myanmar's Wan Pong. The helicopter stayed low, hiding from anyone except those directly below.

Naresuan 261's Rescue Company's Raid Platoon had provided six five-man teams, and the Aerial Reinforcement Unit pilots from the 203rd Squadron transported them in Bell UH-1D helicopters. The aircraft, a modern version of the Huey, carried more passengers and sported better technology, like a turbo engine and double-bladed rear rotor. The other helicopters each carried two raid teams, while a fifth team set up a roadblock on the only road leading south into Thailand's interior. A sixth team had been dropped off on the border to act as a blocking force.

Yakuf had requested delivery near the Chiang Saen Port, which made sense, because beyond Laos and Myanmar lay China's Yunnan Province. The Mekong River was a likely route for him, so the counterterrorism team had also deployed a maritime unit with two patrol boats designed for shallow water. Yakuf would need to circumvent police from four countries to reach China.

He must have a plan.

Pai pressed his Peltor headset against his ear, listening to his internal radio channel, then he spoke into his boom mic and looked at Nathan. Nathan switched channels, and his radio crackled.

"The truck is approaching the last waypoint," Pai said.

"Is surveillance set?"

"They inserted last night."

Pai's commanders had briefed them in the early morning hours. The undercover truck would drive to the meeting location and deliver the shipment to Yakuf. The counterterrorism team had fitted the vehicle with audio and visual recording devices, and above, a Ky Scout U1 drone would provide overwatch. Once Yakuf accepted the drugs, four raid teams would arrest them. The plan seemed reasonable.

But no plan survived first contact.

The command staff around Nathan checked their gear, patting ammunition and adjusting straps. They would land with the assault force and provide direction. The crew chief held up five fingers.

Five minutes.

A familiar mixture of excitement and dread swirled inside Nathan. He'd executed dozens of missions from the mountains of Afghanistan to the streets of DC, but each operation brought risk and uncertainty. He focused, and a professional toughness armored him. He shut his eyes and mentally rehearsed possible scenarios and how he'd react. A calmness stilled him, and he opened his eyes. Whatever happened, he'd be ready.

The helicopter banked, and Nathan leaned away from the opening. He wore a safety line, but falling out of a helicopter wouldn't be a great start, and he needed to exhibit competence to this outfit. Whenever he worked with foreign cops, spies, or soldiers, he represented the United States, and their impressions of him mattered.

The other helicopters came into view, both flying fast and low. The birds turned, then flared above an opening in the jungle canopy. The Kok River flashed behind the trees. The sound of rotors on Nathan's aircraft deepened, and the frame vibrated as the nose lifted. The helicopter banked, and a grassy area appeared below them. They slowed to a hover, then descended. The ground rose fast, and the organic odor of the river and jungle filled the cabin.

Nathan unclipped his safety line, grasped the frame for support, and shimmied to the edge. The skids touched down with a jolt.

Nathan pushed off and dropped into waist-high grass. His light tactical boots thumped on the ground. He kept his head low, took five long strides away from the aircraft, and knelt. Nathan scanned the edges of the clearing as Waldo plopped onto the ground beside him.

Behind him the helicopter's engines growled as its rotors spun faster. The mechanical beast rose and filled the air with floating plant matter. Nathan buried his face into the crook of his arm and closed his eyes as the rotor wash buffeted him and debris pelted his skin.

Then it ended.

The helos cleared the trees and flew away. The chopping sounds faded into the distance, leaving the stillness of the jungle. The infiltration had taken under one minute, making the insertion almost undetectable.

Pai appeared beside Nathan. He'd moved without making a sound—all stealth and tactical awareness. "We must move now."

"How far?"

"Five kilometers."

Nathan stood and checked his gear. He only carried a notebook, camera, and evidence bags. No gun. And despite the knife in his pocket, he felt naked and vulnerable.

Waldo brushed himself off. "Why couldn't we drive in to make the arrest?"

"Lookouts. There's only one road into the meet location, and Yakuf's people will watch it. They'd see us miles away."

Naresuan 261 operators formed around them. They carried .45 Heckler & Koch USP handguns, Franci SPAS-12 combat shotguns, and Heckler & Koch UMP submachine guns. Alpha team took the lead, followed by Bravo and Charlie. Nathan and Waldo stayed close to Pai, his command staff, and their radio operator. Delta team brought up the rear, handling rear security.

They pushed north through thick underbrush, following the bank of the Kok River on their left. They'd landed close to the intersection of the Kok and Mekong Rivers. Narrow leaves of cranium lily, surrounded by willowing water croton, grew out of the sand. A bed of shed java plums littered the ground around jambolan plants. They used the thick vegetation for concealment.

The point man slashed through vines with a machete and the operators behind him trampled down plants. Waldo huffed and puffed and his heavy footfalls were the only sound.

"These *merimbero* are stone loco," Waldo whispered.

"*Merimbero?*"

"*Narcotraficantes*. How they gonna get this into China? Cops from three countries patrol the river, and Burma and Laos don't play with narcos either. Yakuf will have to pass customs somewhere."

"He'll bribe them."

"Jihadis have that influence?" Waldo asked.

"Drugs sales create deep pockets to corrupt officials."

The radio operator glanced at them and shook his head. They were still kilometers away from the meet location, but professionals stayed quiet. Compromising their column would have dire consequences.

The point man led them onto an animal trail, making their progress easier, but as one kilometer turned into five, Nathan heated from exertion. Hiking wasn't hard but stepping lightly, avoiding branches, and staying quiet took a toll. They plodded forward, keeping noise discipline.

The column stopped, and each officer raised a fist, like a militant wave. The radio operator handed a headset to the commander. He listened to a transmission, then whispered something over the tactical channel. Heads around them nodded, but Nathan and Waldo remained in the dark. As foreigners, they weren't given access to the encrypted tactical channel, and even if they could listen, neither spoke Thai.

Pai stepped close to Nathan. "The warehouse is up ahead."

"Does recon have eyes?"

"Three cars pulled into the lot."

"Anyone else there?"

"The warehouse is abandoned."

Delta team filed soundlessly past them and moved north into the jungle —specters floating through the woods.

"You'll wait for Yakuf to take possession, right?" Nathan asked.

"We're deploying now. Delta will form another blocking position, and three teams will execute the arrest when our undercover officers give the signal."

"And us?"

"We wait on the perimeter until they secure the target."

The assaulters slipped off the trail in teams of two. They spread out and formed a line as they moved forward. Nathan and Waldo followed Pai and the command staff. No one spoke as they closed on the warehouse.

Delivering one hundred kilograms of anything brought logistical hurdles, especially with an illegal product, but with an incredibly toxic substance like carfentanil, one mistake could mean death. If this controlled delivery had been in the US, Nathan would have replaced the carfentanil with a harmless sham substance and only included a small amount of the illicit drug. Thailand's Narcotics Act allowed for charging conspiracy, but catching criminals in possession of the drugs made prosecutions easier.

And Thailand crushed drug traffickers.

Pai cocked his head, listening to a transmission, then he looked at Nathan. "Our undercover truck has arrived. Move up."

Pai slipped around a stand of bamboo with Nathan and Waldo behind him. Pai crouched at the edge of a clearing.

Nathan knelt behind a teak tree and peered through the vegetation. Beyond a field of overgrown grass, a dilapidated warehouse stood at the end of a long driveway. The structure's rotting wood battled the elements to keep the corrugated roof from collapsing. Eight men stood around two Toyota Hilux trucks. They carried M16s and Uzis.

Islamic terrorists in Thailand.

Pai looked at Nathan. "Get ready."

Zhao stood erect on the tiled floor of the conference room in Qinzheng Hall in Zhongnanhai, Beijing. Five of the nine members of the Politburo's Standing Committee sat behind a long table and stared at him. General Sun occupied the center, having called Zhao to the meeting. Being summoned like this infuriated Zhao. He had much work to do at this critical time, and he wasn't a prisoner awaiting sentencing. At least not yet.

"And what of your latest technical infiltration?" Chén Weidong asked. He'd invested millions in China's technology sector and his pointed questions never hid his self-interest.

"Chinese companies supply the majority of drones used by American law enforcement agencies," Zhao said. "We've embedded them with spy software that we can access remotely at any time."

General Sun and two of the other members nodded, filling Zhao with pride. This had been one of his most successful tactics. The idea had seemed farfetched, but then, American police departments had willingly purchased Chinese-made drones. It seemed incomprehensible and too good to be true, almost like a trap, but no backlash had come.

"The American police have unwittingly provided us with real-time mapping and imagery of their cities. Their body cameras have allowed us to see inside Americans' homes, and by remotely accessing the footage, we have populated our facial recognition database."

Zhao forced himself not to smile or appear too proud. The simplicity and irony of having those tasked with American security undermine the safety of the citizens they represented had been as sweet as White Rabbit Candy.

"An intelligence coup," Wang Xi said. He wielded enormous political power, and while he mostly used his influence to surround himself with young boys and enrich his relatives, he had been known to lash out when threatened. Impressing him and earning an ally to counter General Sun's skepticism would help. Although staying on any of these men's radar had a downside.

"Beyond collection activities," Zhao said, "we can shut down the systems and take away police departments' aerial ability . . . when the time comes."

General Sun glared. "We have greater information needs than compiling photos of ordinary citizens." He didn't show any appreciation for Zhao's successes. Had Zhao's strategic gambles made Sun defensive, or worse, did he see Zhao as a political rival? "Our priority should be undermining the American military's effectiveness."

Zhao needed to avoid overt confrontation, or Sun would drop the sickle on him, but showing subservience or weakness would diminish Zhao's chances of rising to power in the future. Their perception of his strength could be as important as the actual power he wielded.

"Our surveillance balloons have flown over American military bases for years. We've mapped every building and documented every movement."

"That plan was initiated by your predecessor," Sun said. The man sought to compromise Zhao's authority. Zhao would need to deal with him sooner rather than later.

"That is why we executed Operation Fenghuang," Zhao said, referring to the program he'd named after the Chinese mythological phoenix. He kept his voice even so as not to appear defensive. He had good news to report, and the committee should celebrate his victories. "Our drone fleets have scoured every American base and collected intelligence from tail numbers to images of soldiers."

"Another overly antagonistic operation that landed on the front pages of American newspapers. I don't consider operations exposed to the public as triumphs."

"We tested their responses and determined the ease of attacking with drone swarms when we are ready."

"We have silently infiltrated the West for decades, but now you do so overtly. You pull the tail of the tiger."

"A paper tiger. Their tepid response proves that."

Sun's face hardened to stone. "The FBI has arrested your operatives and exposed your blackmailing operation. Do you consider that an achievement?"

Zhao kept his face placid, but the way Sun had phrased that cooled his core. Sun had subtly directed the focus onto Zhao personally. Clever man.

"Disintegration strategy contains a variety of tactics, and we acknowledged ramping up our activity would create conflict. The result was predictable."

"You predicted failure?" Sun asked.

"Our Bureau anticipated some level of exposure."

"More risk," Sun said.

"The benefits outweigh the danger, and blackmail was necessary to solidify support behind our candidate."

"You find this danger acceptable?"

It took all Zhao's strength to hide his fear. He steeled himself. "Our strategy will raise China to world dominance, many decades ahead of schedule. We will achieve hegemony."

Sun stared a hole through him. "We better."

70

The buzz of insects vibrated through the flora, and the white noise covered Naresuan 261's movements as they concealed themselves in the dense thicket surrounding the abandoned warehouse. Eight armed TIP terrorists milled around beside their Hilux pickup trucks in the driveway. Somewhere nearby, a gibbon whooped.

Nathan peered through the jungle where the Thai operators prepared to charge across the field, but none were visible. True professionals. The blocking team stayed behind the warehouse, using it for cover in case a gunfight broke out and Alpha, Bravo, and Charlie teams needed a clear line of fire. But the two undercover officers bringing the carfentanil would be in serious jeopardy. Luring a team of terrorists into an arrest operation took balls.

Pai touched his Peltor headset, listening to a radio transmission. Nathan leaned in to get an update as movement flashed on the road.

The undercover box truck, a white Isuzu, chugged down the dirt driveway with one hundred kilograms of carfentanil concealed in the enclosed cargo area. The vehicle stopped thirty yards from the warehouse.

The terrorists faced the truck, seemingly oblivious to other threats. They weren't trained soldiers.

The truck's cabin doors opened, and the undercovers disembarked.

Both wore polo shirts with linen slacks. If they were strapped, they didn't show it. Two against eight wasn't good odds, and if Nathan had been undercover, he'd be armed. In America, undercovers often carried backup handguns, like .38 revolvers that didn't flag them as agents. Did the Thai police think the same way?

The undercovers approached the buyers. The officers looked tense, and who could blame them?

Three bad guys headed toward them, while the other five spread out. The thug closest to Nathan scanned the jungle, but the rest focused on the truck. The buyers should be TIP members, since Yakuf wouldn't trust Thai traffickers to accept his delivery—or handle the money.

The undercovers met the three terrorists halfway between the trucks and warehouse. The lead guy looked like Yakuf, but the distance made identification difficult. He put his hand on his hip and waved a finger toward the Isuzu while he spoke—a gesture he'd done with Kei in Shanghai.

Yakuf had come in person to collect his drugs.

He spoke to the undercovers, but their words evaporated across fifty yards of field. The Naresuan radio operator huddled with Pai and their commander and listened to the direct feed from the transmitters worn by the undercovers.

The driver gestured back at his truck, his movements stiff with fear. The undercover knew that teams of armed operators surrounded them, but when they swooped in for the arrest, he'd be exposed. Did a flicker of doubt that the raid teams had arrived gnaw at him?

Yakuf nodded and followed both undercovers back to the truck. They stopped at the tailgate, and Yakuf moved aside as the driver unlocked a padlock and grasped the handle of the roll-up door. The man beside Yakuf raised his M16 rifle barrel slightly. Did they expect a bunch of cops to jump out?

The driver jerked open the door, and its roller wheels screeched. The other undercover passenger climbed onto the tailgate and disappeared inside. Yakuf glanced in Nathan's direction and surveyed the jungle. Nathan held his breath and froze. Yakuf's eyes passed over him.

The undercover came out carrying a box, and Yakuf turned back to him.

Nathan exhaled. The undercover scrambled off the tailgate and laid the box on the ground. He knelt beside it and dug a knife out of his pocket. The terrorist closest to him raised his Uzi. The undercover ignored him and sliced open the box. He removed bags of what looked like coffee and set them in the dirt, then he lifted a plastic-wrapped item that was unmistakable.

A kilogram.

Nathan glanced at the other five men carrying M16s near the warehouse. They'd spread out and crept closer to the truck, but they'd stopped, so their movement was probably driven by curiosity and not an intent to ambush the undercovers.

The ambush would come from Naresuan.

Yakuf gestured at one of his men, a frail man with jittery movements, and the man donned a mask and rubber gloves. He squatted beside the undercover and slit open the kilogram. He withdrew what looked like a narcotics identification test kit.

They had to be careful. A dot of carfentanil tiny enough to fit on the head of a pin could be deadly. An image of the border patrol agent lying in the sand last year popped into Nathan's mind—an unwelcome memory. Nathan shook it away.

The TIP chemist jabbed a scalpel into the package, then gently lifted it, balancing the blade. He opened the test kit and tapped the scalpel to drop a tiny sample of powder inside. He set the scalpel down, then sealed the kit. He squeezed it, breaking the vials, and agitated the package. Everyone watched while he waited for the chemical reaction.

The chemist looked up at Yakuf and said something. He grinned. Yakuf glanced back at his men waiting and waved them over.

Three of the men jogged over as the other two climbed into the Hilux trucks. They parked beside the box truck and flipped back tarps in the pickup beds.

Having Yakuf take possession of the load would create an ironclad legal case, but if Naresuan allowed the shipment to slip away, Nathan's career wouldn't survive it. Neither would Pai's. The risk was high, but Nathan needed TIP to engage in high-level narcotics trafficking to convince Chinese intelligence they had a problem. A future prosecution in the US wasn't likely, because Thailand would bury these terrorists in prison.

Yakuf removed a duffel bag from the truck and handed it to the undercover. That should be the down payment, as Kei had done with Quon. Deals of this size were rarely paid in full at the time of delivery. Yakuf stood beside the undercovers and watched his men unload the boxes of carfentanil. Two of his men kept their M16s out and monitored the offloading.

Nathan tingled with anticipation. Pai's commander should signal the arrest. Why was he waiting?

Something barked nearby, and Nathan looked up. A reddish-brown deer no bigger than a poodle traipsed through the jungle where Naresuan hid. It stamped its hoof in the underbrush and barked again. Beside it, a Bravo operator stood.

Shit.

Nathan looked back at the truck. The terrorists all stared in that direction.

"Compromise," Nathan said as loud as he dared.

Pai stared at him.

"Execute," Nathan said.

Pai leaned into his commander and said something to him.

Yakuf yelled something to the undercover driver.

The undercover stepped back—a tiny movement—but he projected weakness. And the foreknowledge of imminent action. The terrorists would know he'd betrayed them, and that anger could fuel violence, despite the hell it would bring down on them. Shooting an undercover was not a smart tactical move, but emotion often trumped reason.

Yakuf shouted at his men and they aimed their M16s and Uzis at the trees.

71

Time stilled.

The TIP terrorists scrutinized the jungle, staring over their sights into the thick brush. Compromised because of an impossibly small deer that had awoken from its slumber—a damn deer. The undercovers both froze. Nathan didn't breathe.

Then the world exploded.

Yakuf's men opened fire. Muzzles flashed and carbines thundered, and a volley of 5.56mm bullets cracked through the air as rounds pierced the jungle at three thousand feet per second. Lead smacked into wood, sliced vines, and shredded leaves.

"*Ying, ying, ying,*" Pai shouted over the barrage.

The jungle around Nathan erupted as officers returned fire with the distinctive pop of 9×19mm Parabellum rounds from the Heckler & Koch UMP submachine guns and USP handguns.

Nathan's pulse increased, but he'd been in enough gunfights to keep his wits. What a day to be unarmed. Nathan didn't carry a firearm, and he didn't have authority to give orders, so he should hunker down—but the urge to action overpowered his self-preservation.

He peeked around the tree. Four terrorists fired from behind Hilux pickups. Another lay in the dirt holding his leg. Blood soaked his pants.

Yakuf and two thugs stood beside the Isuzu. One fired his M16, but the other pointed his Uzi at the undercover officers. They raised their hands in surrender. He didn't shoot, probably unsure they'd betrayed him. Or he waited for an order from Yakuf, who peeked out from behind the Isuzu, using the engine for cover.

Muzzle flashes lit up the area and gunshots echoed through the jungle. Bullets spider-webbed truck windows and smacked against the metal frame. Rounds kicked up dirt across the field.

One of the Naresuan's SPAS-12 combat shotguns exploded and sent double-aught buckshot downrange. At the distance, the pellets wouldn't be effective, but they might suppress the enemy's fire. The bad guys behind the Hilux trucks continued to fire. They weren't trained professionals, and their fire discipline sucked. How much ammo did they have?

Hiding in the jungle shadows created a feeling of invulnerability, but it was illusionary. Rounds hissed through the canopy and snapped twigs off a tree beside him.

Naresuan bullets slammed into the Hilux truck's frames and punched through their windows. The first truck's tire punctured with a hiss and then leaned to the side.

A TIP terrorist screamed behind the other truck and stood up grasping his face. Blood gushed between his fingertips. He stumbled away from the vehicle, exposing himself. His shirt flapped as bullets pounded into his chest. He stumbled back and collapsed.

A Thai cop shouted something off to Nathan's right. He fell back, holding his hand high. Two bloody fingers dangled, attached only by ripped skin.

Nathan crawled through the underbrush to him. The officer looked up with wide eyes and facial muscles contracted in pain. Nathan knelt beside him and dug through the officer's medical kit attached to his utility belt. Nathan kept his head down as he applied a compress and bandage.

The firefight continued. In battle, everything slowed, and seconds felt like minutes. They'd only been in contact with the enemy for a short time, but life or death hinged on the trajectory of every bullet—and on chance.

Adrenaline made Nathan powerful.

Yakuf ducked behind the undercovers and used them as a shield. He grabbed the driver from behind and clutched him in a half-Nelson head-lock. Yakuf drew a revolver and placed it against the man's head.

"Yakuf's going to murder them," Nathan shouted at Pai. "Shoot him."

Pai continued moving down the line of men directing their fire. He hadn't heard Nathan's warning.

Yakuf fired, and the undercover's skull ripped open beneath a crimson plume. The dead undercover collapsed, and the second undercover bolted. Yakuf raised his handgun and aimed at his back.

Bullets kicked up earth at Yakuf's feet, and he darted for the box truck.

Nathan's pulse thumped in his temples. His role was to observe, but every fiber of him wanted to control the operation and lead these men. Terrorists tried to kill them, and he wouldn't stand by and let that happen—even without a gun.

Yakuf jumped into the Isuzu's driver's seat. The engine roared, and the truck lurched forward. It leaned hard to the right as Yakuf cut the wheel and spun around. He gunned it, and the truck accelerated down the dirt driveway. Yakuf drew some fire, but Naresuan focused on the three remaining terrorists still shooting.

Naresuan had blocking teams to the north and south and their heli-copters could track Yakuf, but they'd expected him to flee north to the river, not south, which increased the risk of escape. And now, Yakuf knew Emerald and Kei had betrayed him.

Nathan couldn't let him abscond with the deadly drugs. Even if Yakuf sold carfentanil to addicts instead of creating a chemical weapon, people would still die—and Nathan couldn't live with that.

Nathan lurched through the jungle, lifting his boot high to avoid trip-ping over a root. He ran parallel to the driveway, using the brush as cover. A chunk of bark kicked off the tree beside him as bullets buzzed through the vegetation. A terrorist had spotted him. Nathan lowered his head and plowed through the tangled growth.

The incoming fire ceased. Had that terrorist been eliminated, or had he switched back to the operators shooting at him?

Whatever had drawn his focus, this was Nathan's chance.

Nathan burst through a stand of bamboo and waist-high ferns and into the open field. Two terrorists remained firing from behind the Hilux, but the rest were dead or dying. Yakuf motored down the driveway. One of its dual tires had ruptured, and the deflated tire thumped against the ground with a melodic drumming. Pieces of rubber flopped off the rim as the truck's weight ripped it to shreds.

Nathan sprinted across the dirt, ignoring the shooters. He moved fast, but didn't beeline. No time. He angled to intercept the truck.

Thirty yards away.

The truck gained speed.

Nathan swung his arms and pumped his legs. He leaned forward and pushed off his toes.

Twenty yards.

Yakuf barreled down the driveway raising a cloud of dust. His heavy load slowed his acceleration, but it would be close.

Ten yards.

The vehicle shifted into second gear, gathering speed. So close.

Nathan approached from the side, hidden from Yakuf's view. He reached for the cargo area and his fingers slid down the aluminum. He grabbed at the rounded corner. His hand slipped off.

The truck blazed past.

Nathan planted his foot and cut hard, turning after it. The truck accelerated a few yards out of reach. The cargo door remained open, and stacks of cardboard boxes toppled over inside. Some of them contained enough carfentanil to wipe out a small city.

The Isuzu plowed down the driveway toward the main road, and the overgrown jungle encroached, narrowing the road. Vines and branches screeched against the truck's sides.

Nathan raced after it. His heart pounded and his body warmed. Sweat trickled into his eyes.

Yakuf slowed as he approached a bend in the road, but he didn't downshift properly, and the truck's engine sputtered. If it stalled, Nathan would have him. But if not, Yakuf might escape.

The truck leaned into the corner and the brake lights illuminated, casting a red glow on the jungle walls. Fluid dripped from the vehicle's undercarriage, soiling the earth. The odor of gasoline stung Nathan's nostrils.

Nathan's muscles screamed from depleted oxygen. He dug deep into that place where mental toughness overcame exhaustion and pushed his body to challenge the limits of endurance.

The gears ground as Yakuf shifted. The engine growled as he found first gear.

Dammit.

The truck rounded the bend, and Nathan cut the corner, catching up. He could leap onto the hydraulic lift gate and climb into the cargo area, but he'd be stuck in there, unable to reach the cab. He had to gamble.

Nathan aimed for the cab as Yakuf accelerated.

He had one chance.

Nathan dug his fingers into the tiny ridge on the aluminum siding and jumped. He landed on the metal connector between the cab and cargo container. His breath came hard, and perspiration coated his skin. The frame swayed beneath him and he steadied himself.

The truck gathered speed.

Branches and vines slapped against the extended mirror, and Nathan eyed Yakuf's reflection in it. He'd spot Nathan any second—unless Nathan acted.

The vehicle rocked over the uneven terrain. Nathan clutched the cab and braced against the cargo container to avoid falling. The truck only traveled fifteen miles an hour, so a tumble wouldn't kill Nathan, but he'd never catch up.

One slip and Yakuf would escape.

Nathan needed to stop the vehicle, and that meant attacking Yakuf. And the terrorist had a gun.

This is crazy.

Nathan leaned out along the driver's door and grasped its handle. If it had an automatic lock or if Yakuf had spotted him and secured it, Nathan would never get to him. He jerked the handle.

The door flung open.

Branches pelted the door, sending leaves into the air. Nathan swung into the compartment. Yakuf's mouth opened in surprise. Blood stained the front of his shirt. He'd been shot.

Nathan clutched Yakuf's neck.

Yakuf reached for the revolver in his waistband.

Nathan had no time to think. He leaned his weight onto Yakuf's arm, trapping the gun. Nathan had to stop the vehicle.

"*Cāo nǐ gè yuán yǎn*," Yakuf shouted with a snarl that conveyed his intent.

Nathan hooked his arm around Yakuf's neck—as the terrorist had done to the undercover. Nathan tugged to yank him away from the wheel.

Yakuf didn't budge.

Nathan was strong, but the terrorist had sunk into his seat, and he clung to the steering wheel. Yakuf tried to jerk the gun free.

Nathan locked his elbow to secure the gun. He squeezed harder to choke him, but Yakuf lowered his chin and protected his air supply.

Nathan twisted and shifted the crook of his elbow over Yakuf's larynx. He tightened his grip over the carotid arteries, interrupting the flow of blood to the brain.

Yakuf's eyes bulged. He squirmed and threw an elbow. It caught Nathan's cheek with a flash of lightning.

Nathan gritted his teeth and squeezed harder. It wasn't working.

Danger tingled through Nathan as he considered something bold. And reckless. Adrenaline dumped into his system.

"Fuck you too."

Nathan leaned back, toward the open door. Yakuf resisted, and his knuckles whitened on the steering wheel. He was too sinewy to manhandle.

Nathan's shoulder injury burned. He needed to end this. He arched his back and then snapped forward and drove his forehead into Yakuf's nose. Cartilage crunched.

Yakuf recoiled and released the handgun. Blood gushed from his nose as if from a spigot. Yakuf was a terror leader, but he didn't know how to fight.

The truck swayed back and forth as Yakuf steered with one hand. Tires thumped over deep ruts, and the jungle's teeming foliage hissed past.

Nathan braced his foot against the steering column. Yakuf tried to resist, but he seemed stunned.

Nathan tensed his bicep around Yakuf's neck and exploded backward.

His quads strained as he hauled Yakuf toward the door. Nathan's body dangled out and palm fronds slapped him, covering him in organic detritus.

Yakuf twisted and came off the seat. He growled something unintelligible in Mandarin.

The truck drifted right. Yakuf held the wheel like clinging to a life raft.

Nathan arched his back and Yakuf turned the wheel. The truck jerked to the right and leaned on two wheels.

Centrifugal force gave Nathan a boost, and he tugged with all his might. Yakuf's grip slipped off the wheel.

They flew out the door and spun into the air.

Shit.

Nathan twisted his legs beneath him, and his boots slammed into the ground. The world turned upside down. Yakuf flew from his grasp.

Nathan rolled and flopped hard on the ground, knocking the air from his lungs. His chest burned, and he couldn't catch his breath.

Metal crunched and glass shattered as the truck crashed into trees on the opposite side of the road.

Nathan lifted his head. Yakuf lay five yards away with his head turned at an unnatural angle. He stared back at Nathan with unseeing eyes.

Yakuf was dead.

The truck came to rest at a forty-five-degree angle, wedged against a giant Petrie tree. Torn metal poked up at jagged angles. Smoke rose in the air, and the odor of gasoline prickled Nathan's sinuses.

Nathan lay back and allowed his lungs to refill. His breath came easier.

Help would arrive after the firefight ended. He should unload the carfentanil before the truck caught fire and destroyed them. Of course, if any of the kilos had broken open, the truck would be a toxic hazard. Or he could—

The gas tank exploded.

Nathan flinched as the pressure wave passed through him. Flames engulfed the truck and black smoke poured out of the cargo container. The drugs were gone.

Nathan crawled away from the deadly fumes.

72

Nathan and Meili strolled around the National Mall to discuss his Thailand operation away from headquarters, and he tried to focus on her words over his pain. He hadn't been seriously injured when he pulled Yakuf from the truck, but bruises covered his body, and his shoulder ached. And physical ailments weren't his biggest problem. The FBI's brass was apoplectic about his rogue operation.

"My goal was to prosecute the Chinese trafficker who supplied carfentanil to the Phantoms," he said.

"You're not talking to OPR," Meili said. "Don't bullshit me."

"It's not bullshit. His drugs killed thousands of Americans."

"Catching him wasn't the point of your little off-the-books operation."

"I had approval to—"

"You mischaracterized it. I know you intended to send a message to the Chinese that opioid production could backfire on them. You wanted to encourage them to limit production and control the industry better."

Nathan couldn't conceal his smirk. She knew exactly what he'd done. Had she figured it out earlier and let him continue because she thought it might work?

"We helped Thailand take out a terror cell," he said, "and we still have evidence to lock up Quon Li."

"That's the only thing keeping you employed. You broke policies, like fronting the dope."

"I told the ASAC Naresuan was supposed to seize it, but it slipped away."

"I spoke with Major Paitoon Shinawatra," she said, "and he said it was a miscommunication. He thought you wanted the drugs to walk."

"Gee, I don't know how he got that impression."

Meili shook her head. "How did your other supervisors deal with you? I have a newfound respect for Rahimya."

"I made significant cases and carried the AF-Pak group's arrests stats."

"You keep bending the rules, and you'll lose your badge. You've only survived because you've succeeded. One failed rogue operation, and you'll be out. Or worse."

She was right. He could only push so far. "Our rules can be our biggest obstacle. Bureaucracy is the problem. When the stakes are high enough, I focus on our mission. That's what the taxpayers want. It's what our country needs."

"You're walking a tightrope."

"I haven't fallen yet, and we have a better understanding of how the Chinese are targeting us."

"You got that right," Meili said. "The deeper we go, the more it's clear the Chinese are our adversaries. And I don't mean rivals. They're our enemy. The CCP wants to destroy us."

"No argument," Nathan said.

She grimaced. "It conflicts me."

"Investigating China makes you uncomfortable?"

Meili looked at her shoes. "I won't deny it has dredged up strange feelings. I don't believe in identity politics, but I have Chinese heritage. I grew up with the culture—the good parts without the dictatorship."

"We all come from somewhere. It's natural to feel that way."

"But I shouldn't. I'm supposed to enforce the law and follow cases wherever they lead, without prejudice. I'm an FBI agent."

"You're also human."

She stared up at the Washington Monument. The sunrise reflected off its stone. "To be honest, I gave China the benefit of the doubt at the beginning of the Havana thing, but the brain injury the Leopard gave me cured my hesitation. I know they're our foe."

"What's the problem? We're uncovering their operations and exposing their evil to the world to stop them from damaging our country."

"That's what's bothering me. You took out Yakuf's team, but the Uyghurs are fighting the CCP too. And they're a minority group struggling against a totalitarian government."

"I agree," Nathan said, "but that philosophy of 'the enemy of my enemy is my friend' can bring serious unintended consequences. We supported radical Islamists to repel the Soviet invasion of Afghanistan, and twenty years later, they crashed planes into our towers."

"We didn't understand what they wanted."

"Some did. One man's freedom fighter can be another man's terrorist, so motivations matter. The TIP are fundamentalists who seek a worldwide caliphate. We may share a common enemy in China right now, but if Islamists topple China, they're coming for us next."

"Islamists don't have a chance of destroying the West."

He snorted. "It's happening right now. They use immigration as a form of jihad. Islamists call it *hijra*."

"Still, you took out people fighting our enemy."

"There's also the ethical argument," he said. "Even if they further our cause, we lose the moral high ground when we support evil people doing bad things. If we enable terrorists, we're no better than the people we're fighting."

Meili beamed.

"What?" he asked.

"Talking to you always makes me feel better."

Warmth crept into his chest. Was this love? "We better head back. Waldo keeps texting me."

"He's worried?"

"Yeah, but I've kept him focused on the lure operation in Thailand."

"Think Quon will bite?" she asked.

"We'll see."

They walked back up 9th Street to Pennsylvania. Waldo stood outside headquarters with a group of FBI personnel. Everyone looked at the sky.

"*Qué pasa*," Waldo said. "You guys talking about me?"

Shadows flickered over the street, and Nathan craned his neck and shaded his eyes with his palm. "What's everyone looking—"

A fleet of drones circled to the east.

"We got an alert they flew over Joint Base Anacostia Bolling," Waldo said.

"That can't be good," Nathan said.

"What are they doing?" Meili asked.

"Nobody knows who's flying them," Waldo said. "Why they in the District?"

"It's target rich," Meili said. "We've got the Washington Navy Yard, the US Naval Research Laboratory, even the Marine barracks."

The drones spiraled downward, like a flock of birds but with perfect synchronicity that only artificial intelligence allowed.

"Assuming their mission is surveillance," Nathan said.

"As opposed to what?" Meili asked.

"Something worse," Nathan said.

"Like?"

"They could be attack drones," Nathan said. An image of the Phantoms' craft firing into Amelia's school flashed in his mind.

The drones flew five hundred feet over the city, and their size became apparent. They were huge, close to ten feet long with massive wingspans. They moved in unison, their engines echoing off building facades.

"Why are they so low?" Waldo asked.

"To scare us?" Nathan said.

"It's working," Waldo said.

The drones moved into a single-file formation and circled the White House.

"They get any closer," Waldo said, "and Secret Service will shoot them down."

"They won't launch missiles downtown," Meili said, "unless the drones dive-bomb the building."

"Think they're armed?" Waldo asked.

Nathan shrugged.

"I guarantee they've moved the president into his bunker," Meili said.

"If he's there," Waldo said.

"Either way," Meili said, "they're in lockdown."

A roar filled the air, and Nathan flinched as two F-16s shot overhead. They passed the drone swarm and circled to starboard. White contrails streaked from their wings.

"This is bad," Waldo said.

"What?"

"China's gearing up for war."

"They could be posturing," Meili said.

Waldo crossed his arms. "This is a clusterfuck."

The drones circled again, then flew east and gained altitude. The F-16s stayed close to the White House.

"You think your new source has insight into this?" Nathan asked.

"She seems to have access," Meili said. "If these drones are a prelude to war, she'll know."

"We need to return to debrief her," Nathan said. "ASAP."

"Agreed. I'll send a message."

"Tell her it's an emergency," Waldo said.

"If we're right," Meili said, "she already knows."

73

Nathan slumped on a moldy seat cushion inside a forty-five-foot fishing trawler off the coast of Ko Samui in the Gulf of Thailand. The pungent odor of rotting fish and contaminated water choked the cabin and induced nausea. The trawler rolled over three-foot waves, and Nathan swayed with the motion. Waldo sat beside him, looking green, and Pai perched on the captain's chair, unperturbed by the odor and motion. His radio officer hunched over a satellite radio on the navigation table and communicated with the Thai Maritime Enforcement Command Center.

"This wasn't my dream when I joined the FBI," Waldo said.

"We'll give it another hour," Nathan said.

Waldo groaned.

Nathan raised Steiner binoculars to his eyes and aimed them out a tiny porthole frosted with dried salt water. No sign of Quon.

"Anything from your surveillance units?" Nathan asked.

Pai rattled off a string of Thai, and his officer transmitted over his radio. The Royal Thai Marine Police had deployed numerous watercraft and an aerial drone supplied by the UNODC Global Maritime Crime Program. They'd called out every boat in the vicinity, but nothing headed toward the rendezvous point that Emerald had given Quon.

The radio officer cocked his head, listening to something on his headphones, then he looked at Pai. *"Mai mee arai."*

Nathan didn't need that translated.

"Nothing," Pai said.

"He's not biting," Nathan said.

Waldo's eyes darted to the head in the bow. Vomiting in front of their Thai counterparts wouldn't instill confidence, but the operation had gone to shit, regardless.

"We done?" Waldo asked.

"I think so."

"Our snitch could lure him to the Maldives."

A sinking feeling weighed Nathan down. Their ruse hadn't worked, and another one wouldn't either. He stretched his back until it cracked.

"Quon didn't show because he's afraid of getting arrested," Nathan said.

"He knows our guy's a snitch?"

"He must. Word of Yakuf's death was bound to spread. We only had a short window to catch Quon. Pai delayed the press release, but a shootout leaving injured officers and dead terrorists was too much to hide. Once the news stories came out, it was only a matter of time. Besides, Emerald made sure the Second Bureau knew what Yakuf tried, and they might have informed Quon."

"What next?"

Nathan sighed. "Another source could set up a new sting. Something unrelated. I don't know . . ."

"That *churro's* got American blood on his hands."

"We'll get him. Eventually."

"You got more faith than me," Waldo said.

"We identified him, we have his photo, and we know what he's doing. He'll pop up."

"If he thinks we're onto him, he'll disappear into a hole somewhere in China."

"He won't stay under forever. He craves power and a life of luxury, and he needs money for that. The same motivations that drove him into a life of crime will help us catch him. It's his Achilles heel."

"And if your wrong?"

Nathan's stomach hardened. "Then the bad guys win this one."

74

Reagan awoke and experienced a fleeting moment of restful bliss before the reality of her cratering career came crashing into her consciousness. The dangerous situation she navigated crept into her brain like a virus. The threat of blackmail, and even physical harm, hung over her like a guillotine. Her guts twisted.

She sighed and sat up.

Another day. Another battle to salvage her career, reputation, and self-worth. She needed help. She glanced at the unwrinkled sheets on Vince's empty side of the bed. He'd left for the Dominican Republic again to extinguish another political fire at the embassy, but who could blame him for leaving? He'd only come home for a few days, and he'd been cast into the rotors of chaos that swirled around her. She wanted to flee too—but she couldn't escape her own life.

"Shit."

She'd canceled her speaking engagements, which left her with little to do, other than calling the long list of donors they'd given her, but she wouldn't do that either. No way she'd support Lemon, especially after the blackmail attempt.

A few more minutes in bed wouldn't kill her. She slid back down and pulled the covers up. She reached out and snatched her phone off the nightstand. She'd covered the lenses on both sides of her new smartphone with masking tape. A Band-Aid covered her new laptop camera too. No way she'd be vulnerable like that again.

"Fool me once . . ."

She entered her password and unlocked her phone. A red sixteen glowed on her text app, indicating new messages. She wrinkled her brow. Another number glowed on her email app showing seventy-one unread emails. That wasn't normal. Was Amelia okay? Her chest tightened.

She clicked on the messenger app displaying a string of text previews.

Oh my God. Who did this?

Are you okay?

Is this real?

Call me!

Reagan couldn't breathe. She opened the first text, which had an attachment. She scrolled down to the photo.

The image showed her twenty years ago, lying on the sand flashing a crooked drunk smile at the camera—completely naked.

"Nooo." A groan slipped through her lips as her stomach cramped.

She clicked on the next text with an attachment. Another nude photo. And another. The blackmailers had released every photo. But how had so many people seen them? She opened a browser and searched her name. She scrolled through hits and landed on a porn site where her blackmailers had uploaded her photos.

Darkness flooded into her. She couldn't catch her breath. The photos would shatter her political career. Worse, her friends would see the photos. And her family. Her daughter.

"Amelia."

The walls closed in. Dizziness overcame her. How would she explain this to her daughter? Would it scar Amelia and damage the way she viewed sex? All because of a youthful indiscretion.

"Oh, God, what have I done?"

She'd never leave the house again. She should hide under the covers and—

The doorbell rang.

Reagan's heart skipped a beat, and she clutched her chest. She lumbered out of bed, stiff with shock. Her world had collapsed.

She pressed her face against the window and looked out. Nathan stood on the front stoop. She flinched. Had he come to berate or console her? She should lock her bedroom door and never come out. But she'd need to confront this eventually, and her shared history with Nathan might make it easier.

Or much worse.

She plodded downstairs without getting dressed, but she'd slept in Vince's enormous tee shirt, and it covered her underwear. She stopped at the front door and took a deep breath. She opened it.

Nathan smiled, a sad empathetic expression, the way you'd look at someone who'd been fired for incompetence. "You okay?"

"What are you doing here so early?"

"I wanted to make sure you weren't freaking out." He'd seen the photos.

"I'm fine."

"May I come in?"

She didn't have the energy to object. She turned, walked into the living room, and plopped onto the couch. He followed and sat beside her. She curled her legs underneath her and held her arms.

"I feel responsible," he said. "I told you to report the blackmail."

"I'd have been screwed if I didn't. Well, screwed worse, though I can't imagine this getting much worse." She rambled like an idiot.

"You had no choice."

"When they didn't release the photos after Anderson's arrest, I thought I'd dodged the bullet."

"This will pass."

Her throat tightened. "They emailed everyone I know."

"They probably hacked your address book."

"They . . . my reputation's ruined." Tears filled her eyes.

"You chose to expose your blackmailers. You fought back. Voters will see that."

"Maybe . . ."

"You're exposing corruption and bringing election interference into public view."

"Even if the voters forgive me, I won't be on any ballots without DNC support."

Nathan rubbed his neck. "You know I don't like either party, but both have some honorable people in their ranks. I'm hopeful patriots will step up and take charge."

"That may be aspirational."

"Aspiring to a better America should be bipartisan. We need to envision a better future."

"I don't see it happening," she said.

"Nothing is permanent, and bad behavior can be corrected . . . in time."

"Time is something I don't have. Politics is all about perception, and I'm persona non grata in the Democratic Party."

"You can serve your country in other ways."

"I tried with the State Department and received a brain injury for my efforts, then they disparaged my credibility by claiming my symptoms were psychogenic. They didn't stand behind any of the victims."

Nathan snickered. "Welcome to my world. Working for the feds is an exercise in frustration, but government isn't your only option."

"You want me to start a business or join a nonprofit?"

"If DNC leadership derides you publicly, use that against them. Most people dislike politicians and elitists who seem completely disconnected from their lives."

"But if they can't vote for me—"

"You can reach more people with your own podcast or blog," he said. "If you want to be an agent of change, grow a platform. You can always reenter politics later."

"I made the decision to fight, and people voted for me."

"It'll be a fight. Whenever you make public appearances, the media will bring up the photos. You'll handle questions about it every time."

"But *you* don't hide from things that scare you."

He nodded. "It doesn't make them less scary."

"Won't they win if I give up?"

He took her hands and gazed into her eyes. "We were married. I care about you, and I want you to be safe."

"What would you do?"

"It's hard for me to put myself in your situation, but my instinct is always to resist. Don't let them silence you."

"Confront them publicly?"

He nodded. "Explain the blackmail. Tell them how your leadership pressured you. Someone hacked you and released your private photos to silence you from speaking out against your party's leadership."

"But the photos—"

"Were taken years ago. We all make mistakes when we're younger. Everyone's done things they're not proud about, so change the conversation. Acknowledge a youthful mistake and then talk about why they targeted you. Use the sensational nature of the leak to focus people on the corruption inside the party machine."

She looked out the window. What did she have to lose?

"Screw it. I'll bring the fight to them."

75

Nathan shut off the Toyota Noah rental van in the Macao Port Park-and-Ride in the shadow of the Hong Kong-Zhuhai-Macao Bridge. Beside him, Meili stared out the window at the massive terminal where people bought tickets to travel across the bridge to Hong Kong. A constant stream of vehicles flowed past on Shun Hang Road. Nathan had parked front end first, so he used his rearview mirror to watch the lot's entrance. Meili's source, Xuannü, should arrive any minute.

"This place is too busy," Meili said.

"Busy is good," Nathan said. "Easier to blend in."

"And harder for us to spot surveillance."

"There's that."

They'd flown into Macao the night before and spoken with Tony over unsecured cellphones and email to schedule a meeting and give them a reason to be in Macao. Hopefully, Chinese Intelligence had been listening. Xuannü was driving down across the bridge from Hong Kong to meet them. She'd suggested their approach from different jurisdictions would provide an added level of complication for Chinese surveillance. Nathan and Meili had valid visas for both Macao and Hong Kong, and their rental car displayed the proper license plates to cross the bridge. If they felt any heat, they could put thirty-four miles of water between them and Macao.

"I thought Tony insisted on joining us," Nathan said.

"He's nervous about this," Meili said. "He's close, on a boat with one of his facilitators. His idea of an escape plan if we need a quick exfil."

Nathan snorted.

"Problem?"

"Not unless he tries to butt into our debriefing."

A bright yellow Honda N-One headed straight for them. The tiny hatchback looked like a clown car. A single female sat behind the wheel. Nathan checked his watch. Right on time.

"This could be her," Meili said.

The N-One slowed behind them and the driver scrutinized them for a split second before backing into the spot beside their van. Xuannü displayed good tradecraft by not hesitating too long, but her car seemed an odd choice for keeping a low profile. She presented a mass of contradictions.

Xuannü remained in the driver's seat, bathed in shadow, with a scarf covering half her face. She glanced around but made no move to exit. She turned her gaze on them and lowered her window, but only an inch.

"I did not want to meet like this," Xuannü said. "It is very dangerous for me . . . and for you." Her words came through the slit like a hiss.

"You agreed to an in-person meeting," Nathan said.

"Things are escalating."

"How?"

A black Mercedes with two male occupants crept past. Had the passenger glanced at them or had he been gazing out his window without purpose?

"There's talk of blockading Taiwan and forcing a reunification," Xuannü said.

"They must know the US won't allow that," Meili said

"They are not afraid of conflict. They have been preparing for the unavoidable clash with America for years. They have flown balloons and drones over your military installations. Chinese-made cars have traveled millions of miles on American roads photographing and plotting maps. They've infected your core infrastructure systems with viruses that can be activated anytime, and they emplaced covert teams who are ready to disable your electrical grid and contaminate your water supply. They—"

"Wait," Meili said. "You're telling us China has infiltrated sleeper cells into the United States—"

"Yes."

"—with the intent of destroying American infrastructure?"

"That is what I say. They have also inserted malware into America's critical infrastructure, like water treatment plants, telecommunications networks, transportation systems, and gas pipelines."

"For what purpose?" Meili asked.

"To disable your economy and throw your country into anarchy."

"That would be an act of war."

"You are at war, but you have yet to recognize that."

"That seems like an extreme characterization," Meili said.

Cold seeped into Nathan's gut. Xuannü had articulated the problem he'd had fighting DC bureaucracy his entire career. Trying to get the DOJ and FBI management to acknowledge facts right in front of them didn't always work, especially when the evidence created political problems. Congress and the White House had the same problem. China actively targeted them, and no one seemed willing to respond.

"The Central Committee is being led down a dangerous path," Xuannü said, "and this may lead to a tragic outcome."

"Meaning?" Meili asked.

"War."

Meili leaned across the seat. "We can't debrief you like this. Sit in our backseat."

Xuannü surveyed their vehicle. The Toyota Noah had plenty of room, and the lightly tinted window offered privacy.

"I prefer to remain here."

Nathan focused on the lot's entrance. Every few minutes, a passenger car would enter and drive around looking for spots close to the massive terminal before eventually parking in an outlying space. A black four-door Mercedes pulled into the lot and turned away from them. Was that the same car that had driven past?

"What has changed?" Meili asked. "What's motivating their aggression?"

"General Ming Zhao."

"The Second Bureau chief?" Nathan asked.

"He has always been an advocate for the guerrilla tactics of China's unrestricted warfare, and he has convinced the Central Committee to accelerate their disintegration warfare strategy."

"But the US will push back," Meili said.

"Will they?" Xuannü asked. "And even if they do, General Zhao won't be deterred. He has staked his career on his strategy's success."

The Mercedes rolled down the opposite row of cars.

"Give us an example of this accelerated strategy," Nathan said.

"They have targeted your elections," Xuannü said.

"How?" Meili asked.

"The Second Bureau has used many of its favorite tools." Her voice tightened. "Blackmail, bribery, coercion, intimidation, even murder."

"Murder?" Meili said. "How can we believe—"

"You are resistant to the truth. I am inside, and I am telling you what they are doing . . . what they plan for you."

"We can't do anything without evidence," Nathan said. "What can you give us that would stand up in court?"

"Stand up?"

"Proof. Corroboration. We need hard evidence showing China's interference in our election."

The Mercedes had circled around. Nathan looked back at Xuannü, then stopped. Something was wrong. He leaned forward and looked past parked cars as the Mercedes turned into their row. What had he seen?

There.

The Mercedes had passed an open parking space opposite the terminal. They wouldn't find a better one—unless they searched for something else.

"The Second Bureau has been influencing your elections for decades," Xuannü said. "General Zhao takes a big risk. He wants to control America from the top. He is—"

"What do you mean by the top?" Meili asked.

"General Zhao wants to bypass normal influence tactics and seize control."

"Of what?"

"The White House."

Movement in the side-view mirror drew his attention. The Mercedes drifted behind them. He squinted and focused in his rearview mirror. Both the driver and passenger stared hard at Xuannü's vehicle, leaving no room for doubt.

They searched for her.

"We've got a problem," Nathan said.

"What?" Meili asked.

"The men in that car. They're interested in her."

Xuannü turned and watched the car continue down the line of cars. She looked over her shoulder, and the scarf slipped off her face.

Adrenaline flashed through Nathan's veins and he straightened.

"What is it?" Meili asked.

"She's not Shen Wang," he whispered.

"What?"

"Xuannü isn't who we thought. She's not the senior member of State Security."

"How can—"

"I glimpsed her face. It's not her. She's way too young."

"You're positive?"

"One hundred percent."

"Shit, shit, shit."

"We were never certain it was her," Nathan said.

"Her role in State Security gave her credibility. Now, we need hard evidence."

"That's why we're here."

Xuannü leaned toward them. "I must go."

"We need the documentation you brought."

"Another meeting."

"We don't have the time for—"

Xuannü put her car into gear and pulled out.

"We can't let her go," Meili said, "not without getting proof."

"We have bigger problems," Nathan said. He nodded down the row. The Mercedes had turned around, and it headed after Xuannü.

76

Xuannü's Honda roared down the parking lot row toward the exit, and the black Mercedes followed.

"Let's get out of here," Meili said.

Nathan scanned the lot where vehicles trolled the lanes, ostensibly looking for parking. A Suzuki Solio raced down a perpendicular lane toward the exit. Was someone rushing to get home, or were a team of counterintelligence agents swooping in?

Screw it.

Nathan fired the ignition, threw the van into reverse, and spun back into the lane. He slammed the gear into drive and stomped on the gas. Ahead, Xuannü approached the exit as the Mercedes closed on her. The Suzuki multipurpose vehicle barreled down on her too.

"Find another exit," Meili said.

"We're not running."

Meili stiffened. "Don't follow her. Head in the opposite direction."

"She doesn't stand a chance."

"The Chinese will throw us in prison for espionage."

His gut tightened. "If they catch us . . . but they'll execute her."

Meili's face tightened to steel. She bit her lip. "If we're with her, they'll have proof she's a traitor."

"They already know."

Xuannü turned onto the access road and headed for the bridge. The Mercedes and Suzuki turned after her. Nathan followed.

"We can't intervene," Meili said.

He shook his head. "We may not have an opportunity, but we can't help if we run away."

Meili dialed her cell. "I'm calling Tony."

"Tell him we're taking the bridge to Hong Kong."

Traffic slowed as it flowed through fifteen access lanes at the Gangzhuao Bridge Toll Gate. Xuannü edged toward the gate, and the Mercedes and Suzuki stopped two cars behind her. Were they surveilling her or planning to make an arrest for—

The Suzuki's passenger door opened.

A lithe man wearing a dark suit and sunglasses climbed out and headed for the Honda. A flash of adrenaline heightened Nathan's senses. Maybe he could pull out and block the man to give her time to—

Xuannü's Honda jerked forward, then she flashed through the gate and accelerated onto the bridge.

The agent sprinted back to the Suzuki. The Mercedes followed Xuannü through the gates, and its engine growled as it gained speed. Sunglasses jumped back into the Suzuki, and it lurched forward and through the gate before he shut the door.

Nathan gave chase. He weaved through traffic, keeping Xuannü's speeding Honda in sight. He closed the gap—but so did the Mercedes and the Suzuki.

They climbed onto the bridge. The fifty-three-mile-long Hong Kong-Zuhai-Macao Bridge consisted of three cable-stayed bridges, a long undersea tunnel, and three man-made islands, making it the longest sea crossing in the world. They rose onto the bridge, revealing views of islands and the mainland. A large dividing fence separated six lanes of north-south traffic, and a guardrail protected the outer lane from a several-hundred-foot drop to the water.

Xuannü passed a truck with pictures of corn on the side. The Mercedes did too, then jerked into the truck's lane and accelerated in front of her. The

Suzuki tried to pass the truck, but there wasn't room, and the truck driver laid on his horn.

Xuannü must have seen their attempt to block her. She swerved out of her lane to get around the Mercedes, but he moved with her, blocking her passage. She cut hard back into her lane. The Mercedes did too, and she clipped his bumper.

The impact spun the Mercedes sideways. The driver hit his brakes, leaving black melted rubber on the road.

Xuannü turned to avoid him and lost control. She crashed into the divider with a bang, and the Honda's front end crumpled against the center divider. Her car bounced off the barrier and spun in a circle with pieces of metal flying into the air.

The truck locked up its brakes, but the driver didn't have time to react. The heavy commercial vehicle plowed headfirst into the Mercedes—crushing it.

The truck leaned over. The driver overcorrected, and it swung back the other way and toppled over. The sound of screeching metal filled the air as the truck slid down the street on its side.

Xuannü's Honda squealed to a stop in the center of the road.

Traffic braked and zigzagged trying to avoid the collision. Vehicles rear-ended others, sending broken cars across three lanes.

Nathan swerved into the far right lane, and a passenger car in front of him locked its brakes and skidded. Nathan yanked the wheel hard, and they lurched to the right. He hit the gas and squeezed between the decelerating car and the guardrail. His passenger mirror smashed against the outer barrier and exploded into pieces. He made it through and stopped.

He peered into his rearview mirror. The truck lay on its side with the Mercedes crinkled against its cab, and the wreckage covered all three lanes. Fluids poured out of the truck onto the street, and smoke billowed out of the Mercedes' engine. The Suzuki stopped in the center lane, and Xuannü's car didn't move.

Nathan opened his door and jumped out.

"Where are you—" Meili asked.

He ignored her and sprinted for the Honda.

He reached it and held his breath as he looked inside. Xuannü looked up at him with her mouth agape and eyes wide. The deflated airbag shriveled in front of her, and white powder covered her face.

He cracked open her door. "Are you hurt?"

She shook her head.

"Let's get out of here," Nathan shouted.

He grabbed her arm and helped her unravel from the twisted seat. They jogged toward his van, and he looked over his shoulder. Sunglasses hopped out of the Suzuki and weaved through the wreckage. He cleared the truck and headed for them.

Nathan and Xuannü climbed into his van. He threw it in gear and rocketed away on the bridge.

Nathan glanced in his rearview mirror. Sunglasses had stopped with his hands on hips and glared after them, then he turned and ran toward the smoking Mercedes. The Suzuki crept through the debris field.

Meili pointed at Xuannü's head. "You're injured."

Nathan glanced back. A trickle of blood dripped down her forehead.

"It is nothing," Xuannü said. "The airbag."

Nathan concentrated on the empty road as he pushed the van to its limit. Towers linked massive cables five hundred feet above, and the choppy water lay a hundred feet below. They traveled as fast as he dared for several more minutes, then the surface angled down and the bridge descended to sea level toward an artificial island.

"Stop here," Xuannü said.

"Negative," Nathan said. "They've probably cleared the wreckage already, and they'll be racing to catch up."

"You don't understand. This is my escape plan."

The island approached fast, and Nathan eased off the accelerator to slow them. Braking at that speed could make him lose control.

"Tell me," Nathan said. "In ten seconds I have to make a decision."

"There's no time. It's my only way out. Trust me."

How would she get off the island? Her life depended on getting away. Hell, they'd all face prison or a firing squad if Chinese authorities nabbed them. He slowed and tapped his brakes as he hit the tiny island. He exited onto an access road and pulled over.

"Let me out here," Xuannü said.

"This is crazy," Nathan said. "They're right behind us."

"And they will be waiting for me at the end too. I chose this bridge because I have a plan. Someone will pick me up. He's waiting on the other side."

"Give us whatever evidence you have, while you can," Meili said. "Don't let them catch you with anything."

Xuannü slipped her hand into her blouse and dangled a thick pendant from her fingers. She unclasped it, revealing a chip. She pried it out with her fingernail and handed it to Meili.

"I didn't want to give this to you . . . but my situation is very bad."

"What is this?" Meili asked.

"The connection you need to remove the cancer." Xuannü opened the back door and stepped out.

"Wait," Meili said. "Who are you?"

"This must stay secret."

"I'm sorry," Meili said, "but that ship has sailed."

"Ship—?"

"They know who you are."

Xuannü recoiled. "It's impossible—"

"They were looking for you," Meili said.

Xuannü's face transformed into sharp angles, and her eyes flittered back and forth.

"I need your name to help corroborate the information," Meili said.

"We're running out of time," Nathan interjected.

Xuannü looked up. "My name is Colonel Ying Luo. I work for General Ming Zhao."

77

Nathan and Meili stayed in their minivan and watched Xuannü jog across the pedestrian area toward the far side of the island. A beat-up Toyota Corolla exited the southbound lane and pulled over. A young man with scruffy hair looked around frantically. His eyes landed on Xuannü. He rolled down his window and beckoned her.

She waved back and waited for a break in traffic. A truck lumbered in her direction with a smattering of traffic around it. She stepped onto the road.

The Suzuki screeched around the truck.

Xuannü didn't notice, but she'd already committed. She darted across the lanes.

The Suzuki accelerated quickly and switched lanes, vectoring for her.

"He's going to hit her," Nathan said.

"But they can't—"

The Suzuki's engine roared as it bore down.

Xuannü jerked her head up. But too late.

The Suzuki's driver didn't touch his brakes. The vehicle struck her at eighty miles an hour. Its grill impacted Xuannü from her knees to her sternum. She cleared the windshield and spun into the air like a baton. Her feet and head rotated as she flew through the air.

The Suzuki's brakes locked, and it screeched as it left thick skid marks on the pavement. Xuannü's shoeless body crashed back to earth as the Suzuki came to a stop.

She didn't move. Her limbs bent at awkward angles. Her head had twisted on her broken neck, and her lifeless eyes stared over her shoulder at him.

Sunglasses and another man scrambled out of the vehicle and sprinted back to Xuannü. They stopped a few feet away to avoid the lake of arterial blood pouring from her shattered legs. Sunglasses turned back in their direction. He pointed at Nathan and Meili's minivan.

They'd been spotted.

"Time to go," Nathan said.

"But Xuannü—"

"She's dead."

Nathan stomped on the gas and spun the wheel. Their tires screeched, and the Toyota leaned as he swung around the access road.

"Shit, shit, shit," Meili muttered.

Losing a highly placed snitch inside the Second Bureau was hard, and seeing a beautiful young life snuffed out before his eyes turned his stomach. The Chinese had killed her without a second of hesitation. They showed no remorse.

Nathan and Meili scooted past the Suzuki and dove into the tunnel's black mouth. A glance in the rearview mirror showed empty road behind them, but that wouldn't last. And what waited for them in Hong Kong?

Halogen lights illuminated three lanes of light traffic with walkways on either side. He accelerated as they dipped beneath the surface. They descended for well over a minute, and even at their high speeds, they still hadn't reached the bottom.

"How deep are we?" Meili asked.

"Why does that matter?"

She bit her lip. "I hate tunnels."

The pitch changed and the front of their minivan rose as they headed for the surface. Nathan stayed in the center lane and goosed the gas pedal. The engine whined as they neared top speed. Lane markings whisked by like in a video game.

Meili's phone rang, and she answered. "Yeah . . . okay. Our source is dead. They killed her . . . I know . . . We're coming out of the tunnel now."

"Tony?"

"He's a little behind."

"He's catching up in a boat?"

"A cigarette boat."

The tunnel's exit glowed in the distance. Nathan lifted his foot off the gas, and they burst into sunlight.

He squinted in the bright light. The bridge wrapped around to the left, and off to their right, the hills of Lantau Island rose out of the water. They were getting close to the end.

A plane flew low over the water, preparing to land at Hong Kong International Airport, which came into view ahead beside the bridge.

"Where's Tony?"

"Status," she said into her phone. She looked at Nathan. "He's close."

"How close?"

"Why?"

Nathan pointed. Red-and-blue lights flickered on shore and a thin line snaked over the bridge toward them.

"The police blocked the bridge," Nathan said, "and they're coming for us."

Meili's mouth tightened.

An idea flared in his mind, and his breathing increased. He scanned the water to the south, in the direction where Tony would come. A black cigarette boat bounced on the tiny waves toward them. Four massive outboard engines powered it as it leapt from crest to crest. Red seats in the bow and stern flashed every time the boat pitched.

"That him?" Nathan asked.

She pressed her phone against her ear. "He thinks he sees us."

Nathan screeched to a stop.

Meili's eyes widened. "What are you—"

"Let's go."

He popped the van's rear door release and leapt out. He flipped up the floorboard and yanked out the spare tire. He carried it to the walkway and balanced it on the safety rail.

"What are you doing?"

"We're jumping."

The color drained from her face. "But ..."

"The surveillance team will arrive any second, and the police are coming. We're trapped. There's no other escape. You confirmed that's Tony?"

She nodded but didn't speak.

"If we're wrong, it's a tough swim to shore," he said.

"I'd never make it."

"Don't say that."

"I can't swim."

A sense of doom weighed him down. "You could have said something before."

"You didn't mention base jumping when we briefed this morning."

He sighed. "Can you swim at all?"

"Dog paddle. I can float."

"That'll do."

He leaned against the railing and looked down. This close to shore, the bridge was lower, which gave them a better chance of survival—but not an absolute one.

"It's too far," Meili said. "The water will feel like concrete."

"We have no choice."

"I can't."

"It's this or a Chinese prison."

The police lights drew closer. He glanced behind them. In the distance, the Suzuki hurtled toward them at high speed.

"Now or never."

"No, I—"

"The water's deep enough. Fill your lungs and hold it. Jump feet-first, and try to keep your body straight. Keep your arms straight down at your sides and blade your fingers. Your speed will carry you under, so start kicking for the surface as soon as you stop sinking."

"This is insane."

He held out his hand. She took it and climbed over. He helped her face outward with her back to the railing. He did the same. The shrill sound of sirens cut through the air.

The Suzuki screeched to a stop behind them.

"Ready?"

"The police will send the harbor patrol."

"One problem at a time."

They jumped.

78

Nathan watched Meili snoring in a Washington General Hospital bed with her leg in a cast. She'd hurt herself during their jump off the bridge, but he hadn't realized the severity of her injury. A fractured femur. *Fuck.* She'd suffered in silence until they arrived in Taiwan, and a doctor who worked secretly for the agency had given her codeine, but she hadn't received proper care until they'd returned home. Codeine had made the long trip possible, and she'd crashed after corrective surgery. She'd been asleep for close to six hours.

She was one tough cookie.

Someone rapped on the door.

"Come," Nathan said.

Lincoln White entered. He nodded at Nathan and stared at Meili. The FBI's Beijing LEGAT had accompanied them on their trip home. He'd been pissed about the havoc their off-the-books operation would cause him, but despite China threatening to declare him persona non grata, he'd insisted on escorting them back to DC. Underneath all his bureaucratic bullshit, he was still a federal agent. And an American.

Nathan had judged him wrong.

"She gonna be okay?" Lincoln asked.

"They caught a mild infection, but she's on IV antibiotics. Her surgery went well, and she'll recover. Her femur had two breaks. She's lucky it stayed intact."

"I've been second-guessing my decision not to fly her to a hospital in Tokyo," Nathan said.

"Too risky. NSA intercepted chatter that China wants to take her out, and they have more influence in Asia. You're a target too."

Nathan nodded. "I'm on their radar for sure, but she's a supervisor and . . ."

"*And* what?"

"She's Chinese, and I have to assume China considers her a traitor."

"Possible."

"I experienced that in Afghanistan. Our Afghan interpreters had higher bounties on their heads than we did. The Islamists considered them disloyal for working with us."

Lincoln approached Meili's bedside and inspected her cast. "At least you're safe here."

"I wouldn't say that."

He glanced back. "China wouldn't try anything on US soil."

Nathan snorted. "They've done it before, with Havana Syndrome."

"That was never proven."

"We had evidence. Not enough to charge them, but we persuaded the National Security Council."

Lincoln adjusted the watch and cleared his throat. He didn't seem convinced. "They won't touch two FBI agents here. They'd start a war."

"This is a fucking war," Nathan said. "Just because Chinese and American tanks aren't firing shells at each other doesn't diminish the conflict."

"China has nuclear weapons," Lincoln said. "A shooting war with them looks like Armageddon."

"Our militaries aren't landing haymakers, but we bump into them, from our naval forces in the South China Sea to their surveillance balloons flying over America."

"My point is war with China would look different."

Why didn't he see the threat? China didn't hide their intention to replace the US as the world's hegemon, and their behavior proved they meant it. How many people needed to die before policy makers noticed the existential battle with a massive global power. Chinese people weren't the enemy, but the CCP controlled the world's largest army. Full-scale war was inevitable. The question was when it would start. To avoid a nuclear exchange, the US had to attack China from within, like they did to America. It wasn't rocket science.

Nathan shook his head. "You're not getting it. The war has started, only we haven't unleashed our military yet. Our casualties are economic loss, a propagandized people, the destruction of institutions, and dead intelligence assets."

A lump formed in his throat. How was this real? How was any of it real? He should have protected Meili. She may carry a badge and gun, but it was his role to defend her.

And he'd failed.

"We're pushing back," Lincoln said. "Cops die every day too, and we're fighting a war of attrition. We'll keep taking casualties. I'm sorry about your source, but that's reality."

A heaviness weighed Nathan down and depleted his energy. He wanted to stop pushing, stop fighting with management, but he had to continue. Americans needed to see the threat, and China needed to be stopped. If he didn't lead the vanguard, who would?

"Stay home and recover," Lincoln said.

Nathan wanted to explode, bang his fists on the desk and grab Lincoln by his shirt and shake him until he understood the danger he faced, the peril threatening them all.

But perhaps Lincoln knew. Had he been corrupted like so many other Americans? How would Nathan fight the Chinese menace if his own agency had been infiltrated? He stood and looked at Lincoln, but there was nothing else to say.

Lincoln seemed to get the point. "Gotta get back to it." Lincoln let himself out.

Nathan walked to the window and stared out. Everything had gone to shit fast. Reagan's political career had imploded, and she stood no chance of rising in the new Democratic administration—if they won the election—and her reputation had been dragged through the mud.

Nathan's career wasn't doing any better. Xuannü had been killed, removing their highly placed source. Hamilton hadn't responded to Nathan's last message, despite Hamilton's claim that he had important information. If Hamilton withdrew his stable of informants, Nathan would be in the dark. Nathan had risked his career on the drug operations, but they had no discernible effect. He could still get suspended or fired, and for what? And now, he and Meili had to look over their shoulders everywhere they went.

Things couldn't get much worse.

79

Nathan and Waldo shuffled through a bureaucratic checkpoint at the Florence Supermax penitentiary. Hamilton's last message claimed he had urgent information, but he hadn't responded to Nathan, so Waldo and Nathan had flown out to talk to him in person. Processing took much longer than during their previous visits, and corrections officers raced around behind bulletproof glass looking agitated.

"Something's going on," Nathan said.

"How long are we staying out here?" Waldo asked.

"You're not enjoying the Mile-High City?"

"We're chasing our tails."

Nathan sighed. "We're close. I sense it. Hamilton's connection in Bangkok was a goldmine, so if Hamilton has something important, we have to come."

"What more can he do from inside? He's not Hannibal Lecter."

"No, he's more dangerous," Nathan said. "He's locked in Supermax for a reason, and his contacts in the criminal underworld and intelligence community could be the key. Nobody else is talking to them."

"Or he's playing us."

Nathan nodded. "We need him to help us contact his networks. Human intelligence could be the difference between success and failure."

They stopped at the secondary checkpoint and handed their identification to another guard, a tubby man with round glasses, whose name tag read, *Hebert*. He inspected their credentials, then the visitor intake sheet that listed Trent Hamilton's name. Hebert scrunched his face.

"Problem?" Nathan asked. Bureaucratic hurdles never ended.

"You're here to see inmate Trent Hamilton?"

"That's what it says. We've been here before."

He scratched his head. "You can't see him."

Anger flared Nathan's nostrils. Did the entire federal government want to prevent him from protecting the country?

"It's all approved by BOP," Nathan said.

"That don't matter."

Nathan closed his eyes and breathed out, but controlling his temper was easier in theory than practice. "What's the problem, officer?"

"You didn't hear?"

"Hear what?"

"Uh . . ." Hebert shuffled on his feet and looked down at the papers.

"What?" Nathan asked with an edge to his tone.

"Hamilton's dead."

An icy chill froze Nathan in place. "Excuse me?"

"They found him hanging in his cell."

"What?"

"This morning. He hung himself."

"That's impossible," Waldo said. "This is a maximum-security facility."

"I shouldn't say anything, but since you're agents . . ." Hebert glanced around, then leaned in. "I heard he chipped the concrete on the wall and used it as a hook. He hung himself with his pants."

"No, no, no," Nathan said. "That's so unlikely, it's almost absurd. Isn't he under twenty-four-hour surveillance?"

Hebert made a face and looked away. "The cameras went down."

"This is bullshit," Nathan said.

"Whatever happened," Hebert said, "you won't be able to see him today . . . or ever."

Nathan and Waldo collected their credentials and left the prison in silence. They climbed into their car, and Nathan sat there without starting it.

"You don't really believe he killed himself?" Nathan asked.

Waldo shrugged. "Guy was depressed. No hope of getting out. He told us life in there was hell. Can't imagine what that feels like, knowing he'd never escape those walls. It'd be *muy loco*."

"He wanted revenge," Nathan said. "China set him up, and he took the bait. Don't get me wrong, he killed Americans, so he deserved to rot in jail, but he finally had a reason to live—vengeance."

"He gave us his theory . . . and Emerald. Maybe he had nothing left, so he offed himself."

"We were using him for analysis, and he had other sources. He told us he had vital information." Nathan sighed. "He seemed better, engaged. I think talking to us gave him hope."

"They're calling it suicide."

"Someone in that prison killed him."

"You think China flipped a guard and got them to commit murder?" Waldo asked.

"Or they looked away while someone else did it."

"In a supermax?"

"Who knows?" Nathan said. "They may have run a false-flag operation, like they did with Hamilton."

"Seems unlikely."

Nathan cracked his jaw. "It's no coincidence that the guy analyzing China's complicity in election interference kills himself when we start making headway."

"Is that what we're doing? 'Cause it feels like we got nothing."

"I'm calling the AUSA. We need a full investigation, and I don't trust the penitentiary to do it."

"It's BOP's jurisdiction," Waldo said.

"Then we'll talk to internal affairs. I'm not taking this suicide bullshit without putting up a fight."

"The cameras were out. What can they learn?"

"That it's a cover-up."

80

Reagan sipped coffee in her kitchen and stared vacantly at the television while a morning news anchor droned on about a ludicrous remark the president had made. The constant outrage on television and social media exhausted her. It never ended.

She wore sweatpants and hadn't showered or done anything with her hair other than pull it into a ponytail. She hadn't worn makeup in days. Sliding into sloth was easy without responsibility, and she'd been in hiding since her public humiliation. Sleeping late had been a welcome break, but her lack of productivity screwed with her mind. She had no purpose.

"What am I doing?"

She should spend more time with Amelia, but their relationship had been weird since the pictures had been released. The poor girl had—

Glass shattered behind her.

Reagan whirled around. The window above the sink spider-webbed around a tiny hole. A hunk of glass fell out and shattered on the counter.

"What the—"

Another hole appeared in the glass and something whooshed past her face and exploded a vase on the counter behind her. Flower petals fluttered in the air. Reagan flinched and stared at the hole.

A bullet.

She ducked as the window disintegrated under a hail of bullets. Rounds thudded against her wooden cabinets. She dove onto the floor and crawled behind the island for cover. What the hell was happening?

The shooting stopped, if that's what it had been. There hadn't been any loud bangs—only muffled pops. It couldn't be real. Was someone trying to kill her?

Her eyes darted to the sliding door. Would the shooter come for her? She needed help.

She slithered back to the table on her belly and reached for her phone. She kept her head down and stayed below the windowsill. She stretched and patted the table's surface. Where was her phone? She glanced back at the broken window. The fall wind whistled through it, bringing a chill.

Her hand bumped the phone, and she wrapped her fingers around it. She dragged it off the table and scrambled back across the floor. Her heart pounded as she dialed.

"Fairfax County Police. What is your emergency?"

"I, uh, I need help," she stammered.

"What is the nature of your emergency?"

"Someone's shooting at me, I think." She leaned around the island. The sliding glass door remained closed.

"Ma'am, are you in immediate danger?"

"Yes, I think, they shot into my house. My kitchen window—"

"What's your street address?"

Reagan gave it to her and stayed on the phone at the operator's request. She stared through the door's glass. Leaves blew across the lawn. Who was out there? Would they smash through it and hunt her down?

Her pulse thumped in her neck. She forced herself to breathe. Had she hallucinated everything? She looked at her damaged cabinets and shattered vase. The shooting happened. Someone had tried to kill her. But who would want her dead?

A siren blared in the distance.

81

Nathan paced inside the Colorado Springs Airport as he finished his call with Reagan. He'd spoken to her three times since the shooting, because not being there to protect her drove him crazy. He slipped his phone into his pocket and joined Waldo at the gate.

"Flight's delayed," Waldo said. "Reagan okay?"

"She's got the sword of Damocles hanging over her."

"Who'd want to hurt her?"

"The animals who hired her blackmailer."

"As retribution for turning them in?"

"Maybe, but I think it's part of a larger, targeted strategy. They tried to coerce her into voting for their candidate, but she refused, so they decided to remove her."

"That doesn't get them delegate support."

"It might if they replaced her with someone friendly to Lemon. But taking her out would have also removed a dissenting voice. Having delegates criticize the Democratic Party's nominee damages the party's credibility."

"You're talking like the DNC was behind it."

"Best case, they have a group forwarding their interests through illegal activity, whether the DNC's directly involved or not. Worst case, they're complicit in planning and executing a massive criminal conspiracy employing everything from blackmail to murder to change the outcome of this election."

Waldo's cell rang, and he answered.

Nathan drifted over to the gate. The Flight Information Display System updated, and their flight was re-listed with a departure in thirty minutes. Nathan confirmed the departure. Between their carfentanil sting, uncovering Chinese disintegration warfare tactics, and protecting Reagan, he had his hands full.

He returned to their waiting area and slipped into a chair. Waldo hung up and pinched the skin on his neck. He'd gone quiet.

"You look like you've seen a ghost," Nathan said.

"That was Isabella."

"Who?"

"The corrections guard who's been flirting with me at the penitentiary."

"You mean the one you've been harassing with unsolicited sexual advances every time we visit."

Waldo didn't smile. "I asked her to put me in touch with Don Wilson."

"The corrections officer on duty when Hamilton hung himself?"

"One of two guards supposedly keeping an eye on him."

"The video camera wasn't recording."

"You said Chinese intelligence either bribed, threatened, or tricked them into helping. I thought that was *loco*, but I don't trust these *pendejos*, so I asked her to track him down."

"*Thought?*"

"Before Isabela called."

"What'd she say?" Nathan asked.

"We can't question him."

"Why not?"

"Wilson's dead," Waldo said.

Nathan's muscles tensed, a primitive reaction to a perceived threat. His subconscious lizard brain processed information quicker than his executive functions.

"What happened?"

"Initial report suggests a carbon monoxide leak in his house. His stove leaked."

"How did you—"

"They briefed Isabella's shift."

Nathan stared out at the tarmac. This was bad, and too much to be a coincidence. "They killed him to cover up Hamilton's murder."

"Keep talking like that, and we'll be wearing tinfoil hats."

"Wilson and his partner . . . what was his name?"

"Henry Evans."

"Yeah, somehow, the Chinese influenced them to murder Hamilton because he was helping us to expose their role in election interference and disintegration warfare."

"You guessing, *Papi*."

"Now one of the guards is dead."

"The guards weren't cooperating with BOP," Waldo said. "I mean, not really."

"It's possible Wilson had a change of heart, or the Chinese wanted to eliminate the possibility of . . ."

"What?"

"If they killed Wilson, they'll eliminate Evans too."

Waldo cocked his head. "If Evans and Wilson were complicit, and if China murdered Wilson . . . then, yeah, Evans might get whacked. But that's a lot of ifs. And killing Wilson could be a warning for Evans to stay quiet."

"Or the motivation for him to cooperate. If he worries the CCP will kill him too, what choice does he have?"

"You gone far down that conspiracy rat hole," Waldo said.

"We're always playing catch up. How many people must die before we get proactive and anticipate China's next move?"

Waldo scratched and stretched. "Okay, I'll play. If you're right, China knows killing Wilson will warn Evans."

"He might not even know yet. We only found out because of your flirtation with . . ." Nathan jumped up.

"What?" Waldo asked.

"They'll murder Evans today, if they haven't already done it."

"You think—"
"It's time to get proactive and punch back."

82

Zhao's encrypted satellite phone jangled on his nightstand. They'd installed classified hard lines in his residence, but he carried the satellite phone everywhere and trusted it more than wired devices. It made little sense to use wireless over wired, but China's enemies had long targeted him, and being under constant surveillance had created a strange form of paranoia. He was self-aware enough to realize this, but it didn't matter. He did what made him happy.

Which explained why Jíng Qí lay naked beside him.

Zhao answered the phone. "Yes?"

"We intercepted a communication planning a terrorist attack," Colonel Chén said without preamble.

Chén had replaced the traitorous Colonel Ying Luo. Her death was little consolation for her betrayal. Oh, how he would have loved to have her alive and in his underground prison. He could have made her pain last for years.

"And?" Zhao asked.

"They're using opioids as a chemical weapon."

Zhao swung his feet out of bed. "When?"

"A few hours ago."

"No, when is the attack?"

"Unknown. From the transcript, it sounds like it's still in the planning stages. The caller mentioned Shanghai, the site of the recent bombing incident."

Zhao looked back at Jíng. She stirred but didn't appear to wake.

"Have you identified the terrorists?" he asked.

"The call originated from an unknown person. Our analyst identified a Shanghainese dialect and traces of other languages. He spoke of the Muslim Brotherhood, as if he represented them."

"Where did the call originate?"

"The Jaiding District in Shanghai. We sent a black team, but the caller disabled the cellular telephone before they arrived. He made the call from an open-air market."

"Video?"

"They are collecting police camera footage now."

"And the other party?"

"That's why I'm calling you at home. The terrorist is tentatively identified as Bai Hu, an active insurgent in the Turkistan Islamic Party. He worked with Yakuf."

Zhao stilled, and his stomach hardened to stone. He glanced behind him. Jíng breathed deeply.

"The Muslim Brotherhood is communicating with the TIP about a terror attack?" Zhao asked.

"Yes."

"And they plan to use opioids?"

"That was the inference, and our analyst's conclusion. I read the transcript, and it seems accurate."

The hair rose on Zhao's neck. Bad enough that Yakuf had been killed with Quon's drugs, but now Islamists planned terrorism using opioids—and he'd approved sales to them. The king cobra coiled in the high grass, waiting to strike.

He cleared his throat. "I want all our people on this. Arrest or kill Bai Hu and seize his drugs before he deploys their weapons."

"Yes, General."

"Islamists have learned their lesson too well. We showed them a new weapon, and now, they plan to use it."

"So it seems."

Chén's tone and casual manner prickled his skin. Chén felt too comfortable to express his unsolicited opinion. Did the colonel sense his vulnerability? Zhao's tactics backfired, one right after another, and his strategy teetered on the verge of disaster. Perhaps Chén planned to betray him and save himself. That would never work, because Zhao's command staff would be executed with him. Did Chén understand that? He'd need to teach him a lesson and put him back in his place.

"Have our agents contact the traffickers we've used for black ops. Instruct them to cease all deliveries to Muslim customers." He paused. No that wouldn't do it.

"Amend that instruction. Order our traffickers to suspend all sales until we can determine where and how our opioids are used."

"All opioid sales?" she asked.

"Cease drug warfare until we can reassess."

"We're indirectly supporting and financing billions of dollars of sales to the West," Chén said.

"What part of my order did you not understand?" He kept a chill in his voice. "Are you unable to follow a simple command?"

"Yes, General. I mean, no, General. I'll see it done immediately."

Fear had crept into Chén's voice. Good. If he couldn't control his own subordinates, what chance did he have of executing a complicated plan?

Behind him, Jíng's breathing rhythm changed, and he glanced at her. She lay motionless facing away from him. He looked beyond her through the open bathroom door. In the mirror's reflection of the mirror, Jíng's eyes were open. She'd been watching him. And listening.

83

Nathan peeled out of the airport car rental agency's parking lot and glanced at Waldo. "Where we going, partner?"

Waldo waited on hold. "The BOP won't release Evans's address."

"We're trying to save his life. Fucking bureaucracy." Nathan took out his phone and dialed the AUSA Sam White's office.

No answer.

He dialed Sam's cell, and the call went straight to voicemail. "Shit. Isabella's got the hots for you, right?"

Waldo looked out the window. "Like I told you—"

"I'm not matchmaking. Call her at the prison and get Evans's home address. She'll understand the urgency."

Waldo opened his recent calls, found Isabella's and hit redial. "*Hola*, it's Osvaldo . . . Uh-huh, yeah, I wanted to call too."

Nathan smiled and focused on the road.

"Yeah, *también*, we can talk about that later, okay, *bonita*?" Waldo listened for a minute. "*Gracias.* We think Wilson's death wasn't an accident. We have a theory—" He pressed the phone against his ear. "I'll explain later, but right now, I need his partner's home address . . . *Si*, Evans."

Waldo glanced at Nathan and flashed a thumbs-up. Thirty seconds later, he sat upright. "Yeah, got it. *Muchas gracias. Si, si*, yeah, uh, me too. Okay. It's a date." He hung up.

Nathan smirked at him. "Get the address, lover?"

He lives in Pueblo on the 1700 block of 7th Street East. It's forty minutes south.

Nathan stomped on the gas.

They raced down Interstate 25 from Colorado Springs toward Pueblo. Nathan sped as fast as traffic would allow, alternating his attention between the road and the map on his phone.

"You really think they coming for Evans?" Waldo asked.

"Hamilton is dead."

"Could be suicide."

"Not a chance. It's an impossible coincidence that the corrections officer monitoring Hamilton would kill himself the next day."

"*Si*, it's unlikely, but maybe he felt guilty for—"

"A million-to-one shot."

Waldo stretched out his legs and exhaled. "*Me rindo*. I know when it's useless to argue."

Waldo stared out the window and didn't speak for at least ten minutes. Then he sat up and looked at Nathan. "Hey, *amigo*. If you're right, shouldn't we request backup?"

A sinking feeling passed through Nathan. He hadn't been thinking clearly. It could be the jet lag, fatigue, or the complicated conspiracies fighting for attention, but he needed to do everything in his power to save Officer Evans.

"Call 911," Nathan said. "Tell them a corrections officer's life may be in danger. Send them to his house. If we're wrong, I'll take the heat."

Nathan accelerated through thickening traffic while Waldo called the police and requested a welfare check. Ten minutes later, they screeched to a stop behind a black-and-white SUV with gold lettering and a low-profile light bar. Two officers in black uniforms walked away from Evans's dilapidated, single-story house. The paint peeled off the siding and brown grass and weeds covered the lawn. A shithole. What financial strains had eaten Evans's federal salary? His living in poverty made Chinese bribery more feasible.

They met the officers outside the house and showed them their credentials.

"You guys call this in?" the younger officer asked.

"We have reason to believe Officer Evans's life is in danger."

The cop smirked at his partner. "And why is that, sir?"

"The high-profile inmate in his custody allegedly committed suicide last night, then his partner was found dead this morning."

The cop hooked his thumbs on his gun belt. "We knocked on the door. Doesn't look like anyone's home."

"He didn't show for his shift today."

"Maybe his partner's death screwed him up. Could be sleeping one off."

"They didn't find his partner until this morning."

The second cop wrinkled his nose. "Something *could be* wrong."

The first officer crossed his arms. "There's no sign of a crime, and we don't have permission to enter. We don't have the right to knock down his door."

The second cop nodded. "I guess—"

"You don't have to," Nathan said. He headed for the house.

"Uh, sir," the cop called after him.

Nathan kept going.

"Agent," the cop tried again.

Nathan ignored him.

The officers and Waldo followed Nathan to the front door. Nathan tried the handle. Locked.

"I told you we checked it."

Nathan looked from them to Waldo. He shrugged.

Waldo shook his head, anticipating.

Nathan smiled, then turned and kicked the door. His heel impacted the wood below the doorknob, and splinters flew into the air with a crack.

The door swung open.

The younger offer raised his palm up. "We can't let you—"

Nathan drew his Glock and slipped across the threshold into a living room.

"Sir!"

He moved down a hall into the kitchen. Nothing. The lights were off and the place stunk like hot dogs and stale beer.

Nathan moved down a side hall with doors on either side and one at the end. He paused at a bedroom, then stopped. He'd glimpsed something. He leaned back into the hall as the two officers and Waldo came around the corner.

There. The bathroom door was ajar and something pink poked out.

A finger.

Nathan sprinted down the hall and eased open the door. Evans lay naked on the floor with empty bottles of medication scattered around him. A thin stream of blood oozed out of his head and stained the white tile.

"We're too late," Waldo said.

Nathan knelt beside Evans and leaned close. Evans's chest rose, and he gurgled.

"He's breathing. Call an ambulance."

"Shit," the younger cop said. He keyed his mike. "Dispatch, X-ray fourteen. Roll a bus, code three."

84

Nathan and Waldo showed their credentials to the Pueblo police officer standing guard outside the hospital room where Corrections Officer Henry Evans fought for his life. The cop was officially there to protect Evans, at the request of BOP, but no one wanted Evans walking away either. Evans had awakened after a short coma, but he wasn't out of the woods yet, and this could be their only chance to interrogate him.

But Nathan and Waldo weren't the only investigators interested in speaking with Evans. Agents from the Office of the Inspector General and the Office of Internal Affairs in the Bureau of Prisons both wanted their shot at him. Hamilton, a high-profile inmate, was dead of a suspected suicide, one of his guards had died under suspicious circumstances, and now this. The situation stunk, and everyone knew it.

They entered the room where the IG and IA agents sat in blue plastic chairs at the foot of the bed, talking to Evans, or more accurately, at him. Evans didn't look good. His skin had taken on a yellowish hue, indicating the drugs he'd ingested had damaged his liver. His eyes wandered around the room while one of the agents read questions out of a notebook.

Seriously? The investigator wasn't even watching Evans while he asked questions. The other investigator, a plump man with worn brown shoes, sat on the edge of his chair with his elbows resting on his knees. He looked around the room through narrowed eyes and shifted uncomfortably and glanced at the door. The man did not want to be in a hospital room.

"... and you didn't notice anything wrong with the camera at the beginning of your shift?"

"I already answered that," Evans said.

"But ... I mean, when did you notice it wasn't working?"

Heat flushed Nathan's neck. The agents' inability to read the situation infuriated him, as did their juvenile questions. The interrogation felt like a student exercise at Quantico.

"We weren't told the camera was out until after we discovered the deceased inmate," Evans said in a weak voice.

The investigator flipped the page in his notebook. "Did Hamilton threaten suicide before?"

"No."

"Did he say anything that suggested he may want to hurt himself?"

Evans turned his head and stared at the wall.

"Officer Evans?"

"I answered these questions before. They grilled us after the suicide."

"This is the internal investigation."

Evans closed his eyes. "I'm not feeling well. Are we done?"

"Uh, let me see." The investigator flipped the pages in his notebook. "You, uh—" He cleared his throat. "Why did you try to kill yourself?"

"I didn't."

"But the pills—"

"An accident. I got drunk and took too much."

"So you didn't attempt suicide?" the other investigator chimed in for the first time.

"No."

The investigators looked at each other. The first agent exhaled and grunted as he stood. "That wraps this up. You get some rest and feel—"

"Are you kidding me?" Nathan asked.

Everyone looked at him.

"The camera on Hamilton's cell goes down the night he allegedly kills himself, then one of the guards monitoring him dies from carbon monoxide poisoning and the other attempts suicide on the same day. You're buying that?"

"The carbon monoxide poisoning was confirmed and—"

"Are you that incompetent to not see what's happening, or is it willful blindness?"

"Now hold on a second," the first investigator said. His jowls reddened. "We're conducting a thorough—"

"I don't have time for this shit," Nathan said. "Our country's under attack."

"What do you mean—"

"Listen to me, Evans," Nathan said. He crossed the room and leaned close.

"Hey, I don't gotta talk to you."

Nathan held out his badge. "Nathan Burke, FBI. I'm investigating a widespread Chinese attack on the United States, and you're involved."

"I don't—"

"Save it. What's your plan here? Lie to us about Hamilton's death to avoid a charge? And then what?"

"You didn't try to kill yourself, right?"

"I said—"

"Don't bullshit me about an accidental overdose. The guys who paid you off to either kill Hamilton or look the other way tried to murder you."

Evans pressed his lips together. He looked away.

"Hey," the second investigator said. "You can't accuse him without evidence of—"

"We have circumstantial evidence," Nathan said. He glared at the investigator, then turned back to Evans. "But you shouldn't worry about a murder charge."

Evans cocked his head, and a glimmer of hope flashed in his eyes.

"We're not your problem," Nathan said, "because the Chinese are gonna kill you."

Evans flinched.

"You're only alive because we figured it out and kicked in your door. If you survive, it's only because we saved you."

Evans's mouth opened. He didn't know Nathan and Waldo had rescued him.

"We'll protect you if you cooperate, but if you stonewall us, Chinese intelligence will finish the job the second you're released. You won't last a day."

"I don't know what you're talking about."

Nathan studied Evans's face. He'd showed genuine surprise at Nathan's mention of Chinese involvement.

"You didn't know your master, but the only people who wanted Hamilton dead were the Chinese."

"He worked for them," Evans said. "That traitor sold us out to China. Why would they kill him?"

"They used a false-flag operation to entice his treason. They do the same to you?"

Evans blinked rapidly. "I'd never work for China."

"You helped them murder Hamilton, without understanding who gave the order. That's how it went down, right?"

Evans's cheeks bulged. He glanced at the door.

"You leave, and you're dead."

Evans's eyes shifted back and forth.

"They tried to kill you."

He closed his eyes.

"They'll do it again."

"I know."

Nathan didn't breathe. "They want to silence you. We're your only hope. Give them up."

No one spoke.

Finally, Evans opened his eyes and stared straight ahead. "I was drinking, like I said, but I only had half a glass of whiskey, like I do every night. Then I woke up here."

"They drugged your whiskey?"

"Must have. It hit me hard. I thought I was having a stroke. I reached for my phone, but I didn't make it. That's the last thing I remember."

Nathan nodded. "They dragged you into your bathroom and spread out the pills to suggest a suicide."

"Fuck."

"And Hamilton?" Nathan asked.

"We broke the camera."

"*We?*"

"Me and Wilson. They told us to disable the one covering Hamilton's cell."

Nathan vibrated with excitement, like he always did when he flipped a criminal. This was an inflection point that could break the case.

"*Who* told you?"

"He called Hamilton a traitor who deserved a beating. He never said nothing about killing him."

"What was this man's name?"

Evans looked at Nathan. I don't know, but he was an older bald guy . . . and he showed me a badge."

"What kind of badge?"

"FBI."

85

Nathan plowed through endless paperwork at his desk, a Sisyphean bureaucratic task that throttled the effectiveness of federal law enforcement. Agents stuck at their desks feeding red tape into the machine weren't out investigating bad guys. Administrative requirements never ended.

Evans's cooperation had led them to forged visitor logs, and the footage taken from a series of cameras show the ingress of a man Wilson had escorted to Hamilton's cell and left him alone for what Evans claimed was supposed to be a beating but had turned into a suicide—and was now classified as homicide. An enlarged frame taken from the employee's entrance revealed an image of an old friend.

The Leopard.

They'd limited the intense internal investigation to a handful of FBI agents working with a DOJ prosecutor under the watchful eyes of agents from OPR and OIG. An internal investigation like this required oversight, and Nathan welcomed it, as long as they could keep it secret in light of the deep Chinese infiltration.

Nathan's cellphone rang, and he answered. "Burke."

"This is Ali from Crypto," the FBI analyst said, referring to the Cryptanalysis Unit in the Laboratory Division. She'd been trying to access the data on the microchip Xuannü had provided Nathan and Meili before her gruesome demise.

"Talk to me."

"We cracked it."

Nathan's heart raced. "What did she give us?"

"I'm sending it to you on the high-side now."

Nathan waved Waldo over, and his fingers fumbled over the keyboard as he logged into his classified computer. His fatigue had disappeared.

"*Que pasa*, partner?" Waldo asked.

"They decrypted the information on Xuannü's disk."

Waldo's eyes widened. "Anything *bueno*?"

"Let's see if she died for nothing."

Nathan opened Ali's email. She opened by detailing the decryption process, which he'd have her explain on the witness stand if this case ever went to trial. He skimmed over it and opened the attached files.

The first was a photo of an internal Second Bureau memo, but everything was in Mandarin, and he'd need to have it translated. Meili had been discharged from the hospital and was at home recovering, so he'd print the image and sneak it over to her. That would be a security violation—but only if they caught him. Without bending the rules, it could take days to learn what it said.

Waldo leaned over Nathan's shoulder. "That looks important."

"We'll see."

Nathan opened the next document, and telephone tolls popped up on his screen. He scrolled through the call detail, cell site information, and other data, then returned to the metadata at the top.

"Who does that belong to?" Waldo asked.

"Let's find out."

Nathan swiveled to his unclassified computer and pulled up the Criminal Justice Information Services Shared Enterprise Network database. He plugged in the number and gasped.

"*Que?*"

"It comes back to the DNC," Nathan said.

"Someone from China called a number at the Democratic National Committee?"

"Yep."

Nathan would subpoena the phone providers for subscriber information, then if he had enough probable cause, he'd seek search warrants for any retained SMS information that hadn't been deleted. But he needed to know who used that number right now.

Nathan grabbed his desk phone and dialed Reagan. She answered on the first ring.

"You never call with good news," she said.

"I need some quick information. I have a DNC number and I want to know who uses it."

"I don't have that information."

"But you can find out."

She sighed heavily into the phone. "Let me have it."

He passed the number, hung up, and turned to Waldo. "Let's get an analyst up here and start digging into this information."

"You're optimistic?"

"Xuannü gave her life to get it to us. She said it's the evidence we need, and I have no reason to doubt her."

Nathan returned to the email on his classified system. He opened the last attachment—an audio file. He hesitated before opening it, because it had come from a foreign source, but tech had scanned and scrubbed everything before putting it into their system.

He opened it. And a man's voice speaking in hushed tones came through the speaker.

"You will need to fire twenty percent of your staff."

"If I win," a woman said.

"*When* you win. We've taken the necessary steps to ensure victory. Once you're ensconced, we'll clean house."

"Of course."

"This will be the final preparation before we fight for hegemony."

Nathan hit pause. His heart pounded like it wanted to come out of his chest. He recognized the female voice.

"Is that . . .?" Waldo asked.

"One hundred percent." Nathan tapped the keys on his desk phone.

"Who you calling?" Waldo asked.

"We can't sit on this."

Waldo shifted on his feet. "Shouldn't we wait and confirm—"

"It's her."

"*Es posible, pero*—" His eyes widened. "What if it's a deepfake, and they want us to think—"

"No."

Meili picked up on the second ring. "I'm going crazy sitting in bed all—"

"We cracked into Xuannü's chip."

Her rapid intake of air came out of the speaker. "What's on it?"

"Call details, photographs, recordings. There's a call where a man is giving orders to a woman to clean house after the election."

"Who?"

"Darcy Lemon."

Meili didn't speak.

"Did you hear me?" he asked.

"You're sure?"

Waldo leaned close. "Hey, boss, Waldo here. It could be a fake to set us up?"

"To what end?"

"Create confusion?" Waldo asked. "I don't know."

"The call data will give us more, and I still haven't listened to the other recordings, but we have enough to corroborate this. Her voice can be authenticated, at least to the level we'll need in court."

"Court?" Waldo asked.

"Darcy Lemon is a Chinese spy," Nathan said.

"But—"

"It all makes sense," Nathan said. "This has been a long play by the CCP. They inserted their mole into the government to gain credibility while they blackmailed and bribed members of both parties, then after the last election, they tried to get their candidate into office. As a failsafe, they prepared to kill the other potential nominees. That's why we found explosives in the barber shop."

"We need to take this to the attorney general," Meili said.

Nathan's core tightened. "I don't know . . ."

"What's your hesitation?" she asked.

"The infiltration is so deep. If we present this to the wrong person, they could bury it or discredit the evidence . . . or worse."

"Good point," Waldo said. "We shouldn't share this with anyone until we know more."

"We need to take her out," Meili said. "We're on the verge of an election, and a Chinese spy could become president. We have no time to hesitate."

"Agreed," Nathan said.

"Then what's your plan?" she asked.

"We go public," Nathan said. "We dump everything onto the internet. We send it to newspapers and podcasts and radio stations. We let the American people know what's happening."

"Bad idea," Waldo said. "This will rip the country apart. The conspiracy nuts will go *loco*."

"Only this time, the conspiracy is real," Nathan said. "Let's release this evidence today."

Meili sighed. "Take the bitch down."

86

Zhao slumped in the Tactical Operations Center and listened to clacking keyboards as intelligence officers decoded communications. They glanced his way, trying to intuit his mood, but he didn't possess the energy to project strength. Not today. He should laugh in the face of adversity, but the failures of the past weeks had worn him down.

A young major eyed him from behind a classified terminal. Zhao glared at him, and he looked away. Zhao had built a culture of fear, and that maintained his authority, even through his recent defeats.

Colonel Chén leaned over a SIGINT computer with a classified red phone pressed against his ear. He listened and then his body stiffened. Chén looked at him, and Zhao spread his hands in a question. Chén shook his head.

Another problem.

Chén hung up and walked across the room. He stood in front of Zhao.

"Report," Zhao said, not wanting to hear more bad news.

"We received a message from the Sky Fox." Chén took a deep breath, and his hesitancy threatened to tear a hole in Zhao's stomach.

"Out with it."

"The Sky Fox reports the FBI have exposed our connections to Darcy Lemon."

The room darkened and Zhao's temples throbbed. "They have evidence?"

"The Sky Fox believes they can't yet make an arrest, but they've discovered the trail of breadcrumbs. They know."

Zhao sighed. The significance of events over the past days weighed him down. General Sun's presence hovered over him, even when the man wasn't there, as if he saw everything. Judged everything.

"We need to withdraw," Zhao said.

"Withdraw?" Chén asked.

"A tactical retreat. Disassociate from election influence. Abort operations, cease communications, close the offshore accounts."

"The Americans have already uncovered our interference."

"We must cease black ops targeting electors, politicians . . . any elected officials."

"We have many plans in progress across—"

"The damned FBI had stumbled on good fortune and uncovered our hand in their democratic process. Direct links to our intelligence will bring diplomatic reprisals."

"Won't we deny—"

"We can disavow everything, but even a single spark can ignite the fire. Evidence of our direct involvement could lead to embargoes, debt dismissal, blockades, open support for Taiwan . . . The potential punishments are endless. This could lead to open warfare."

"Isn't that the plan?"

Zhao shouldn't allow his subordinate to question him, but Zhao's mind had grown fuzzy, and talking out loud helped. Besides, others could hear, and they needed to understand the urgency to react and the severe consequences if they failed.

"We will go to war when we have the advantage. But first, we must hollow out the West from within so they crumble when we apply pressure. The time is not right. We are not ready."

"What are your orders?"

"Withdraw from the battlefield."

"But General Sun—"

"We need damage control before this becomes an international incident and General Sun removes me, guts the Second Bureau, and destroys our chances of defeating the West."

"And the rest of our disintegration warfare?"

"Keep applying pressure in other areas . . . until the United States breaks."

Chén nodded, and worry lines creased his face. Chén understood the gravity of the situation. They stood on the edge of a cliff, and every bad report edged them closer to the abyss.

And if Zhao fell, his staff would perish with him.

87

Reagan hovered her finger over her laptop's keyboard, then stopped and reached for her wineglass on the end table beside the sofa. The hotel room offered a small suite, yet the walls still seemed to close in on her. At least Vince could leave for work, but she was stuck there. She took a long drag of sauvignon blanc, a New Zealand grape with a green-apple finish. Her claustrophobia lingered.

Vince shot her a disapproving look from the chair across from her. She probably had been drinking too much, but he'd do the same thing if he'd been disillusioned, blackmailed, and almost murdered.

"What?" Reagan asked.

"That brazen shooting explains their motivation," Vince said.

"Yeah, it proves they want to eliminate me."

"It reveals why your blackmailers allowed the hacker to meet you."

"I don't follow," she said.

"If the shooter had succeeded . . ." His face hardened. "If they'd killed you, they'd have created a huge controversy."

"It's all over the news now."

"That's what I mean," he said. "Exposure was predictable, either way. They don't care about the publicity, and that clarifies why they took a chance and let the blackmailer meet you face-to-face. Even if police caught him and exposed their election interference plot, they'd still achieve their end."

"Which was?"

"Chaos."

"All this death and destruction to screw up our election?"

"They wanted to install their candidate. If their coercion and fraud had gone unnoticed, they'd have controlled our government. But if their efforts failed, they'd still create distrust in our elections and make people question the system. They'd undermine our government's credibility."

Reagan sighed. America was under attack, her party had been infiltrated, and her reputation had been smeared. Now her life was in jeopardy. How would they survive?

She returned her attention to her computer and looked at her official delegate email. She'd avoided it since the pictures had hit the public, but now the shooting had been in the news, and the coverage had gone national, because it provided another chance for the media to talk about lewd photographs.

Her inbox showed 623 unread emails. The amount of hate must be off the charts. She grabbed her laptop screen to slam it shut, then stopped. She couldn't hide forever. Being a delegate brought duties and responsibilities, and that meant acknowledging voters' concerns. Entering politics was her choice, and if she ever ran for a national office, this came with the job.

She took another sip of liquid courage and opened her inbox. She stared at the subject lines and cocked her head. Not what she'd expected. She opened the first email to be sure.

"Huh?"

"What's that?" Vince asked.

"Something's going on."

Vince looked up and sighed. "Another problem?"

"The opposite," Reagan said. "They're . . . on my side."

Vince came across the room and looked over her shoulder. She scrolled through them, reading subject lines and the email content previews. The senders consistently offered condolences and expressed empathy for the way she'd been targeted.

Reagan opened one.

It's a disgrace that you have been attacked. Thank you for doing the right thing and exposing corruption in our party. I stand with you.

Reagan's throat tightened and tears welled in her eyes. She clicked through more emails. A few called her horrible names for posing nude, and one lamented the shooter had missed her, but the rest were positive. No, they were more than that. She'd received an outpouring of support.

"Unexpected," Vince said.

"They're thanking me for not changing my vote and reporting the blackmail to the police. They're commending me for not submitting to coercion."

"They recognize the courage it took for you to do the right thing, despite the public humiliation you knew you'd face." Vince put his hand on her shoulder.

She looked up at him, and he smiled. He hadn't touched her since the scandal broke, not until he'd hugged her after the shooting, but this was different. He seemed to understand the dilemma she'd faced, and he acknowledged her bravery in coming forward.

She placed her hand on top of his. "I didn't have enough faith in the American people. They have the ability to forgive, and they're smart enough to see the corruption. Maybe I can make a difference. There's hope."

88

Ming Zhao exited the Second Bureau's headquarters, and his boots thumped against the bricks as he strode across the courtyard. Jíng hustled to keep pace. He didn't trust her, but after Luo's betrayal, he suspected everyone. He'd let Jíng get too close, and she could ruin him.

Tonight, he'd send her to a watery grave.

Zhao's stomach churned. His discomfort could be from last night's squid soup, but Luo's betrayal and his suspicions of Jíng had tied his intestines in knots. As had his failures in America. He'd stuck out his neck to seize power, and his gambit had not succeeded.

They approached an old factory that had once produced farm equipment, and had then been transformed into a mental institution. Now, the Second Bureau repurposed it as a black site to incarcerate political prisoners.

Jíng raced ahead and showed her identification to a guard. The man snapped to attention and opened the door. Zhao returned his salute and entered the building. He stopped at a security desk encased behind bullet-proof glass, where even Zhao had to show identification and sign the log.

Zhao followed Jíng down a wide hallway that reeked of ammonia. The fluorescent bulbs hummed, and the glare off the tile pierced his brain. They showed their identification to a third guard, and the man let them into an industrial elevator. He activated it with a key and hit the button of the ninth subterranean floor. The elevator groaned as they descended at a maddeningly slow pace. Zhao focused on the door and tried not to think about their descent over one hundred feet below the surface of the earth.

The elevator jerked to a stop, and Zhao stepped out into another brightly lit hallway. A guard snapped to attention and saluted. Zhao returned it and entered the first of six interrogation rooms, and the only one where prisoners weren't tortured. Zhao used it to tell prisoners their fate.

"How long?" Zhao asked.

Jíng spoke into a microphone attached to her sleeve, a technical accessory she used whenever they moved about the Second Bureau's compound. She cocked her head, listening to the response, then looked at him. "Two minutes."

He nodded and turned away. His strategy had backfired in unexpected ways. Using Islamists had been a proven tactic since Kaiser Wilhelm II radicalized Muslims before World War I. The Soviets, Iranians, and even the Americans had done it too. Zhao had simply repurposed China's dominant opioid production into a weapon to bring the American economy to its knees. But China's own Islamist radicals had learned from the Phantoms' example, and they planned to use carfentanil against the homeland.

What had gone wrong?

Jíng touched her earpiece and looked up. "He is here."

"Bring him."

Jíng slipped out the door, shutting it behind her. A murmured conversation came from the hallway, then the door opened and she reentered. Behind her, two guards led a man in a prison uniform into the room. A chain connected his handcuffs to leg irons, and it jingled as he moved. They stopped and pushed the man forward.

Quon Li.

The white strips on the chest and shoulders of Quon's blue uniform had yellowed from sweat. The prisoner number affixed to his uniform, 115-968, referred to the 115th year of the Chinese Communist Party and the sequential number of his incarceration in the Ministry of State Security's special prison for the most notorious and treacherous political prisoners.

They had yet to reach one thousand inmates that year, but each man—and a few women—posed the highest security threats.

Quon stared back with red-rimmed eyes above dark, puffy circles. Bruises from multiple beatings colored his skin—a palette of color from light blue to dark purple. A flicker of pity tickled Zhao's belly. The guards hadn't been told to torture him. Perhaps Quon had caused trouble, and they'd taught him a lesson. Beating wasn't necessary, because Zhao would inflict the ultimate price.

He had no choice.

China's involvement in the Phantoms' carfentanil attacks must be hidden. Even though the Americans suspected Chinese complicity, the extent of China's involvement could never be exposed. Zhao would have imprisoned Quon long ago, but the man had stayed below the radar, and he'd proved useful. But delivering carfentanil to Turkistan Islamic Party members was the ultimate act of treason. And the death of Hasan Yakuf had made international news, which meant Quon's role could be discovered.

He had to go.

"You know why you are here?" Zhao asked.

"Something has gone wrong."

"You supplied drugs to Islamists to be used as terroristic weapons against your own people."

"I have no knowledge of this."

"You supplied the Muslim Brotherhood, and they support traitors in our midst."

"I informed you the Brotherhood approached me."

"You didn't say they supported the Uyghur uprising."

"I traffic drugs. I don't engage in politics. My opioids are intended to intoxicate people, not kill them."

"Your Islamists disagree."

Quon's jaw bulged.

"You want to say something?" Zhao asked.

Quon shook his head.

"This is your only chance."

Quon looked up and his shiny eyes showed fear.

"Out with it," Zhao said. Somehow letting prisoners unleash their anger and speak their mind made him enjoy what came next even more.

"You taught Islamists to deploy carfentanil as a weapon. You introduced radicals to chemical warfare, and they've turned on you. You blame me for selling the drugs—something you have encouraged and enabled—and now you blame me because the monkeys you taught to kill come after you?"

That was it. Treason, insubordination . . . enough to pass judgment. And more than that, Quon was a link to a part of the drug warfare strategy that had gone horribly wrong, and he could implicate Zhao. That could never happen.

Zhao straightened his shoulders, milking every inch of height out of his diminutive stature. He wanted to project the full authority of his position. The order he was about to give demanded it.

"Prisoner 115-968," Zhao said, "for your crimes against the People's Republic of China, you have been sentenced to death."

"But—"

"The matter is closed. You have committed treason."

"I did as the CCP demanded I—"

"The verdict is rendered."

Quon Li's eyes danced around the room, flickering like a tiny bird. Did he hope to find an escape? He returned his stare to Zhao. "When?"

"Now."

89

Darcy Lemon went from presidential hopeful to federal inmate in a flash. She was treasonous but also intelligent and savvy, and she'd immediately cooperated with the FBI. Her insider knowledge led to dozens of arrests. A cascade of corrupt politicians accepted plea deals and became witnesses, because nobody wanted to hold out while others received reduced sentences. The prisoners' dilemma unraveled China's election interference scheme.

But spies remained in place.

The morning sun hung low in the east and streaks of pink colored the sky as Waldo parked outside Nathan's condo. Nathan walked to the driver's side, and Waldo lowered his window.

"Getting in?" Waldo asked.

"Take a walk with me," Nathan said. "There's something I want to discuss in private."

"We've got a meeting in an hour."

"This is important."

Waldo sighed and shut off the engine. They strolled along the concrete pathway in Stanton Park, which was deserted that early in the morning. The air bit Nathan's skin.

"Something's bothering me," Nathan said.

"*Que pasa?*" Waldo asked.

"Chinese intelligence is good, but they can't be this good."

"Not following you, *amigo*."

"They anticipated our actions, almost like they knew what we'd do."

A woman walking a terrier entered the far side of the park. She glanced in their direction.

"The presidential candidate was a spy," Waldo said. "China infiltrated the top levels of government."

Nathan nodded. "I'm talking about tactical decisions. The Second Bureau stayed ahead of us."

"Their moles dug in everywhere, including in the Bureau."

"The Leopard knew we were coming."

"Tampa blew that surveillance," Waldo said.

"Chinese agents crashed my first meeting with Xuannü, but they didn't arrest her. It's as if they knew we were meeting a source but didn't know who. Then they killed her."

"That sucked," Waldo said, "but she played a *peligroso* game."

"The Chinese sent the Leopard to kill Hamilton."

"He flipped on them. They must have accessed our debriefings."

Nathan nodded. "That's true, but I never filed the reports."

Waldo scratched his head. "We had travel itineraries and signed into prison . . . someone found out he dropped a dime on China."

"I agree. They framed Meili's defector before we started using him, and something spooked Quon when we tried to arrest him."

"We waited too long. You said it yourself."

"I thought that was the reason," Nathan said. "But why blackmail Reagan?"

"Anderson explained it," Waldo said. "To compel her support."

"I understand their scheme to blackmail, bribe, and coerce politicians, but why choose her, specifically. Most of their targets were higher placed."

"To get Lemon elected. Reagan got mouthy about the party, and they wanted to shut her up."

"By trying to kill her?" Nathan asked. "And how does an assassin miss a stationary target sitting at her kitchen table? They found rifle casings twenty yards away."

Waldo shrugged. "*No sé, Papi.* Maybe they thought she would cause problems."

"Or her being my ex-wife had something to do with it."

Waldo slowed for a step, then resumed his pace.

Nathan stopped and faced him. "That's the final piece that made it clear to me. Our investigation was compromised at every turn."

Waldo scowled. "What you saying, partner?"

"You and I are the only commonality between Reagan, Quon, and Xuannü."

Waldo put his hands on his hips. "You're forgetting Meili. She's a commie bitch who—"

Nathan punched him.

Waldo stumbled back and fell onto the hard ground. Behind him, the woman stopped with her dog and stared at them.

"What the hell?" Waldo said.

Nathan stood over him. "I know it's you."

"What the fuck are you—?"

"Some of our failures could have been caused by infiltrators, but not all of them. It's too coincidental. The leak came from us, and I'm not a spy."

"This is bullshit," Waldo said. "And you can't prove—"

"Oh, I'll prove it. Now that I know you did it, I'll discover how you communicated. We have dozens of Chinese cooperators, and one of them will provide what we need . . . or you can be a man and admit it."

"Whatever you're thinking—"

"It's over, Osvaldo. Give it up."

Waldo rubbed his jaw. He sighed. "I'm in debt. Deep. I owe some bad people."

"You could have come to me for money."

Waldo snorted. "You don't got that kinda *dinero*."

"How much?"

"Over a mil."

Nathan shook his head. "Son of a bitch. How did you—"

"I needed one big score to get even. I kept betting, and I kept losing. I couldn't cover the vig."

"Gambling is a disorder. We could've gotten you counseling." Nathan said *we* intentionally to convey they were in this together. Waldo was desperate. Who knew what he'd do?

"You still don't get it, *compadre*. They would have killed me. They told me they'd give me more time if I fed them information."

"About our cases?"

Waldo's eyelids lowered, and he nodded. "About everything. I updated them on our open cases."

"How could you—"

"They threatened to tell OPR about my gambling. I would have lost my security clearance and my job."

Nausea spread through Nathan's stomach. "What did you give them?"

"Not much at first. A hint about our Havana investigation, something I overheard about Chinese counterintelligence. I tried to stall, but they knew I was holding out. They turned the screws, and I had to respond to specific requests for information."

"That's why you were reading other China cases?"

"*Sí.*"

An image of Xuannü flashed in Nathan's mind and rage fired adrenaline into his system. "People died."

"People die all the time."

"You passed secrets to our enemy, and they killed our source. You're a traitor."

Waldo grunted and rolled onto his hands and knees, facing away. He lumbered to his feet, then turned around.

He held his Glock in front of him.

"Think this through," Nathan said.

"It's easy for you to pass judgment. You're the big hero with the cute kid and the hot girlfriend. You're dating your boss and not telling anyone."

Nathan's mouth dropped open.

"Didn't think I knew about that, did you? What would the Bureau do if I told them?"

The adrenaline coursing through Nathan's veins fueled his anger. "You can't bargain with me. I break rules, but I do it to accomplish our mission—not to betray it."

"So high and mighty. I was a good cop in Florida, better than you, and I'm a solid agent."

"Except for the treason."

"I knew you wouldn't play ball. I should have taken you down a long time ago." Waldo glanced around, then raised the Glock's barrel and pointed it at Nathan's chest.

The woman walking her dog had taken out her phone and was speaking to someone. Nathan needed to keep Waldo talking.

"You're a murderer now?" Nathan asked. "Spying on our country wasn't enough?"

Waldo clenched his jaw, signaling imminent violence. Nathan's gun was on his hip, and he was a fast draw, but Waldo only needed to squeeze his trigger. He'd light up Nathan before Nathan's gun broke leather. Nathan needed another plan.

"Gambling is an addiction," Nathan said. "It led you to a bad place. They blackmailed you, same as they did to dozens of politicians. You would've lost everything, but they offered you a way out. Nobody can blame you for taking it."

"I'll go to jail."

Nathan nodded. "Yeah, you will, but if you help us fight them, you'll get a break. You can handle a couple of years in a minimum-security prison."

Waldo wrinkled his nose, probably running through scenarios. At least he considered alternatives. They'd throw the book at him. No AUSA would give a sweetheart deal to a federal agent who revealed secrets to a foreign power, but if he cooperated, he'd get a reduced sentence. The minimum-security suggestion was probably a pipe dream. Waldo must know that, but a desperate man would cling to any lie.

"You're not a bad person," Nathan said. "You ended up in an impossible place."

"Cops don't survive jail."

"They'll put you in a special housing unit. Someplace safe."

"I'm a cop. It's who I am."

Nathan mustered and empathetic expression. "It's who you *were*. You stopped being a cop the first time you passed information to your handler."

Waldo swallowed hard.

"You can't run. They'll play *Where's Waldo* and find you."

"*Posible.*"

"You'll die in prison. But you have a chance here. Flip on those assholes."

Waldo adjusted his grip on the Glock. He could go either way. Nathan had a five-shot .38 strapped to his ankle. If Waldo shot him, Nathan could draw it as he fell, but his chance of survival wasn't high.

"The Chinese may have rigged games to make you lose your bets."

Nathan diverted responsibility away from Waldo to help him save face. Not getting shot would be nice too.

Waldo rolled his tongue inside his cheek, close to a decision.

A police siren yelped a few blocks away.

"Let me help you," Nathan said.

Waldo's eyes snapped to his. "Why would you do that?"

"Because you've been my partner. Because you have a disease, and China exploited you."

"DOJ will agree to a deal?"

A glimmer of hope lightened Nathan's chest. "Only if you help catch these guys. Set a meeting with your handler, and we'll grab him."

Waldo looked down.

Nathan could draw and have a chance, but talking was working.

Waldo's shoulders slumped, and he dropped his muzzle. "I'm sorry."

"I know."

"You'll help me."

"Let's catch those fuckers together."

A police car screeched to a stop beside the park. Waldo tossed his gun onto the grass.

90

Darcy Lemon's arrest—an unprecedented moment in American politics—had thrown the country into political turmoil. Reagan sat in the first row of a suite at Nationals Park, high behind home plate in a box reserved for VIPs. She leaned over the railing and scanned the 41,000 people in attendance to see Archibald James—the third Democratic presidential candidate in a matter of weeks.

James stood on a platform constructed over the pitcher's mound and addressed the crowd. A close-up image of his face filled the jumbotron, and his voice echoed across the field as he tried to reassure Democrats that their party would recover.

Despite the nightmare she'd endured, excitement bubbled inside her. Any minute, James would announce his running mate. A dozen names had been floated, and talking heads speculated, but James kept the information close. He'd demanded complete autonomy in selecting his vice president.

". . . and I'll do my best to win this election." He took a deep breath and scanned the audience. He came around the podium, abandoning his notes and the teleprompters. "Let me speak from the heart."

Was this political theater or genuine?

"The past weeks have left a dark stain on our party, and on our country's electoral process. We lost good people when foreign-backed assassins murdered Mayor Gavin Harrison and nineteen others."

James rested his hands on his hips and looked up in her direction. Was he speaking directly to the delegates in her box?

"I don't know if we can win," he said.

The stadium stilled. Not a sound.

"We're starting at the last minute, with little time to answer questions or share our message. People are reeling from the scandal. The head of our party worked for a foreign power, and now we're asking those party members to trust us . . . trust me. It's a big ask."

Networks televised his speech live. Had any other politician publicly admitted he might not win just days before voters took to the polls and made a decision? Would Democrats even bother to vote on election day?

"Our party needs to heal. Our country needs to heal. For far too long, we've let tribalism and partisanship divide us."

Forty-one thousand people didn't move or speak. The audience seemed in shock. They waited to hear what James would say next. His words didn't feel scripted, but if he'd memorized this speech, he was a brilliant actor.

"We can have legitimate differences of opinion on economic policy, foreign entanglements, and the role of government—but we need common purpose. Let's come together around values we share, not focus on what divides us."

He leaned back and cracked his back, as if he spoke to people on his front porch. All pretense and formality had gone. He was either a master manipulator or he truly believed what he said.

"I honestly think the Democratic Party has moved far from the beliefs of everyday Democrats. The change happened gradually at first, but it accelerated, and we're in a bad place." His face tightened, and he set his jaw. "That ends today."

A few people cheered. The officials around Reagan looked uncomfortable. When had a presidential candidate spoken so honestly?

"The Republican Party has changed too, and it's led by elites who don't represent the average American. I ask them to follow our lead."

That elicited a cheer.

"That is why I've made a historic pick for my running mate. For the first time in American history, a Democratic presidential candidate will have a Republican vice presidential candidate on the ticket."

Electricity crackled through her. Was he serious? A Republican? He'd chosen a member of the opposing party? The enemy?

"I make this choice to the great consternation of my party, which, I might add, made my point. We need a change. I've reached across the aisle and invited my good friend and colleague to join me on this journey toward our common goal to unite us."

Someone whooped, and a smattering of applause passed through the crowd, but most people stood silent, waiting. Reagan held her breath.

"Please welcome my vice presidential pick . . . the Republican senator from Georgia . . . Doyle Knight."

Knight emerged from a group of aides who'd been hiding him. He mounted the steps onto the platform and waved to the crowd.

The audience applauded, tepid at first—this was, after all, a member of the opposition and someone they'd demonized for years—but then their reaction grew. Knight stood next to James and put his arm around him. Their enthusiasm caught on like a contagion.

"If we're lucky enough to win," Knight said, "I pledge to help President James usher in a new political era, when we don't demonize our opponents. Instead, we'll encourage civil and intellectual debate. An informed electorate will create better decisions and lead to a stronger country. We will unlock the potential of the United States and put Americans first."

Was any of this real?

Knight's voice reflected off the stadium walls around Reagan. It resonated inside her. Was that physics or hope? The country craved candidates with morals and common sense. People who believed in American exceptionalism.

"Today is the dawn of a new era," James said. "A moderate conciliatory government that strives to create policy and govern for its citizens. No longer will we cater to the extremes of either party."

It could all be empty promises, or . . .

Reagan smiled.

91

Traffic crawled down M Street NW past the Francis Scott Key Memorial, a park situated on the northern end of the bridge by the same name. The gray November sky darkened and the fresh scent of rain hung in the air. The conditions cloaked the surveillance.

Nathan knelt in the unmarked van and watched camera feeds over a tiny black-and-white monitor. The split image came from both a long-range camera mounted on their van and a pre-positioned camera hidden in the park.

Waldo stood in that park—waiting.

Six SWAT team operators sprawled on the van's benches and eyed the monitor. Four more SWAT members staged in a nearby truck, a tiny quick reaction force designed to isolate the operation from the FBI.

Secrecy meant everything.

The tactical team would execute the arrest, but Nathan was present because Waldo had insisted. Somehow, after everything, Waldo believed Nathan would protect him.

The sad part was, despite Waldo's treason, he was right.

Agent Davis, the SWAT commander, hunched beside Nathan and monitored the tactical channel. "This is old-school meet," Davis said.

"The Chinese have compromised so many American electronic

communications and database systems, it's made them paranoid. Waldo told them he had information too sensitive to pass over the email they gave him. He also gave them reason to send a special handler."

"Waldo?"

"Osvaldo Falcón, the cooperator."

"Your former partner, right?"

"Yeah."

Nathan's stomach sank. He'd breezed over that part in the earlier briefing. Had Davis implied Nathan should have seen the betrayal sooner, or was Nathan being paranoid too? He carried enough guilt for not catching Waldo's duplicity sooner.

Waldo had surrendered with Meili and Nathan at his side. Waldo chose a public defender he'd known for years, and they'd met the AUSA away from the US Attorney's Office to minimize the chance of his arrest leaking. An FBI deputy director and an OPR agent had attended the proffer when Waldo had revealed everything about his recruitment by Chinese intelligence.

Nathan looked up at the SWAT commander. "Waldo told his handler he knew William Kremelberg orchestrated Hamilton's 'suicide.'"

"Who's Kremelberg?"

"An FBI ASAC from the Public Integrity Section."

"Ironic."

"Waldo warned his handler that we're close to identifying him, but said he slow-played the investigation to buy time. He demanded the mole meet him so they could strategize on how to protect both their identities."

"The Chinese buy it?" Davis asked. "If I was a double agent, I wouldn't show."

"Desperation forces bad choices. We'll know the answer in a minute. If he—"

Davis touched his headset. "Movement. Surveillance has a heavyset white male moving across the bridge. He matches the description."

Nathan leaned forward and focused on the monitor. On the screen, Waldo faced M Street. The man stepped into view and surveyed the park. He took his time approaching. He stopped a few feet from Waldo.

"That him?" Davis asked.

"No doubt. It's William Kremelberg."

Kremelberg settled his attention on Waldo. Neither man spoke. The drizzle intensified. A cloud of vapor blew over them. A moment later, the gust rocked the van.

"Meeting in person is dangerous," Kremelberg said.

Nathan pressed the headphones against his ear, straining to hear. If Waldo gave the codeword "motorcycle," the SWAT team would race in to save him.

"Had to do it," Waldo said. "I'm concerned about my safety . . . about being found out. You and I are in the same boat."

"Do they know about me?"

"Yes."

"My name?"

"Not yet."

Kremelberg nodded. He looked around again. "You have something for me?"

"I copied the files."

"I could have done that too."

"Not without exposing yourself," Waldo said. "And I did something you couldn't. I copied Nathan Burke's notes. I have his thoughts, his hypothesis, and his plans."

"Good, that's good."

A shadow moved behind Kremelberg. A man had entered the park.

"Where the hell did he come from?" Nathan asked.

"Don't know," Davis said.

"I don't like this."

"It's a public park. Could be anyone."

"It's raining."

The man slunk down a path behind them. He didn't approach Waldo and Kremelberg, but he crept along, in no apparent rush. He wore a black jacket and black pants, and he didn't look homeless, so why did he wander through the park in a light drizzle? Something about him looked familiar, but his distance from the camera gave him an ethereal appearance, like a specter floating through the mist.

"If that fucking corrections officer cooperates, I don't have a way out," Kremelberg said.

"He doesn't know your name," Waldo said.

"He knows what I look like. They'll ID me, eventually."

"I mess things up when I can."

"They'll catch you," Kremelberg said.

"I'm careful."

"If they can arrest Darcy Lemon, none of us are safe."

Waldo nodded. This was the moment. The entire point of letting them talk and not swooping in to arrest Kremelberg was to develop evidence and intelligence. As a highly placed asset, Kremelberg could shine light on the depth of Chinese penetration.

"How many agents does China control?" Waldo said.

Nathan flinched. The question was too on the nose, and it wasn't something a co-conspirator would ask. It came out awkward. Rehearsed.

Kremelberg stepped back. "What?"

"How many of us are in the Bureau?"

"You fuck."

"*Qué?*" Waldo asked.

"You miserable, stupid fuck. You're wearing a wire."

"No, I—"

"Barcelona," Kremelberg yelled.

"I don't understand," Waldo said.

The shadow moved into the frame behind Kremelberg. Nathan leaned close to the screen. The man's face came into focus.

The Leopard.

Nathan gasped. The operator Nathan had chased through the streets of Tampa—the team leader who'd attacked Meili years ago—was yards away.

"It's a trap," Kremelberg told the Leopard.

"Shit," Nathan said. "Waldo's burned. Go get him." Nathan stood and banged his head on the van's roof.

"Take them," Davis said into his radio.

The van doors opened and the SWAT members disembarked.

A handgun appeared in the Leopard's hand as if he'd conjured it.

"Gun," Nathan broadcast on their tactical channel. "The second guy is a Chinese assassin."

The Leopard pointed his gun at Kremelberg.

Kremelberg raised his hands. "Not me—"

The Leopard fired.

Kremelberg looked down at the bloody stain spreading across his chest, then he collapsed.

The Leopard aimed at Waldo.

"Motorcycle," Waldo said, his voice a resigned whisper.

The Leopard fired. Waldo's head snapped back as blood misted the air. He fell to the ground.

Nathan ripped off his headphones and leaped out of the van. He chased the SWAT team across M Street. He drew his Glock and snatched his radio off his belt.

The Leopard disappeared into the trees and fled toward the Chesapeake & Ohio Canal at the bottom of the hill behind the park. The rushed radio calls came through Nathan's speaker as the SWAT team pursued the Leopard.

Nathan raced into the park and stopped. A SWAT member covered Kremelberg, who lay on his back staring up into the light rain with wide eyes. Kremelberg's chest rose and fell rapidly.

Nathan stepped around him and knelt beside Waldo, who had face-planted in the dirt. The back of his skull had disappeared and a pool of blood thickened around his head. Nathan laid two fingers over his carotid artery. No pulse.

Waldo was dead.

92

The SWAT member aimed his MP5 at Kremelberg as his team chased the Leopard through Georgetown. Nathan ripped open Kremelberg's shirt. Two tiny flaps of bloody skin revealed entry wounds where the Leopard's bullets had punctured his chest cavity. They'd entered over his heart. Kremelberg didn't have long.

Davis's radio transmissions came over the tactical channel as he vectored his team through the canal.

Nathan switched to the main channel. "Base, Whiskey 34-06."

"Go ahead Whiskey 34-06."

"Shots fired. Two agents down. We need a bus at the north end of the Key Bridge."

"We have fire and ambulance rolling," the operator said.

"Copy."

Normally, they'd have pre-staged an ambulance, but the secret operation limited all their resources. Agent Davis only had his squad to chase down the Chinese operative.

Nathan looked up at the SWAT member. "Go help your team. I got this."

"You sure?"

"Kremelberg's not going anywhere. Catch that killer."

The agent jogged through the park to the stairs that led down into the canal.

Nathan holstered and opened his personal med kit. He removed a roll of gauze and pressed it against the puncture wounds. He applied pressure, but the lethal bleeding happened inside, and from Kremelberg's raspy breaths, blood already constricted his lungs.

"Hang on," Nathan said. "Ambulance is coming."

"I'm dying," Kremelberg said in a voice devoid of emotion.

Nathan had seen enough mortally wounded people to know when a victim said they were dying, he should believe them.

"Do you want to tell me anything?" Nathan asked.

"Confess?"

"Clear your conscience. Help us root out other moles."

"How would I know?" Kremelberg asked.

"You've been in China's pocket for years, like Darcy Lemon and countless other politicians and bureaucrats."

"That's simplistic." He coughed, and a drop of blood hung on his lip.

"Corruption isn't complicated."

"Your kind always see the world in black and white. Every politician takes money—" He grimaced in pain, then coughed. "Wealth doesn't recognize borders. Corporations manipulate governments wherever they do business."

"There's a difference between corporations donating money to candidates to secure favoritism and a foreign government buying influence."

"You're naïve."

Sirens rose in the distance. The ambulance would arrive soon.

"Businesses fight for their interests," Nathan said. "China's trying to destroy us."

"Politicians seek money and power." Kremelberg's voice faded.

"That's why we need to return to small government."

Kremelberg sneered. "We're never going back. We're headed for a world government."

"That won't happen."

Kremelberg's eyes clouded.

"Kremelberg?"

He refocused on Nathan. "We already have an elite shadow government led by billionaires, oligarchs, and politicians."

"We can change that."

"You can't."

Nathan's radio crackled. "Tango One, Whiskey 34-06," Davis transmitted.

"Go for Whiskey 34-06."

"We got him," Davis said.

"Alive?"

"Affirmative."

"Copy. Good job."

Nathan looked back at Kremelberg. "See, even the Leopard couldn't escape—" He stopped. Kremelberg stared into the rain, unblinking, with dilated pupils. He was gone.

Something moved in the bushes and caught Nathan's eye. A dark shape slipped through the shrubs bordering the bridge.

Could the assassin have brought an accomplice? Nathan's heart raced.

Nathan checked his radio. He hadn't switched back from the main channel to the tactical one. Dammit. He twirled the knob back to the local frequency.

"Break, break," Davis transmitted. "Whiskey 34-06, Tango One, emergency traffic."

"Go for Oh Six."

"We do not have jackpot. Repeat, negative jackpot."

"Tango One, Oh, Six, you confirmed you had him."

"We grabbed a guy running from us and wearing the same clothes, but it's not him. He's a decoy."

Nathan's eyes moved to the bushes. The shadow moved away. If SWAT had collared a decoy, then this could be—

Sirens filled the air as police cars, an ambulance, and a fire truck raced down M Street. Nathan started for the shrubs, then cut right toward the sidewalk. He burst out of the park as the man vaulted the retaining wall and turned onto M Street.

The Leopard stumbled to a stop five feet away.

The Leopard pointed his silenced handgun at Nathan, but he held it loosely, like a television remote. Nathan surpassed the urge to charge him. The operative wasn't lazy or sloppy, his casual manner came from extreme comfort with violence. Preparing to kill was his normal state. He'd probably take a life and go out for lunch.

Time stopped.

A police car screamed around the corner from 35th Street onto M Street. Nathan dove behind the wall as the Leopard's gun spit. A round ricocheted off the brick.

Nathan landed hard on the ground and rolled. He drew his Glock and aimed at the opening in the wall, but the Leopard didn't appear. Nathan peeked over the wall.

The Leopard backed across the street, then turned away from the oncoming emergency vehicles and headed toward a gas station on the corner. Nathan jumped the wall and gave chase.

A Volvo skidded to a stop, and the driver laid on his horn. Nathan pivoted around the hood of the car and sprinted for the sidewalk to cut off the Leopard's egress. The Leopard only had one path to escape.

Knowing DC was Nathan's secret weapon.

The Leopard dashed toward a steep, seventy-five-foot staircase—made famous in *The Exorcist* movie. The Leopard raced up the stairs, and his shoes thumped on the concrete like a drumbeat.

Nathan reached the bottom of the stairs. Above, the Leopard scampered upward like a cat. Nathan vaulted onto the steps and pursued. His thighs burned and his breath came hard.

The killer had already scaled half the staircase. How was he so fast?

"Fuck this," Nathan said.

He stopped with his left foot on the step above and braced his elbow on his knee. He dropped his sight onto the Leopard's back.

"Stop," Nathan yelled. He applied pressure to the trigger.

The Leopard twisted and the black hole of his barrel poked out beneath his arm.

Nathan squeezed the trigger. His sights jerked as a round exploded out of the chamber. Flame flashed from the Leopard's barrel and the round buzzed over Nathan's head—amazingly close for a no-look shot.

Nathan pulled the trigger three times in succession.

The Leopard's back arched and he stopped. His handgun dropped from his hand and clattered down the steps. The Leopard wobbled on the steps with his arms splayed out. He toppled over backward.

Nathan dropped his sights and followed the Leopard's body as it tumbled down the steps. He came to a rest thirty feet above Nathan. Blood cascaded down the steps like a hellish waterfall.

Nathan climbed toward him. But without rushing. He'd killed the Leopard.

93

Zhao stared at the back of the guard's head as the industrial elevator descended to the prison's ninth subterranean floor. He ignored his new assistant, Bai He, a striking young woman who had replaced Jíng. Zhao had no proof Jíng spied on him, but the nagging feeling in his gut wouldn't disappear—so he made her vanish. A pity, really, because she'd served him well as an assistant, but a fresh recruit was exactly what he needed to distract him from his troubles.

Zhao focused on the problem at hand. Who was the prisoner the Central Committee needed him to interrogate, and why did they require Zhao to do it himself? The Central Committee's demand that he attend to the prisoner had been odd—unprecedented. A high-risk security threat, such as a prominent public official, would demand this type of security.

But another thought raised his hair.

What if the party's internal security apparatus had arrested someone who knew Zhao's involvement with Quon Li. What if they'd uncovered Quon's attempt to supply carfentanil to Hasan Yakuf and the Turkistan Islamic Party?

The elevator groaned, then jerked to a stop. Zhao shook the thought away. The American agent had killed Yakuf, and Zhao had executed Quon before he could talk. No one in the prison even knew Quon's identity.

But still . . .

The elevator doors groaned as they opened, and Zhao exited and displayed his identification to a guard. Bai held out her badge too.

"She is mine," Zhao said. He smiled. How true.

The guard inspected their identification, matching the photographs to their faces. Were his officers this thorough with everyone, or was this theater to prove their efficiency? He should order an internal review. Zhao led Bai down the long corridor to the first interrogation room, the place where he'd condemned at least one hundred men.

Another guard snapped to attention. Whoever waited for Zhao inside required extra security. Zhao straightened and steeled himself in preparation for an important interrogation. The guard opened the door. Zhao entered and stopped.

General Donghai Sun stared at him.

Sun sat behind the desk. Zhao's desk—his throne from where he passed judgment on prisoners.

The memory of standing in this room and sentencing Quon Li to die flashed in his mind. Every instinct urged Zhao to flee—but that wasn't how generals behaved. And he had no chance of escape. If the Central Committee wanted to imprison him, or worse, he could do nothing to prevent it.

"General Sun, welcome," Zhao said. "They did not tell me you would be here for the interrogation."

"You had no need to know."

Alarm tingled the base of Zhao's skull. This situation brought peril.

"Who is the traitor you wish me to break?" Zhao asked.

Sun glowered but said nothing.

An icy chill settled in Zhao's bones. "Which prisoner, General?"

"You are the prisoner."

Zhao tried to keep his fear off his face, but sweat moistened his skin. "I do not understand what—"

"Girl, leave us," Sun commanded.

Bai slipped out. The guard shut the door behind Zhao but he stayed in the room.

"General, I think there has been a mistake," Zhao said.

"You have exposed our homeland in disastrous ways. Your covert operations exposed our high-energy weapons to the Americans, and now they suspect our collusion with the Phantoms' terrorism."

"I eliminated the links in that chain."

"All but one."

An acidic taste filled Zhao's mouth, and the floor shifted beneath him. His ambition gave way to the primal instinct to survive. He needed to keep his wits about him.

"My strategy requires more time," Zhao said.

"More time to supply the Turkistan rebels?"

"How did you hear about—?"

"An intercepted communication between an FBI agent and someone in your office."

That jolted Zhao. He cocked his head in disbelief. "But—"

"We implemented disintegration warfare strategy for decades, but your reckless acceleration of operations exposed us . . . and your tactics failed."

"Our strategy requires time to see its effects," Zhao said. "Lack of vision will endanger our success."

"You gambled and lost."

"But I—"

"The time for talking has ended." Sun motioned to the guard. "Take him away."

A cold fear seeped into Zhao's belly and settled there like winter frost. How many times had he been on the other end of this conversation? Despite his experience, fear spread through him like wildfire.

"What will be my punishment?"

Sun glared at him. "Death."

94

Reagan sat beside Vince at the back of the dais and gazed at the raucous crowd. In the most shocking presidential election in history, Archie James and Doyle Knight were voted into the White House. They'd done it with a thin electoral win, but they'd won the popular vote, which gave them a mandate. If the polls were accurate, voters were fed up with divisive partisan politics and radical ideologies, and they wanted a moderate ticket to perform basic duties of government.

They wanted common sense, and a Democrat-Republican ticket offered that.

But why had she received a seat at James's first rally? She'd publicly supported him, because he was a level-headed and moderate Democrat who could take the party in a new direction. Picking a Republican running mate had proven that. Many considered it a Hail Mary pass after a historically chaotic election cycle, but it had been a brilliant appeal to independent voters and moderate Republicans. By picking Knight, James proved he wouldn't let the Democratic machinery dictate his decisions. That was a very good sign.

The curtain behind her parted, and President-Elect James strode confidently to the podium. The crowd roared as he lowered the microphone. He was shorter than he appeared. Force of personality did that.

"Thank you for coming," James said. "This election marks a new beginning for America. Vice President Knight and I appreciate your votes, and now, we want you to do more. Support us as we rein in government spending, deregulate, and limit legislative overreach. It's time to diminish governmental interference in your lives. We . . ."

James's victory astonished everyone, and the DNC had probably only succumbed to his vice presidential choice because they assumed he couldn't win. But they'd underestimated the simmering frustration in a populace sick of tribalism and political bickering. People wanted better lives, and they expected their politicians to help. Republicans sought smaller government while Democrats wanted to expand it, but both agreed that hyperbolic rhetoric and demonization of opponents had reached intolerable levels. Enough was enough.

". . . and there will always be differences between Democrats and Republicans, and that's healthy," James said. "We can only learn the truth by having our ideas challenged. But disagreements over policies are just that—differences of opinion. Your neighbors may disagree with you, but that doesn't make them your enemy."

Vince reached over and held her hand. She smiled at him. He leaned over and whispered in her ear. "I never thought I'd feel optimistic about a Democrat in the Oval Office."

"I always expect positive change, and I'm always disappointed. This time, I have hope."

James waited for the crowd to settle down. "Doyle and I give you our solemn promise to reduce radicalism from both our parties and make our government leaner and more efficient. We will represent the values Americans want, not the outsized voices of extremists."

Reagan scanned the dignitaries around her. Many of them she recognized from interviews on television. A few had served the previous Democratic administration, but most came from other walks of life—a refreshing change from the career politicians who had dominated the party for generations.

"We promise free speech, free markets, and a compassionate government that will care for those who can't take care of themselves. And when we disagree, we'll do so with civility and empathy."

The crowd cheered. James had hit a nerve. Conservatives and liberals had become dissatisfied with government that only claimed to represent them. Voters wanted to be heard.

"Doyle and I will work hard over the months before we take office to put together a strong team. We will hit the ground running, because change can't come fast enough."

More applause.

"Many people aren't aware that our administration will make four thousand appointments, and twelve hundred will need Senate confirmation. We must select our cabinet, deputy secretaries, undersecretaries, assistant secretaries, and heads of agencies that will keep the government running. It's an effort, but appointing the right people is critical, because leaders' personalities influence organizations and set the tone. We will demand transparency, effectiveness, and efficiency."

The crowd cheered, and their enthusiasm became contagious. Was James's rhetoric more empty promises, or did he really plan to make changes?

"Let me introduce a few of the people who will help us lead America into the future. Some of tomorrow's leaders are seated behind me now. Thomas Scott will be my secretary of defense. Margaret Taylor will become my Labor Secretary. Olivia Lewis . . ."

Nerves tingled Reagan's stomach. Being seated with people who lead the country was such an honor.

". . . and Leo Milani will head the Department of the Interior. We will have more announcements coming soon, and be prepared to see fresh faces fill our administration . . ."

James began to wrap up his speech, and Secret Service agents moved into position, preparing for his departure. Was he in more danger than previous presidents because of the recent assassination and blackmail, or would his moderation make him less of a target. If he—

"Before we say goodbye," James said, "I want to thank Reagan Cabrera, who is sitting behind me."

Reagan's heart jumped. She cocked her head. Had James mentioned her?

James turned and looked at her. "Mrs. Cabrera is a delegate from the

Commonwealth of Virginia. I salute her courage in standing up to corruption and exposing the foreign influence within our party."

"What's happening?" she whispered.

"Everyone's watching you," Vince said. He beamed.

"We all know the personal toll her decision to fight for our country has taken on her and also on her family," James said. "But she didn't bury her head in the sand. Instead, she chose to do the hard thing and fought those who would subjugate us. That is the strength and moral courage I want in my administration."

What was he saying? Had he invited her to the event to invite her into his administration?

"I don't know where I'll use her yet," James said, "but she'll be on our team. Most politicians would run from her after her scandal, but forgiveness for past indiscretions is a moral good, and courage is a rare commodity that's needed in government. Please thank her for standing up for election integrity and shining a bright light on the bad actors trying to influence our political parties."

The crowd roared, and Reagan filled with . . . What was she feeling?

Hope.

95

Nathan and Meili cuddled on his living room couch drinking a Lebanese cabernet while Amelia sat across from them and played on her laptop, engrossed in something.

Amelia sat upright. "Dad, the ChatteringHen app is gone."

"Do you know what I call that?" Nathan said.

"What?"

"A good start."

"Not funny, Dad."

Meili swatted him playfully. Amelia dialed her phone and padded into the kitchen in her socks.

"ChatteringHen is one of a thousand cuts," Meili said. "China's bleeding and on the retreat."

"We smacked them pretty hard in the chops," Nathan said, "but they won't be deterred for long."

"They lost their Manchurian candidate, and we've exposed their strategy to public scrutiny. It'll be harder for them to hide."

"Ironically," Nathan said, "China's decision to murder Hamilton helped prove their conspiracy. Flipping Evans and recording Kremelberg gave us real evidence."

"And Reagan's blackmailer," Meili said.

"Now we have a moderate president who wants to unite us. If he pulls it off, a unified front will help us expose the CCP's strategy."

"Did you see the latest?" Meili asked.

"What?" Nathan said.

"China announced a major crackdown on opioids. They've exerted national control over all fentanyl production. Instead of giving provinces quotas and letting local officials administer production, they've assigned commissars to watch over legitimate companies."

"That's positive," Nathan said.

"You did it."

"But nobody can ever know."

The smile slid off her face. "Part of me wants you to receive credit, but I'm still pissed you went off book and violated policy."

Nathan smiled and shrugged.

"You keep running rogue operations, eventually one will blow up and you'll be in big trouble."

"I'm trying to accomplish our mission."

"They could fire you . . . or worse."

"It's worth the risk."

She sighed and leaned against him. "It's hopeless trying to change you."

"Change me?"

"Stop you from taking risks."

"I won't. Not while our country's surrounded by enemies."

"I know." She sighed. "That's what worries me, but it's also what I love about you."

"Love?"

She smiled. "Love."

Nathan warmed. Things were starting to look up.

The Uganda Protocol
Nathan Burke Thrillers #4

Terror strikes from inside America's own institutions, turning one agent's manhunt into a fight to save everything that matters.

FBI Special Agent Nathan Burke expected a routine prisoner transport. Instead, he finds an airplane full of corpses and his most wanted terrorism suspect gone without a trace. The investigation plunges him into an international manhunt for Imam Omar Yemeni, a man whose network runs deeper and deadlier than anyone imagined.

Meanwhile, Iranian immigrant Leila Kabiri works as a court interpreter, building a new life for her neurodivergent son Darius after fleeing her homeland. But when colleagues start disappearing and foreign operatives make contact, Leila discovers the American justice system itself has been compromised. Someone is watching her every move, and they want something only she can provide.

What Nathan doesn't realize is that Yemeni's escape was just the opening move in a much larger plan—one that targets the most vulnerable and threatens mass casualties. As Nathan races across continents tracking his fugitive, Leila finds herself trapped between protecting her family and doing what's right. When their paths finally converge, both will discover that the most dangerous enemies are the ones hiding in plain sight.

Perfect for fans of Michael Connelly, David Baldacci, and Vince Flynn, this pulse-pounding international thriller delivers high-stakes action and unforgettable characters in a race against time where the cost of failure is measured in thousands of lives.

Get your copy today at
severnriverbooks.com

30% Off your next paperback.

Thank you for reading. For exclusive offers on your next paperback:

- **Visit SevernRiverBooks.com** and enter code **PRINTBOOKS30** at checkout.
- Or scan the QR code.

Offer valid for future paperback purchases only. The discount applies solely to the book price (excluding shipping, taxes, and fees) and is limited to one use per customer. Offer available to US customers only. Additional terms and conditions apply.

ACKNOWLEDGMENTS

I write all my books for my brilliant wife, Cynthia Farahat Higgins.

I'd like to acknowledge the many other people who supported this work. My parents, James and Nadya Higgins, who always read to me at bedtime and encouraged my interest in books. I owe my love of story to them. My grandfather, Nejm Aswad, was an author, philosopher, and poet, and I carry his storytelling genes. I'm grateful to my mother-in-law, Sanaa Nessem, who showers me with love and support.

Thanks to Andrew Watts, Amber Haddock, and the entire Severn River Publishing team. Special thanks to Publisher Julia Hastings for shepherding my book through the process and to Lisa Gilliam for editing my manuscript.

Last, but not least, thanks to my readers. If you enjoy this thriller, I'd appreciate a rating or review on Amazon. I love seeing readers' comments. You're also welcome to email me at Jeffrey@JeffreyJamesHiggins.com. Thanks for your support!

ABOUT THE AUTHOR

Jeffrey James Higgins, author of the Nathan Burke Thrillers, is a retired supervisory special agent who writes thrillers, short stories, scripts, creative nonfiction, and essays. He has wrestled a suicide bomber, fought the Taliban in combat, and chased terrorists across five continents. He received the Attorney General's Award for Exceptional Heroism and the DEA Award of Valor. Jeffrey has been interviewed by CNN, National Geographic, and The New York Times. He's a #1 Amazon bestselling author and has won numerous literary awards, including the Claymore Award, PenCraft's Best Fiction Book of 2022, and a Reader's Favorite Gold Medal. Jeffrey is an active member of the Authors Guild, The Virginia Writers Club, International Thriller Writers, Sisters in Crime, and the Royal Writers Secret Society. His first three thrillers are *Furious, Unseen,* and *The Forever Game.*

Sign up for the reader list at
severnriverbooks.com